Girl on a Plane

CASSANDRA O'LEARY

Second edition (2023) published by Cassandra O'Leary.

Paperback ISBN: 978-0-6484227-4-7

Ebook ISBN: 978-0-6484227-5-4

Previously published (ebook, first edition) by HarperCollins UK, 2016.

Cover design by Deborah Bradseth at **dbcoverdesign.com**

Interior book design by Cassandra O'Leary using Atticus.

Cassandra O'Leary, Author

Melbourne, Australia

cassandraolearyauthor.com

Praise for Girl on a Plane

'Cassandra O'Leary's writing is captivating'
— **Readers' Favorite 5 star review**

'A sizzling, emotional read that's perfect for pool, beach or sofa!'
— **Phillipa Ashley, bestselling author**

'Fasten your seat belts . . . Girl on a Plane is a charming debut that's sure to fly high.'
— **Amy Andrews, *USA Today* bestselling author**

'Girl on a Plane is a charming debut that has everything I love about romance – sizzling chemistry, real-life emotion and a swoon-worthy happily ever after. I highly recommend it!'
— **Stefanie London, *USA Today* bestselling author**

Content note

Dear readers,

Overall this book is fun and light-hearted, including some laugh-out-loud scenes.

But please note that this book contains themes that may be upsetting to some readers. These include descriptions of domestic violence and controlling behaviour occurring in the past, and a confrontation with a stalker who has been following the heroine, Sinead. There is also discussion of parental illness including Alzheimer's disease. Gabriel, the hero, has been caring for his mother for several years and he has health concerns of his own.

However, as I mentioned the tone of the book is positive and more of a romantic comedy than a serious tome! I do hope you'll enjoy it.

Happy reading,

Cassandra x

Contents

Chapter One

Mermaid Airlines Flight 180, Melbourne to London

Showtime! Sinead Kennealy sucked in a deep breath and squared her shoulders. Time to get it over and done with. The molly-coddled first class passengers wouldn't entertain themselves, apparently.

She sensed her colleagues Yuki and Deanna on either side of her usual position, centre front of the cabin. Yuki flicked her shiny black ponytail over her shoulder and flipped on the PA system. The airline's theme song, a hackneyed rendition of the "Macarena", blared from the plane's speakers.

Hey! Mermaid Airlines.

Sinead's heart sank like a stone dropped in a bucket of water even as she plastered on the airline's trademark happy smile. Her jaw ached with the enforced perkiness, all day long. It was only breakfast time and she had a crick in her neck. A few more hours and they'd land in Dubai. She might have time for a massage at the hotel spa.

She shimmied forward in a practised and synchronised routine. The move she hated. The booby shake. A couple of mature men eagerly watched her from their premium seats with an over-excited gleam in their eyes.

One of the men mumbled, "Shake it, baby!"

Heat crawled up her throat to her cheeks and she wanted to slink away to the bathroom. Surely she couldn't die from embarrassment. But it was a close call.

How much more of this job could she take? As an eager twenty-one-year-old recruit with Mermaid Airlines (*The funnest airline in the world!* so the tag-line went) she'd been bouncing off the walls with glee. The travel! The glamour! The most exciting job ever. Five years on, either her patience had run out or her expectations had grown.

Shimmy, shimmy, shake!

She kicked her leg. Shook her hips. A grown woman. Fluent in French, German and English, plus a sprinkling of Gaelic. A first-aid expert. Calm in an emergency. She had some mad skills these days. She'd even talked down an over-zealous pilot keen to initiate her into the Mile High Club. But look at her shaking her money-maker. Was it too much to ask for something more challenging?

Shimmy, shimmy, kick!

While she was ranting, why didn't her male colleagues ever have to shake their tails to keep the high-flying passengers happy? Fecking Damian smirked at her over the passengers' heads, from the rear of the cabin. Skiving off again. She gave him the evil eye, a slight pinch of her eyebrows the passengers wouldn't notice. But he sure noticed, and scurried away like a little mouse back to the galley where he was meant to be preparing breakfast. She'd deal with him later.

Shimmy, kick!

She bowed. Enthusiastic applause from the whole cabin drowned out the roaring engines as the music died. She grabbed the microphone from Yuki.

"Thanks ladies and gentlemen. Welcome to Mermaid Airlines flight 180 from Melbourne to London via Dubai. We will be serving breakfast shortly. In the meantime, please watch this short safety video."

Mirroring the gestures in the safety video, she pointed out the nearest exits. Her arms went off on their own merry way, demonstrating on auto-pilot. A yawn rose up in her throat. So tired. She could have shut her eyes and slept where she stood. But her lips stretched upwards, and she nodded at the passengers in front of her.

A mixed bunch today. Business people mostly. One younger man in dark glasses who might have been a football player. Yuki would know, she was always up to speed on celebrities. Older Aussie gentleman in 5K, already showing signs of downing too many beers in the airport bar. And it was only eight o'clock in the morning. *The heckler*. She'd keep her eye on him.

She held up the airline's safety card and waved in the direction of the oxygen masks.

A couple of other passengers stood out. Young professional-looking mother in 16G, dressed all in black, travelling alone with her baby. Was she wearing a Chanel suit? A different world, these rich people lived in. Who wore Chanel when they travelled? Let alone when they'd likely be covered in baby vomit in no time at all?

No matter, the bub was bound to annoy the first and business travellers. She'd help out by holding the baby when Mummy needed to go to the bathroom. He looked a sweet little thing. The random baby cuddles were a definite perk of the job.

She glanced towards Deanna. Her friend was well into robot mode, her dark eyes bright and blank.

Sinead scanned the rest of her passengers, letting her gaze slide over the business people who all looked much the same. Except...

Well, hello there.

Shockingly handsome young man with a perfectly sculpted face, full, kissable lips, sparkling blue eyes and dark blonde hair in 3A. Her belly fluttered and flipped. She was experiencing mild turbulence. Because of him? Her gaze tracked down his long, lean form, from broad shoulders to slim hips under a sharply cut suit. The man knew how to wear a suit.

And the man stared directly at her with intent—anyone would think he wanted to pounce on her and eat her alive. *Yowza.* Her stomach performed its own little dance and flipped over in the most peculiar way. As if she was falling.

Her hands formed into fists at her side and she sucked in a soothing deep breath. She was all hot then cold, goosebumps pebbling down her arms. The last thing she needed was another man who wanted to own her. But not all muscular and *fit* men were like Padraig. She'd left her mad ex-boyfriend years and thousands of miles away. Why couldn't he stay there, out of sight, out of mind?

Don't engage the crazy. Calm blue ocean. The image of a tropical Thai beach popped into her mind and calm washed over her like gentle waves against the shore.

She was still staring at Mr Hot Stuff in 3A. Rubbing her arms, she hastily looked away.

It was nearly time for the coffee and tea service, not the time for the distraction of a handsome man with a James Bond-ish air about him. Who looked like he would be able to handle himself . . . and a woman too.

What would it feel like, to let him handle her? *Oh, Lord.* She had a sneaking suspicion it would feel mighty fine. Heat crept up her throat and surged across her cheeks. The last thing she needed was a blush lighting up her face like an emergency beacon.

She lowered her arms and finished up the safety demo. And stood there staring for a few seconds too long. She'd better catch up to Yuki and get the beverage cart stocked. Time to crack on.

Gabriel cocked his head to one side and stared as her skin changed from pale porcelain to hot pink. The platinum blonde flight attendant was having some kind of reaction to him. Damned if he could tell whether it was good or bad. He gripped the iPad tighter in one hand where it balanced on his lap, as her red glossy mouth popped open and she inhaled deeply.

He'd first noticed her at the boarding gate, walking away from him towards the large wall of windows overlooking the runway. Her body had been framed in silhouette—the outline of long, slim legs and a shapely backside in her tight skirt drew his gaze and fired his imagination.

She seemed so confident and in control, a woman to be reckoned with. It had been a while since he met a sexy woman who wasn't a complete pushover. Someone to spar with. He let the idea percolate as she headed off towards the staff area, behind the curtain at the front of the plane. The sway of her hips as she walked down the aisle was definitely some of the best inflight entertainment he'd seen in a long time.

He stopped gawking and let his gaze drop to his iPad and the designs for his company's new travel blog. Something was off with the style but he couldn't put his finger on it. The main Global Village website was doing fantastic business, especially since his deal with the major airlines flying through the Asian region.

But the demands from the board and shareholders were taking a toll. He rubbed his right temple with his forefinger, tiny circles, round and round. There was pressure to expand the business too quickly, pressure to push into new markets, and the constant pressure to make more money.

He'd commissioned a cutting-edge digital advertising agency to develop the new Asia blog. But they weren't getting it right.

What the hell was going on? He'd have to step in. Talk to the designers, get them to start from scratch. As if he didn't have enough on his to-do list.

It was so hard to let go.

After starting a business fresh out of university and building it into a global brand, it wasn't so easy to hand over the reins. Now the business was expanding from his home city of Melbourne to London. He should have stepped back and allowed the new Europe and Asia-Pacific regional managers to do their jobs. Instead he was on a flight to London to supervise the set-up phase for the new office.

He wasn't sure he should have left his mum, even if it was only two weeks. He'd promised to always be there for her. The guilt and stress threatened to devour him if he let it take over. He pushed it down till his gut ached. He needed a break. Some downtime to decompress.

It had been so long since he went on a proper holiday. Gabriel pictured the top of the range surfboard stashed somewhere in his Mum's house. He'd love to take off surfing and drop-out for a while. Not likely in sunny London in February. He could try to take a weekend trip to Spain or down the coast back home. Surfing was the only personal time he seemed to get these days.

The other flight attendant pushed the drinks cart down the aisle and stopped beside his seat. She was pretty with her black glossy hair and even blacker eyes. Wide eyes. She looked younger than the other hostess. *Yuki*, he read on her name tag. He'd have a bit of fun with her, cheer himself up. He liked to flirt, hopefully she'd be into it too.

"Coffee or tea this morning?" Yuki asked.

"Let's see. Is the coffee likely to be any good? On a scale from one to ten—one being sludge scraped off the bottom of the Yarra River to ten being nectar of the gods—how would you rate it, Yuki?"

She blinked, pausing for a second. "Ah, I believe the coffee is good, Sir. Would you like a cup?"

He raised his eyebrow. She was no fun. "You didn't answer my question. If you give it a six or higher I'll try it."

"Right. I'd give it a six or seven." Yuki poured the cup of coffee and set it on a small plastic tray, ready to pass across to him. He waved it away.

The tall blonde approached behind Yuki to help with the drinks service. His eyes instantly snapped to hers and then his gaze moved lower, to the name tag pinned above her perfectly round, high breasts. Wicked thoughts flitted through his mind, which she could obviously read in his expression. A pinched crease formed between her eyebrows, then her tongue darted out and licked across her soft-looking lower lip. Half-annoyed, half-interested?

Sinead. He noted her name in his memory bank. She had a musical Irish lilt in her accent when she'd made the announcement over the PA. Very sexy.

"Can I be of assistance?" Sinead's voice was a little husky. Very sexy indeed.

Yuki nodded to Sinead and stepped past her, continuing to serve the next passenger.

"I was asking Yuki whether the coffee was any good. What do you think, Sinead?"

"Well, it's hardly Jamaican Blue Mountain, but it'll do in a pinch." She winked at him, actually winked.

He liked this woman. His mouth tugged up at the corners. Too long. It'd been too long since he'd met a woman he wanted to banter with.

"You know all about Jamaican Blue Mountain coffee, do you?"

The condescending comment was out of his mouth before he could stop it. Scorn dripping off his tongue seemed to be his default setting when talking to women lately. Too much time spent with his mother, nurses, doctors, all women telling him things he didn't want to know. He had to snap out of it. Charm came easily when he tried. He hadn't always been a grumpy bastard.

Her lips twitched and she leaned a little lower over his seat. "As it happens, I do. Blue Mountain coffee beans come from a tightly controlled region in Jamaica and are considered the best in the world by many critics. We don't currently stock it on board, but I can recommend a few excellent cafés in London serving it, for when you arrive."

"Really? Do tell."

"There is Tomtom in Belgravia of course, but my personal favourite is Nude Espresso in Soho Square."

"Nude Espresso?" Gabriel raised his eyebrows. Was she flirting with him? Things were looking up.

"Yes. Nude." Sinead's cheeky half smile answered the question.

Hello, Irish fling. Definite interest there.

He chuckled, stretching out his legs. "Hmm, I'll keep it in mind. But right now I'll take a pot of tea."

"Of course you will. Sir." Sinead muttered the last word, reaching for the tea on her cart. The frown crossing her face was a kick in the guts, before she beamed like a little ray of sunshine.

He should've known better. In her mind, he was nothing but another rich arsehole, and she was used to serving them without a second glance. Unless he could show her he was different.

He wanted to be different. He didn't want to be a man who would ruin a woman's day. He'd like to make Sinead smile. Now wasn't that a surprise?

Three hours later, Sinead slumped down in her jump seat next to the galley at the rear of the first-class cabin. She gazed out the window on her much needed break, feet aching, with her head up in the clouds. Which pretty much summed up her life at the moment. So much of her life was spent in the clouds. Fifty per cent. It was a strange realisation and she still wasn't fully comfortable with it, even after five years of flying almost every day. Floating, gliding through the air.

Although she understood the basic mechanics of how a plane worked and concepts like wind resistance, it was somehow magical to travel through the sky in a metal box. So far above the earth and removed from everyday reality, as tiny people went about their lives below. She was somehow apart from them, removed. Sometimes it felt like she was on a different planet from most people.

The clouds today were different than usual, darker. Or was it a reflection of her strange mood? No, she'd flown in all sorts of conditions and knew a lot about weather these days. The clouds were dense and gathering quickly.

The plane lurched and bumped, and she grabbed hold of the armrests. Her stomach rolled over. Not a good sign. She was right about the clouds being different. Probably the tail of the storm system the captain mentioned during the pre-flight briefing. She needed an update on the weather conditions. As the lead cabin crew member on the flight, she had to understand what was happening to brief the others. She pushed herself upright and swayed into the partition.

On her way to the cockpit, the plane tipped sharply to the right, causing gasps and murmurs from the passengers. Sinead stumbled and tripped forward, grabbing hold of the nearest thing. A strong, muscular shoulder. *Oh, no! The coffee man.* She watched his blue eyes blink and open wide, his lips tugging up into a half smile. A surge and drop in an air current rattled the cabin, tray tables shaking. She pitched forward, pulse thumping loud in her ears, until she clutched the headrest beside his face.

Her boobs were lodged right in front of his head. Looking down, she saw his eyes widen and he took in the view straight down her now gaping neckline, between *the girls*.

She squeaked like a frightened mouse. Between the weather and the man, she was all off-balance and her heart was aflutter.

Somehow she had to move. But she was captured by his ruffled beachy blonde hair with the goldy highlights. Those baby blue eyes had her hooked, searing hot this close, only inches away.

She inhaled a full whiff of him. His scent shot straight from her nose to wrap around her good-feels receptors. Delicious, citrus and spice and all things nice, like some kind of tropical island spliced with man. Her blood was flowing too fast, or something. But it wouldn't pump properly, having turned sticky in her veins, full of throbbing heat.

Danger. Pheromone alert.

It had to be him. *Him* being Mr Tall, Dark Blonde and Handsome, or Mr Anderson, as stated on the passenger list. So, she found out his name. It didn't man she was interested in him. She had a split-second to admire him and breathe him in again before . . . A sharp drop in altitude. It took her down with it. Toppling over, her stomach connected with his armrest.

Oooof.

Oh, Lord. She toppled right on top of him. Her face was dangerously close to his groin. It was the closest she'd been to that area of a man's anatomy for quite some time. What must he be thinking? She must look like a complete idiot. He sucked in a deep breath.

Robbed of breath, possibly a few brain cells too, she tightened her grip on his seat and hauled herself upright. She rubbed at the sore spot on her stomach, which would probably become a nasty bruise.

His eyes followed the movement of her hand. "I wouldn't refuse a lap dance, but are you okay?"

Such a crude comment. She had thought he was a better class of man than most, at least, good for a bit of flirting and ogling. But maybe not. The airline overlords expected them to put up with the odd comment or 'joke' but it did tick her off. *Men.*

"I'm fine, thank you." She clenched her teeth and pushed back, out of his orbit.

Standing tall, she shrugged her shoulders and tugged at her shirt, making sure the girls were tucked in, then knotted the silk scarf come loose around her throat. She pulled herself together. Somehow, she'd forgotten where she was going. Cockpit. Right. She nodded, but her legs stayed put.

He nodded too and raised his eyebrows, crinkling his forehead in apparent concern. He ruffled a hand through his cropped hair and mussed it appealingly. What would it feel like, to run her own hands through his hair? To smooth her hand across his brow, then muss the man properly.

What was wrong with her today? Had she bumped her head on the way down? There was just something about him.

An unwelcome pang of something – regret or desire, she wasn't entirely sure – shot through her belly. A certain something likely to lead her into temptation and end in trouble.

Her heart *ker-thumped* out of rhythm and the air huffed from her lungs. Straightening her skirt, she hurried down the aisle to get away from him, swaying and bumping along with the turbulence.

Sinead entered the cockpit and nodded at the co-pilot she didn't know well. He tipped his chin at her, but directed his attention back to the radar image. She hung back, hearing the tense tone of Captain Arrowsmith's voice. "Acknowledged. We'll await further instructions."

Tom, as he'd asked her to call him when they first met, sat perfectly straight with his back to her, his spine rigid as he worked the controls and hung on for air traffic control. He was one of the good guys, always so professional. Not to mention a fine-looking older man. A silver fox. He spoke to her as an intelligent person, not a serving wench as some pilots did.

The disembodied voice of an air traffic controller crackled through the radio. "Flight 180, you are being diverted. You are go to Singapore. Repeat, you are go to Singapore."

"Acknowledged. Repeat course correction."

The rest of the conversation was a muffled blur against the backdrop of her mind. The storm was developing fast and air traffic control was clearing the airspace. Not a good sign. Everything was reminding her of the worst day of her travel career, a flight to the Philippines that went awry. Her breathing sped up and she wiped her palms against the wool fabric of her skirt.

Tom swivelled around, a frown creasing his forehead. His usual warm expression was missing. "Okay, Sinead. We have a confirmed tropical storm and it's getting stronger, possibly a typhoon developing. We'll need to de-plane. Please inform the cabin crew and then I'll make an announcement to the passengers."

She nodded. "Yes, Captain. Tom, I mean."

Her heart raced ahead and her mind played out worst-case scenarios as she stepped out of the cockpit.

Stay calm. She slowed her pace, walking on wobbly legs down the aisle back to her colleagues. She passed Mr Coffee with barely a glance, concentrating on the job at hand.

Minutes later, she'd assembled her crew mates in the galley for a briefing. They stood in a circle as she relayed the captain's message, the bare facts. Yuki's mouth popped open and Deanna leaned against a trolley, arms crossed tight across her chest. They were no doubt worried but trying to remain professional.

The rest of the crew looked at their feet or stared at her and nodded, silent as the grave. *No.* Not a grave, definitely not a grave. Silent as some other silent but lovely thing, like rainbows or butterflies. Sinead was working hard to think happy thoughts, anything other than a terrifying typhoon blowing a plane full of passengers off course.

Her crew were all okay. None of them were panicking. They'd remember their training and help the passengers however they could.

Damian was the odd man out. Pouting, his poufy black hair bouncing as he shook his head. He looked put out. Sinead knew he coveted her senior crew member position, which made him unmanageable at times. Damian wasn't a happy camper, but she wouldn't waste any more time on him. He muttered something under his breath and then kept quiet.

She had a whole cabin of passengers to calm, to reassure, to make comfortable. Even when she was feeling less than calm and comfortable herself. She'd developed a sixth sense when it came to emotions, honed by years of anticipating and meeting other people's needs. It didn't make the work any easier. It was emotionally as well as physically exhausting and that was without the added stress of a tropical storm.

Half the time she was a flight attendant zombie, an honorary member of the walking dead. A new wave of tiredness washed over her and she rolled her shoulders and stretched her neck. Then she snapped out of it. She stood tall and got going again, showing the other crew members she was on top of things. Leading by example.

A loud but calm voice burst through the PA. "Ladies and gentleman, this is Captain Arrowsmith speaking. Apologies for the unexpected turbulence. We have been asked to divert course and make an unscheduled stop in Singapore due to an approaching tropical storm front. We'll make our descent in approximately three hours. At this stage we only expect a short delay but we will be required to disembark. Please remain seated and fasten your seat belts. I'll provide another update shortly. Thank you for your attention."

The crew took off in all directions, no messing about, back to work. She grabbed Yuki's arm before her friend disappeared. She worried about her. A mother hen instinct, or a desire to help her settle in as a newer crew member with only six months in the air. Yuki had never experienced a tropical storm while flying.

Sinead spoke quietly in Yuki's ear. "Are you all right?"

Yuki nodded, then her lips stretched in a tight grin. It didn't reach her eyes. She pressed her lips together and shook her head in disagreement with herself. "I don't know. What are we going to do if the storm hits mid-flight? Do you think we'll make it into Singapore in time?"

"Of course we will. The captain's got it all under control. We need to make sure we do our jobs and stay calm. All right?" Sinead hoped her voice conveyed all the confidence she herself was trying to muster.

The plane dipped and Sinead ignored the nausea rolling through her own stomach as she held on to Yuki's arm. She closed her eyes for a second. Lord, she'd kill to be on holiday. Thailand. Warm and exotic. Relaxing without a care in the world, drink in hand, stretched out on a sun lounge by the pool. *Three weeks to go, and counting*.

Yuki's face crumpled in concern. "I'll be okay, Sinead. Let me know if you need me to help with anything."

She'd lighten the mood with talk of shopping. That always worked a charm with Yuki. "Don't worry. Before long we'll be in Singapore. We might even have some time for shopping in Orchard Road, spending all our cash in those gorgeous shopping malls."

Yuki's expression brightened. "Oh! How could I forget? Daniel's in Singapore. He could meet us. I wonder if we'll have to stay over? I can invite Daniel to our hotel."

Sinead's tired brain ached at the idea, but she nodded. "Sure, why not?"

She'd covered her hesitation pretty well. Yuki's boyfriend was a medical student who still lived with his parents in a crowded high-rise apartment. So reunions always happened in Yuki's hotel room, adjoining Sinead's room with paper-thin walls. The close quarters never seemed to worry the pair of them, but the wall-banging, making-up-for-lost-time loving got on her nerves. It cost her precious sleep and only brought home the reality of her own lack of sexy times.

She clanged plates and cups together, concentrated on stacking trays and tidying up, to make sure things didn't go flying in the turbulence. It was a thankless task, but it had to be done.

All the while, Yuki prattled on. "He's so handsome, I miss him so much . . ." *Blah, blah, blah.*

Then Yuki stared up at her from her crouched position by the cart, her huge dark eyes bright with mischief. "Speaking of handsome men, what did you think of coffee-guy in 3A? Gabriel Anderson. I recognised him. He's an Aussie CEO, some kind of website genius, according to the BRW Young Rich List. Gorgeous, loaded and single. You should go for it."

Sinead rolled her eyes. Yuki's addiction to reading up on eligible bachelors was legendary. Yuki had memorised *Business Review Weekly* magazine's annual list of the richest Australian business people under the age of forty. Some girls wanted to marry a rock star, but Yuki was set on snagging an up-and-coming businessman.

Sinead ignored her friend's odd hobby of virtual stalking and organised containers of sugar. "Sure, I pick-up arrogant rich men all the time. I collect them. Have my wicked way with them, then stuff them and hang them as trophies on my wall."

Yuki stood with her hands on her hips. "Make jokes all you want. You might want to try taking one home once in a while. You're only getting older. Tick, tock." She tapped the designer watch strapped on her wrist.

Sinead dropped a handful of spoons on the cart with a clatter. "Oh. My. God. What did you say? I'm only twenty-six." She playfully pushed Yuki on the shoulder.

Yuki shoved her right back. "And you're hot, in your prime. Get out there and have some fun. You might regret it later if you don't."

Sinead sighed as Yuki walked away, then gripped the wall as the floor vibrated underfoot. Her friend might have had a point. At no stage during the last few years did Sinead think she'd be a twenty-six-year-old flight attendant flitting across the globe, but locking herself into a series of cells, alone each night. Celibate as a nun. She might as well wear a habit instead of her uniform and call herself Sister Sinead.

How depressing. She pulled her shoulders back and marched herself back into the cabin and got to work.

Somehow, the crew got through the next three hours of increasing turbulence, pitching and rolling. Sinead had handed out nearly the whole stock of sick bags, and that distinctive smell was getting to her. Passengers were whinging and she'd caught a coffee pot that had nearly bonked Yuki on the head in the galley.

Sinead was walking down the aisle handing out hot towels when a hand shot out and grabbed her hip. She froze. Goosebumps raced down her arms. Not the good kind of goosebumps. The creepy kind. She stepped back a pace so the man's hand dropped away.

"Darlin', how about you get a bloke an extra blanket and come keep me warm?" It was the heckler, making his presence known again. His speech was slurred. They'd cut off the booze earlier but he'd only become stroppy. He'd yelled at poor Deanna until her eyes went watery, close to tears.

Sinead took a closer look at him. Bald shiny head, red-rimmed eyes and even redder nose. His suit was shiny at the knees and elbows. He was the type of passenger she hated, who used a first-class ticket as a pass to act entitled and obnoxious.

She gritted her teeth then called up her nice-as-pie expression. "Of course. Wait a moment."

A grinding noise and a dip in the plane to match had her stumbling down the aisle again. Little bubbles of nervousness rose to the surface of her mind, then popped and disappeared.

He was standing by the bar at the rear of the cabin, watching her again. Mr Anderson. Her mind blanked. Blue eyes stared back at her. Blue as a summer sky over a tropical island. His gaze was as warm and decadent. Yuki was right, he was gorgeous. She could feel his eyes on her as she swayed on down the aisle to the storage cupboards near the restrooms.

Next thing she knew, the heckler was there. Banging against the closed restroom door a few paces away from where she stood with an armful of blankets. He rattled the lock until she feared it would snap.

She stepped away from the cupboard and turned to see what he was doing. "Excuse me, do you need some assistance?"

But it was too late. With a loud crack, the heckler pulled the restroom door clear off its hinges. He staggered back, the door in his two-handed grip, then he fell on his arse. The door clonked him on the head, good and hard.

Her hand flew to her mouth. It was hard not to laugh, but she held it back. She pressed her lips together tightly and popped her armful of blankets on the floor before offering a helping hand.

"Oh, sir, are you alright?" She bent forward and tried to drag the door off him. But the door didn't budge. It was heavier than it looked, and kind of wedged between the walls of the small space. The heckler grunted, legs flailing about. It served him right. She wished she could leave him there, but that wouldn't do.

Then *he* was there. Mr Blonde CEO, Too-Hot-To-Handle, Anderson. He wrenched the door off the prone man, as if it weighed nothing at all, and leaned it against the wall beside her. Then he dusted off his hands and managed to still look perfect in his swanky suit. All in a day's work, apparently. There was grumbling from the man on the floor as he sat up, but she was staring at the helpful passenger.

"You okay?" Mr Anderson's forehead crinkled attractively.

She blinked, wondering if it was appropriate to thank him for being handsome. "Ah, yes, thank you."

"Good." He nodded once and sauntered back to his seat.

An odd one, Mr CEO-To-The-Rescue. Surprisingly helpful, if a little un-talkative. With an arse she'd like to sink her teeth into. *Oh, Lord*. He was definitely a distraction she didn't need.

The heckler was up on his feet, stumbling towards the re-stroom further down in Economy. At least he was out of her hair for a while.

She faced the gaping hole of a doorway, the restroom on display. What was she going to do? People would still need to use the facilities, and she couldn't see how she'd re-attach the door mid-flight. She didn't exactly carry Superglue or an electric drill around. All she had handy was a pack of Hollywood tape. While it might keep her boobs in place in a low-cut dress, it probably wouldn't do the trick on a six-foot door.

Out of the corner of her eye she spied Damian, standing back down the aisle, pretending to tidy up with a garbage bag in hand. He'd no doubt been watching the shenanigans, but had avoided helping her. Time for him to do some actual work.

Her quick hand signal meant *get over here now, lazy bones*. He raised his perfectly groomed eyebrows in that insolent way of his. But he strolled over to her, taking his sweet time.

"Here, Damian. I need a big strong man. But you'll have to do. Hold this door for me." She shoved it towards him and he caught it awkwardly, stumbling back a step.

His head snapped from side to side, looking at her, then the door. "But, what? How long for?"

"Until the flight's on the ground, I expect. Hold it in place when someone needs the loo. Good man."

Before he could close his gaping mouth or refuse, she'd left him to it. One more problem dealt with. She almost tripped over the blankets by her feet, so she grabbed them and headed towards the heckler's seat. She left him a couple of blankets to head off further complaints.

On her way to catch up with Yuki, who was checking the luggage was secure in the overhead compartments, Sinead heard a tiny wail like a trapped kitten. Then she spotted him. *Poor little man*. The baby boy with his lone Mummy. The woman was standing and jiggling him in the aisle, bub draped over her shoulder. The wails grew louder, and his face was red and blotchy. The mother caught Sinead's eye as she was about to pass her.

"Here, take little Jack." The woman shoved the baby at Sinead, none too gently. "I need the bathroom."

Sinead grabbed for him, tucking him into the crook of her neck, one hand under his tiny onesie-clad bottom. "Sure, happy to help."

It was part of her job, doing whatever was needed to help the first-class passengers. Anyway, she quite liked getting to cuddle the babies.

Baby Jack's cries grew piercing as the plane dipped. She clutched the little one close, his face nuzzled into her neck. The soft and sweet smell of baby actually soothed her, while she tried to sooth him. Her belly lurched and her ears popped painfully with the sudden change in air pressure. Horrible to an adult, aware of the situation, let alone a tiny child. On cue, he let out an earth-shattering wail.

Sinead shooshed and spoke softly. "It's all right, little man. Your Mummy will be back in no time."

She kissed the top of baby Jack's head, downy hair tickling her nose. She giggled and patted him on the back in a slow rhythm. Raising her head, her gaze connected with a certain gorgeous CEO a few metres away. He was watching her. Again. Eyes alight but darker now, if such a thing were possible. His face was flushed, a touch of pink across his cheeks. She could've sworn he was interested in her.

Something warmed deep inside her belly. She found she didn't mind his attention at all. It was nice to be appreciated. Her lips stretched upwards and she blinked.

He clenched his jaw so a muscle twitched near his ear, then shifted his gaze away.

Okay then. Not so interested. It didn't matter. What would she do with a man like him? A series of naughty images flicked through her mind before she woke up to herself, with a tap on her shoulder.

Baby Jack's mother was back and Sinead handed him over. "He's a treasure."

The elegant woman's formerly tense expression softened. She actually grinned. "Thanks so much, I think so."

Sinead joined Yuki in making sure passengers' hand luggage was safely stowed. Then the captain's announcement grabbed everyone's attention.

"Ladies and gentlemen, we're about to begin our descent into Singapore. We anticipate turbulence as we pass through some cloud. Please fasten your seatbelts and ensure you follow the directions of the crew. Thanks for your understanding. Cabin crew, prepare for landing."

Sinead and the rest of the crew went about the routine tasks, preparing for landing. All the safety checks were double and triple checked for good measure.

The flight took a turn for the worse as they hit the heavy cloud bank. Battling for footing as the cabin trembled and shook with the gale-force winds, she and the crew got everyone ready for landing. Sinead did her job and did it well. A model of calm in a crisis, on the outside at least, when the passengers could see her. Inside was more panicky mayhem.

The descent into Singapore was an adventure in itself, but one she wouldn't want to repeat in a hurry. The plane was pummelled by horizontal rain and buffeting winds as they plunged through the clouds. It was dark as nightfall although only early afternoon. The passengers were all on edge, even the crew. It reminded her a little too much of a flight to the Philippines, when one engine had failed . . .

No, no, no. Don't think about it. A freak incident. It will never happen again.

She sat beside Yuki as they entered Singapore airspace. Her friend grabbed Sinead's hand atop the armrest and dug her fingernails into her skin, leaving little half-moon shaped indentations. The pain provided welcome distraction from the images running through her head.

Yuki murmured, "I'm going to see Daniel again. It will all be okay."

Sinead shuddered, cold creeping across her skin, then pressed back into her seat and closed her eyes.

If the worst were to happen, she had no one special to say her final goodbyes to. How pathetic. Her family back home in Dublin popped into her mind. They'd all but disowned her years ago, but still it hurt her heart to think of them. Sometimes she missed them. Her little sister anyway. Bridie was a good egg in a bad batch. She'd better call Bridie once she got onto *terra firma*.

As the plane began its final descent, Sinead crossed her fingers and prepared herself for touchdown. The engines screamed through her head along with the mantra: *I will make it through this*.

With a thud, the wheels connected with the tarmac. A jolt, and they were on solid ground again. Only it didn't feel so solid, the way the plane skidded down the wet runway. They finally came to a complete stop and the passengers burst into spontaneous applause, followed by sighs and deep breaths. Their collective relief was palpable.

Sinead breathed deeply and resisted the urge to drop her head between her knees. She was alive and her whole life was ahead of her.

Why did it suddenly seem such a lonely prospect?

Chapter Two

Changi Airport, Singapore

"What the hell do you mean there's no flights out of Singapore?" Gabriel's blood pounded in his ears where he stood in front of the customer service desk.

The London office was counting on him. His mother was counting on him. And here he was stuck in the middle, no bloody good to either. Useless. His palm was slick with sweat where he gripped his carry-on bag.

"If this is how Mermaid Airlines treats its first-class passengers, I'll have to rethink the online clients I swing your way. So I suggest you check your computer again and find me a flight."

The customer service officer behind the first-class counter practically cowered behind her computer monitor. She was kind of young, could be new on the job. Once, he'd been like her, working retail, serving people all day long. He shouldn't be a grumpy bastard. But being a pushover wouldn't get him anywhere. If they were trying to pull the wool over his eyes, he wouldn't stand for it. There had to be a flight out.

"I'm so sorry, sir. But as I explained before, there are currently no flights leaving Singapore. We're waiting on a further announcement, but we expect long delays and cancellations. It's a safety issue. But we'll let you know as soon as possible about alternative transport or evacuation." The tiny redhead blinked, awaiting his response. Her bottom lip trembled.

God, he was being a mean prick. The type of self-important arsehole he came in contact with growing up poor in an upper-middle-class suburb. The type he swore he'd never become, even as he built his business and earned more money. The last thing he wanted was to be the type of man to make a woman cry. What would his mum say if she knew? He let a long breath out of his lungs, allowing some of the tension to ease from his shoulders.

Time to change tactics and turn on his trademark charm. It worked every time when dealing with women.

"Okay," he said, and checked her name tag. "Tania. Here's what we're going to do. We're going to work something out to keep me happy and you in a job. Sound good?"

Gabriel flashed his teeth. His smile usually had women eating out of his hand, or offering to do all sorts of other tasty things. Tania nodded, her face flushed and stunned-looking.

He leaned forward on the counter and whispered, "I know you only want to help me."

Tania sighed and dropped her shoulders, then tapped at her keyboard. He waited and pushed down his earlier anger, schooling his expression into a mask of cheerful reasonableness.

Nothing to see here, folks.

"I've made an appointment for you to meet our head of customer relations, Mr Peter Lim. He'll see you in his suite in a few minutes. Jennifer will show you the way."

Another staff member appeared beside him. A younger woman, around twenty-two, dark hair, slim and attractive in those toppling high heels they made them wear. To appeal to men like him. It didn't exactly work. He coughed on a half-chuckle. She was harmless enough.

He didn't have a flight, but maybe it was progress. Mr Lim might have an ace up his sleeve for high rollers like him. Maybe a charter flight. "Not so hard, was it? Thank you very much for your excellent service. I'll be sure to mention it to Mr Lim."

To top it all off, he winked at her. The action reminded him of the cheeky flight attendant, Sinead. Would she be relaxing in some hotel room now? Why was he still thinking about her?

Tania's pale skin flushed and she stammered a response he barely heard. He was already homed-in on young Jennifer, leading the way towards the airline's offices.

He'd managed Tania, like he managed everyone and everything in his life—with a perfectly planned strategy and the right amount of emotion to swing things his way. It was the only way to keep everything running smoothly, to keep everything in balance so it didn't come crashing down and fall in a heap on top of him.

Worked every time. *Usually.*

A crowded airport. Stranded, weary travellers as far as the eye could see. An angry storm. An even angrier man, right beside her. To unwind from the harrowing flight, Sinead had escaped to the relative privacy and quiet of the frequent travellers' lounge with its cushy sofas and buffet of delicious food. She was waiting on word from the airline, there were delays but flights weren't cancelled yet.

But instead of being allowed to curl up and read her new romance novel, a tall, blonde and stunning hunk of Australian surfer-in-a-suit style gorgeousness had decided to plonk himself in the chair next to her. It was him again—the handsome coffee connoisseur from seat 3A. Mr Anderson, it was indeed.

The way he looked at her, slowly running his gaze up and down her body, gave her a little shiver of delight. But no, he wasn't chatting her up. He was complaining. Loudly.

"Can you believe the 'Customer Service Manager' had the gall to call security and 'escort' me here to the lounge? If that's how they handle complaints, they've got a lot to learn. For all they know I've live-tweeted the whole incident. There's plenty of other airlines I can do business with."

She tried valiantly to block out his voice and concentrate instead on his brilliant blue eyes and broad, muscular-looking shoulders, but without much luck. He was truly obnoxious. What a waste of perfectly good man candy. They could be stuck here for hours yet. She could have used a handsome distraction.

The Sky News report blaring on the TV screen in the corner warned of a typhoon rated Category Scary, or something. It was expected to hit hardest in Malaysia, not far from Singapore.

He stopped talking. *Thank God!* He stared at her with one eyebrow raised, as if he'd finally noticed she wasn't paying attention.

"The least you could do is listen. I am a disgruntled passenger after all," Mr Grumpy said.

Enough. She couldn't listen to another word. Sinead broke out her winning hostess-with-the-mostest smile. "Mr Anderson—"

"Gabriel, please."

"Gabriel. Such a lovely, angelic name. Shame it doesn't match your personality." With those words, she stood and grabbed her bag, then marched towards the buffet.

Sure, what did she need a man for? Coffee would always be there for her.

"C is for coffee." She mumbled under her breath.

Foods and drinks beginning with the letter 'c' were her favourites. Naming and cataloguing them all was a little game she played to pass the time in the unfamiliar places she found herself around the world. Her favourites were coffee and chocolate, but from champagne and croissants in Paris to Chahan fried rice in Tokyo, her c-for-comforting foods never let her down.

She made a passable espresso using the coffee machine with the little pods. What to do next? Perhaps some tax-free shopping. She should stay close to the airport seeing as she was on-call for a few more hours. In case the weather improved and they received clearance to fly.

Unlikely. Glancing out the full-length windows, she craned her neck as the rain appeared to be falling sideways. It slashed across the runway in sheets, blown by typhoon winds with terrifying force. The planes on the ground shuddered with the impact. No, those planes were not going anywhere.

Something occurred to her, a light flicking on in her head. So many people were stranded. The hotels near the airport would be booked out soon, especially if all flights were officially grounded. She didn't want to be left hanging in the airport, especially with Mr Grumpy who didn't seem to be going anywhere.

Yuki had taken off to the Orchard Road hotel as soon as their flight landed, although she probably should have stayed put. She was on call too. But Yuki was anxious to get to Daniel. Sinead was more than happy to leave them to have their fun privately if she didn't have to listen to them. If Sinead didn't take action now, she may end up sharing a room with Yuki and Daniel, which didn't bear thinking about.

Balancing her coffee in one hand, she moved to a more private lounge chair and grabbed her smartphone. A few clicks later, she'd booked a junior suite at the airport's five-star hotel through the airline website. All the standard rooms were fully booked, and the suite was over her hotel allowance – it bordered on more than she could comfortably afford – but she'd pay the excess. It would be worth it.

Oh, the luxury of sleeping in a quiet room with a comfortable bed. She'd pretend it was a mini-break holiday, order some room service and watch a movie on satellite TV. She'd take a bubble bath. Proper girl time to relax and unwind was something she'd been sorely lacking.

The phone in her hand seemed to stare accusingly at her. She should probably send a message to her family. They might see the news reports about the typhoon and worry about her. At least her little sister Bridie might worry, if she wasn't too busy with her latest boyfriend. She sent a quick text to Bridie. She texted Ma too, before she could rethink it. She wasn't sure whether to expect a response.

Finishing her coffee, she grabbed her wheelie bag and strode out of the lounge. No time to lose, she had to check in to her hotel and ensconce herself in luxury while she could.

Gabriel pretended to read his copy of the *Financial Times* while he peered over the top of the paper and watched her across the room. The stunning Irish flight attendant with platinum hair. *Sinead*. He'd certainly blown it with her. What had he been thinking? Ranting about turbulence and the diversion to Singapore adding a day to his trip to London, plus the idiot airline manager. She'd taken the full brunt of his frustration, but none of it was her fault.

Just as it wasn't his fault life had become nothing but a series of commitments and obligations, lined up, one after another. An endless to-do list. He barely had time to pause for breath, let alone meet a woman to spend time with. No wonder he was so rusty. When was the last time he'd even been out on a date? Six months ago? The stunning lawyer in New York. Gillian. She'd wanted more and he couldn't commit, not even to a next date.

Sinead on the other hand would probably understand the problems of dating when you're always busy, always getting ready to leave. She was always travelling. He hadn't exactly bowled her over though. Far from it.

He'd been completely unprepared for the effect of talking to her—the scent of her hair was distracting. And she was so freaking hot. Up close, she had the most amazing creamy skin which looked so soft. Then there were her legs—so long and elegant. When she crossed her legs and her skirt rode up her thighs, he couldn't help but watch and wonder what sort of underwear was underneath. She'd completely thrown him off his game.

With most women, he practically had to fight them off. Once they realised he was a company CEO, young, single and not horrible looking, they pinned him as husband material. *Not bloody likely.*

Still, he couldn't stop watching her. She was using her phone, probably texting someone special. Of course she'd have a boyfriend or a husband, although he hadn't seen a ring on her finger. There must be someone worried about her back home. Did she live in Ireland? It wasn't too far to fly there from London. If he could get her talking again . . .

It would be fun to have a fling on this trip, especially if he had to hang around in Singapore. All work and no play was making him a very dull boy lately. According to his best friend Ryan, he was a workaholic robot headcase. The guy didn't mince words.

He needed to feel human again. To feel something other than stress. He needed a plan to get him into Sinead's good books and, ideally, get her into his bed.

Oh hell. He was so distracted, he hadn't even organised a bed for the night. It was already four o'clock and the weather was getting worse. What kind of an online travel expert was he? He should have been onto a hotel booking as soon as Mr Lim had made it clear he couldn't help with a flight. Something, or someone, had obviously rattled his brains.

He looked at his phone on the coffee table. He finally had reception. But before he had a chance to browse his go-to hotel websites, his messages popped up. Twenty-three emails and voicemails too. He took a deep breath and ran his fingers through his hair, then rubbed his temples. Even at a glance, they didn't make fun reading.

Some shit-storm had blown up the company website while he'd been in the air during a typhoon. How appropriate. Looked like his personal life would have to wait while he dealt with it. Business as usual in other words.

Gabriel glanced at Sinead as she crossed the lounge to the exit. The stunning flight attendant had apparently walked out of his life. Too bad.

She was dying for a long soak in a bubble bath to ease her tension. It had been a rough day, keeping calm and in control during the turbulent flight. Her phone buzzed in her pocket as she pushed open the door to her hotel suite.

It was an email from the airline. All flights were grounded until they received a further update from the authorities about the storm later that evening. Which meant down time. Excellent. She was so glad she'd booked her room in advance.

Sinead entered the suite and wandered through the main sitting area *(it had a separate sitting room!)*, kicked off her high heels with a sigh of relief and dumped her bag by the bed. The suite was all soothing earth tones and plush velvet with silky trimmings, a delicious hint of vanilla scented candles hanging in the air. Much nicer than the usual smaller hotel rooms or apartments.

She skimmed her fingertips along the silky edge of the caramel-coloured quilt and then flopped onto the king size bed.

"Oh, how divine," she moaned.

Snuggling into the thick quilt and the feather-top mattress beneath, she closed her eyes. She could have happily crashed for a full eight hours, but there was a possibility she may have to fly again tonight. It was best to keep awake and somewhat alert. At least she could get comfortable and she wouldn't have to worry about another run-in with Mr Grumpy.

When she was able to get vertical again, she checked her phone for messages. Nothing from the airline, not that she expected it so soon. But there was a message from her mother.

That job will be the death of you.

Short and not so sweet. Probably the best to be expected. At least Ma wasn't harassing Sinead to lend Bridie more money. To be fair, Bridie hadn't really asked for help, but Sinead had felt obligated.

Then another text popped up.

WHORE.

She sucked in a breath like she was being pulled underwater, drowning, gasping for air. It was from an unknown number. But she knew who sent it. Her whole body knew. Her fingers trembled as she deleted it and dropped the phone on the bed. She couldn't deal with it now. When would he move on and leave her alone? It had been years. She couldn't deal with *him*. Not again.

Needing a distraction, she explored the rest of the suite, especially her ensuite bathroom. An expanse of white marble tiles led to a massive, glass-walled shower with two massage-type shower heads. There was an inviting designer bathtub which looked like a sculpture of a giant egg and it called Sinead with its siren song. But what if she fell asleep in the tub? She'd miss work, if not risk drowning. The fancy shower would have to do. She stripped off her uniform and tossed it across an armchair near the bed.

She reached for the cotton balls to remove her mask of work makeup. A door slammed, so loud and so close, she jumped.

Jayzus!

She wrapped herself in a towel, then dashed in her bare feet on the slippery floor out of the bathroom. Catapulting through the bathroom doorway into the bedroom, she came to a stop near the bed, only to be confronted by a man. A tall, blonde and looming man, standing beside her bed.

It was the passenger again. The dishy ride of a man. The coffee nut. *Gabriel*. A moment ticked by, pure stunned silence as she stared at him, and he stared right back.

She clutched her towel, then screamed bloody murder.

"You! What in the name of all things holy are you doing in my suite?"

"Your suite? This is *my* suite." He waved his key card around and dumped his overnight bag by his feet. As if that proved anything.

"Look here. I'm about to have a shower in *my* suite. I've half a mind to call hotel security right now. Explain yourself."

"I can see you're going in the shower," he paused, but made no effort to hide the way his gaze slid right under her towel as he mentally undressed her. "I'll call the concierge and sort it out."

"You can get out while you do it." She placed her hands on her hips. The towel slipped slightly.

"I don't think so. You can't kick me out of my own suite."

"My suite. Mine! Get out!" Lord, was the man actually crazy?

"Settle down, sweetheart. Why don't you put some clothes on and lose the attitude?"

Her attitude? What about his? Busting into her room, then telling her what to do. "Why don't you bite me?"

"Feisty. If I thought you really meant it, I'd bite you all right." His eyes twinkled in such a playful way, all the fight went out of her.

Sinead huffed out a breath and sagged down onto the bed. The interloper took it as his cue to sit next to her. She stared, hardly believing his audacity. The bloody cheek of it. Then he picked up his phone and called the concierge as if he hadn't a care in the world.

"Hello, this is Gabriel Anderson. I just checked in and there's a mix-up with my suite. There's a woman in here." He laughed, low and throaty.

Everything under her towel clenched and tingled. That's all she needed. Traitorous libido, getting all uppity.

He glanced at her and grinned. "No, I didn't order a woman."

"You cheeky bastard . . ."

"No, I don't know her. Except from the flight. She works for the airline." He paused and she tried to listen in to the voice babbling on the other end of the phone. "I see. The airline usually books the suites in case of emergency. Double booking. Right. We'll discuss it. I'll get back to you."

Gabriel's expression lit up with the kind of smile which could melt her knickers. If she'd been wearing any.

"We both have a valid booking. You, through the airline, and me, through my corporate account. I guess we're stuck here together," he said with a shrug, as if this were a perfectly acceptable situation.

"You guess wrong. You have thirty seconds to get out before I call security and scream 'stalker'." Sinead stood and marched towards the door, holding her towel firmly across her breasts. She opened the suite's door and waved him out into the hall. "Thirty, twenty-nine, twenty-eight . . ."

He raised his hands in the air. "Okay, I'm going. But you'll see me again soon." His grin was infuriating.

She rolled her eyes. "Not if I can help it."

"Sooner rather than later, sweetheart."

He walked through the door and she slammed it in his smug, sexy face. Her towel dropped to the floor and she groaned in frustration. All kinds. The *I've-had-enough-of-this-day* kind and definitely the *I-haven't-had-sex-in-a-year* and *I-can-feel-it-all-over-my-naked-body* kind. Time for a shower. She scooped up her towel from the floor, checked the door lock and retreated to the luxurious bathroom. She locked that door too.

Many long minutes later, she emerged dripping wet, clean and refreshed, but feeling ever-so-slightly dirty. It was one of the best showers of her life. She may have fantasised about a certain blonde man with a grumpy disposition. *Gabriel*. She loved his name. But she didn't understand why she was attracted to him when he was so annoying. It hardly mattered now. It was unlikely she'd see him again. He probably had the means to rent a hundred suites and then charter a private jet out of Singapore.

Would they have liked each other if they'd had time to talk? She'd have liked to get to know him, intimately. Up close and personal. There was no point in denying it. And he'd been helpful on the plane when the heckler was giving her trouble. He'd watched her during the flight, then again in the lounge. His gaze almost searing her, sending sparks flying through her body. Then he had to go and ruin it by being a grumpy-pants. As she towelled her skin dry, the ache of lingering want low in her belly bothered her.

It had been a long time since she'd last touched a man. Over a year since her ex-boyfriend, Brian The Banker, left. Even before they broke it off, they hadn't been together often. With their busy work schedules, it was amazing they'd managed to get together every few weeks. She'd known it hadn't been working, even before he pulled the plug by announcing he was moving to New York. Brian hadn't suggested she go with him and she hadn't broached the subject either. Since then, she'd been foot-loose and fancy-free, and more than a little lonely.

She stood naked in front of the large bathroom mirror and applied a few dabs of an expensive perfume sample, a freebie on the bathroom vanity. In the mirror, her reflected body looked pretty good. *Not bad*. Not as taut as she'd been at twenty-one, but slim and tall, with decent breasts and nice hair.

Why did she have so much trouble meeting a man who wanted a real relationship with her? It was what she wanted, eventually. But she wasn't even seeing anyone. No man had sparked her interest for years, Brian included. She'd gone for a different type with him. Safe. Undemanding. Boring. It hadn't worked out so well.

She was the first to admit she'd been scared to get into anything serious, after Padraig. She'd been scared and alone and almost broken. But now she was strong and independent. So she told herself every day.

Was it something about her personality scaring the men away? Her mother would say so. Ma had always loved to criticise her, like a kind of hobby. She would've said Sinead was too quick to speak her mind. But since when was honesty a bad thing?

She shook her head to dismiss such depressing ideas and wandered through to the living area. Rifling through her bag for fresh clothes, she made a snap decision to get dressed. She didn't want to stay in her room moping all night. She put on her off-duty clothes. Nice lingerie, skinny jeans and a funky silk top. She styled her hair so it hung in loose waves down her back.

It was so good to express her own style and feel unconfined after hours of having her hair pinned back, dolled-up like Barbie in her straight-laced work uniform.

As she bent to pick-up her phone from a low coffee table, she stumbled, lightheaded, as a wave of dizziness hit. She'd forgotten to eat lunch on the plane and then left the airport lounge after only a coffee. On a whim, she decided to check out the dinner menu at the restaurant downstairs.

After a quick pit-stop at the mirror to apply some lip gloss and mascara, she zipped on her ankle boots. She was good to go.

Chapter Three

D *amn it!* Gabriel couldn't believe his luck. His flight status had officially changed from delayed to cancelled, along with every flight scheduled for the evening. He was stuck with nowhere to stay, like your typical cattle-class passenger. He'd backed down with Sinead, let her take the suite. He didn't want to scare her or snatch the room when she was clearly there first. Just a few floors up from where he now sat in the hotel bar. She was probably in the shower.

He left another furious message for his PA in Melbourne, then punched at his iPad and tried to make hotel rooms magically appear. No luck. Of course the Global Village website was down too. Just perfect.

The airport hotels were both fully booked and there wasn't a taxi or a bus in sight to take him to the heart of the city. He'd tried to charter a flight but had missed his chance. He wasn't going anywhere for at least twelve hours. The airport was officially closed.

News reports on the bar's TV screens advised everyone to stay indoors. The weather was much worse and they were in the thick of it at the airport. The rain beat hard against the windows facing the street at the hotel bar, pounding like someone urgently banging on the door, begging to come inside. He was stuck, sure as shit.

Gabriel signalled to the barman from his prime barstool and ordered a Tiger beer. He checked out the bar, full of stranded passengers like him. Except most of them probably had comfortable rooms upstairs. Rooms they would actually get to sleep in. As he sipped from his tall frosty glass, he spotted a new patron entering the bar. A tall, curvy vision of a blonde bombshell. His night instantly improved.

Hello again, Irish.

Sinead walked into the bar looking like a hot rock chick. This look was even better than the flight attendant uniform, and that was something. Tight jeans clung to her long legs and fine arse. A slinky shirt skimmed the curves of her absolutely outstanding breasts. Long blonde hair hung loose and tousled like she'd rolled straight out of bed. *His* bed. He could still be in with a chance to convince her to share the suite.

His pulse thrummed wildly and he tried to get a grip. How should he play this? His standard *treat 'em mean, keep 'em keen* approach hadn't worked. She was smart enough to see through it. Time for Plan B. His mum had always said flattery would get you anywhere. It was worth a shot.

"Sinead!" Gabriel shouted loud enough for a few heads to turn his way.

Her head snapped round too and she met his eyes, but with eyebrows raised sky-high. She was wary of him, based on their last conversation. Fair enough.

"Come and join me." He tried not to sound desperate. Not cool.

"Hello again. Ready to haggle for the suite, are you?" She sighed and sat on the stool next to him. Then she looked up at him from under long eyelashes. She was obviously pissed-off and exhausted, but the fire in her eyes nearly burned him alive.

Wow. His voice caught in his throat and he swallowed, hard. "Look, I'm sorry about earlier. Let me say, you look stunning. I thought it was you, but I had to double-check."

"Are you saying I didn't look good earlier? Because I had a pretty hard day and I don't need to hear it."

This was not going according to plan. "No! I meant you looked so neat and perfect in your uniform and then you were in nothing but a towel." He cleared his throat. *God, that towel*. "Now you look . . ." He reminded himself to be charming. He didn't want to put her off. "You're absolutely smokin'. Stunning. Beautiful."

"Well, thank you. It's the nicest thing anyone has said to me all day."

She moved closer, hitting him with a dazzling smile and leaning an elbow on the bar. Warmth rolled through his stomach. She might like him. Her body language was giving him the go-ahead.

He gestured to the bar. "Can I buy you a drink?"

"Um, I haven't eaten and I'm not sure if I have to fly soon, so I'd better not." But she scanned the printed wine list on the bar. She was tempted.

"Didn't you hear? The airport's officially closed. The typhoon's moved closer."

"Really? The update must have come while I was in the shower."

Gabriel instantly pictured her naked under the shower, her luscious skin dripping wet. So very distracting. But definitely in a good way. He gave his body a talking-to. *Down boy*.

Sinead pulled her phone from her clutch purse and checked her messages. "Yep, everyone's grounded for the night. Grand, I can relax. I'm so glad I booked a hotel room earlier. I had a feeling I might get stuck here." Her lips pursed, the expression was so smug. She was obviously winding him up.

"I tried every hotel I could think of and everything's booked. Too bad I don't have hot-chick superpowers to steal a suite from an innocent man." He graced her with his cheesiest grin, reserved for occasions when he had to pull out all the stops.

Sinead rolled her eyes at him. Strangely, he found it cute.

"Superpowers aside, I know how to book a hotel room. I've been stranded before. I soon learned to beat the stampede of passengers looking for a bed for the night. First in, best dressed, Gabriel."

Her husky voice as she half-whispered his name and all her talk about being first into bed, or whatever she said, had his pulse racing again. Add the flutter of her eyelashes against her cheeks and the fact she mentioned her hotel room, and he was losing his mind. Maybe she was interested.

"I still haven't snagged a room. But I could get lucky. If there's any cancellations, I mean. Let me buy you dinner to apologise for busting into your suite. You said you're hungry, right?"

She titled her head, then shrugged. "Sure, why not?"

Gabriel reached for her hand as she slid off her stool. Their fingertips connected and the charge between them was instant. Hot, electric. This was new. He glanced down and searched her face. She blinked slowly, then stared, her eyes wide.

Oh yeah. She felt it too, the wild pull of attraction. He took her elbow and led her through to the restaurant. And he didn't want to let go.

He was so transparent. Sinead blinked in disbelief as Gabriel led her into the restaurant, squiring her on his arm like the lord of the manor. This turnaround in pretending to be nice and throwing a few compliments her way was so obviously a ploy to get into her bed. Actually, he probably planned to steal her bed out from under her, beds being few and far between during a typhoon. He'd lost out. She'd won.

But she'd play along, if only to tease him. Her instinct said Gabriel usually had women falling into his bed as soon as he looked at them. Not her. As much as she might like to.

The slight contact when he took her hand, and now the feel of his large hand on her bare arm, had heat suffusing her skin. The sensation was delicious and it had long-neglected parts of her body humming with pleasure. But she didn't trust it. She'd eat a good meal, ogle a handsome man and then get a good night's sleep in her big hotel bed. All alone.

The only problem was, she was tired of sleeping alone. It would be wonderful to snuggle all night next to a warm, strong man with his arm wrapped around her, holding her close. After she'd shagged him senseless.

Whoa, Nellie!

She tried to rein in her errant sexy thoughts. She'd need to be on guard with Gabriel. Her footsteps stuttered as he pulled out a chair for her at a secluded corner table. She took her seat, keeping her head down so her hair curtained her face, hiding the rosy glow no doubt lighting up her cheeks.

Gabriel's fingertips grazed her bare shoulder as he pushed in her chair. Shivery anticipation zipped across her skin, a sensation hard to ignore. She liked it. Her body liked it, but her head told her to be careful.

A Singaporean waiter stood nearby, dressed in trendy black from head-to-toe. It was a modern Asian-fusion restaurant and aromas of chilli and fragrant jasmine rice wafted from nearby tables. Her stomach grumbled, reminding her to eat something soon. The manly vision in front of her was distracting. Earlier she didn't think she'd ever see him again, but she didn't mind running into him. At all.

Sinead stealthily admired Gabriel as he took his seat. He looked a little rumpled. His hair was ruffled and stubble dusted his jaw, blondish brown against tan skin. He'd lost his jacket and tie. His white shirt was open two or three buttons, revealing smooth skin and the outline of broad shoulders beneath, narrowing to a slim waist and hips. A swimmer's build – he was in great shape. She'd like to unwrap the rest of him. It was okay to fantasise.

Her eyes snapped back up to meet his gaze and a gasp hitched in her throat. He'd caught her checking him out. A self-satisfied smirk crossed his face.

"What do you feel like eating?" he asked.

You. The answer popped into her head uninvited. Luckily she didn't voice it.

"Let's see." Sinead picked up a menu and held it up to hide her blush. How embarrassing. "The Curry Laksa and Hainanese chicken both sound good." She lowered the menu and ran her finger down the dessert list. "I like nearly anything, but especially foods beginning with the letter 'c'. Coffee, chocolate, champagne, they're my favourites. What do you like?"

"Oh, I could be tempted by many things, Sinead. But tonight, I'll let you choose."

Her mouth popped open and heat charged through her system. She'd run with it. She was attracted to him. Whatever this thing was between them, why not let herself have some fun for a change?

"Then let's get both dishes and we'll share. And I think a drink is overdue." She waved at the waiter. Sinead was about to order white wine but the waiter suggested cocktails.

"For the lady, we recommend our specialty, the Singapore Sling. Very popular." The waiter hovered with a pen poised over his notepad.

"Sure, sounds good. Gabriel, how about you?"

Gabriel cocked his head to one side and seemed to consider the idea carefully. Finally he nodded.

"All right, I'm game. Sling me."

The waiter left them alone. Sinead pressed her lips together as nervousness hit. She folded and re-folded her hands in her lap and tried to think of something to say. It'd been a while since she last went on a dinner date. Not that this was a date. Or was it? Either way, small talk wasn't her favourite way to pass the time.

She glanced across the table at him. "So, Gabriel. I gather you're some kind of businessman. What do you do exactly?"

"I run an online travel company called Global Village. You might have heard of it?" He raised an eyebrow as if waiting for a big reaction.

She'd heard of it, it was a major company. But she wasn't overly impressed by his success or the fact he had money. He was a first-class passenger and she met men like him every day at work. Except most were not quite so handsome.

She gazed into his bluer-than-the-ocean eyes and stopped a sigh escaping her lips by a millisecond. Apparently those eyes had the ability to render her speechless and reduce her insides to a gooey puddle of warm, liquid caramel. With an effort, she concentrated on the conversation.

"Aye, I've heard of it. It's a good website. You run the company? Must keep you busy."

"Yeah, to put it mildly. I started the company and built it to this stage. Now I'm setting up the Europe branch in London. It's . . . flat out. It doesn't leave much time for anything else."

"I feel the same sometimes. I obviously don't run a company but I'm always on the go. Always arriving somewhere to be leaving again. It can be lonely."

Now why had she said such a thing? She didn't want to sound like a sad old spinster.

Luckily, the waiter returned with their tall, cherry-coloured cocktails and placed them on the table so they were perfectly aligned on red cardboard coasters. She raised her glass to propose a toast. What to say? To hell with it. She'd take a risk.

"To Singapore, to typhoons and to meeting a handsome stranger."

A mischievous glint lit up his eyes as he raised his glass. "To Singapore, to typhoons and being stranded with a beautiful woman. Cheers."

They clinked glasses and she had the uncanny sense of having struck a bargain of some kind. Probably a deal with the devil. She swallowed a giggle and then she took a long sip of her cocktail. After a few moments, it began to work its magic. Her limbs loosened up and her head buzzed with pleasure. She needed to eat something, and soon.

Gabriel snagged her with his gaze. "I've been wanting to ask, is there a Mr Mermaid Airlines? Someone you met on your travels or back home?"

He drummed his fingers on the tabletop. He was nervous, even if he was trying not to show it. Could he actually be interested in her, not just playing a game?

Her body couldn't help but react. Her breath hitched again and she struggled to focus on keeping her hands steady.

"No, nobody special. I'm based in London at the moment, but I don't really know a lot of people there. I had a couple of fellas chasing me when I used to live in Melbourne and back in Dublin. But it's been a while between drinks, you could say." She took another long sip of her cocktail to illustrate the point. She was definitely thirsty.

"I'm surprised no man's put a ring on your finger. You're quite the catch."

"Really? It's sweet of you to say." Her cheeks flamed and she probably had a silly grin pasted on her face. Which no doubt wobbled when Gabriel's knee nudged hers beneath the table. Her blood pumped extra fast through her veins, heating every inch of her skin.

"What about you? Is there a girlfriend or Mrs Online Travel Guru?" She managed to keep her voice steady, but hung on for his answer.

He hesitated. "No. I don't really . . . I haven't done that before."

"You don't mean to tell me you're a virgin?" She was all wide-eyed with faux innocence.

Gabriel spluttered and nearly choked on his drink. "Hardly! I just haven't really gone in for relationships, a partner, whatever."

"Oh, right."

Sinead caught his drift and couldn't help feeling disappointed. She'd hoped his answer might have been different, like he was looking for Ms Right. Then again, maybe he hadn't met any suitable candidates. Although he must have his pick of beautiful, highly qualified women—a veritable temp agency of talent at his beck and call wherever he went around the world. Best not to think about it.

"Why don't you do relationships? I haven't had the best luck, but I still want to find someone special. Don't you?" Hadn't she always believed in honesty when dating? It was the only way to build a real relationship with a man. It hadn't worked out for her so far, but she'd test out her honesty theory with Gabriel. Put it out there. Would it scare him off?

"As a kid I saw first-hand what a bad relationship can do to a woman. I don't want any part of it."

She was surprised he'd say something so honest. It must be something in the air tonight.

Gabriel looked away from her for the first time since they sat down to dinner. His gaze darted around the restaurant. His posture was tense, from the firm line of his jaw to his raised shoulders and tendons pulling taut in his neck.

She was tempted to jump the table and offer to massage him, to ease his tension. Instead she changed tack, hoping to steer the conversation back to more pleasant territory.

"I'm sorry. Why don't you tell me something fun you like doing? What have you got planned in London?"

He chuckled deep in his throat but without humour. "There isn't much fun stuff on my agenda right now, apart from having dinner with you. I've got a major office opening in London in a couple of weeks and it'll be round-the-clock getting it up and running. I want to step back a bit soon. But it's probably not going to happen." He gripped his glass in a choke-hold then took a long sip.

He sighed and crumpled in his chair, as if the weight of a thousand worries crushed his bones. "Honestly, the pace is getting to me. I love running my own company and it was brilliant a few years ago, when it was still growing in Australia. But now it's taken on a life of its own. I'd like to have time to go surfing once in a while, you know?"

She nodded. She'd never been surfing but she'd like to try it. There'd be freedom out on the ocean. And she'd always had a mermaid fantasy. So, she fancied herself as Princess Ariel. A girl could daydream. She was embarrassed to admit that's why she'd wanted to work for Mermaid Airlines in the first place.

"Apparently I now work twenty-four hours a day, whenever one of my staff has a problem they can't sort out." He shook his head. "Sorry, I don't know why I'm telling you all this."

She was surprised by his willingness to share, but she liked it. She liked him. He wasn't quite as slick or as annoying as he seemed at first glance.

"It's okay, I'm interested. Why don't you step back? It's your company. Surely you can hire some people to help. I meet a lot of businessmen in first-class, sometimes we get talking. What puzzles me is why so many work themselves into an early grave when they don't love it."

His eyes narrowed slightly, a crease forming between his eyebrows.

Sinead toyed with the cherry decorating the rim of her glass. She rambled on. "It could be the chase, trying to reach the mythical state of having 'made it'. I don't know, the material things don't mean much to me. There's better ways to spend your time on this earth. Give me a beach any day. At least I'll be on holiday in a few weeks. Thailand, here I come."

Anticipated pleasure flooded her body. The white sand between her toes as she strolled along perfect beaches, swimming in water as warm as a bath. She'd try all the exotic foods and shop for bargains at the night markets. It was all waiting for her.

She snapped back to the here-and-now. Gabriel stared intensely into her eyes. It was a bit unnerving. What was he thinking? Had she overstepped his comfort zone with her pop psychology?

"I'm so jealous. Thailand is amazing. Have you ever been to Koh Chang? I reckon it's one of the most beautiful islands in the world. Lonely Beach is my favourite spot. I'd like to take some time off to hang out there again."

The wistful tone in his voice caught her off-guard. Like a little boy lost, adrift in the big bad world. Exactly how she felt, half the time.

"I've never heard of Koh Chang, but I'll add it to my list. Still, I've got a few flights to get through before my holiday. Including a trip home to Dublin I could do without." It already made her spine tense, even two weeks before the visit.

"I know how that goes, believe me." Gabriel looked so sad then, heartbroken even. His forehead creased in horizontal lines, jaw clenched so hard she swore she heard it click. But the way he closed his eyes, it nearly slayed her.

She didn't try to fill the awkward moment with words, but reached for his hand, surprising him. It surprised her too. His hand stiffened, then relaxed. He opened his eyes and gently squeezed her fingertips, rubbing his thumb across the back of her hand.

Holy moly. Tingly pleasure ran from her fingertips to the most surprising places.

She stared at his hand resting on hers. It was hot and heavy and *manly*. The pull between them was compelling. When she raised her chin and their eyes locked across the table, there was something there. A real connection.

She was almost one hundred per cent sure. Well, at least sixty per cent. Sinead slowly withdrew her hand from Gabriel's.

The food arrived, carried by another black-clad waiter. He placed the dishes on the table with a flourish of his hand, as if to say *voila*. Sinead glanced at him as he backed away without a word, trying not to disturb them. So efficient and silent, some sort of dinner ninja.

She didn't want to disturb the mood with Gabriel. She looked up into his eyes. His gaze had a weight to it. It was demanding. Intense. Burning right down to her soul, or some such nonsense.

He hid there, behind those eyes. A vulnerability most people wouldn't see, which made him all the more appealing. Mad as it was.

Perhaps this wasn't a harmless flirtation after all, for either of them.

So soft, so sweet.

Gabriel meant to say something, but he was barely coherent. The feel of her hand in his, skin-to-skin, had been magic. Intoxicating. She'd scrambled his brain like eggs with one touch. But it was only a fraction of the contact he wanted, of what his body demanded. And she'd touched him first. She'd reached out to him.

Who knew why he was talking about his childhood or his overwhelming business schedule. He never talked about those things, not with anyone. His weaknesses. In business it was best to conceal any vulnerability. Half of the trick to his success was the veneer of capability and strength, the smooth shell he showed to the world. Normally he wouldn't allow the shell to crack, especially with a woman he'd just met.

He'd cut the conversation short, before he revealed too much. Who cared about half a lifetime of poverty or a sick mother now he was successful? No woman ever had, and he had no reason to think Sinead would be the exception to the rule.

She watched him closely. It had him on edge. Did she want him to make the next move?

"Should we eat this dinner or let it go cold?" His weak attempt at a joke eased the tension between them.

A hint of amusement made Sinead's lips twitch. "Definitely eat it. I'm actually ravenous."

The possible double-meaning to her words had him staring at her mouth, as she licked along her plump lower lip.

An instant kick of arousal charged through him in response. Lucky the table covered his reaction as his body stiffened. He had to get a grip, they were in a public restaurant.

He wanted to stand up and grab her, then push her hard up against the wall behind them. Kiss those lips, strip her bare and explore her body until she begged for more. To make her his. He gripped the edge of the table until it made an angry red crease in his palm.

Bloody hell. What was that about?

He'd never had such a strong reaction to a woman, especially someone he hardly knew. And he wasn't a Neanderthal.

Sinead reached for the serving spoon. She served the food from shared plates in the centre of the table for both of them.

Gabriel was having a meltdown and she was fine, going about her business, serving dinner. His skin still tingled where she'd touched him. He tried to compose himself. Breathed in, then out.

He was the one who knew how to control any given situation. Throw him into a room with a bunch of business executives and CEOs in a crisis and he'd have them hanging on his every word, looking to him for advice. Now he was in real danger of losing control.

What would it mean, to totally lose control when he was with a woman? He'd never got close, never really let go. There'd been flirting and fun, but this could be something else.

A plate of food appeared in front of him with a clunk, and snapped his attention back to her. She'd served him a mixed plate of the meals they'd ordered and it smelled sensational. He ate automatically, the spoon moving from the plate to his mouth.

She looked at him, a glint of laughter in her eyes. "So, there's a sign in the bar advertising karaoke later. I'd like to give it a try. Do you want to join me?"

"Karaoke? Really?" He sighed and leaned back in his seat, ruffling a hand through his hair. "If you're into it, okay."

She grinned. "You sound sooo excited."

"It's fine. I'd like to hear you sing."

Right then, he would have done anything to extend the time they had together. He'd even sing karaoke. Without his own hotel room, he'd be stuck hanging around in the bar or the foyer all night anyway.

Sinead leaned toward him, then waved her hand at him. "Gabriel, you have something on your face. Here, let me get it."

He was spellbound when she reached over and traced the tip of her index finger across his lips. Shuddering under her touch, he closed his eyes for a second. When he blinked his eyes open, her lips were parted. Her cheeks were flushed a gorgeous shade of pink. A stop sign? Maybe he should back off.

If she regretted touching him for a second, what would she think if she could see inside his head? If she knew exactly what he'd been imagining doing to her, she'd probably run straight upstairs without him.

She sat back in her seat. "You had a little curry on the corner of your mouth."

His heart had some kind of malfunction as she raised her fingertip to her own lips and licked the curry off her finger. Slowly. Painfully slowly.

Everything pulsed and throbbed. *Bugger and damn*. He was so close to losing control of the whole situation.

As a distraction, he ordered another round of Singapore Slings from the passing waiter. Then he flicked through his saved phone messages. He was using any excuse not to look at her face again. Not yet, when his brain was stuck in slow-motion. Replaying Sinead sucking her finger between glossy lips and licking it clean. The finger she'd swiped across his own mouth. The intimate act sent his nerve endings wild. Then he looked up to find her eyes locked on his face.

"Aren't you hungry?" She glanced down towards his mostly untouched meal.

His voice cracked. "You have no idea."

Picking up his chopsticks, he ate. But he barely noticed anything he tasted. All he wanted to taste was her, for dessert.

Sinead shook her head at his offhand comment, but really, she had no bloody clue what he was thinking. A couple of times during dinner, she'd seen something in his eyes, like desire. Then it retreated behind his cool facade. Not Mr Grumpy from earlier in the day but a different Gabriel. She guessed it was his businessman 'game face'. Why he was showing it to her, she wasn't sure. He was so hard to read.

If only she could control her body's response. Her heart pounded beneath her breasts like a wild animal thrashing against a cage, fighting for release. When her fingertip made contact with his lips, so slight a touch, desire flared inside her. She wanted his kiss on her lips, on other parts of her body. Everywhere.

It'd been an age since her libido raged through her body with a will of its own. Her body demanded to be touched. By Gabriel. Immediately.

What a pity her brain was busy hosing her down from the top.

The man was ignoring her in favour of checking his phone messages. It was certainly a blow to a girl's ego.

The waiter delivered two more cocktails to their table with a clink and a bow. *Thank goodness.* She needed to cool down. It might not be wise to drink so much so quickly, but she needed to take the edge off the hormonal rush whipping through her body. She was mad. Of course the alcohol would make her want him all the more. But still, she drank. Anyway, it gave her something to do with her mouth.

She sucked the cocktail through her straw and rolled it around her tongue. "Mmm, delicious." Cherry flavour laced with a hint of something naughty.

Gabriel sighed and she didn't know what to make of it. Was he disgusted with her for drinking too much?

"Sinead, what would you say if I told you you're not the sort of woman I usually take out to dinner?"

She froze. Was he saying she wasn't good enough for him? *The bloody hide of him.*

"What do you think I'll say to such a question? I'm perfectly good enough for any company, including yours, thanks very much. I may be a working-class girl from Dublin, but I've a brain in my head and I've made a good career for myself. I didn't expect to hear snobbery from an Aussie like yourself." She slammed her glass down on the table for emphasis. Her head spun from the impact. She was a little tipsy.

"No, I didn't mean anything negative. I'm hardly a snob. You're refreshing. You're real. Not like some of the women I meet at business functions. They're always preening and pouting, putting on a show. I can't stand it."

Right. So he was slumming it with her? She straightened her spine. Gabriel Anderson may have been rich and handsome, but he wouldn't make her feel bad about herself. He'd put a pretty spin on it, but she wasn't fooled.

She wasn't any man's fool. Not anymore.

He'd killed the conversation. *Idiot.* Gabriel pressed one hand to his temple as he leaned on the table.

"Sinead?"

She'd gone so quiet, the silence was thick as snow on the ground in Aspen when he'd last gone skiing. She did it again, staring at her lap, folding her elegant hands over and over each other. A nervous tic.

He wanted to smooth things over but he was rusty at this kind of thing too. "I'm sorry. I didn't mean to upset you. I've been having a great time so far."

She looked up and offered a hint of a smile.

He'd have to put her at ease again. He grasped at a familiar and relatively safe topic. Work. "Tell me about being a flight attendant. I'll bet you love the travel. You must have been to some amazing places."

Sinead frowned. What was her reaction about? Work might not be a safe topic after all.

She shrugged. "It's a good job. I've seen half the world and know my way around an airport with my eyes closed. But it's been five years and I could do with a change. More of a challenge, I suppose. Not to mention I live in a tiny shoebox in London that doesn't feel like home."

Her eyes flicked sideways, avoiding his gaze.

"Sinead, are you all right?"

She smiled for a moment. "Aye. Sorry about that. It must be the jet-lag talking." He doubted it. She was upset about something. It wasn't his place to ask, but he could help cheer her up. Show her a good time.

Thinking fast, he stood and reached for Sinead's hand.

"What do you say we go check out the karaoke? Little known fact about me: I can really belt out a show tune." He grinned and raised his eyebrows. It had the desired effect, even if the thought of karaoke made him want to cut and run.

Sinead laughed, clear and true, chiming like crystal glasses striking in celebration.

She grinned and shook her head "Oh, is that so?"

Then she was on her feet, standing in front of him. She took his hand, wrapping her fingers around his. It was perfect, their hands pressed together, like they fit.

He couldn't believe he hadn't done more of this. Talking, spending time with a woman, holding hands. He never realised what he'd been missing.

Raising her hand to his lips, he kissed the smooth skin on the back of her hand. Only the briefest contact, but it raised his temperature, and hers too, judging by her reaction. Her quick intake of breath, the way her breasts rose and fell, the flare of heat in her eyes. That was something.

He wanted more. More of her laughter, more of her heat. He wished he could take her straight upstairs to *their* suite.

Chapter Four

Gabriel held onto her and led her through to the hotel bar. Sinead's heart was still fluttering like it was being brushed by fairy wings, dancing in her chest. Tinkerbell and her friends were having a party in there. The way he'd kissed her hand. Heat pulsed through her body, making her legs weak.

Oh my goodness. She'd had past encounters of the naked and horizontal variety which had barely raised her pulse. Gabriel on the other hand . . . *Wow.*

He was full of surprises. Based on their first couple of run-ins, she'd never have picked him as a gentleman. Gruff and sexy, demanding and handsome—check, check, check and check. But gentlemanly? Not exactly. He'd upset her with his comments about being different to the women he usually dated. But she'd judged too soon. He'd apologised and now he was taking her to karaoke, although it probably wasn't his cup of tea.

Was it really only a matter of hours since they met? It seemed like days ago already.

They found a table against the wall of the crowded bar. She slunk into the leather seat and kept her eyes on him as he settled in opposite her. He folded his long, limber self into the metal framed chair and crossed his arms on the dark wood table. His forearms were on full display with his sleeves rolled up, strong muscles and tendons taut and tempting. A wave of warmth rolled up her chest and neck to flush her face. God, even his arms were making her blush.

She hoped their evening was only getting warmed up. But she never did this. Meeting a man, talking for a while, then seriously entertaining ideas of how best to separate him from his clothes. And wrap herself around him instead.

She'd never had a one-night stand. The more the idea rattled around her brain, the more she wanted it. Wasn't it something every normal, red-blooded, woman of the world should experience?

Rationalising her bad behaviour, or so her mother would say. *No.* The voice of doom had no place in her head tonight. In her Ma's book, she'd probably burn in hell simply for looking at a man like she'd been looking at Gabriel. Seeing as she was already on fire, it was a little late to start worrying.

A screech from the front of the room had her whipping her head around. A woman was belting out a tune on the small stage at the end of the bar, furthest from the street entrance. Her high voice was muffled by the feedback from the speakers. It was a bit squealy.

"So, Gabriel. What do you think?" She didn't like it. The whiny pop-song might have been top of the charts in Asia, but she couldn't get the gist of it. And that was before the woman on stage murdered it.

"Man, that's some crooning. What's the word for it? Warbly?" His cheeky grin was highly flammable, or so it seemed to her lady parts.

"What's your type of music then? You mentioned show tunes. Something like *Oklahoma!* or *CATS*?" Her lips tugged up at the corners.

Gabriel answered with a full-throated chuckle which rumbled across her skin and through her belly like a roll of thunder.

He didn't laugh often, but when he did there was such an open and sunny look on his face, it was almost boyish. It was addictive. She loved being able to turn his frown upside down. She wanted more of his laughter, his humour.

"Oh, no. My musical taste is eclectic, but it runs more to the Nirvana side of the equation, with a bit of Hilltop Hoods thrown in. How about you?"

"Little known fact about me," she mirrored his earlier comment, "when I was a teenager I followed a couple of punk bands around the festival circuit, Glastonbury, Reading, the whole scene. I even shaved off all my hair like Sinead O'Connor. My favourite band of all time is The Sex Pistols. But I love my pop songs too."

"I never would have picked you as a punk. I'm impressed. Although I don't think I approve of your being a skinhead. I can't imagine you without your beautiful blonde hair."

She stilled, afraid to break the spell as he reached across the table and stroked his fingers through the lengths of her hair. Already trembling, she gasped under the light but sensual touch. She couldn't hide her reaction, but bit her lip to keep from groaning.

His hand hovered next to her cheek for a split second as if to touch her face, to feel her skin. "You have beautiful skin too. Irish cream."

She wanted him to touch her, willed him to. It was so strange, she'd never been so drawn to a man in her life.

He dropped his hand down onto the table in front of him. Her heart sank with disappointment.

"I reckon it's time for another drink. What do you say?" Gabriel avoided her eyes.

She could have sworn he was blushing too, even through his suntan.

· ❤ · ❤ · ❤ · ❤ · ❤ ·

Two Singapore Slings later and Gabriel's head was about to explode. Not from sitting so close to Sinead, although she was definitely getting under his skin. It was an all-too-familiar foe. A migraine.

He was an idiot, it was official. Too many drinks in his system and probably one of his food triggers. He should've checked the ingredients of the meal. It must have contained MSG.

The synapses in his brain were firing randomly and a full-blown migraine was coming. But he didn't want a bloody headache to ruin his night with Sinead. He pressed his hand to his forehead. The acupressure move was supposed to help. No luck so far.

The darkened bar was completely packed, spotlights illuminating the stage. A bunch of people stood jammed in near the stage, swaying and shouting. He'd agreed to karaoke, mostly so he could stay close to Sinead a while longer. Now it was hurting his brain.

The MC called for more volunteers and Sinead's hand shot straight up in the air. Okay, then. He'd cheer her on. People nearby clapped and hooted. She jumped up and was almost away before she cupped her hand to his ear. Her warm breath rushed across his neck and he had to tell himself not to reach for her. Not to kiss her.

"Wish me luck?" Then she was off, weaving through the crowd.

"Luck!" He wasn't sure if she'd heard him, but she looked back and winked over her shoulder.

A wash of heat stole over him. Damn, she owned him with a wink.

Now he was eager to see her in action. She was a wannabe rock star and she'd really loosened up with the potent cocktails.

She bounded up to the low stage. The crowd was lapping it up, shouting and applauding after the last act, or victim. He could do without more pounding bass beats, keeping time with the pounding inside his head.

He sat higher in his seat and craned his neck for a better view. She spoke to the MC and chose a song from the database. The music started and he groaned. Not because of the throbbing pain in his head, because of the song.

"Not bloody Kylie," he whispered. The singing budgie wasn't his favourite Aussie export. He rubbed his temples with both hands.

Sinead was centre stage with a microphone in one hand, doing the weird dance from the music video. Even though he wasn't a fan, it was the type of song your brain absorbed by osmosis. She wasn't wearing the famous white jumpsuit with the plunging neckline, but he pictured it anyway. She already looked damn fine up there, shimmying and shaking, even sexier than when she'd danced to the Macarena song back on the plane. The Kylie outfit would be the icing on the cake though.

"*La, la, la, la, la, la, la, la . . .*"

She launched into the song and as she started on the lyrics, he had to admit she wasn't half bad. At least she was giving it everything she had.

Gabriel's ears pricked up at the words of the song. Could the lyrics be meant especially for him? She couldn't get some guy out of her head, and his loving was all she could think about. This song wasn't so bad after all.

Sinead strutted across the stage like a real rock chick. Her tight jeans gave him a fine view of her assets, along with every other bloke in the bar.

One guy yelled out. "Hey Kylie! Wanna do the locomotion with me?"

Laughter broke out from the punters near the stage. A jolt of jealousy struck him like a punch in the gut. He couldn't stand the idea of these guys looking at her, let alone laying their hands on her. Weird, seeing as he'd never experienced anything like it. Jealousy.

Sinead seemed to be oblivious to the effect she had on the guys in the crowd. She was in the zone. Now Sinead sang about wanting the guy every day and every night. Asking him to stay.

Absolutely. He wanted to stay with her and he was going to get her. Now. He stood up and steadied himself. Most of his body was ready to leave, but his brain, and a killer migraine, had other ideas. The hazy aura in the corners of his vision slowed him down. This migraine was going to hurt. Based on past experience, he reckoned it would hit full-force in about half an hour.

Then so many things happened at once, he wasn't sure what came first. Sinead fell off the stage with a massive crash, singing as she went down.

"La, la, la, la, laaaaaahhh!"

Shit! She'd taken a headlong stage-dive into the crowd. He had to help her. No one had any warning. No one had tried to catch her or help her to crowd-surf, not like at a music festival.

Bloody hell.

"Sinead!" His voice got lost in the crowd.

He was on his feet and moving, pushing and stomping his way through the mass of people. A space opened in the crowd at the front of the stage but he still couldn't see her.

Then from behind him, a sound like tearing metal and cracking glass made him spin. He swivelled on the spot and took in the scene. A window had shattered at the bar's entrance. Shards of glass and half a palm tree had blown inside. The typhoon had hit. Literally. Wind rushed through the open windows, howling and creaking.

People screamed. A woman somewhere behind him laughed hysterically. He staggered back from the windows like everyone else, as water rushed across the floor.

Where the hell was Sinead? He had to get to her.

Everyone was going nuts, running around, bashing into each other, looking for the nearest exit. Through the hustle of the crowd in front of him, he spotted a flash of white-blonde hair near the floor, a few metres ahead.

He shoved past people and tripped over a table. He groaned, the air whooshing out of him as he righted himself.

Shit, shit, shit.

He looked up, and there she was. Finally. Sprawled across the floor on her front, half propped-up on her elbows. Looking lost and scared. He skidded to her side and dropped to a crouch.

"Gabriel? Is everyone freaking out because I can't sing and I fell off the stage?" Her voice was tiny.

"Of course not! Are you hurt?" He pushed her hair back from her face and cradled her head in his hands. She looked beautiful, but too fragile.

"No, I'm okay.

He breathed a sigh of relief.

She sat up, still resting against him. "I didn't see what happened. What's going on?"

"It's the typhoon. The windows shattered and the bar's flooding. We need to get out of here."

He wrapped an arm around her waist, loving her softness, having her close. Heat prickled across his skin. She hooked her arm through his as he helped her to slowly stand. His hand squeezed tighter, holding her steady.

She winced. "Ow, my knee." Bending, she rubbed the sore spot.

"Hurt?"

"Bruised, or sprained. I'll survive."

He nodded. An emergency siren sounded. The *woop-woop* noise nearly split his ear-drums and didn't help his damn headache. His whole skull vibrated with the clanging. He grasped his forehead with both hands.

"Are you all right? What happened to you?" Sinead tilted her chin up, still holding onto his arm.

"It's a migraine. I get bad ones sometimes." This wasn't how he imagined things going, but he had to try. "It's a big ask, but I might need to share your suite after all."

Sinead dropped her hand from his arm like he'd zapped her with electricity. Not the good, panty-melting kind. The drop your hairdryer in the bathtub kind. The shock could kill you.

God, she was stupid. Of course it was the bed he really wanted. Most likely he wanted to shag her *and then* steal her room.

Migraine, my arse.

She stepped back a pace and yelped when her knee throbbed, and a shot of searing pain zipped up her leg.

He stared at her, face crumpling like a balled-up tissue. "Sinead? Did you hear what I said? I'm seriously about to fall flat on my face."

What to do? Screams and shouts rang out around them, standing still as statues while the crowd flowed around them. People were skedaddling, that was for sure.

A puddle of water formed around her feet and she sploshed as she shifted on the spot. She breathed in deep and caught a strange whiff of ozone. Jesus, Gabriel was right about one thing. The storm was barging in, flood water heading their way.

It was like a scene from *Titanic*: some people losing their marbles and others fleeing and pushing others out of the way. Only she wasn't buying Gabriel in the role of Jack. Not selfless enough.

Locking her fingers together in front of her, she told it to him straight. Kind of. "I'll need a hand getting upstairs. Then we'll see about getting you settled."

It was the truth as far as it went. She didn't mention the part about him not having a hope in hell of getting into her bed.

He moved close to her body. She could've purred and rubbed against him like a cat. But that would be bad. A bad, bad idea. She couldn't remember why, or much of anything, when he wrapped his arm around her waist. She could feel muscles on his muscles, for goodness sake.

He spoke low and deep in her ear. "Here, lean on me."

She'd flake out at his feet if he kept that up. Her mind went places she wasn't supposed to be going. Gabriel talking low and dirty in her ear, naked and hovering over her, kissing her deep and slow, waiting for her to . . .

"Are you coming, or not?" He squinted and sounded puzzled. The question nearly had her laughing, except it wasn't funny at all.

So, she hadn't had a boyfriend for a year. Not even a man to hold her hand or put his arm around her. There was no need to become a quivery mess, a volcano filled with molten lava, ready to blow at the slightest touch.

Nope, no need at all.

She let him lead her across the bar, their footsteps falling in sync. He was going slow, helping her balance. Her knee throbbed like it was huge and red. It was hard to see in the low light. Glass crunched underfoot and she sloshed through water to her ankles—her little boots would be ruined. *Stupid thoughts. Stupid boots*

They reached the side exit, where a long line of people were jostling and shoving, trying to get out. A man near her staggered into her shoulder. She glanced up and she nearly lost her dinner. *Oh, no.* He was bleeding from a great gash in his head, red rivers down his face and droplets on his shirt.

Gabriel tugged her towards him. "Let's go, right now. Are you with me?"

Was she with him? It was a good question. One she didn't have time to ponder as he yanked her arm and pulled her behind him into the hotel foyer. It was like a transplanted refugee camp right off the evening news. Hotel staff in black uniforms handed out pillows from huge trolleys, stacked high. Blankets and air-bed mattresses too. Emergency services were just arriving, pushing through the front doors with stretchers.

Gaze skimming the open area, she took in the families, small children huddled on the floor wrapped in blankets, more than a hundred people altogether. The hotel foyer was dripping with opulence, plush carpets and marble staircases, chandeliers and all. Now it was oddly practical and hospital-like. People with bandages around their limbs, a makeshift first-aid area near the reception desk.

She must have gasped, because Gabriel spoke all reassuring and hot in her ear again. He squeezed her waist, making her skin tingle through her silk shirt. That was one way to get her mind off the chaos.

Glancing at her, then to the crowd near reception, he rubbed her back. Up and down. "Don't worry, we'll be fine."

She shivered under his touch and hoped her reaction wasn't obvious. "I know, it's bad though. All these people. I hope nobody's stuck outside in the storm."

Their heads swung to the full-length windows facing the street. Staff were taping them with sheets of cardboard. It probably wouldn't make a lick of difference. Through the uncovered panes of glass was a torrential downpour the likes of which she'd never seen. As if a hundred high-pressure fire hoses exploded and rained down on the hotel from all directions.

With a tug on her upper arm, Gabriel pulled her with him, towards a bank of elevators. Her knee twinged as she struggled to keep up. Gabriel stormed ahead of her. She frowned and stopped to catch her breath. "Hey, weren't you supposed to be helping me along?"

He stopped and looked back, his expression tense, jaw clenched. "I didn't mean to rush you."

"Sure, I'm fine." Nodding, she kept walking, trying to keep an eye on his back, and on the floor at the same time.

Was he was thinking about the bed waiting upstairs? The one with her name on it.

Hers, not his.

Chapter Five

His brain was about to explode, which would leave a nasty mess all over the silk-covered walls for some poor cleaner. A bastard of a job. How did you clean brains off silk?

Bloody hell, he was losing it.

He was descending into that weird twilight stage before he blacked out. Images more like dreams played through his mind, noises amplified twenty times louder than normal. The light burned his retinas.

They were at the suite before Sinead spoke.

She tipped her head to the side. "So, thanks for your help getting me upstairs. I'll be okay now." Her hair hung over one shoulder, glowing silver in the moody lighting.

After the elevator ride where she'd given him the silent treatment, Gabriel didn't like the tone of her voice now. She was trying to get rid of him. *Like hell.*

He was sick, about to get a whole lot sicker. It was mayhem downstairs and he didn't have another option. This was his suite as much as hers. There were times when it might pay to be a gentleman. This wasn't one of them.

"Right. I'll take the couch. I only need a spare pillow and blanket. I'll stay out of your hair."

She crossed her arms over her chest. "Ah, I don't think so. It's been a pleasure, Gabriel. But I'll be getting to bed now. Alone."

Subtle as a sledgehammer. He could be plenty blunt too. "If you're worried about your virtue, My Lady, I promise not to defile you. Not even with my eyes. I feel like death warmed up and I'm about to fall down flat with a migraine. Happy now?"

Her narrowed eyes said *don't mess with me*. Then she composed her features into a sweet expression, fluttering her eyelashes. "Aye, I'm bursting with sunbeams and there's rainbows coming out my arse. But I'm still not letting a strange man in my bedroom."

She unlocked the suite's door with her swipe card quicker than he could blink. Then she flicked her rose-petal scented hair over her other shoulder. "Goodnight, Gabriel."

She slammed the door in his face.

What the . . . ? Had she really kicked him out and left him in the hall for the night? All signs pointed to yes.

He stepped back and stared at the door. Really stared. Like if he concentrated hard enough, she'd take pity on him or he'd summon her by telepathy and she'd let him inside.

When he heard a click and the door actually opened a crack, he blinked a couple of times to make sure it wasn't his mind playing tricks. Light spilled into the hall through the narrow gap, then it widened. Sinead stuck her head into the doorway, then a pale hand followed, dropping something that landed at his feet with a hushed plop.

One pillow, and one blanket. Exactly what he'd said he needed from her. Nothing more, nothing less. His gaze roved up, searching for some sign of reprieve in her face. There was none.

The door clicked shut. Sinead was still on the other side of it. The comfortable side. He was not. Which left him with precisely no options, except to slide his sorry butt down the opposite wall until the floor connected with it and jolted his tailbone.

He sat for a while, resting his head on his hands, knees drawn up to his chest. His head pounded ominously.

About time he called Ryan. He didn't want to talk about work, he only wanted to talk to his best mate. He couldn't call his mum because she was so far gone, she wouldn't recognise his voice. He found his phone in his shirt pocket and scrolled through his contacts, then hit Ry's name.

The call rang out. The message tone sounded, and he went blank. What to say? He'd been kicked out by a woman he hardly knew, who he liked more than he should. Plus, she was his best prospect of a bed for the night. He was sleeping in the hall like a vagrant. And if all that wasn't bad enough, he had a banging migraine and he was stuck in Singapore in the middle of a typhoon.

Not the sort of stuff a bloke dumped on his friend in a voice-mail message.

He ended the call, kicked the door with a clunk and sank down on his side. He stuffed the pillow under his aching head.

Thoughts raced through his addled mind. Where the hell were his migraine meds? On the plane in his checked luggage? No, of course not. He'd dumped his carry-on bag in the suite when he'd barged in on Sinead earlier. The meds were in his bag, on the other side of the door. Resting comfortably by Sinead's bed.

He kicked the bloody door again for good measure.

Sinead pulled back the covers and arranged a pile of pillows on the bed, making it all pretty and perfect. A thud from the hallway told her Gabriel had flopped in a heap near her door. Most likely. She wouldn't risk sticking her neck out again to check. She was annoyed at him for trying to trick her. So she told herself. Maybe she was also slightly worried she might invite him inside and wrap herself around his hard body.

Things weren't going at all to plan. She'd failed in her bubble bath and girly night-in goals, letting him talk her into dinner. Then she'd ended up at karaoke with him. She'd almost invited him upstairs, but then he'd pulled the invalid card. She should have tested her high heel sprinting skills and made a dash for it long before the Singapore Slings.

Rounding the end of the bed, she tripped over something low and square. Gabriel's overnight bag. *Shite*. He'd probably be looking for it.

Flight attendant school hadn't prepared her for this scenario. She'd earned an A+ in tray carrying and advanced smiling, but this? Stranded with a handsome first-class passenger who wants to sleep with you, and you've locked him outside your hotel suite without his luggage or a place to sleep. What do you do next? She didn't want to take it out to him. If she were sitting a test, she didn't think the correct answer would be 'search through his bag and personal belongings'. Actually, it would probably get her fired.

She stared at the offending bag and willed it to disappear. Her X-ray vision obviously wasn't working. Who knew what he had in there? Work papers, a laptop? Probably a change of underwear and snacks.

Nothing important, surely. It would keep until morning. And there was absolutely no reason for guilt about holding onto the man's bag or for making him sleep in the hall. No reason at all. Her stomach twisted a little, but it was probably all the cocktails going down.

She strolled into the bathroom and took care of necessities, then stripped off her clothes. In her own bag, she found a deliciously clean and fresh white T-shirt and matching knickers.

Once she was changed, she fell into bed. Sure, she was exhausted, but she still had a tiny bit of energy to make snow angels with her arms and legs in the perfectly neat hotel sheets. 1000 thread count, no expense spared. The fabric was smooth and soft as her hair when the fancy hairdresser in Paris ironed it straight.

Curling up on her usual left hand side of the bed, scrunched in a tight ball, she hugged herself. Gabriel popped into her mind, probably sprawled on the hard floor outside with his pillow and blanket. Part of her was tempted to ask him in. Scrunching her eyes closed, she dismissed the thought. She'd be smart, not soft and emotional. She let the sounds of the storm carry her off to dreamland.

"Good night," she whispered.

To no one in particular.

Thunk, thunk, splice.

Gabriel squinted his eyes open, letting in the bare minimum light. Weren't brains meant to be soft and squishy grey matter? Not sharp and stabby swords of torture tearing his skull open. He had no bloody idea where he was.

Cold, dark space, a hard floor and thin blanket. Pins and needles down one side of his body, a numb leg on the other. His head was kind of jammed against a wall. He'd guess his office floor (it wouldn't be the first time), or jail (it *would* be the first time), except the blanket covering him was plush and warm with an expensive feel, like cashmere.

He raised himself up to sit, rubbing his dead leg with the palms of both hands, rasping over the blanket and his trousers. Looking around, he registered more details. He was in a corridor, outside a hotel room door.

The night's events rushed back with the sound of the howling, whipping wind. The storm. Sinead. Drinks and karaoke.

The hotel suite and a door in his face. Last but not least, a killer migraine.

His vision splintered, red and black. Searing pain burned behind his eyes, scrunched tightly closed. *Meds*. He needed them, now.

He remembered now. The meds were in his bag, on the other side of the door. He lifted his head and concentrated. It wasn't too far away, only a metre. Then he'd tackle getting inside and crossing the room. How would he get in? The concierge would open the door if he could find his phone. Slipping his hand into his back pocket, he found something else. His key card to the suite. He'd had the damn thing the whole time.

"Bingo." He slipped it out of his pocket and held it up in the dim light. He doubted Sinead would've opened up if he banged on the door, but since he had his own key, he'd use it.

He dragged his butt to the door and opened it with a soft click. At least Sinead hadn't locked the inside latch. His head was pounding like someone had taken a meat mallet to his temple.

Doof, doof, doof.

Then he got the shakes. *Crap*. If this kept up, he'd be flat on his back in a second. His fingers trembled as he pushed the door open with his palm, cool wood giving way until he almost fell through the doorway. He managed to stay on his feet. The last thing he wanted was to wake Sinead and freak her out, thinking he was some kind of creeper. He might end up in jail after all.

The room was dead silent. Only a gold ribbon of light from the bathroom draped across the bed and lit his path to where she slept. His bag was right beside the bed, he could see it now in the low light. His footsteps faltered. She looked tiny, all curled up on one side of the king sized bed, draped in white cotton sheets. And so damn beautiful it was hard to breathe. The weird clench in his gut happened again, like he was being tugged towards her. As if there was some kind of connection between them.

Crazy. He rubbed his aching right temple.

Concentrating on stealthy footsteps on the thick carpet, he made his way to her side of the bed and his bag, a black blocky outline. He was only inches away from her now. He bent down and grasped his bag, trying to open it. The bag's zipper tore like a fault line through the sleeping earth. An earthquake would've been quieter, even with the wind still howling outside. He glanced up at Sinead, whose eyelashes fluttered, but she still slept peacefully.

He opened up his bag. Fumbling for his wash bag inside, he found the small box of pills. He hated taking painkillers, but he needed them. Man, he needed them.

Gripping the pills in one hand, he quickly stood upright. Big mistake. Burning, searing, red-rimmed light filled his vision.

He had to sit down. He found the edge of the bed and lowered himself onto it. *Just a second*. He'd be okay to move soon. Maybe. His head fell into his hands and all the air whooshed from his lungs. He groaned.

"Gabriel?" Sinead's voice cracked and she sat bolt upright. "What are you doing in here?" She held the sheet up to her chin and her eyes were wide.

Damn it. He'd scared her, the last thing he'd meant to do. He met Sinead's gaze and shook his head, but immediately regretted it. The room tilted and went blurry. With his head in his hands, he closed his eyes and groaned again. "Sorry, it's the migraine. Needed my meds."

"Are you okay?" Her voice was so soft he could've he'd imagined it. "Do you need water?"

Suddenly she was at his side, sitting on her knees with a glass of water in her hand. An angel all in white, her hair a halo of silver. He took the glass gratefully, gulped the water and got the meds down.

Then he was flat on his back. Not sure how, but there was the ceiling straight up. She was there, whispering. Shooshing and stroking. Touching his forehead. Something cool. So cool. So good.

His shirt came off, her fingers making quick work of buttons and pushing it open, when he couldn't. Then the cool, down his chest. A cloth with cool water. Her fingers followed, the lightest touch.

Gabriel wanted to thank her. But the words wouldn't come out right. "Sorry I – I didn't mean to scare you. I just need to rest." He gripped his head, right hand covering his eyes. The sharp pain blocked out everything. Until he focused on her voice.

She leaned in, over him. "It's okay, it's okay." Her words repeated over and over.

Strands of hair brushed his shoulder. Her lips, softer than air. A tug on his lower lip. A kiss. Was he hallucinating now? No, he could feel the trace of her kiss on his lips.

"Rest now." She spoke near his ear, warm breath against his skin.

Sheets and blankets covered him, her hand smoothing them down.

Everything went black.

Her eyes popped open to blackness. No, not total dark, a sliver of light fell across the bed. It was late at night, close to dawn. Sinead lay still, curled on her side. Something woke her. The harsh sound of the wind and rain beating relentlessly at the windows. She closed her eyes again. Her body felt too heavy, and her head ached with exhaustion.

She shivered and rubbed her hands up and down her bare arms sticking out of rumpled sheets. Dread crept over her skin like a shadow. It could have been a hangover from her dream—flashes of lightning and twisted, tangled limbs, glimpses of a man's strong chest and back, defined and highlighted by lamp light. A deep, rumbling voice calling her name.

She'd dreamed of him. Gabriel. Finding him at the bottom of her bed, looking after him. Taking off his shirt and seeing him stretched out, abs and golden skin on full display. The touch of him under her fingertips, soft and hard at once.

Someone groaned. "Sinead – you there?"

She flipped over and whipped her head up. This wasn't a dream. Her gaze snagged on fleshy ridges of muscle, the type of torso Yuki called *abtastic*. A sound came out of her throat like a strangled cat caught on a barbed wire fence.

Man. Hot man. Hot, half-naked man. In my bed.

She pinched herself on the thigh, hard. He was still there, and she was fully awake. So she scuttled up the bed like a startled crab when someone lifted up its rock, exposing its hidey-hole to the world. Pulling the bedcovers up to her chin, she leaned back on the bedhead and gave him a proper looking over.

He was most definitely there, and most definitely asleep. Her gaze tracked upwards from the sheet at his waist, over hill and vale of man pecs and shoulders.

She reached a sculpted jaw, full lips and the eyes she knew were as blue as her lonely heart, though they were closed.

Gabriel. Shirtless and stunning, making her want him. Making her want *things* beyond all reason.

A ridey ride of a man.

He stretched his arms above his head and clutched his forehead. Her heart pounded at a gallop. Ridey or not, he was waking up. And he was clearly out of order being in her bed.

"Get out of my bed or I'll box your head off!" She pointed at him, waving her hand around as if to shoo him away.

Her brain was bombarded with questions, banging around in there, trying to get out.

Why was he in her bed?

How did he get in the room?

Why did he have to be so delicious?

Why did her resolve to stay away from him melt like a scoop of gelato in the sun as soon as he looked at her with half an eye?

And shouldn't she be scared of him?

"Good morning." The words dragged out of his throat, snagged on something solid, like chunks of testosterone. He opened one eye, only a crack, and his lips tipped up in a micro-smile.

Words tumbled out of her mouth. "What do you mean 'good morning'? I seem to recall you being on the other side of the door last night. Did you break in to my room? I've a good mind to call the police."

Both his eyes popped open "The police might be busy with restoring order and directing traffic, but go ahead. I didn't so much break in as use my swipe card to enter the suite which, you may have forgotten, is registered under my name through my business account. All above board and legit."

"Oh." She twisted the ends of her hair around her index finger until it cut off the circulation. She let go, so the strands unfurled and the tip of her finger went from blue to pink again. "There was still no reason to barge in and *sleep* with me. So rude."

"You didn't seem to mind last night." His lips tipped up in a knowing grin, so dimples appeared on either side of his lush mouth. The dimples were overkill. And what use did a man have for such full lips? Actually, there would be a few kissing-related purposes. Hidden parts of her body heated and tightened.

La, la, la. Not thinking about kissing. Not any kind of kissing.

And what did he mean, anyway, she "didn't seem to mind last night"? Oh, God. What exactly had happened between them?

She shook her head. "I didn't know you were here."

He nodded and his lips twitched. "Ah, so it was someone else who got me a glass of water to take my migraine meds. Someone else who took off my shirt. Sponged my head and chest with a wash cloth to cool me down. Right. Must have been some other gorgeous blonde woman who's always being kind and taking care of people."

Oh, wow. The memory came back to her in black and white images, not quite fitting together. She had helped him. She'd touched him. Unbuttoned his shirt and laid him down on the bed while she knelt beside him, then she'd practically given him a sponge bath. He'd been burning up with fever. Now she remembered.

Still, there was no reason for the image of her palms sliding over the contours of his damp chest, down the ridged path of his abs. Her eyes slid over his body again. Yes, her ab-memory was correct.

Ribbed, for her pleasure.

He even had a golden happy-trail of raspy hair from his chest to the waist of his trousers. Probably lower. His skin was tanned a toasty colour too, everywhere she could see. Her fingers twitched where they clutched at the sheets.

But wait, did he call her gorgeous? He had to be trying to butter her up. Of course. He wanted to stay.

The crazy storm blustered on outside, rattling the windows, and here he was lying in her bed without a care in the world.

He sat up, leaning on his elbows. "You didn't remember any of it, did you? I wondered if you were half asleep. Or drunk. Too many Singapore Slings, I guess. That explains it."

"Explains what?"

"The kiss."

"What kiss?" Shivers passed over her skin like phantom fingertips, stroking all over her body in tiny circles.

"You kissed me. Then told me to rest and tucked me into bed."

She gasped, pressing her fingers to her lips. "I did not. If I'd kissed you, I'd remember. I'd know how soft your lips were. I'd know whether they tasted like ice cream and the beach the way I imagined . . ."

Oh. My. God.

She'd kissed him all right.

Now he grinned at her like the cat who'd got the cream. Except he hadn't, of course. Gotten any. No cream, not even a lick of it. It didn't even count as a real kiss when one of them was half drunk and the other out of his mind with a migraine. Although from what she remembered, it had been a gentle, delicious kiss.

She shook her head again. "If I'd kissed you properly you wouldn't be so smug. You'd be begging me for another kiss and all sad and mopey because I won't."

"Won't what?"

"Kiss you again."

"Kiss me again." He bit his bottom lip. It was all damp and glistening. Lord, she did want to kiss him.

She stared at him—his eyes, his mouth. His face was dead serious now. The smirk had dropped right off his dial, replaced by a tense-jawed concentration centred on her lips. His eyes burned with white-hot laser beams, searing her from three feet away. Although he was suddenly closer. When had he moved closer?

He hadn't. *She* was the one who'd moved closer. She wasn't sure how it had happened, but she couldn't stop herself. She was leaning into him and breathing too fast. Should she kiss him?

She hovered, still leaning towards him. The sheets pooled around her legs, leaving her sitting beside him in a semi-sheer white T-shirt which did nothing to hide the hard points of her nipples. At least she was wearing knickers this time and not a towel. Still, she was more naked.

He raised one eyebrow and stared at her. "I dare you to kiss me again."

She blinked. "What? How old are you, Gabriel Anderson?"

The grin was back. He looked like a teenager when those dimples showed themselves. "A few years older than you, I'll bet. But I still remember some things. Like when a girl kisses you, it's a good sign. It means she likes you."

"I do not like you. I find you infuriating and annoying. And too *Australian*." Seriously, he was like a commercial for surfing and barbeques. But he was certainly good looking. Even more so without his shirt on.

"You like me. I can tell." His gaze strolled lazily down her body and landed on her breasts, circled there until her flesh swelled and pushed against the soft cotton. "I like you very much, Irish."

Lucky she was already sitting, because her legs evaporated. She kind of fell forward until she had to grab his hard shoulder to steady herself. Months of pent-up desire wreaked havoc on a girl's muscle control.

His eyes reeled her in. "Kiss me again. I double-dare you."

So, she did. Of course she did. Not because of the dare. She wanted to. No one could blame her. Not even her brain, which fled on a little holiday as soon as her mouth brushed his too-full, too-succulent lips.

Delicious man.

Gabriel hadn't expected the kiss last night. He'd sunk into heavy sleep with the taste of her, teasing him. Sending him on dream adventures where he'd wrapped her in his arms on some tropical beach and kissed her until she sighed and moaned.

And he didn't expect the kiss now, even though he'd goaded her into it.

But she leaned into him and her scent surrounded him, wrapped right around him, blocking out the rest of the world. Some kind of flowers, sweet and light as springtime. Her lips touched his and he groaned.

The noise had a weight to it, reverberating all the way up from his stomach and shaking his bones. She licked across his lower lip and hummed into his mouth, like she was singing a song only for him. He was a goner.

When she gripped his shoulder and leaned over, pushing him down into the mattress, he could only go along with it. Her tongue flicked into his mouth, tangling with his.

Next thing he knew, Sinead was rising up above him and straddling him, lowering herself over his body. She flexed her hips and pressed her soft heat into his groin. Only a tiny scrap of white cotton covered her. Heat surged through his system and all the blood rushed south, so he lost his damn mind.

A goner? He was dead meat. Lying powerless at her mercy, waiting to be taken to heaven.

What a way to go.

Her lips opened and she tasted him. His mouth, his lips, his tongue. Sweet and salty and so, so, good. The way he stared up at her, as she pressed herself into his body . . .

He was all open, boyish innocence and wide eyes, blue as the summer sky. Not the arrogant CEO now. Not half.

Jaysus.

She thrust her tongue into his mouth. Tasting him, wanting more. Kissing with eyes wide open, soaking up his admiration and handsomeness like a sponge.

That look of his was almost enough to tip her over the edge. Her body, her sanity, balanced on a precipice, teeter-tottering on the point of no return. Heat drummed through her belly and legs, pulsing at the point between her thighs. She almost had him where she wanted him, but not quite. She hadn't taken her clothes off, but she didn't have time for minor details like that.

He groaned and God help her, she pressed her hips into him. The hard, solid length of him still clad in trousers. Fizzy tingles of pleasure fanned out from her centre to every nerve she had. If her body had wiring, she would've lit up like a Christmas tree strung with lights.

Ding, twinkle, flash!

Shifting slightly, a wave of pleasure rolled through her. She gasped, an incoherent noise in her throat.

He broke their insatiable, ongoing kiss and chuckled darkly. All deep and rumbly. "Slow down, Irish."

"Oh, Gabriel. I don't think I can." She didn't think she could stop now, even if she wanted to. She rocked her hips and pressed into him again.

His eyes rolled back in his head and he tightened his grip on her hips. "You're a firecracker. I want you too," he whispered.

She squirmed as he kissed the delicate skin along her throat and licked the shell of her ear. Shivers danced over her sensitized skin as he blew hot air over the damp spot where his lips had been.

Then he hypnotised her with whispers about the things he wanted to do to her. Dirty things. Delicious things.

So fecking sexy.

The pressure built inside her, swirling and brewing like a storm. He reached under her shirt to cup her bare breast. She leaned into his touch and he rolled her hard nipple between his fingertips. She gasped at the sensation, his slightly rough fingers rasping over her sensitive skin. Tingles zipped here, there and everywhere. It was almost too much. It had been so long, and Gabriel seemed to know how to push all the right buttons.

He thrust his hips forward and she moved with him, then her mind went blank.

She gasped, and closed her eyes as she fell over the edge. Floating. A surge of hot pleasure overtook her and she rode it, she rode him.

Warmth washed over her whole body, like a wave lapping at the shore. Finally, she collapsed across acres of his hot, bare chest. Her lungs burned, full of heat but no air.

After about fifty years, she came to. Inch by inch, she regained her senses and found herself back in her body, in possession of limbs. She'd flopped over him, boneless as a jellyfish washed up with the tide. Very attractive.

She found her arms, her hands, and pushed up over him. "How embarrassing. I didn't even get to undress." She glanced down at her own body, at the front of her T-shirt which was hanging off one shoulder. She hadn't undressed, but she wasn't wearing much of anything.

"You were *so* hot. And I'm ready to go anytime." He laughed, the rumbly rolling sound making her belly flip.

He took her hand and placed it over his thick erection, straining against the thin fabric of his trousers. So hot and hard, all for her.

She breathed out, a long sigh of a breath which said she hadn't quite finished with him. Not even close. It had been a long time since she'd wanted to worship at the temple of a man's holy place. But she wanted to. Whatever madness had gotten into her, it wasn't done with her yet. She was more than ready to return the favour with Gabriel. In fact, she was itching to unwrap him and bask in what she hoped would be a glorious sight.

"Let me take care of you, Gabriel." She sat up slowly, unbuttoned and unzipped, setting him free.

He closed his eyes and sighed. "I'm all yours, Irish."

She stroked him, lightly at first. Her fingers trembled, and so did he. Then she took in the view before her. The whole shebang. The entire package. All his glory. Everything tightened and heated inside her again.

This was going to be fun. She was a lucky girl. Very lucky indeed. So, she went to town on him.

Chapter Six

T he dream gripped him by the throat, even as he opened his eyes and blinked back the shards of daylight piercing the darkness. He was trapped inside his own body, unable to speak. Immoveable as a stone. Helpless. Lying in a hospital bed. He fisted the sheets in his hands.

Gabriel swallowed hard, but couldn't catch his breath. His heart pounded too fast.

Slowly, he moved his legs. The weight lifted, feeling returned. Then he unclasped his hands and sat up. He leaned back against the bed frame and propped a pillow behind him. And breathed deep.

When his breathing slowed, the prickles at the back of his neck calmed. It was only a dream. A nightmare.

On cue, the wind ripped past the windows and shook the entire building and he tensed again. It was the storm, playing havoc with his imagination. Nothing more. Nothing to worry about.

Breathe. In, and out.

God, he should be relaxed after what Sinead had done to him. The way she'd moved above him, touched him and tasted him.

So bloody beautiful. She'd let loose, taken him in her hot little mouth and gone wild. She'd given him the best orgasm he'd had in years. Damn, it was amazing. Then she'd fallen asleep before they could go again. She'd better bloody well remember him when she woke up this time. A man's ego could only take so much.

He lay down, stretched out on the amazingly comfortable bed and enjoyed the view. Sinead, asleep beside him, was simply stunning. She was curled up on one side, facing toward him. Half-naked with only a sheet covering her to the waist, her white T-shirt stretched across those impeccable breasts. There was still a lot of gorgeous soft skin on display where it rode up her stomach. Skin he'd like to taste. Still a lot of her to experience. He hadn't even been inside her yet. That thought made his body tense again. He had to push it out of his mind. For now.

He turned to her, lying beside him. Her expression was so sweet and peaceful. Rosebud lips and eyelashes fanned out over her cheeks. She looked younger and carefree when she slept.

She was posed like a model, but he didn't want to share this image with anyone. If he was a great artist or a photographer he'd capture the way she looked right now and keep it for himself. To hold onto the memory. He'd remember Sinead like this when they inevitably went their separate ways. He'd remember the wild, wanton woman too. Of course he would. How could he forget?

Part of him wanted to wake her, no prizes for guessing which part. He could surprise her with a good morning gift. He was definitely ready for action again after a short rest.

The higher reasoning part of him knew he should leave her to sleep. They'd still have time for fun later. Hopefully, more energetic fun if she was well rested. Although even exhausted, she'd blown his mind.

First things first. He was starved. He'd need some fuel for what he hoped was still to come with Sinead. Stretching his arms above his head, the tension ebbed out of his sore back and shoulders. He rolled out of bed and onto his feet.

Stalking across the room naked, he found the room service menu and phone on the desk by the windows. He pulled back the heavy curtains, shaking his head at the thunderous sky, pelting rain and wind like the end of the world. He wouldn't be going anywhere for a while, and he was glad.

He flicked his focus back to the menu and called the order through. Enough breakfast options for two. Coffee, croissants, bacon and eggs, fruit salad. No more weird ingredients to mess with his head or his stomach.

Next most important thing on the agenda: get work off his plate for at least another day or two. It was unusual for him to get a whole day to himself and he intended to make the most of it with Sinead.

Grabbing his phone, he gripped the edge of the desk and braced himself to call his PA, Martha. She was a tough as nails older woman with indestructible-looking iron grey hair and an unforgiving attitude towards time-wasting. He loved her for it. She could be a handful, but she was an absolute gem and made his working life – basically his whole life – so much easier to manage.

"Martha, good. I'm glad you're there."

"Gabriel, you had me worried. I'm watching the news about the typhoon. It's much worse than you let on yesterday. Are you all right? Did you find somewhere to stay?" Her voice went up in a high inflection. A sign of her concern.

He was rattled to hear the motherly tone, coming through loud and clear even over the phone. Martha reminded him of his own mum at times. The way she used to be. He'd been expecting to be told off for being rude yesterday.

"It's okay, I'm fine. I made a friend on the flight and we're sharing a room at the airport hotel. No harm done."

His gaze swung around towards Sinead, still dead to the world in their big bed. *Friends*. He didn't usually have such debauched thoughts about his friends. The things he'd like to do to her... Anyway, they weren't friends. It was only a casual thing. Something in his stomach clenched at the thought and he stared out the window again.

"Actually I'm calling to ask you to rearrange my schedule. I'm obviously stuck in Singapore and I don't know when I'll be flying out. And I had another migraine last night. I need some downtime to recover. Let's say, two days?"

Martha tutted in his ear. "You poor thing. Consider it done. The website palaver was all sorted out last night by those new IT guys in the London office, no problem. I'll let everyone know Ryan is acting CEO while you're in Singapore. Now you rest, Gabriel. No checking your messages and worrying about work. I won't stand for it."

"Thanks Martha, you're the best. I'll call Ryan later to check in. Why don't you hand over some of your normal work to Katrina and take the afternoon off too? Go and get your hair done, a facial, whatever. Book the fancy spa place you like, I'll pay. I'll text my hotel details so you know where to reach me."

"Listen to you, still giving orders. But I'll obey the one about the spa. Do you want me to book a doctor's appointment for you?"

He shook his head. "No, thanks." He planned to avoid the doctors as long as possible. He'd spent far too much time in hospitals lately.

"You need to look after yourself better. Get back to bed and rest. Bye, Gabriel."

He raised his eyebrow at Martha's bossy tone but didn't dare talk back. He fully intended to get back to bed as soon as possible. With Sinead.

"Bye, Martha."

Work would be okay. Ryan was more than capable. Both as the new head of the European office, and as his best friend and business partner. Considering he'd known Ryan since their university days and they ran the business together, he was comfortable in handing over the reins. Temporarily.

The thought of Ryan made him remember to let his friend know where he was, and basically confirm he was alive. Gabriel pulled on his boxer shorts, grabbed his phone and moved to the living area, leaving Sinead to sleep. She looked perfect where she was.

Settling into the sofa, he tapped out a text message. Ry responded quickly, telling Gabriel to rest and make sure his migraine cleared before he got back to work. He'd obviously been talking to Martha already.

He almost hit the call button—Ryan would be a good guy to talk to about Sinead. Years ago, Ry had met a woman on holiday. They'd ended up dating for over a year. Noelle from some finance company in Europe. Nice woman, pretty too. Gabriel had never heard the end of the story about why they broke up, although he suspected it had something to do with Ryan's past.

His friend had been in love once. Properly, madly, stupidly in love. Ryan had thrown himself in head first, since he'd been too young to know better. When it ended, tragically, Ryan had been in pieces. Gabriel had done his best to get Ryan involved in work, in building something. To give his friend purpose again.

No way did Gabriel ever want to have his own heart crushed and his life destroyed the way Ryan's had been.

A drumming knock made him jump. He glanced at the door. The breakfast order. He searched through cupboards in the hallway and found a white cotton bathrobe. Slipping it on, he cracked the door open wide enough to accept the tray of food.

The bill caught his eye, flapping in the breeze from the air-conditioner, held under a plate, the total circled in red pen. The food was pricey. The whole place was. He didn't want Sinead forking out for this. He'd treat her. She'd probably get an allowance from the airline, but not enough to cover all the extras. Well, he could afford it.

He called down the corridor to the retreating hotel staffer. "Excuse me, I have a question about the account. Do you know, can I pay in advance? For the suite and the room service. I don't want to leave it for Ms Kennealy."

The young man hurried back and stood in the doorway. "I'm sorry sir, I don't know. But I could ask the front office staff."

"Yes, thanks. Wait a minute. I'll give you my corporate account details."

He stepped inside and deposited the breakfast tray near the TV, then found his wallet and a business card. Back at the door, he jotted down his account details and handed over the card.

"I'd like the suite and any additional costs charged to my account—Gabriel Anderson. I'm a friend of Ms Kennealy's. I don't want to bother her while she's sleeping, but I'll take care of it. The front office staff know me. I stay here all the time for business." He signed the receipt.

"Very good, sir."

"Thank you. I'll drop in downstairs later."

The staffer nodded and disappeared down the corridor.

Gabriel wandered back into the suite feeling lighter. No work for two whole days, his head had stopped aching and there was a stunning woman sharing his suite. Now he didn't have to worry about her paying for it.

He always paid his debts. One thing about growing up poor, he always made sure he wasn't under obligation to anyone. He already owed Sinead big time for looking after him overnight, but he couldn't let her, or anyone, take care of him long term.

Inhaling a long slow breath, he took a metaphorical breather and poured himself a coffee. The grey haze through the window wasn't clearing. They were definitely stuck for a bit longer.

Storm or no storm, right then, he couldn't think of another place he'd rather be. Grabbing his breakfast and dumping the tray on the bedside table, he joined Sinead back in bed. He cast his eyes over one long, slender leg, now exposed by the tangled sheets.

He trailed his finger from the tip of her pretty silver-polished toes up the outside of her smooth leg to her hip bone, over the edge of her white underwear. Her gentle, sleepy sigh made him relax back into the headboard. Her response to his touch was perfect.

They'd be perfect together, at least for now. They had a couple of days before he'd be on his way. With heat prickling his skin, he imagined the possibilities. If he kissed her again, if she let him closer. If he touched her so she lost her mind, the way she'd done to him. If only.

He'd make sure their *layover* was memorable. He didn't have time for anything more.

Sinead sat bolt upright. The huge expanse of white-sheeted bed was empty except for herself. She glanced around the suite, but sure enough, he was gone. It was quiet, save the groaning wind outside. Pins and needles ran up her arms and legs, and she shivered.

Had he upped and left as soon as possible? She'd kill him. Well, if she knew where he'd gone and she got her hands on him, she would've happily killed him.

Who left a cosy luxury hotel during a typhoon? More to the point, who disappeared after some heart-stopping, although hardly enough, action between the sheets? Apparently, Mr Hot-Shot CEO, love 'em and leave 'em, *arsehat*, Gabriel Anderson.

Did he have any idea what might happen if the storm grew worse? If the windows actually blew in? If he was caught outside when a building fell?

So, he knew some travel tricks and he'd been to Singapore before. It didn't mean he knew the first thing about surviving in an emergency. She did, having experienced the full force of two typhoons before. The nightmare time trapped in a shuttle bus in the Philippines was not something she wanted to relive in a hurry.

She wanted him to be okay. And it might have been stupid, but she didn't want to be alone. Then she spotted the scrawled note he'd left on the pillow beside her, and growled when she read the message.

Good afternoon Irish. You look edible in our bed. Breakfast near the TV. Gone out to find you a treat. Back in a bit. Don't miss me too much. G.

So annoyingly smug. *Our* bed. The cheeky thing. At least he intended to come back.

How long had he been gone for? Her head ached. But she was also loose-limbed and sleepy, in a good way. Of course, she'd kind of fallen on the man and used his amazing body. It had been wonderful, as far as it went.

Oh yes, perfect.

Gabriel, stripped of his remaining clothes, shuddering beneath her as she closed her eyes and bent over him . . . She'd definitely like to go there again. He was so attractive, and almost *nice*. There was no harm in a little fun, since they were stuck here together.

Anyway, she was exhausted. She must have fallen asleep for a while after expending so much energy.

She tumbled out of bed with a clunk that rattled her bones. Thank God she wasn't suffering 'the fear'. A monster hangover was the last thing she needed, even if she deserved it after all the Singapore Slings.

Grabbing her phone from the bedside table, she checked her messages. She crossed her fingers and hoped for no news from the airline. Good. Only one message from Yuki, last night. She and Daniel were tucked up in bed in the apartment-hotel, and she'd wanted to make sure Sinead was safe. A quick message back, and she was done.

I'm snug as a bug. This suite is luxury heaven! Amazing bed. Speak soon. xxx

She left out any mention of Gabriel's presence.

Why did she feel the need to keep him a secret from her friend? Was she embarrassed about jumping into bed with a man who was practically a stranger? Yuki had encouraged her, after all. She suspected she wanted him to belong to herself alone for a little longer. But Gabriel had gone and ruined it by dashing out of the hotel like a lunatic in the middle of a typhoon.

She shouldn't worry about him, but she did.

She did, she did, she did.

All that *weather* out there. And the note might be a tricky-man ruse. What if he never intended to come back?

Her gaze skittered around the room. She needed a distraction. Pulling on her rumpled jeans, she switched on the TV news reports about the typhoon. Not many casualties, but people were missing. The busy work of heating up coffee and croissants in the microwave kept her mind off him. Two of her favourite foods. He'd paid attention to her last night. The man was a genius, as well as dead-sexy.

Scoffing her breakfast sitting in bed, flashbacks of sexy times danced in her head. Long, lean and lovely, he was. He'd been so hot and hard under her hands and between her thighs, as far as it went. And she was all riled up again.

Really, he was inconsiderate rushing off. She needed him back ASAP to pick up where they'd left off. If she had his phone number she would have sent him a memo or scheduled an appointment. She giggled. How best to phrase her calendar appointment for the important businessman?

2pm-3pm, Ultimate shagathon - Make Ms Kennealy scream with pleasure.

On second thoughts, one hour wouldn't be long enough.

The click of the suite's door lock shook the silliness out of her.

Thank God.

He stood framed in the open doorway and her heart didn't skip a beat, it jumped rope. *Skip, thwack, skip, thwack.*

Her heartbeat settled as relief washed through her system, then a whole lot of rolling heat. She was stupidly aroused at the sight of him.

"Irish. Did you miss me?"

Irish. She sighed at the cuteness.

His expression shone like a starburst, then he shook his head like a dog after a swim in the ocean. Water droplets formed a halo around his face and shimmered in the harsh fluorescent lighting from the corridor. His wet, white shirt stuck to the contours of his chest and shoulders, outlining every perfect detail. Gabriel's hair was slicked back so it defined his face, the sculpted cheekbones and startling stormy blue eyes. He'd been out in a typhoon and he came back looking gorgeous. How was that fair?

She was gobsmacked. But only for a moment.

Crossing her arms under her breasts, she told him off. "I thought you were dead. How dare you scare me so badly?"

He raised his arms in surrender and presented his surprise. Champagne in one hand and a box of fancy chocolates in the other. Belgian, by the look of the box.

"For you. Food and drink beginning with the letter 'c'. Only the best, of course." He shrugged.

Wow. He was earning some massive points with her.

"Thank you. Get back to bed this instant!" She assessed his wet and bedraggled state. From top to toe. "But first, let's get you out of those wet clothes."

One of his eyebrows shot up. "Anything you say."

"Actually, I changed my mind. I'm feeling a little bit dirty. I think I need a shower."

His other eyebrow joined the first one up around his hairline and he stepped towards her.

She rose from the bed, her eyes locked with his. She pulled her T-shirt over her head and dropped it on the floor. Her breasts were bare, exposed to his gaze. A thrill rushed through her, hot and tingly, at his low moan. Then she unzipped her jeans and pushed them down her legs, stepping out of them with only a little stumble. Standing straight as a supermodel, she winked.

Now his groan blended with his trademark chuckle. It did all sorts of good things to her insides.

Continuing her slow striptease, she hooked a finger into the edge of her knickers, pulled them down and stepped out of them. She bent down and then flipped her hair back over her shoulders.

Gabriel stared, his lips parted, a crease between his eyebrows. Another part of his anatomy strained towards her, obvious through his wet trousers. Sinead huffed out a breath. *Hello again*. She was very glad to see him, especially in such a state.

Completely naked, Sinead stalked up to him, took the champagne and chocolates from his white-knuckled grasp and placed them on the coffee table. She returned to stand in front of him, placing her hands on his firm chest. Spreading her fingers wide, clutching at muscles under wet cotton, she set to work and unbuttoned his shirt. Ever so slowly.

He watched her fingers. "Bloody hell, you're killing me here." His gaze flicked up to meet hers. But he didn't move another muscle.

"So, help me then."

Seconds later, he'd stripped off his sopping clothes and tossed them aside.

Her long, shaky breaths stuttered as her gaze travelled the length of his glorious naked body. She'd not get sick of looking at him in a hurry. In fact, she toyed with the idea of licking him all over, to memorise his contours with her tongue.

Interrupting her naughty catalogue of ideas, he reached out and pulled her hard against him, crushing her breasts against his chest, wrapping strong arms around her back. They stood there heart to heart, staring at each other. Electricity zinged between them like lightning, wild and out of control, signalling the latent power before the storm.

She could have sworn her heart actually stopped and, instead, Gabriel's heart beat beneath her skin.

"Shower, now," Sinead ordered.

He licked his lower lip. "Yes, Ma'am."

She took him by the hand. The chocolates and champagne could wait until afterwards.

She was so sexy. So confident and beautiful. Powerful.

Gabriel usually took charge with women, but letting Sinead call the shots had been mind-blowing so far. What they'd got up to in the early hours of the morning had been a gourmet appetizer, but it was time for the main course. Hopefully one of many dishes. A ten-course degustation menu to be tasted and savoured. Hours and hours of feasting.

She pulled him into the bathroom and flicked on the jets in the enormous shower.

"Wait a sec." She slipped her hand out of his hold and rushed off towards the basin.

The way her butt and hips swayed from side to side was a thing of beauty. If she didn't act soon, he wouldn't be able to control himself. She rustled around in her cosmetic bag and retrieved a foil packet, then waved it in the air in victory.

"Come here, you big dirty man."

His lips stretched upwards. "You think I'm big and dirty?"

Her eyes were wide and innocent as she nodded. "Oh yes, very big. Very filthy."

Gabriel swallowed when she bit her lip, her gaze roaming down his body. *Shit.* At this rate, the show would be over soon. He was so hard already it verged on painful. His groin tightened further and he clenched his hands into fists by his sides. He tried to control the tension inside him.

She swayed over to him. He had to touch her, if only her shoulder. Stroking her silky skin made his breath catch in his throat. Her little gasp was music.

She ripped open the little packet, reached out and slowly sheathed him. Now he groaned so loud, she laughed, light and tinkling.

His hand hovered over hers, then he grasped her fingers and stopped the stroking movement she'd begun. So close. He'd lose it if she kept it up. Without another word, he took hold of her hips and lifted her so those long, slim legs wrapped around his back.

"I want you inside me, Gabriel," she whispered.

The blood pounded through his veins and his heartbeat resonated in his ears. He wanted her so much. But he teased her, kissing her mouth, stroking against her until she shivered. Then he pressed inside her. No more waiting. His breath leaked out, it felt so good. He almost gave in to the impulse to drive her hard and fast.

No, she'd have her pleasure. He wanted her to come apart in his arms.

Good Lord, he's a sex god.

She clenched her inner muscles and held on for dear life. His hardness throbbed deep inside her. Everything cried out for release. Every inch of skin, every cell in Sinead's body.

He somehow walked them into the shower, warm water pounding over her as he pinned her against cool marble tiles. A wall of muscle pressed into her breasts and belly. He stroked into her, slow and steady. Playing her like an instrument. She arched her back, wanting more. Trembles broke out everywhere.

With one arm pressed against the wall, his other hand glided over her slick skin. Ocean waves of pleasure followed in the wake of his touch. He skimmed rough fingertips over her right breast, then lifted it, weighing it in his hand. She kept her eyes on him as he lowered his head. He kissed her flesh and licked rivulets of water from her skin. Then he took her breast into his mouth, licking and teasing the tight peak of her nipple.

She gasped at the intense slivers of sensation slicing through her. "God, yes."

"You taste so good." His eyes met hers, looking up at her as he licked around her areola. "I want to make you come again."

His jaw clenched. *Oh, God. That look.*

Her bones liquefied and he grabbed her tight.

She clasped his shoulder with one hand, and the tight curve of his butt. Her world tilted as Gabriel thrust inside her, his mouth on her breast. Licking and tasting her, rasping his tongue over both nipples in turn. Back and forth. She pulled him closer. Their bodies aligned perfectly.

She'd never had such a man. Never like this, never this good. She'd stay with him forever like this, joined together. Wanting him, then having him.

He rose and kissed her mouth, tugging at her bottom lip with his teeth. It'd be fair to say she devoured him. His taste filled her senses, like spring rain and the finest chocolate. He broke the kiss and moved even deeper inside, filling her.

So good, so good, so good.

She trusted him, gave herself completely over to him. Tension built until she could barely stand it. Her thighs shook, her lower belly tightened.

She stared deep into the ocean of his eyes. "Yes, Gabriel," she gasped.

Sinead rocked forward and heat flowed over her skin. She arched again. The tension broke and sweet power rushed through her, vision darkening, sparks igniting like silver stars. He surged inside her with a final thrust. They tipped over the edge together, crying out as one. She clung to him then, resting her head on his shoulder, inhaling his clean, spicy scent.

After a minute or two, the pummel of water brought her back to earth. The touch of his lips on her forehead made her want to weep. He'd slipped out of her body, but she throbbed inside still, where he'd been. She loved it. She'd never been taken there before, so close to another person, yet floating away.

He'd marked her as his own, from the inside out.

She'd been aching for him since she first noticed him. Now she knew. He was addictive. As hot and delicious as coffee. He could be the best thing ever, essential as breathing.

If she had to go without, he could be her doom.

Amazing. Incredible.

Gabriel wracked his mind for superlatives super enough, but none came close to describing what just happened with Sinead.

He helped her slide down his body until she stood on her own shaky legs. Holding her close and supporting her with one arm, he reached for a towel. He wrapped her carefully, like something precious. Head and body hadn't quite rejoined, but he couldn't remember ever feeling such a strong connection with anyone.

Tenderly kissing the top of her head, her cheeks, her lips. He didn't want to stop touching her. He disposed of the condom and dried himself, then stood close behind Sinead, fitting his body to hers. With another towel, he dried her hair. Long, pale strands, with a scent like flowers from his mum's old garden. Roses and jasmine.

He breathed in her clean, airy scent at the side of her throat. The spot beneath her ear made him want to bite her. He could kiss her all day. Every day.

What the hell?

One time with a woman and he was losing his reason. He couldn't be feeling . . . some emotion he didn't even have words for. It went to show how hopeless he was at feelings, and stuff.

Before he said something dangerous, he wrapped his arms around her waist and squeezed her tight. "How about that champagne, beautiful?"

"Sounds perfect."

He led Sinead into the other room. She sat on the bed, pulling the crisp white sheet up over her gorgeous body. It was so tempting to whip the sheet right off her. Instead, he found the champagne and rustled up glasses, then popped the cork and proposed a toast.

"To my sexy Irish date." He poured them each a glass.

She paused for a moment, biting her damn lip, then raised her glass. "Sláinte!" The Irish word sounded wonderful on her lips.

Gabriel climbed into bed next to her, sitting up against a pillow. He tasted his champagne and wrapped an arm around her, needing her close.

He let out a breath and leaned back so he spoke to the ceiling. "Sad as it sounds, I reckon this is the best date I've ever had."

She nodded. "Me too."

"Really? I would've imagined you'd have proper dates lined up around the globe. Hearts and flowers and stuff."

"Not so much. Anyway, all I need is a big dirty man who knows how to make me feel special. You, Gabriel." She poked him in the chest, then stroked his arm.

Her touch was hot. Fiery.

Gabriel didn't know what to say. No one had ever said he made them feel special. He liked it. He liked *her*, more than he probably should. He didn't do relationships and hearts and flowers. Anyway, he had to leave tomorrow. They each had their separate lives on opposite sides of the planet. But he liked her, and there was no reason he shouldn't make the most of this time with her.

"What do you want to do now?" He'd purposely lowered his voice, pressing his lips against her throat.

She shivered. "Honestly? I'd like to cuddle."

"Cuddle?" He rolled the word around his mouth and the unfamiliar concept around his mind. "Cuddle. Okay, show me."

Sinead put her glass on the bedside table and curled up on her side. "Now you lie behind me and spoon me."

"Spoon you?"

He raised his eyebrows but did as was told. Snuggled up behind her, his arm around her waist, he realised the position had its advantages. The feel of her butt pressed against him, not to mention access to those incredible breasts if he let his hand wander. Definite advantages. Spooning for the win.

He stroked one of her nipples which instantly peaked, and nuzzled her neck. "Like this?" he asked.

She breathed out on a sigh. "Oh, yeah."

He was getting hard again. Holding her close made him want to lose himself with her, to get even closer. Would she think he was a sex fiend if he made another move?

She'd gone quiet. Was she trying to ignore him? He leaned over to examine her face. Her eyes were closed, long lashes fanned against her pink cheeks. She was asleep in his arms. With any other woman, this turn of events would freak him out. But now, with Sinead, it felt right.

Trying not to disturb her, Gabriel lay beside her and let his own tiredness win. It had been a long couple of days.

He needed a rest. Understatement of the century.

Sinead wriggled, the press of manly flesh at her back, fingers clasping her naked hip. His hand was massive, a great hulking claw of a thing. So hot. Was there anything more wonderful than a strong male body pressed up against her? So safe and warm. At least, it seemed so.

She could wake him with a kiss, or more than a kiss. But he'd been unwell the night before. She'd let him sleep a while.

She staggered out of bed to the windows. The weather situation probably wasn't worse, but it wasn't better either. Pressing her palm to the cold glass, the vibration of pelting rain made her teeth chatter. A couple of trees had been uprooted, splayed across the road.

Shaking her head, she moved to the bedside table and checked her phone. No messages, no airline updates. She wasn't sure when Gabriel would be leaving, but it seemed they'd have another night together. Gabriel was asleep, so she would have her planned girl time. It wasn't quite as appealing as it had been earlier, before she realised she had other, nakeder options.

After visiting the bathroom, she dressed in her clean white T-shirt and underwear and hummed contentedly while she made a cup of coffee in the tiny kitchenette. A milky coffee was a perfect complement to the chocolates Gabriel brought her earlier. She hopped into bed beside him with her treats.

Next, she needed a chick flick to watch on the flat screen. She flipped through the channels with the remote.

"No boring sports, thank you." She kept flicking, then stopped and clapped her hands with delight. "Yay! How lucky is that?"

Love Actually, starting right now. Her favourite romantic comedy of all time. Bliss.

She sighed, watching the famous scene of people arriving at airports, being welcomed home by the ones they love. Such joy on their faces. It's what she wanted to be perfectly happy—someone to love her and always welcome her home.

Wherever in the world that might be.

· ♥ · ♥ · ♥ · ♥ · ♥ ·

Gabriel woke, his head heavy as a tonne of bricks. Sinead sat in bed next to him, chilling out, watching TV. This was the type of relationship he could get on board with. Wait, what was he thinking? It wasn't a relationship. Just a casual thing.

"What's on, Irish?" he mumbled, propping himself up with a pillow.

He feigned ignorance, but he knew the movie. He owned the DVD. He'd bought it for his mum a few years back, but he'd ended up watching it more than once. He liked the movie, although he hadn't admitted it to anyone but his PA, Martha.

Sinead turned to him and smiled, lighting up with happiness. "*Love Actually*. It's my absolute favourite."

It was the part where Emma Thompson found the necklace her husband had bought, and she assumed it was her Christmas present. But he'd bought it for the skank secretary who was trying to steal him away. This part of the movie was so sad, he flicked his eyes away from the screen. He had no intention of blubbering in front of Sinead, but watching her expression was nearly as bad. She looked like her pet kitten had died.

"This bit is so sad. I hate the skanky secretary," Sinead commented.

Was she plucking thoughts directly out of his head now?

"It's a silly movie. Hugh Grant's dancing ruins it for me." Stupid mistake. Too late to rein it back in. Being overly familiar with the plot was a dead giveaway.

He covered up by leaning over and running his fingertip along her cheekbone. "How is my naughty little trolley dolly this afternoon?"

Sinead met his gaze, her mouth hanging open. "What did you call me? What a rude way to refer to a professional flight attendant."

"Naughty. Little. Trolley. Dolly." He punctuated each word with a hot kiss—on her earlobe, her throat, her cheek, her lips. Then lower, lifting her T-shirt and pressing kisses on her belly.

"Oh," she moaned. "But don't you want to watch the movie? It's your favourite too, isn't it? Go on, admit it."

"Stop talking."

She giggled. "You're distracting me."

He pressed his body into hers and she gasped.

Oh yeah.

"One big hard distraction, coming right up." He aimed to please.

Sinead lay in Gabriel's arms, stroking her bare belly. *Mmmm.* So deliciously satisfied. The room service dinner had been delectable, the hot man in her bed, even more so.

She scanned the room, now in total disarray. First she glanced at the sofa, a blush heating her cheeks at all the mischief they'd managed. He'd taken her there. Next she peeked through her fingers at the coffee table. He'd taken her there too. Then the bed – she'd taken control that time – and he loved it, going by his moans of appreciation.

Gabriel rustled the sheets and stretched out beside her, displaying finely honed chest muscles and contoured abs. He was in peak physical condition. Quite the marathon man. And she didn't mean running!

She flicked on the bedside lamp and glanced at her phone. After 10 p.m. And there was an email briefing from the airline. She sighed. She snuggled back against Gabriel's body. He smelled so good. A musky, spicy scent. Was it weird that she was sniffing him? She didn't care. It would be nice to be stranded here a bit longer. A few days, maybe a month.

But no such luck. The briefing said the airport would most likely re-open at 5 a.m. A new flight schedule would be posted in the morning too. Her heart thumped in her chest at the thought of leaving Gabriel.

The conversation she'd been putting off couldn't be avoided much longer. They needed to talk about what happened next. They couldn't stay in the hotel suite forever, locked away from the world in their isolated bubble, even if she wished to. But she didn't want to say goodbye and fly back alone to her tiny flat in London.

She wanted to keep him.

Wearing her rational hat, Sinead knew it wasn't going to happen. He'd already said he didn't do relationships, he never had. Anyway, he lived in Melbourne and she was based in London, in the completely wrong hemisphere.

She could move to Melbourne. *Ridiculous.* The idea flitted through her head anyway. She'd lived there for three years while working for the airline, before London. It had been her home. Old friends still lived there. The airline would probably approve a transfer flying the Melbourne to London route.

She huffed out a breath and pinched her arm, hard. She'd only known Gabriel for a couple of days. It was stupid to want to uproot her whole life because of him. Then again, some of her 'smart' choices over the past few years had ended up being big mistakes.

The hot man stirred beside her. Gabriel stroked her arm and kissed her shoulder, sending shivery tingles shooting down her spine.

He was so lovely, now she'd got to know him a little, which made it all the harder to leave.

"What are you thinking?" His voice was croaky.

"You really want to know?" She sighed as he nodded against her shoulder. "I don't want to go home to London without you. I want to keep seeing you, Gabriel."

His body went still, tension emanating from every inch of him. It was all the answer she needed. He spoke anyway, his eyes fixed on the ceiling.

"I don't think it's a good idea. I don't do relationships. For good reason. I don't have anything to offer. My company takes up all my time."

She watched his face in profile. "It doesn't have to. Other people have jobs and still have partners and families. What makes you so different?" Why did she even bring it up? She didn't bother to hide her annoyance.

"It's the way I am. I work long hours, travelling for days or weeks at a time. Sometimes I go surfing or skiing for a few days. That's all. It's been working fine for me."

"What about women? Love? Don't you want someone special in your life?" *Don't you want me?* She bit her lip and willed it not to wobble.

He faced her, his lips thinned and jaw clenched. "There have been a few women, but no one *special*."

Sinead didn't want to hear anymore, it hurt her insides. But he turned to her and continued. "I'm always leaving. I can't offer you anything more. You know how it goes."

He sounded defeated. For whatever reason, he wouldn't even consider a relationship with her. Wouldn't take a risk and try to make it work between them. For a smart man, he was obviously kind of stupid when it came to his personal life. It made her want to kick him, or hug him. The kicking instinct was winning.

"Yes, I know how that goes."

She tumbled out of bed and stood, keeping her back to him. Retreating to the bathroom, she closed the door and leaned against it. The cool wood panel at her back grounded her.

"Why'd you have to be a typical man?" she whispered.

She ran a bath and leaned on the rim, waiting. He didn't come to her. She sniffled and swooshed fancy lavender bath oil into warm water. Oil and water didn't mix. The elements separated, pretty swirls of rainbow decorating the surface, but never going deeper.

Tears threatened to spill over her cheeks, the hot prickle behind her eyes felt like gritty sand at the beach. She rubbed at her closed eyelids with the backs of her hands. A few minutes of privacy, that's what she needed. The chance to think back on the last two days with some distance from Gabriel's overwhelming presence.

At the same time, he was only on the other side of the door. She could call out for him if she wanted to. But she couldn't. She wasn't so brave, or so confident she wouldn't be completely rejected.

In the morning, they'd both be getting back on a plane, then he'd be beyond her reach. It was already too late for anything more.

Bugger it.

Gabriel had totally stepped in it. When Sinead walked away, his heart pounded in his chest. When she closed the bathroom door behind her, his stomach churned. He'd made a mess of things again, like every time he'd met a woman he liked. And Sinead was different – he already liked her more than any of the other women he'd dated. He couldn't make it worse by going after her.

The click of the lock echoed in the silent room and it sounded so final. He only had himself to blame if she didn't want to talk ever again. He'd dismissed her like an employee who'd failed him. Standard operating procedure for a guy who'd become a workaholic loner.

He rolled over in bed, grabbing her pillow and slamming it down over his face. Her scent surrounded him, sweet jasmine and her sleepy, warm skin. A groan rose up from deep inside. It could've been a scream if he let it out. He sucked in a deep breath and threw the pillow back down.

They couldn't get involved, there were plenty of good reasons. The biggest one, the one worrying him most, was the state of his head. He wasn't losing the plot, it wasn't so extreme, but the migraines were coming on fast and furious. It was time he took his health more seriously. His doctor had warned him months ago, stress was a major migraine trigger. Without some lifestyle changes, the situation would go from bad to worse. The 'worse' part of the prognosis had him clenching his jaw.

What if he ended up like his mother? She was totally unaware of her surroundings, unable to recognise him or her lifelong friends. It'd been years since she was able to look after herself financially. He'd stepped up, of course. But who'd step up to look after him, if he needed it?

It was the real reason he couldn't tie himself to any woman. She might end up looking after him as if he was a child. He wouldn't be such a bastard. The type of man who marries a nursemaid.

Sinead was on the other side of the world, but he had to stay in Melbourne for his mum's sake. A short trip to London was one thing, but he couldn't jump on a plane and disappear. When he got back from this trip, he had to sort out the situation at home. He'd put it off as long as he could.

A girlfriend couldn't be expected to understand the baggage he dragged behind him through life. Even someone special, someone caring. Someone like Sinead.

Gabriel's hands formed fists in the sheets. Staring blankly at the ceiling, willing a solution to magically appear, he let his mind fill with the swish of wind and steady beat of rain on the windows. Sleep would help, only it wasn't going to happen in a hurry.

Rising, he headed towards the bathroom, one foot in front of the other, heart in his mouth. He needed to apologise to Sinead and see if he could smooth things over.

He turned the door handle with a squeak. It wasn't locked after all. Maybe she wouldn't shut him out.

A dripping wet Sinead reclining in the bathtub filled his vision. Heat thudded through his veins. With her eyes closed, pale hair fanned out over her shoulders, she looked like a dream. Swirls of colours on the water's surface barely covered her breasts. The rose pink tips taunted him. He wanted to lick them, lick all of her. But this wasn't helping him sort out his head.

She didn't speak, but she didn't tell him to get lost either.

Stepping forward, his footsteps a hushed whisper on the marble floor. "I'm sorry."

He hoped she believed him. The last thing he wanted was to leave in the morning with this weird vibe between them.

"Are you?"

"Yes, more than you know." He waited for a response.

Her eyes popped open. She looked up at him and gasped, then promptly squeezed her eyes closed again. "Blimey! Gabriel, you could have put on a robe or something."

"It would have ruined the effect."

"Which effect?"

"The naked man wanting to show you how happy he is to spend one last night with you."

He was relieved when she opened one eye and peered up at him, scrunching her face adorably. Then her face blanked. Coldness washed over him.

"Go, Gabriel. Just go." She shook her head and turned away, wet strands of hair sticking to her cheek.

The flame flickering inside him was snuffed out. It'd been too much to hope that she'd want to be with him again. Too much like good luck.

There was something about her – the way she'd taken a chance on him – that made him wonder. What if he could have someone in his life? Sinead was passionate and fiery, the type of woman who'd keep him on his toes and call him out when he was being a grumpy bastard, which was most of the time. But he couldn't expect her to fit in with his life, with all the issues he was facing. He wouldn't do that to her.

He clenched his fists by his sides. "I'll take the sofa." He walked to the door got out of the room.

He grabbed a pillow and lay down alone, as per usual. Waited for sleep to come.

He was so tired. So damned tired.

She sat alone in the now-cold bathwater. The last remnants of ridiculously good loving still vibrated through her body. Sinead shivered, gripping her knees.

Her marathon man had wanted her, but she'd sent him away. What kind of idiot was she? The kind who'd been disappointed before. The kind who'd learned to protect herself.

Padraig had made her distrustful, made her hesitate, even when something good was right in front of her. He'd made her doubt her own intuition about men. And she hated it. Hated the way her horrible ex was still inside her head after so many years. *He was still sending text messages.*

She squeezed her eyes shut and forced her mind back to Gabriel. His teasing words, his come-on, may have been meant to soothe her, but she doubted it. He denied his own emotions, had probably done so for years. He was scared, for some reason, just as she was. It hurt to think of opening herself up to heartbreak again. And Gabriel could break her heart, she had no doubt. The connection between them, the physical spark was so strong already.

She had to let him go tomorrow, before he became a regret.

Even as a short-term thing, her time with Gabriel had been worth it. In her opinion, anyway. No matter what he said, no matter his denial, nothing would erase the time they'd spent together. It would be branded white-hot in her memory forever. Gabriel would always be a part of her.

Whether he liked it or not.

Chapter Seven

T he room was darker now. Colder. Gabriel rubbed his sandpaper-dry eyes and recalibrated his mind. He checked his phone for the time. 6.35 a.m. Almost time to get going again. An email from Martha had him tentatively booked on a re-scheduled at 1 p.m. He wasn't sure yet when Sinead would have to leave.

She'd stayed in the bath for a hell of a long time last night, but then she'd crept up beside the sofa and told him to come back to bed, to go to sleep. Sinead had crashed almost immediately. It hadn't been like earlier. He hadn't touched her again and she'd curled up in a ball on her own side of the bed.

But he'd slept in Sinead's bed again. Staying with a woman two nights in a row was completely unprecedented for him. Big news, as Ryan would say. But not an unwelcome development. At least, now he'd got used to the idea.

He wasn't sure where that left them this morning.

She was curled up beside him, her long, smooth legs entwined with his. It had to be accidental. He didn't think she'd meant to reach out for him. Gabriel raised himself up on one elbow.

So beautiful. Her expression was unguarded now. He hadn't noticed earlier how her smile masked her thoughts.

He reached towards her—he couldn't help himself. He ran his fingers through her long white-gold hair. So soft. The scent was exotic, yet also familiar. Her rosebud lips, slightly parted, tempted him to kiss her, taste her.

A powerful gust of wind whipped past the windows. A tremor followed, reverberating through the building. It brought him to the here and now, and woke Sinead in the process.

She stirred and stretched her arm across his chest. "Mmm."

He chuckled at her inarticulate moan. "Top of the morning to you, Irish."

Sinead's eyes popped open, sleepiness instantly wiped off her face. "Shouldn't that be my line? Where's my phone?" She almost leapt out of bed, away from him.

His pulse picked up pace. "What's the rush? You have somewhere to go?"

She sashayed across the room, her bare bottom peeking out from under her white T-shirt. Making him want to reach out and grab her. He resisted, since he didn't think it would be welcome. She seemed to have no interest in hanging around with him, let alone anything more.

Fiddling with her phone, she didn't meet his eyes. "Yes. We'll be clear to fly soon. I'm scheduled for a 10 a.m. flight."

"Oh, right." A surge of disappointment rolled through his gut.

Their seclusion together was nearly over. Time to get back to reality. His business, setting up the London office. Everything so important to him a few days ago. It was still important. Life went on. But maybe work wasn't the be all and end all.

Sinead bit her lip, then crossed the room to the bathroom. She closed the door behind her.

He rolled over and stared out the window.

Now he realised what made him nervous. Sinead was dangerous. She could tip the careful balancing act he'd created in his life. But she was the type of danger he wanted in his life. Not wanted, *needed*.

Sinead was someone who'd challenge him. She might be someone he could talk to. With her, he might even feel something besides pressure and stress. Feel. Like a human.

He needed to talk to her, to smooth over any rough edges left hanging after their weird conversation the night before. He'd shot her down when she talked about seeing each other again. What he'd said seemed wrong, even while the words were spilling out of his mouth. He knew the truth now.

They were meant to be together. It was a cliché but he didn't care. It was completely new to him. Sinead inspired him to want more in his life—a real relationship, someone to be close to, to come home to. Someone for himself alone.

Of course, he wasn't ignoring the physical side. He'd never been so exposed and raw after being with a woman. *Unbelievable*. They were combustible together, an unstoppable wildfire. She was getting naked behind the door and it was driving him mad with anticipation. He wanted her again, back in the bed, under him, over him, it didn't matter.

What mattered was her, being with him. Whether it was in London or Melbourne, Dublin or bloody Japan, he'd see her again.

Somehow they'd find a way to make it work. She'd become necessary.

Sinead showered, moving under the water, quick and restless. Nothing like the memorable shower the day before. She shivered, goose bumps racing everywhere on her body. Every nook and cranny. Some of those crannies still ached. Her fantasies of being with Gabriel had been far outstripped by reality. Before they all crashed down like a nightmare.

She dressed in the bathroom, hurrying into her slightly crumpled uniform. Gabriel wouldn't have the chance to see her naked again. If he gave her that look, the filthy, come-hither look full of carnal intent, which he could absolutely deliver on, she'd totally succumb to his charms. Melt like ice-cream. Dissolve like a spoonful of sugar in steaming hot coffee.

Oh Lord, give me strength, or give me caffeine.

If she was going through with it, she needed fortification. She couldn't hang around though. The longer she left it, the harder it would be.

It was the coward's way out, but she'd decided in the early hours to get going as soon as possible. To leave Gabriel before he had a chance to break her heart. She'd hoped to be out of there early, before he woke, but she'd fallen asleep next to him. Sleeping beside him was so comfortable, so cosy. When she'd opened her eyes and found her legs tangling with his, she knew she had to go. Before he reached for her again and unleashed all his manliness on her.

She'd known men like him before. Too gorgeous, too rich, too smart – too much altogether. It never ended well for the women in unequal relationships, with so much more to lose.

Anyway, men like him couldn't be trusted. When she was only nineteen, she'd learned the lesson the hard way. She sucked in a deep breath and let it out slowly, calming herself. The brute didn't deserve another thought.

Hesitantly opening the bathroom door, Sinead spied Gabriel sitting up in bed, the hard contours of his chest and biceps flexed on full display, making it hard to stick to her resolution, or concentrate on anything at all. He was simply beautiful, like the classical studies of the male form she'd seen in Rome, statues carved in marble for everyone to admire. But he wasn't made of stone. He was hot and human, vulnerable and strong, all at once. She sucked in a cleansing breath. All the dwelling on the beautiful man wasn't helping.

She forced her legs to move but it was like wading through knee-deep sand, walking through to the bedroom. Gabriel sat wrapped in a sheet, his forehead crinkling madly at his phone.

She kept her voice light and sunny. "Problem, Mr Serious CEO?"

"Nothing the London team can't manage. I'm officially off-duty today." He glanced up, hitting her with his cranky face. "Why are you dressed?"

She couldn't stop a giggle escaping. "You've obviously got one thing on your mind. I'm guessing it's not breakfast."

"That's where you're wrong. How about I peel off your uniform and see what's on the menu? I swear, I'll eat it all up."

She shivered when Gabriel knelt on the bed and reached towards her, letting the sheet slip down his body. Her eyes automatically tracked south. *Oh, goodness.* He was pleased to see her, uniform or not.

He hit her with a killer, lopsided smile sending her stomach flipping over, like the first time she'd noticed him on the plane. She squeezed her eyes closed and backed up a step, putting some distance between them.

"No, I can't. I have to get ready. I still have to do my hair and makeup and it takes a while." Her gaze wandered all over his body though.

"Really? I can't tempt you with breakfast and dessert rolled into one?"

She shook her head and crossed her arms under her breasts. His gaze followed the action.

She cleared her throat. "Sorry, not going to happen."

"Hell. I'll have a shower then. A cold one."

Gabriel rose from the bed and strode towards her, grabbed her by the hips and planted a deep, lingering kiss on her lips. The kiss left her legs shaking and her lips wet and swollen, along with other places. Her pulse throbbed in her temples and between her legs, the need for him making her head swim. Making her doubt her decision.

"To be continued." He said it as if it was a certainty, like he knew they'd see each other again. He strolled into the bathroom and shut the door.

Horrible, icky black guilt lined her stomach, as he traced his thumb across her lower lip. Such a simple gesture, but filled with some unspoken emotion.

She needed to remember her plan, the get-out-quickly-and-relatively-unscathed plan. It was getting harder to resist him. The spark between them was undeniable.

When he'd touched her yesterday, there was something else going on, more than skin-deep. When he'd shown her his vulnerable side, he'd shaken her, like the building which might've fallen down around them.

She was tempted to ask him for more, to give it another shot. But she couldn't risk it. If he pushed her away again, something inside her might break.

Sinead ducked and gathered her tossed clothes from the night before under one arm, hiding from Gabriel's stare and the sight of his perfect body. She heard the water running in the bathroom. Good. She needed him occupied with something other than her naked self.

She called out to him. "They say the airport should re-open by eight o'clock. I'd better pack."

She had a few minutes up her sleeve. He was in the shower now and she was packing, as far as he knew.

"Okay, Irish." His muffled but cheery reply echoed through the door, against the rush of water.

He wouldn't see the tears trickling down her cheeks, or the half-packed bag she'd put aside last night while he slept on the sofa. She stuffed the last of her belongings in her bag.

Sinead glanced at the bathroom door over her shoulder as she left the suite, taking her bag with her. Leaving not a trace of her physical self behind. Only a trace of her heart.

· ♥ · ♥ · ♥ · ♥ · ♥ ·

"Un-bloody-believable."

Gabriel circled around the suite's living area once more, wearing only a thick white towel wrapped around his waist, fresh out of the shower.

Drip, drip, drip. The drops of water hitting the shower floor were a ticking clock, or a countdown to an explosion.

Sinead was gone. No sign of her stuff in the whole suite. She hadn't even left a note. Her toiletries had vanished and her wheelie bag was nowhere to be seen. Her clothes had been strewn across the armchair, now they'd disappeared.

She'd done a runner, packed and taken off. The most beautiful woman he'd ever seen, the hottest he'd ever touched. Also sweet and gentle. Really funny and smart too, even if she didn't see it herself. Probably the one woman he could make a go of it with, if she'd given him a second chance.

Gabriel rubbed his temples. A slow pounding built behind his eyes. The remains of the migraine, or the build-up of the stupid things he'd said the night before. Now he was questioning all of his assumptions and she'd already left.

He didn't even know her address in London. Luckily he'd grabbed her mobile phone number yesterday before he went out in the storm. She hadn't asked for his contact details.

Sinead, where are you?

There were only a few options. Sinead could have met her friend Yuki – he knew she was in Singapore too. The only logical place she'd go was the airport terminal, a few hours earlier than she needed to be there.

But why would she leave without saying goodbye?

Thinking back, she'd jumped out of bed like she was on fire. He'd sensed something was wrong, but now his hindsight was twenty-twenty. The way she'd shut herself in the bathroom and reappeared fully dressed in her uniform. All reserved and pushing him away. He'd been thinking about getting her naked and back in bed with him, where she belonged.

The whole time, even when he kissed her, she must have been thinking of leaving. He wasn't too proud to admit it cut like a knife in the gut.

Why the hell did he let her go without putting up a fight? Because he was an idiot. He needed to find her, to talk to her and make it right.

He threw on creased but clean clothes and chucked his other gear in his bag. A quick pass around the room to check for anything important and he was out of there. He almost sprinted down the corridor to the elevator.

Heart pounding from the exercise he'd been sorely missing, he closed his eyes and sucked in a few deep breaths as the elevator lowered to the ground floor. The drop in his stomach as the doors opened could have been from the quick ride down, but he didn't think so.

In the foyer, he stopped at reception. Great to see a familiar face working there. The perpetually smiling Su, who often greeted him on business stays.

"Hello Su, can you please tell me if my friend Ms Kennealy has checked out? She was in a hurry and I think I missed her."

"Yes, sir, I believe she checked out about twenty minutes ago. Let me see." Su pulled up a record on her computer monitor and frowned. "She left you a message." Su rummaged in a pigeon hole on the wall behind the desk and pulled out an envelope.

Gabriel reached for the envelope in Su's hand, then stared at it. Concern and confusion were at war in his head. He tore open the seal and quickly read her message. The handwritten note barely explained anything, but added to his unease.

Gabriel,

Thank you for covering the cost of the suite, but you shouldn't have.

Best we each go our own way. I had a nice time but I wasn't up for goodbyes.

Sinead x

A nice time? It sounded like something he'd said to her last night. It didn't sound like Sinead, it was too cold and remote. She was brushing him off, like he'd done to her. But that was before he'd realised he needed her. He hadn't only sunk into her heat and tasted her. He'd almost drowned in her arms. The thing was, he had a feeling they could learn to swim, together. No way had he had enough.

Heat flooded his body and sent the blood rushing out of his brain. The way she'd stared into his eyes. She'd made him look deep down into himself and back at her too. She'd cracked him wide open.

The need to find her and talk to her was like a pulsing red light inside his head. It wouldn't be ignored. He could probably catch her at the airport if he hurried.

Maybe it wasn't too late. He didn't want to think about the alternative.

The airport was gloomier than usual as driving rain slashed across the large windows overlooking the tarmac. The typhoon had been officially downgraded but the storm hadn't yet passed. The weather reflected Sinead's grey mood as she waited in the staff lounge for an update from Mermaid Airlines head office.

The tall latte and chocolate bar in front of her barely helped fight her fatigue. She needed to be alert – all the flight attendants had to be ready to fly as soon as the authorities re-opened the skies. She was there super early though.

As much as she tried to focus on work, all she could think about was Gabriel. She could hardly believe she'd done it. She'd checked out and left him behind in the hotel. When she'd spoken to the reception staff, she found he'd already settled the account.

It went to show his train of thought – he couldn't wait to get out of there. The note she'd left him was heartless and filled with empty spaces for the words she wanted to say to him. She was sure she'd regret it later, not telling him how she was feeling.

It was fine.

Fine, fine, fine.

She tapped her fingernails against the side of her coffee cup. She'd left before she made a scene and asked him to keep in touch, to see her again soon, and before she begged him to kiss her and take her back to bed. Why didn't she stay with him a while longer?

Then her ex-boyfriend Padraig's voice popped into her head, as it always did when she most wanted to forget. She was a selfish bitch who wouldn't stay home and look after her man. She was always leaving, one foot out the door. How could she forget?

She pushed that old hurt out of her head. It didn't matter. He was behind her now, she'd moved on. She was a grown-up, professional woman, in control of her own life. Sinead checked her appearance, her mirrored compact in her shaking hand, and applied more scarlet lipstick. She tidied her hair, pulled it back and pinned it into a sophisticated twist. Her reflection grimaced, a Halloween version of herself.

She breathed deep and made herself relax. The carefully con-trolled, regulation-level of grooming and attractiveness was in place. Barely a visible hint of the turmoil stirring beneath the surface.

It was nearly showtime again. She knew exactly what she had to do. It helped her fragile heart and state of mind to have a plan, however simple. Get back on the plane, do her job, fly home to London and then collapse into a bottomless pit of chocolate ice-cream. An excellent plan.

Sinead's phone buzzed in her pocket as she gulped down the last of her latte. She guessed it was the pre-flight clearance alert. Her stomach contracted when she read the name on her phone's screen. Gabriel. He had her phone number. Sure, she

had it written on her luggage tag and it was on the hotel regis-
ter. Maybe this meant he wanted to keep in touch? Her heart
fluttered a little at the idea.

*Irish, come to the frequent flyer lounge. Need to see you before
we fly out. G*

She'd already been second-guessing herself all over the place
and she didn't need him to ask twice. Stilling her shaking hands
with an effort, she managed to text back a quick, *OK*. The
fluttery wings in her chest took flight again. Why did she think
she'd be able to leave without saying goodbye to him? She owed
him that much.

Standing, then tripping over her own high heels as she
lurched forward, she gathered up her makeup and her wheelie
bag. Forget cool, calm and collected. She rushed to meet him.
She only needed to hold it together long enough to properly kiss
him goodbye. She'd hold on to their kiss when he was gone and
she was drowning in the chocolate abyss.

She ran down the concourse pulling her bag behind her,
nearly colliding with passengers staring at the departures
boards.

Move it, get out of my way. Emergency goodbye kiss pending!

Skidding in her heels, she rounded the corner of the lounge.

There he was, his back to her as he stood by the windows
watching the dismal weather. The outline of his broad shoulders in his business suit, slim hips, strong thighs and long legs,
slightly parted, made her want to whimper and wrap herself
around him. But she was strong. She stopped a few paces away.

She panted his name. "Gabriel."

He faced her, blue eyes sparkling and crinkling up at the
corners. So ridiculously handsome.

"Irish, what were you were doing running off?" His sly smile
was everything cheeky and delicious.

"I had to get going. No need to hang around for soppy goodbyes, right?" She could have smacked herself in the head for the
sarcasm in her voice.

His expression turned serious, his trademark frown was back. "Don't. We had a good time, didn't we?"

"A good time. Sure. But you don't want to see me anymore. You made it crystal clear last night. So what's to talk about?"

"I think . . . I spoke too soon. I like you, more than any woman I've ever known. We could meet up again in London, if you like?"

A thud in her chest meant her heart liked the idea. Only, her head was shaking. "That's it? A maybe? Sorry, but a half-arsed hook-up isn't enough for me."

His face crumpled.

Oh, God. It hurt her insides.

She hesitated, then inched towards him, concentrating on placing one foot in front of the other. She needed a goodbye kiss. For closure.

"Goodbye, Gabriel." She leaned in and placed a feather-light kiss on his surprisingly soft lips. She wanted more. But it couldn't happen.

He grabbed her waist and hauled her into his body. She gasped, but then his lips crashed down onto hers, shocking her into kiss-powered submission.

Delicious. Devastating. Minty fresh.

She opened her mouth to speak, to protest or ask for more, she wasn't sure. Only a squeak escaped when Gabriel circled his tongue around hers. He pressed himself into her, chest to hips, his hardness obvious beneath his clothes. The tips of her breasts peaked and the burn of arousal fired in her belly again. It would be so easy to let it get out of control.

Then he pulled back and broke his hold on her.

"Remember that kiss. You have my number if you change your mind."

His lips were parted, his angel's face marred by an angry scowl. She didn't want it to be her last memory of him, but he brushed against her, then stormed away. Gone.

Sinead stood with her mouth hanging open. Reeling from his kiss. She should call him, make him talk to her, but she was frozen in place. Her legs were made of stone and wouldn't shift. The tears she'd pushed back earlier rolled freely down her cheeks now.

Makeup ruined.

It was the least of her worries but stupid thoughts were apparently rising to the top of her mind. Rushing off to the ladies bathroom, she concentrated on repairing the damage, at least on the outside.

Gabriel clenched his jaw so hard he'd probably break a molar. His feet echoed on the tiled floor of the lounge as he stomped away from Sinead. He couldn't get into it with her now, not in public.

She seemed determined to push him away and never see him again, making him so angry, red haze blurred his vision. He wasn't angry at her though. It was all on him. A guy like him wasn't made for these types of conversations. He had no idea how to tell her what he was feeling, so he'd show her. But it would only work if he could get her alone.

Sinead was a lingering dream he couldn't shake from his head. Her taste was still on his lips, like wild honey. He'd never met a woman who'd shaken him up so much. *Damn*. He wanted her again. His body definitely hadn't caught on to the fact she was out of his life.

He needed a plan. Plans and strategies were things he understood. Marching up to the first class counter, he prepared for battle with the airline, or whoever tried to get in his way.

First: he'd get to London and deal with the new office set-up. Judging by emails from Ryan and Martha, everything was under control. He had to keep it that way. Next: he'd find Sinead, talk to her and show her he meant business. If necessary, he'd camp outside the Mermaid Airlines lounge at Heathrow until he found her.

As plans went, it was pretty basic. Actually, he realised his priorities were in the wrong order. Sinead came first. He'd get to London and then talk to her again. Really talk. Put himself on the line. Then he'd take her somewhere private and kiss her like crazy, get her motor running. Hopefully. He needed a slightly earlier flight, but he wouldn't gatecrash the one Sinead was scheduled to work. He didn't want to scare her off.

Clenching his fists by his sides, he looked up to find a startled-looking redhead at the first class counter, staring at him. The same woman he'd told off a couple of days ago. He'd apologise and play nice. He needed practice in convincing a woman to like him, if not love him. There was a scary thought. He shook his head. Best not to think too far ahead, or shoot for the impossible.

He cleared his throat. "Hello again. I'm sorry for the way I spoke to you the other day. I was under a lot of stress, but it's not an excuse. I want today to be a much better day. The best. And it all starts with you. If you'll help me," he said.

The woman's expression softened and Gabriel knew. Sinead had already changed him for the better.

Chapter Eight

London, UK

Sinead was bone-tired, her feet aching with blisters and shooting pain in her Achilles. She slipped off her high heels while waiting for a taxi. The London night air was frosty seeing as it was past midnight. Her stocking-clad feet were like ice blocks on the concrete pavement, but her feet thanked her for the opportunity to stretch out flat.

Exactly what the rest of her would do at home. She'd stretch out, lie like the dead on her own bed. *So tired*.

After the thirteen-hour flight from Singapore she was back to being a flight attendant zombie, going through the motions to exist but unaware of her surroundings. Incapable of higher-order reasoning. She hadn't eaten anyone's brains yet, but if one more passenger had asked her an inane question about typhoons or travel insurance, she might have gnawed someone's face off.

She was finally at the front of the queue at the taxi rank. A pudgy security man she vaguely knew chatted to her about the weather, of all things. She'd had enough weather to last quite some time.

The security man took her bag for her and wheeled it to the front of the line. She watched the row of black cabs align themselves like a row of shiny beetles. Then she pictured her flat in an old council house and the dreariness hit her full-force. Her sigh must have been world-weary.

"Are you all right?" The security man watched her, concern etched on his forehead.

"Honestly, I don't know. It's been a rough couple of days." Her lips twitched and she attempted a happy face. She'd been thinking of Gabriel all through her long flight. She missed him already.

She pulled her wheelie bag towards the black cab waiting at the front of the queue. Her name echoed in the distance. Was she hallucinating? She heard it again. The deep voice, so commanding and infuriatingly sexy, it could only be one man. The last man on earth she wanted to see. God, she was lying to herself. As much as she'd tried to push him away, she wanted to see him. She could stare at him for hours.

Sinead closed her eyes and breathed, willing him to be a figment of her imagination. If he was really there, he was likely to do something mad like kiss her into blind, shaking submission. Then turn tail and leave again.

She might do something equally mad, which scared her. Like telling him that she loved him after two fecking days. That kind of mad.

"Sinead!"

His voice was hoarse from a combination of a lack of sleep and a worse type of exhaustion. He'd been run over by a spunky Irish steamroller named Sinead and crushed into the dust. But he was up and running again.

Tania from the airline had come through, organising for him to board a charter flight with some other first-class passengers. He'd made it to London only a few minutes behind Sinead. He'd send Tania some hotel vouchers or something as a thank you.

She was at the front of the taxi queue. He was sure it was her, although he could only see her from behind. Truth be told, he'd be able to identify her perfect arse in a line-up from farther away.

He ran to catch her, his feet pounded the footpath with thuds like an elephant. He huffed out a breath, a cloud of fog billowing. The scent of rain hung in the air, or was it snow? Freezing London weather, exactly what he needed.

Sinead was a mirage hovering out of reach on the edge of his vision. Hopefully she wouldn't disappear like a puff of fog. Her spine straightened and she held herself perfectly still. She seemed to have heard him, but wouldn't look at him. His feet kept up the pounding until he caught her with a touch on the shoulder. Her muscles tensed under his hand.

"I found you. Don't run off again." He didn't like the pleading edge to his voice but his emotions were out of control around her.

She glanced over her shoulder at him. "If I remember, you're the one who kissed me and stormed off in a huff."

The security guard snorted in amusement.

Gabriel ignored it, speaking close to her ear. "Only after you said goodbye. It's not what I want."

She shivered and took a step back. "What the hell do you want? Make up your bleeding mind."

"Share a cab with me? Hear me out."

Her piercing glare was sharp enough to cut glass.

"Please."

Air leaked from Sinead as her whole body deflated. He'd begun stroking her back. Soon he could be massaging her, minus her uniform and short black overcoat. If he was lucky.

"All right. Get in the cab." She spat out the words. He guessed asking nicely had softened her up, but she was still pissed-off.

Opening the door for her, he let her slide into the back of the cab, while the driver dealt with their bags. Gabriel climbed in beside Sinead. A tantalising flash of the top of her stockings caught his eye as her skirt rode up. How was he supposed to concentrate on talking to her with that view?

She shuffled back into her seat and smoothed down her skirt, then hit him with a smouldering glare. *Yeah, okay.* He'd better behave himself or she'd send him packing again.

The cabbie got into the driver's seat and looked at them through the glass partition, apparently picking Sinead as the person to ask for orders.

"Where to?" The cabbie tipped his chin at Sinead.

"Roehampton." She gave a few directions.

"Right you are." The cabbie switched his attention to the road, starting the engine with a grumble and then pulling into the light traffic.

Gabriel at least knew vaguely where she lived now, on London's fringe, out towards Wimbledon.

Sinead faced him and stared him down across the back seat, crossing her arms under those gorgeous breasts, doing interesting things to her cleavage. Mighty distracting. He choked on a dry mouth, unable to swallow.

"So, talk." Her words were sharp and he shrank back like a small boy in trouble with his favourite teacher. Gabriel's face heated like a naughty schoolboy. *Oh man.* He needed to stop where that fantasy scenario was headed, before he asked Sinead to spank him.

"Sinead, I'm sorry about how we left things this morning at the airport. But I'm especially sorry you felt like you needed to run away."

He shot a glance through the barrier at the driver, who seemed engrossed in watching the road. Still, the guy was probably listening to everything they said.

"Gabriel, have you gone shy? This is new." Her teasing expression and twinkling eyes became more serious, her eyes narrowing.

"You want me to talk, then you need to talk too," he said.

She nodded. "Fair enough. I won't lie to you Gabriel. You hurt me. I already feel more for you than I would for a casual fling. I wasn't prepared for you to break my heart. So I left, before you had a chance to do it."

Gabriel's own heart jumped as he heard the truth behind her words. He reached out to her, wanting to hold her hand in his. Wanting any sort of contact.

She backed away and raised a hand in warning.

He sighed and shook his head. "I understand and I'm sorry. But you didn't give me a chance to talk to you this morning. I want to keep seeing you, for real. I just realised . . . you're the best thing that's happened to me in a long time. Or you could be, if we give it a chance. It's a big decision for me. I've only known you a couple of days and you've shaken me. You're the only woman I've ever met who's made me want more."

He didn't know if he'd said enough to convince her to give him a chance. *Damn it*. He wished he'd paid more attention to all the stories his mother told him years ago about how his father had romanced her. Before she'd found out he was a two-timing bastard. The stories were too painful to listen to and he'd blocked them out.

Sinead glanced at him, then her eyes slipped down to her hands, now crossed in her lap. "I want to believe you. There was something in your eyes last night. But—"

He didn't like the sound of the "but". There was never good news to follow when a woman said it that way.

"But?"

"But I think I need to lay down a couple of ground rules." She grinned. "Yes, some rules to keep you honest." Sinead gazed at him and seemed to dare him to respond.

She made him nervous, but she was so gorgeous at the same time, he wanted to pin her down in the back of the cab and show her who was boss. If she'd let him. God, she had him confused.

He cleared his throat. "Rules?"

"Yes. Rule number one will be no touching. I think we got a bit ahead of ourselves in Singapore. We should take it slow for a while."

"No touching? Not even . . ."

He didn't finish the sentence but his gaze tracked to her mouth, then before he could stop himself, it dropped to her sensational breasts, straining against the white shirt she wore under her unbuttoned coat.

Sinead's gasp woke him from his hazy fog of arousal. He looked up to find her shaking her head. But the glint of fire in her eyes said she enjoyed his attention.

"Are you sure, Irish? Because the things I want to do to you . . . Singapore was only a taste." How the hell did she expect him to hit the brakes now, when he knew how amazing they were together?

Her slow exhalation of breath gave him confidence. She wanted him. He'd play along with her wacky rules and wait it out.

"I'm sure. Rule number two is, you will treat me with respect and like a lady at all times. Non-negotiable."

"Absolutely. I wouldn't want to negotiate on that one." He studied her face, her lips set in a straight line. Had he not treated her with respect? His mum had raised him to be a better man than that. He'd have to lift his game. "Can I ask, how long will these rules have to remain in place? Number one in particular. I can be patient when I'm going after something I want, but I won't wait indefinitely."

Her lips quirked up at the corners. "We'll play it by ear, but I'd say at least a month."

"A month? You really are trying to kill me."

He gripped the edge of the cab's back seat, forcing himself to do anything but reach over and grab her. And kiss the words right out of her smart, cherry red mouth.

Sinead pressed her lips together to keep from giggling. Any anger towards Gabriel had long since dissolved in the warmth spreading through her body. He was trying to offer her something, trying to make her happy. Her gaze raked over him. He was clenching his jaw so hard he looked like he might either pass out or hit something. She settled back against the back seat of the cab and squeezed her thighs together, enjoying the throb between her legs.

Seeing Gabriel so obviously struggling for control when he wanted to touch her did good things for her self-esteem. Yes, he wanted her all right. Only it wasn't enough to pin her hopes for a relationship on physical attraction. She'd had it once before. A long time ago. She'd still never found a real connection with any man.

She wasn't entirely sure she was doing the right thing though. *A month?* What had made her come out with such a thing? She wasn't sure she could wait so long, he was so beautiful and manly with a thinly veiled temper.

But she had her reasons for slowing things down. She wanted to keep seeing him, to get to know him properly without clinging onto him for dear life. There was more to Gabriel Anderson and she wanted him to show her what he usually kept hidden from the world. And she wanted him to be invested in a relationship with her from the outset.

"Sinead? Are there any more rules you're laying down?"

"That's it, for now. But I reserve the right to invent new rules, if and when required."

She enjoyed his small groan of frustration and the crinkly lines which crept across his forehead. She might have been mean but she got a thrill from causing the big hunk of overconfident man to squirm.

"Okay. You should have been a lawyer. You have a real knack for contract negotiations. I have a question. Under these new rules, am I allowed to take you out to dinner?"

She nodded, enjoying a thrill of sparkly pleasure in her belly. "Yes, you may."

"Would you do me the honour of accompanying me to dinner tomorrow night? Or tonight, seeing as it's already after midnight."

"Yes, thank you. You can call me after lunch, when I've had some sleep."

Gabriel nodded and she noticed him loosen his death-grip on the seat. She sighed happily and stared out the window.

After a few minutes, the cab exited the motorway and the familiar lights and streets of her neighbourhood came into view. More than usual, she looked forward to getting home to her flat. This time, after a long and tiring trip she had something, someone, to look forward to seeing.

After giving a few directions to the cab driver, they pulled up in her street. She paid the fare after refusing Gabriel's attempt to do so, and moved to get out of the car. Quick as you like, Gabriel shot out of his side of the car and went round to her door, opening it for her.

"My lady." He dipped his head in a half bow.

She laughed. "Thank you, kind sir."

"Let me walk you to your door."

The cab driver had deposited her bag on the footpath. Gabriel grabbed it, shooing her away when she attempted to carry her own bag. After a word to the driver, asking him to wait and take him to his hotel, Gabriel followed her.

They walked up the cracked concrete path to the two-storey red-brick house, now divided into four separate flats. Her place was nothing impressive, but it was home, for now. She refused to be embarrassed by her humble abode, even if he was used to the finer things in life.

She waved her hand at the house. "So, this is me. Goodnight Gabriel."

"Goodnight."

He moved forward to kiss her, then a shadow crossed his face. Apparently he'd remembered the rules. For a moment she wished he'd forgotten himself. But if this plan were to work, he'd have to play by the rules. They both would.

He stepped back and handed over her bag. "I'll see you to-morrow night."

"Till tomorrow."

Her laughter couldn't be contained, it bubbled up and escaped in a rush. It must have been contagious because Gabriel's wide smile took her breath away as she unlocked her front door.

It would be stupidly frustrating waiting until tomorrow evening to see his face. But considering only that morning she'd never expected to see him again, she couldn't believe her luck.

She hoped it was luck. As she closed the door behind her, she decided luck was only part of it. She had a plan, and the rules.

Gabriel downed his third espresso of the day and tapped impatiently on the cold black lacquered board room table. The long-winded budget update from his London team was making his ears bleed and figures were swimming before his eyes on his laptop screen. Five hours' sleep hadn't been enough, lying alone in his new hotel bed.

He'd woken several times overnight and reached for Sinead, finding the other side of the bed cold and empty. Somehow, in two nights and half a day, he'd become used to sleeping with a warm, soft woman pressed up against him. Not just any woman. *Sinead*.

Hopefully he'd break down her defences soon and she'd be back in his bed, in spite of her infuriating rules. But that wasn't all he wanted from Sinead. Not anymore. Something else had been driving him to catch up with her in London. The possibility of something *more*.

A voice floated into his brain. "The marketing budget is coming in slightly over, but we expected the outlay in the set-up phase."

Gabriel blinked and lifted his chin. His attention had been anywhere but on his best friend, Ryan McKinlay, acting in his new role of European regional manager. Ry looked sharp, his dark hair slicked back and his grey suit Saville Row stylish. Unlike Gabriel. He was rumpled and exhausted. Not his usual style.

Ryan's last comment required some sort of response, but for the life of him, Gabriel couldn't work out what he was meant to say. Clearly, his head wasn't in the game. That was unusual too.

"Gabe, are you with us?" Ryan smirked, clearly amused by Gabriel's lapse in concentration.

Gabriel blinked and opened his eyes wider. "Sorry mate, I'm jet-lagged. I think I'm done with absorbing information for today."

"Okay folks, show's over. I'd like everyone to email their reports to Gabriel and myself by close of business. Thanks." Ryan dismissed the team with his usual confident and friendly way, chatting with people on their way out.

A procession of four men and two women filed out of the conference room and Gabriel struggled to remember their names. It would click into place once he read their written reports. Hopefully.

Ryan flopped back into a swivel chair and stretched out, hands behind his head. His dark hair flopped over his eyes as he stared at Gabriel.

"Come on, spill the beans. You're on another planet today and I reckon it's more than jet-lag."

Ryan had always been insightful, which made him a great people-manager. But Gabriel didn't feel like sharing. Especially since he himself didn't understand what was going on.

"Is it your mum?" Ryan's question was hesitant. Gabriel hated to think his friend might be afraid to raise the subject.

Gabriel had been otherwise occupied and the situation had almost slipped his mind in the past few days. It had been a relief. But now the guilt hit him hard, right in the gut. "No. The worry's always there, but she's all right for now in respite care. I might look into permanent care at the centre."

Sinead was still occupying his thoughts. He should talk to Ryan. His best friend was probably the only person who'd understand what Sinead's presence could mean in his life. He closed his laptop and avoided his friend's eyes. "I um, met someone. A woman."

Ryan sat up straight and his familiar grin appeared. "I'm surprised. One of your hook-ups?"

Gabriel's head shake and raised eyebrows got a laugh out of Ryan. "Sinead's something else."

Ryan leaned forward in his seat. "Now I'm intrigued. Give me the low-down."

"Flight attendant, Irish accent, long blonde hair, fantastic breasts. She's hot, but she's more. Funny and sweet. She's got me agreeing to all sorts of crap to keep seeing her."

"Like what? Bondage, discipline? Cavorting naked in a field?"

He snorted, but enjoyed Ryan's joking. It'd been too long since they'd hung out. Gabriel hadn't had the time lately. "No, but I wouldn't put it past her. She's making all these rules. No touching for a month."

"Oh man, you'll be out of your mind. You agreed? She must be special."

"Special." Funny, Sinead had used the same word. It was growing on him. "Yeah, you could say that. Lucky we already got down and dirty in Singapore, so I know it's worth waiting for. It'll be hell in the meantime though."

Ryan chuckled and got up from his seat. "Good luck, mate. I'd like to meet her sometime."

"She's in London, so you might. Anyway, I'm taking her out tonight, so I'd better get onto booking a restaurant for dinner."

"If you want my advice, don't overthink it. It sounds like she wants to get to know you. Talk to her. Try not to be your usual *charming* self."

"Sarcasm. Nice."

Ryan laughed hard on his way out.

Gabriel was aware of his reputation with women. Some would call him a womaniser. But that wasn't fair. He'd never led anyone on, and only chose women who wanted some fun. And he could be charming. The charm was something he utilised for business reasons, or when it was warranted. But with Sinead, he wanted something different. He wanted to *be* different.

Sinead *was* special, there was no point in denying it anymore.

Gabriel drummed the tabletop again. Working the way he had over the past twelve years, like a machine, hadn't left any time for a real relationship. He'd always avoided ongoing commitments with women, to spare them the complications in his life. And he'd always assumed no woman would want him if she understood the issues he faced with his mother.

Tonight could be the right time to open up to Sinead, at least for starters.

Coffee, fabulous coffee.

Sinead thanked the god of caffeine for her fix as she waited for Yuki. Shot Espresso off the Fulham Road was a sweet little Italian café, perfumed with the scent of real, fresh roasted coffee beans, a balm to her soul. It was the perfect spot for brunch with her friend, and a debrief on the Gabriel situation.

She hadn't confided in Yuki about her new man, so far. It had happened so fast – it was only four days since they'd first met. Although with the typhoon and jet-lag, she'd entered some type of alternate universe where time stretched out like a giant rubber band. Everything had happened in fast-motion, then been jammed in place before things snapped back, not quite in a straight line. Now she was back to regular life, everything was strange and wobbly.

From her seat by the café windows, she spied Yuki heading her way. Yuki had been scheduled on a different flight back to London, so it seemed to Sinead as if she hadn't seen her friend in weeks.

Sinead waved and Yuki answered with a tinkling laugh she could hear from inside. Her friend looked happy. Yuki's days in Singapore with her boyfriend, Daniel, must have made her beam. Yuki pushed open the door, jingling the old-fashioned brass bell.

"Hi Sinead! It's so good to see you. I was worried about you."

Yuki swished her curtain of black shiny hair over her shoulder as she hugged Sinead. She sat in the opposite chair and rolled her shoulders, as if to release some tension.

"I'm grand, but it's good to see you too." It really was a relief to see her friend safe and well. And to have someone to talk to. "So get yourself a cup of tea and prepare yourself. I've a story to tell."

"Oh, interesting. Sounds like I need a whole pot of tea." Yuki ordered English Breakfast tea from the young waiter, a man with Italian good looks and a bright white flash of teeth. "I'm ready. Tell me this story."

Sinead told the tale from the beginning, the flirty exchange with Gabriel on the original flight out of Melbourne, and how they met again in the airport lounge. The twinkle of excitement in Yuki's eyes was contagious.

"Oh, I remember. A top prospect from the Young Rich List. He was gorgeous! A bit cranky but definitely a spunk. Did you do the deed?"

"Aye, we did the deed, and how. You know it'd been a while for me. I nearly tackled him to the ground when I got him alone in my suite. Turns out he's a marathon man and more than equipped for the task." Sinead giggled.

Yuki squealed and clapped her hands in delight. "Yay! Sounds like exactly what you needed. Are you going to see him again?"

Sinead held her tongue as the waiter arrived with Yuki's tea. He poured the steaming brew into a china cup with tiny rosebuds painted around the rim. Then he left them alone again.

"I'm seeing him tonight. But there are a couple of other things I should tell you. I'm not sure if I've lost my mind."

Yuki's eyes widened at Sinead's explanation about Gabriel's aversion to relationships and his attempt to fob her off. She left out some details of both their delicious lovemaking and rampant shagging, and the way she'd tried to run away.

Sinead sipped her latte and sighed. "It's been years since I felt anything close to what I already feel for him. So I decided to give him a chance. But I wanted to make sure he was really interested. So I invented some rules. Number one is already freaking me out—no touching for a month."

Yuki clutched at her heart. "Whoa. You may be shooting yourself in the foot. He's hot stuff. Don't you want some touchy-feely time?"

Sinead groaned and rolled her eyes. "Of course I do. I'll probably have to sit on my hands to stop myself grabbing him at dinner tonight. It's just I want him to be a gentleman and treat me like a lady. I think I deserve it."

"You do." Yuki placed her hand on Sinead's and then her mouth stretched in a wicked grin. "But some rules are made to be broken. It wouldn't hurt to tease the man a little. Let's go shopping for a dress that'll have him picking his tongue up off the floor and begging to lick you like a lollipop."

Sinead snorted and barely stopped a mouthful of coffee from exploding across the table. "You're on. Shopping for tongue-lolling outfit. Excellent plan."

"I don't think I can get it over my head. Help!"

Sinead twisted and squirmed, trying to make an impossibly small 'body-conscious' dress fit over her head and flailing arms. She spoke through the fabric. "I don't think this overstuffed sausage skin look will win me any beauty contests."

Yuki burst in from the next cubicle in the posh boutique's changing room. Her squeal of alarm also alerted the haughty shop assistant who came rushing over.

Sinead huffed out a breath then sucked in her belly. Her less than glamorous yet sensible white cotton knickers were making an appearance. The ones with the unravelling elastic, reserved for when she was feeling jet-lagged or pudgy. Or when she'd got back from her travels and hadn't had a chance to wash her clothes.

The shop lady poked her ribcage with a bony finger. "You are aware there is a side zipper, I presume?" Ms Haughty-Pants enquired. Obviously Sinead hadn't seen the zipper or she wouldn't be in her current predicament.

At least Haughty was helpful, releasing the stuck zipper and Sinead's head with it. Yuki helped to wrench the dress off, thrusting it at the shop lady with unnecessary force.

"Here, why don't you go find my friend something delectable to wear? She wants her new man to try to lick her all over, although she's not going to let him."

The shop lady sauntered off with a barely disguised look of disgust. Sinead giggled and patted Yuki on the shoulder. Sinead picked up a tiny bandage dress from a pile on the chair in the corner, but Yuki slapped her hand away.

"Wait! No more sausage dresses. I have the perfect thing."

Yuki dashed into her original cubicle and was back quick as a flash, closing the door behind her. She waved a bright red silk dress, swaying from the hanger with a pleasing *swish*.

Sinead admired the intricate swirl of fabric at the front, like a rosette. Sliding her fingers down the length of the dress, she let out an *oooh* at the softness. "I don't know, it's more your style." Sinead went for modern, edgy styles, while Yuki liked feminine, retro fashions a la Audrey Hepburn.

"Try it on. I'll bet your fancy-man will love it."

Sinead was sold on the dress the moment it slipped over her head with a whisper against her skin. It fell with a low v-neckline, gathered under her breasts, then it floated down to her knees. A naughty split was hidden under a fold at the centre seam.

"Your boobs look awesome in it. Gabriel's going to be dribbling on you before you finish dinner," Yuki said.

Bubbles of excitement rose in her belly until she almost popped. Her lips tipped upwards. "I guess it's a winner."

Sinead's happy face slid downwards when her phone chiming from the depths of her cavernous tote bag. She fished it out and glanced at the caller's name on the screen, then mouthed to Yuki. *It's him.*

"Hello Gabriel. It's a pleasure to hear from you."

He had the perfect evening planned. When he should have been concentrating on work, Gabriel had spread out the contents of his briefcase across the spare executive desk and studiously ignored it. Instead, he'd called in a couple of favours to snag VIP tickets to a sold-out Slammers gig at an exclusive club he'd never heard of, and booked a table for dinner at the Italian wine bar, North.

It was enjoyable, trying to work out what type of date would appeal to Sinead. A mixture of fun and glamour, he guessed. He grabbed his phone and dialled her number before he knew what he was doing.

When she answered, he could have sworn he heard giggling in the background. What was she was up to? He could picture her, face lit up with internal sunshine, radiating from her creamy skin.

"Hello Gabriel. It's a pleasure to hear from you."

Relaxing back in his leather chair, his lips stretched upwards. "The pleasure is all mine, believe me. What are you up to?"

"I'm trying on a pretty dress which apparently makes my boobs look awesome."

Heat spread from his neck up to his face at the image she conjured. He was pretty sure his eyeballs were bugging out. She was teasing him, trying to get a reaction, he could tell by the lilt in her accent. It was damn well working.

"Oh Irish, will you wear it for me tonight?" His voice was huskier than usual due to a serious case of dry-mouth syndrome.

"Why yes, I think I will wear it tonight."

How was he going to get through a whole evening with her in some super-hot dress with all the boob action, with no touching? He cleared his throat.

"I can hardly wait. I've got some surprises lined up for you too. How about I pick you up from your place at seven?"

"Seven o'clock sounds grand. Looking forward to seeing you all handsome. Bye."

"Bye."

He ended the call and found himself staring out the window. Grinning like a kid who'd been allowed to lick the last traces of cake batter out of the mixing bowl. He had to go and think of licking things. Sweet and tasty things.

The heat that'd spread over his face now rushed downstairs and overheated matters. What the hell? No other woman had ever had such an effect on him. Uncomfortably hard, he shifted in his chair and stretched out his legs.

Sinead had better not leave him hanging for long. He was trying, making an effort to be the gentleman she wanted. But he wasn't known for his patience.

Chapter Nine

The doorbell trilled from downstairs and Sinead leapt from her bed to her feet, hurriedly pulling on her ever-so-hot black leather boots. The combination of the knee-high boots and the more demure dress was a winner, especially as the dress hugged her curves so well and showed a hint of thigh through the split when she moved.

She couldn't wait to open the door and gauge Gabriel's reaction. But she slowed down. It probably wouldn't do to seem too eager. Even though she was.

Stopping at the mirror to slather on another layer of cherry lip gloss, she stopped mid-pout. What would she do if he tried to kiss her tonight? She wanted to hold her ground, but she'd probably melt if he gave her that look. That dirty, I want to make you scream my name look.

The memory popped into her head – Gabriel half-naked and sated in her Singapore hotel bed, complete with devilish look. Eyebrow raised, like he knew all her secrets. At least, he looked as if he'd pin her to the bed until she gave them all up to him. Or vice versa. She'd be happy to pin him down and have her wicked way with him again. But not yet.

Her heart thudded like a jackhammer as she picked up her clutch bag and coat.

On slightly shaky legs, she bounced down the narrow stairs with the creaky wooden boards and out into the small entry hall.

She sucked in a cleansing breath and silently repeated the mantra: *Don't grab the handsome man, don't grab the handsome man.*

Opening the door with a trembling hand, she stopped stock-still at the chilly blast of the night air and the sight before her. Gabriel, wearing slim-fitting black jeans and a dark blue T-shirt which could've been sprayed onto his broad chest. No jacket, just bare biceps from here to kingdom-come. It was far too cold not to be wearing a jacket, but she suspected he was showing off, for her benefit. It had worked, she couldn't look away.

Her slow inspection took in the complete picture, from top to toe. Hair kind of ruffled, the way she liked it, down to black biker-style boots. All the good things in between. Gabriel gone casual, in the most alarmingly attractive way. And he smelled wonderful, like cinnamon and spices with a hint of clean, freshly showered man.

"Oh." The breathy sound escaped her lips with a will of its own. Her mouth was hanging open, but her body refused to catch up with her brain's command to close it.

"Irish, you look good enough to eat. We could skip dinner and you could grab me a spoon. Or some chocolate body paint."

"Stop it, you naughty man. We're going out on a proper date and you promised to be a gentleman. Where are you taking me? Am I overdressed?"

Self-consciously smoothing her hands over the red silky dress, she glanced up to find Gabriel's gaze following the action, staring at her hands passing over her hips. He cleared his throat.

"You're fine. I mean, you look stunning. We're going to a Slammers gig then onto dinner. You're perfect."

His broad smile caused her heart to sputter, it was so full of . . . what? Pleasure, anticipation, something more? The something more almost did her in.

"That sounds grand. It's good to be seeing you again." *I missed you*. So she meant to say.

She avoided his eyes, shrugging on her coat.

It was then she noticed The Car. It sat by the curb putting everything around it to shame. It was the fanciest, sleekest piece of machinery the neighbourhood had ever seen. It wasn't a horrible neighbourhood, but it was an extremely fancy ride. It suited such a ridey man. An Aston Martin? *Good Lord*. He really was James Bond, or possibly Batman.

"Is that yours?" She waved vaguely in the direction of the curb. She could have kicked herself for the idiotic question. Who else would drive a work of art? Nervousness was making her stupid.

"Actually, not really. It's a rental, but I'm loving it. Can I take you for a spin, my lady?"

She giggled, breathless. "You may."

Although how she would manage to breathe in the close confines of a sexy beast of a car, sitting right next to a sexy beast of a man, she had no idea.

Striding towards the car behind Sinead, Gabriel couldn't help the way his eyes were glued to her hips, swaying in a red dress. She wore a short coat over the top, but it didn't ruin the effect. Blasted icy English weather. He wished they were in Melbourne, where it was the height of a balmy summer. Her luscious skin would be on full display. Those knee-high black boots weren't something to wish away – there was a hint of dominatrix about them. Something about that idea made him sweat.

Letting Sinead take control in the bedroom was definitely something he'd like to explore further. If she ever let him touch her again.

She was already firmly in control.

He lost his concentration, stumbling over a crack in the concrete path. He righted himself and re-centred on the here and now. Jogging ahead, he stopped and opened the passenger door for her, resisting the urge to touch her lower back to usher her into her seat. She was only a few inches away and the tug towards her was almost overwhelming. He breathed in her scent, the floral concoction making his head spin.

Sinead dropped her gaze, almost shy, except for the way her lips twitched up at the corners. She ducked her head to get into the low-riding car and he had a clear view down the front of her dress. The curves of her upper breasts. A hint of a red lace bra. Counting slowly to ten and looking straight up to the cloudy night sky, he struggled to control his breathing . . . and other parts of his anatomy.

She giggled. "You can shut the door now, I'm safely seated."

Why was she torturing him? She seemed to know exactly what effect she had on him.

Slamming the door, he stomped around the front of the car and got in the driver's seat. Once he sunk into the leather-upholstered seat and breathed in the authentic new car smell, he'd regained some semblance of calm.

He glanced at Sinead, who was staring at her hands in her lap. "Let's hit the road."

The drive was silent torture, only broken by the growl of the Aston Martin's engine as Gabriel let it rip on the main road heading into the city. Sinead's skin tingled and heated. She'd underestimated how hard it would be to sit so close without touching him. Her hands clutched at the skirt of her dress.

She'd somehow forgotten his magnetic pull and the way his presence filled every space he was in.

Several times she found herself staring at his long legs and powerful thigh muscles encased in black denim. Then his hand would shift on the gearstick and she watched the play of muscles and tendons in his forearms. The man looked so fine it was doing all sorts of disturbing things to her self-control.

She wasn't second-guessing her self-inflicted rules, but third- and fourth-guessing. Gabriel pulled up near a busy corner. They were somewhere in Covent Garden, outside an old, serious-looking building made from blocks of stone. He switched off the engine and placed both of his large hands on his knees.

She nodded towards the building. "What is this place? Aren't we going to see a band?"

"We are. It's the Hospital Club and we're headed up to The Oak Room."

Wow. She'd heard of the club, since some of her favourite bands had performed private shows there and recorded in the studios. She'd never imagined she'd go to a gig at a place like this. Obviously Gabriel had access to places she'd only ever dreamed of going, and he wanted to take her along for the ride. So he was showing off a little. But it was kind of a thrill.

Sinead schooled her features into her serious face and nodded. "I'm suitably impressed."

Gabriel's expression brightened, then he shrugged. "I'm glad I managed to impress you."

She and Gabriel both seemed aware of the awkward, heavy silence blanketing them. He leaned towards her. She held her breath and her gaze dropped to his mouth. Then he let out a rough breath, falling back into his seat.

Sinead closed her eyes for a moment. He'd been about to kiss her. She wanted him to kiss her. The ache deep in her belly had nothing to do with food. It was all about a deeper, more primal hunger. How on earth would she get through the whole evening without flinging herself at him?

The car door clicked and her eyes blinked open. He bent and ducked his head to get out of the car. She didn't look too closely at his tight arse in those jeans. No, she barely noticed it at all. The roundness or the firmness.

He was at her door. Like a perfect gentleman, he opened it for her and stood back, shrugging on a black blazer. Swivelling her legs to the side, she tried to lever herself out of the low seat with some kind of dignity. She wasn't winning the battle. Snagging her high heel on the rim of the car door, she half-fell towards the gutter before grabbing the door's inner armrest for balance.

Gabriel suddenly stepped forward and tugged her upward by her free hand. The feel of his rough-hewn hand enveloping hers was too much. His skin rasping against hers, too intoxicating. Exactly what she'd been trying to avoid. Her stomach flip-flopped and she tried to tug her hand away.

"No. Now I've got hold of your hand, I'm not letting you go."

He bumped the car door closed and handed his keys to a waiting parking valet. She supposed there was a VIP parking garage nearby. Part of his rich-man world she knew little about. Gabriel exchanged words with the young man, but she heard none of it. Her brain was fixated on Gabriel's hand grasping hers. Such a simple touch, but it shook her senses.

She shivered and fought the cold by clenching her teeth to stop them chattering. His skin was so warm, she welcomed his heat seeping into her own skin.

When his gaze locked on her, he searched her face. That muscle twitched in the corner of his jaw. Somehow she knew if she pulled away again, it would feel like a rejection to him. It would be important.

She lifted her chin and caught his eyes. "It's okay. Let's relax the rules a little."

She loved the way his eyes lit from within. His lips quirked up at the corners as if he was laughing at a private joke. He probably was, laughing at her rules or the way she was already bending them. Never mind, the evening was going so well it would be a sad shame to ruin it by being stubborn.

He kept his grip on her hand as they entered the lounge bar outside The Oak Room. He wouldn't let her get away. There would be no escaping his clutches. He'd play the role of the super-villain if necessary. Chuckling, he ushered Sinead through the mingling crowd towards the bar.

The cool factor at this club was off the charts. It wasn't the kind of place he usually hung out. But he wanted to impress Sinead, like a lovesick teenager.

Not keeping up with celebrity gossip of the English tabloid variety, he wouldn't know who was hot or not. But the slim woman with the short black hair and even shorter silver mini dress was getting plenty of attention. She could be a soap-opera star. But he wasn't interested in anyone except the woman at his side.

Plenty of men were interested, checking out Sinead as they walked through the lounge. He didn't think they were only wondering if she was the new 'it girl' around town. She was simply stunning. A primal male surge of pride roared through his body at the knowledge she could was his. Technically she wasn't his yet, but he wanted her to be. He was working on it.

"You okay?" He wanted to check in with her. And look at her some more. She'd done something to her hair so it flowed around her shoulders in soft waves. He itched to touch it. But he'd make do with holding her hand for now. It was a start.

She bounced on her high heels. "I'm great. This place is incredible. I can't wait for the show. Oh my God, is that Sadie Frost? I love her dress!"

His lips stretched out in a smile, then he shook his head. "Er, not sure. Glad you're enjoying yourself though. Let's get a drink."

London's trendy nightspots often made him uncomfortable, when interior designers went mad with untouchable surfaces and Star-Trek-inspired chairs. It could be scary to sit down. But this club was warm and inviting, with oak wood panelling, low coffee tables and long soft sofas in yellows and greens. It wasn't a huge space. The fifty or so people chatting and hanging around added a buzz of excitement.

He led Sinead to the bar, still grasping her hand, enjoying the soft touch of her skin. It seemed somehow forbidden, which was working for him in a big way. She wrapped her fingers through his.

"So, what would you like to drink?"

She wagged her finger. "No Singapore Slings. They make me behave like a wanton woman. Champagne?"

"I rather liked the wanton woman, but champagne's good. I could do without another migraine."

Ordering the drinks, he leaned across the polished wooden bar but didn't let go of Sinead's hand, not for a second. She stood so close. Close enough for him to be constantly aware of her scent and the hum of anticipation vibrating through his body.

The barman placed two crystal champagne flutes on the bar in front of them and the sparkling liquid in the glasses reminded him of Sinead. Golden, bubbly, even magical. His head was spinning from her nearness before he'd even taken a sip. He passed her a glass, their joined hands falling near her hip.

"To you and me, the rules, and possible negotiation." He raised an eyebrow and his glass, daring her to contradict his toast.

"To you and me, the rules and possibly some wiggle-room. I wouldn't presume to negotiate with you, Mr Big Time Businessman."

A laugh rose from his throat as he clinked his glass against hers. "You can be surprisingly persuasive. Cheers."

"Cheers."

He sipped his drink, then before he had a chance to say anything more, he was accosted from behind. A long, thin arm snaked around his waist and he could feel a female body pressed against his back. But it wasn't a snake he pictured in his mind whenever this woman appeared, it was always a big cat. It wasn't only the name, more her predatory nature and superior attitude.

He clenched his jaw and spoke through gritted teeth. He turned to face her. "Kitty, you're here."

Kitty preened her dark shiny hair. It didn't move. Her forehead didn't move when she smiled either, or grimaced. Her black dress was tight, with an expensive designer-ish look. But it was funereal. Nothing about Kitty attracted him, in fact she made him want to go wash his hands.

Glancing at Sinead, he caught the pinched line of her mouth. Not good. He needed to nip this in the bud.

A high-pitched voice grated in his ear. "Gabriel, darling, so good to see you."

Kitty planted a sloppy kiss right on his neck. He could've throttled her. If he didn't need her business contacts in London's high-society set, he'd be tempted.

Grumbling under his breath, he watched Sinead as he spoke. "Kitty, a little distance please."

Thankfully, Kitty dropped her arm and stepped to his side. Still too close, but better.

"This is Sinead, the one I told you about on the phone. Thanks for organising the tickets. We're looking forward to the show."

Kitty's gaze ran up and down Sinead's body. He wanted to wrap Sinead in his arms and drag her away, but he settled for squeezing her fingers tighter.

The other woman practically purred. "My pleasure, anything for you. So this is the girlfriend. Will wonders never cease?"

His spine stiffened. Catching Kitty's eyes, he stared her down. "Yes, Sinead's my girlfriend. I'll see you at our meeting next week."

The unsubtle hint for Kitty to leave hung in the air. Sinead was silent. Then she dropped his hand. *No bloody way*.

Sinead stretched out her hand to Kitty, inviting her to shake. "It was nice to meet you, Kitty. Any *friend* of Gabriel's is a friend of mine."

He let out a staggered breath. Sinead was dealing with the situation graciously.

Kitty looked at Sinead's outstretched hand for a few moments longer than was polite, before shaking it briefly and slinking away into the crowd. Disaster averted, for now.

Sinead stared at Gabriel, as a host of strange reactions washed through her. Heat pulsed in her temples, and a sick roll lurched through her belly. Defiance made her stand taller. What should she make of the last few minutes?

Kitty was everything Sinead was not, from her posh upper-class accent to her perfectly coiffed brunette hair, little black dress, pearls and even a bloody Gucci handbag. A stereotypical London socialite like a cardboard cut-out fashion dolly.

Kitty must be an ex of Gabriel's, not that he went in for relationships. More likely just a sex thing, a hook-up. Her belly pitched and rolled again. The woman was too confident and brazen with Gabriel, rubbing up against him like an alley cat. Sinead could hardly come to any other conclusion.

But Gabriel called Sinead his girlfriend, right in front of Kitty, which kept her from lashing out at the pair of them. She'd liked his comment a tad too much. Her heart contracted. No need to get too excited. They'd known each other such a short time.

Still, the vulnerable side of her soul was crying out for reassurance. She took a cleansing breath and put it all out there.

"So, I'm your girlfriend now?"

"Yes, absolutely. Before you ask, she's a business contact. An events manager."

She nodded. "Okay then."

He tipped his head to one side. "Don't you have more questions? I know she's . . . inappropriate." Gabriel looked so uncomfortable, staring down at his boots, she was almost sorry for him. Almost.

Her hand rose in a stop-sign motion. "No, don't tell me. I don't want all the gory details."

He glanced up again. His forehead was all creased. "Honestly, there aren't any details. She comes onto me, I tell her to back off. That's it."

Sinead's relief had her shoulders relaxing. Reaching across the few inches of space between them, she took his hand again and entwined their fingers. Gabriel rubbed his thumb across the back of her hand and her pulse sped.

She fixed her gaze on their joined hands. "I believe you. But I know there'll be others, so I need to deal with it."

"Others?"

"Other women who want you. I can't fight them all, so I'll have to put up with them."

"I won't cheat on you. I don't want anyone else."

She breathed out on a sigh. This new side of Gabriel was sucking her in. Making her want him so much it hurt. But she still had to be careful. "I want to believe you."

The small performance space was intimate in the darkness. Sinead could barely contain her excitement. Her knee bounced up and down until she smoothed her hand over it. She'd never been this close to a band during a performance, even when she used to hang out in the standing room only area at music festivals. This was different.

It was an exclusive showcase performance for selected journalists and society movers and shakers, people like Gabriel and Kitty. Sinead, not so much. Resentment still burned through her belly when she let herself think of Kitty, making her feel out of place, like an imposter at Gabriel's side. But she was the only one with him now. He was making her feel wanted.

She and Gabriel lounged on a low sofa, only a couple of metres away from the lead singer, glowing under the single spotlight over the small stage. Brody Nightingale. Long black wavy hair, green eyes, pale skin with a few freckles across his nose. He was going all out with the rock star look, wearing leather pants and a loose, unbuttoned white shirt. He was undeniably hot. She'd had a crush on Brody a few years back. He'd fronted another band and she'd seen them live in Dublin.

Brody's voice was hypnotic and the lyrics he wrote were like poetry.

Betrayed, by a rose
My love unbound
Her name on my lips
No more

His voice hovered above the crowd on an extended high note, like something belonging to another realm. Ethereal. When the piano accompaniment twinkled on, she sighed.

Five years ago, she would have been fan-girling all over Brody in an embarrassing way. Now, she could admire him and his talent, but her mind was fixed entirely on the man sitting so close beside her. An urge to curl up and snuggle into Gabriel, to let him wrap his arms around her, wound through her body.

Why didn't she reach for him? *The bloody rules, right.* There was a reason she'd invented them, but it was hard to remember. Especially when he invaded her space, brushing his thigh against hers and then squeezing her hand. His scent taunted her too, a spicy warmth reminding her of twisted sheets and soft sighs.

Sinead slid a glance across at him, and his lips quirked upwards as he watched the stage. He knew exactly how to get to her.

She sank back in her seat and focused on enjoying the music. And ignoring Gabriel, if humanly possible.

The show was excruciating but not because of any tension with Sinead. Not the music, the band was impressive. The singer was great and Gabriel was blown away by the feeling of the floor reverberating beneath their seats when the drummer performed his solo. As the music washed over him, an unexpected and uncomfortable rush of emotion rose in his throat, tears prickling behind his closed eyelids.

What the hell? He didn't want to analyse it. The amount of stress he'd been under was probably getting to him. There was no *probably* about it. The only times he'd relaxed in the past few months had been the days spent with Sinead. Those days had pushed back the tide of sadness threatening to engulf him.

To distract himself, he accidently-on-purpose brushed his leg against hers, making her tremble. He loved her reaction, even when she was trying to play it cool.

When the last note of the last song faded and the house lights rose, Gabriel was calm. Composed. He still grasped Sinead's hand on the seat between them. Her palm was warm and soft. Sinead brushed her hair back from her face and grinned, her happiness pure and contagious.

"It was incredible. I've never seen a show like it."

"I know. I'm so glad we came."

Sinead sighed, then pure joy rolled across her face. "Do you think I could get an autograph from Brody?"

"The singer? I guess so." The muscles tensed in his gut at her excitement to meet the guy. He glanced at the musicians still hanging around on stage. "Some people are talking to him already."

Sinead made a noise, a combination of a squeal and a yelp, then jumped to her feet, dragging him along too.

He staggered after her, gripping her hand, this time to keep his balance. They walked a few steps to the front of the stage and waited behind another couple, the man chatting to Brody and slapping him on the back as if they were old friends. Sinead vibrated with excitement, bouncing on her heels again.

The other couple left, then Brody nodded to them, beaming. "Enjoy the show?"

Brody had vaguely aimed the question at both of them, but his eyes were all over Sinead like a rash. *Bloody arrogant rock stars.*

Sinead beamed, oblivious. "Oh, we loved it. I'm a big fan, all the way back to the Glitter Stomp days. I saw you in Dublin once, but this was my favourite gig ever. I'm Sinead, this is Gabriel."

Sinead's babbling was cute and Gabriel wasn't the only one who thought so. Brody's eyes lit up. The singer's gaze wandered down Sinead's body, landing on her cleavage. The guy needed to step back or he was going to have a problem in a minute.

Brody spoke low, almost a whisper. "Sinead, I'm so glad you enjoyed it. Sometimes these showcase gigs can be a bit quiet, with the media stiffs and all. But I could hear some shouting over there. Was it you?" Brody grinned like a loon.

"Yes! It was so great. Would you sign an autograph for me, if it's not too much trouble?"

Brody bared his teeth, grinning with extra smarminess. Gabriel breathed, and silently counted to three. "Anything for you, Sinead."

The same bloody words Kitty had said to Gabriel earlier. The irony was not lost on him. Now he was the one seething with jealousy. He could admit it, he was jealous. This guy obviously wanted Sinead, and Gabriel was starting to feel like a third wheel.

Gabriel squeezed her hand. "Sinead, we'll have to leave if we're going to make our dinner reservation." His comment grabbed Brody's attention. Gabriel stared him down unapologetically.

She stepped into Gabriel's side, patting the back of his hand. "Just a second."

Sinead pulled her ticket out of her purse and passed it to Brody for his autograph. The guy's hands brushed her fingertips and lingered a bit too long. Gabriel couldn't help his frustrated grunt. *Seriously*.

As soon as Sinead had her damned ticket signed, Gabriel pulled her by the hand in the other direction.

"Jealous, are we?" Sinead's voice rang with glee.

His grumble was hardly an answer, so he forced the words out. "Guess there'll be others. I'll have to get used to it."

The tinkling sound of Sinead's laugh lifted him up, out of himself. At least she helped keep the full-blown grumpiness at bay.

The restaurant wasn't what she expected Gabriel would choose, but then he kept surprising her. It was casual, with dark wood tables decorated with little tea-light candles and exposed red bricks along the wall behind the bar. It seemed popular with people who seriously liked their food and wine.

On second glance, the place reminded her of Italian bistros she'd dined at in Lygon Street, Melbourne's Little Italy. She'd love to go there with Gabriel sometime.

Sinead folded her linen napkin in her lap and looked up to enjoy the view. Gabriel, front and centre, leaning over the table towards her. Wanting to tell her something. She could practically see the words forming in a cartoon speech balloon and then retreating back into his mouth. The scowl of consternation on his face was charming. Cute as a button.

"Spit it out, would you?" Sinead took a bite of her delicious chicken cacciatore, an old-school dish which also, serendipitously, happened to start with her favourite letter 'c'.

"Spit what out, exactly?"

Swallowing a mouthful of deliciousness, she put down her cutlery with a clink. "Whatever you want to tell me. Out with it."

He looked down at his plate of seafood linguini. "It's a long story. I want to tell you about my mum."

She sat straighter in her chair, interested now. It wasn't what she'd been expecting. No, she was expecting an argument about the rules, or a grumpy comment about Brody's flirting at the club. This sounded like details. Depth. Exactly what she wanted from Gabriel.

"You can tell me. Whatever it is, I'm a good listener."

His forehead creased. "My mum's sick. Has been for years. Ever since I was at university."

"Oh, Gabriel, I'm so sorry. Your poor Ma. Is she on the mend now?"

His face went weird, his jaw clenched then released. Again Sinead had the sense words would come tripping off the tip of his tongue. But they didn't. His head dropped down and he took a long sip of his red wine.

She tried not to stare at the way his fingers shook. What she really wanted was to wrap him up in her arms.

Finally he looked up and nodded. "She's okay. She had a chest infection but the doctors caught it before it turned to pneumonia. It's been rough for a while though."

"That must have been hard. Is it some kind of chronic illness?"

Gabriel nodded. "Yes. It's a progressive disease. I have to face the fact she won't get any better."

Her heart pinched in her chest. "Is this what's been worrying you? Not your work?"

He paused again, gripping his glass too hard. "Both. I wanted to explain why I said we shouldn't see each other again. Back in Singapore."

She nodded slowly. This could explain some of his behaviour in Singapore. Gabriel leaned back in his chair. His shirt pulled taut across his chest. He really was delectable. She bit her lip, then forced her eyes up to meet his. She had to stop ogling the man. This was important.

"So, have you had to look after her?"

"There's nurses, but a lot of it has fallen to me. It hasn't been easy. But I don't want to go into it now." Gabriel sighed, then leaned in as he spoke. "I just wanted to explain. There's demands on my time from every direction. I can't promise I'll be available for you. Not like you deserve." He drank from his water glass this time.

"But you still want to sex me up?"

He spluttered, water dripping down his chin. "Irish, what the hell?"

"It's a simple enough question. Do you still want me?"

"Shit. I mean, yes. Absolutely."

Crossing her arms, she considered the man before her. The long, lean length of him. The frown was nearly a constant feature. Yes, there was more going on than he'd admit. She'd bet her life on it. But should she gamble on him? It was a risk. A risk she'd have to take again sometime, if she ever wanted to win.

"Well, I'd say we have something to work with. You'll talk more when you're ready."

He looked stunned. His mouth hung open and he ruffled his hand through his hair.

She finished the last morsel of her dinner, chewing and swallowing, savouring the flavours. Lifting the menu from the table, she scanned the tempting Dolce list. She'd order dessert. Sometimes you had to live a little, give in to temptation. Even if it wasn't strictly good for you.

She looked up, catching his wide eyed stare. His gaze dropped to her mouth. Temptation was the order of the evening.

Walking Sinead towards her front door, awkwardness overpowered him. Gabriel wasn't sure where to look, what to do with his hands, his feet, anything.

He'd wanted to open up to her. He'd tried to. He hadn't been able to talk to anyone except Ryan for nearly ten years. Since his Mum became too distant to really listen to him. But at dinner, he'd backpedalled as fast as he could. Gunning his own engine into reverse.

The puffy white mist of his breath on the cool night air disappeared into the dark. He nearly crashed into Sinead, who'd stopped abruptly on her front doorstep. The lightbulb overhead glowed with dim yellow light and flickered.

"So, we're here." Sinead's words were strung out slowly.

She stood in front of him, her pale skin glowing softly like the moon. So beautiful.

"I had a great night. Thanks for giving me another chance. For listening."

"I had a great night too. Thanks for letting me in. Even if it was only a teensy bit."

Her lips parted, as if she was considering what to say. He understood. Something had changed between them and he needed to tread carefully.

She pushed her hair back from her shoulders and tilted her chin. "I have to get back to work tomorrow. I'm flying the Melbourne route again via Dubai and Sydney. But I'll be back in London in a couple of days."

Gabriel stuffed his hands in his jeans pockets to stop himself from wrapping her up in his arms. He wanted to hold onto her so she wouldn't disappear again. He hadn't realised she would be leaving so soon. But this is what it would be like all the time. He'd be constantly missing her.

"Okay, I have to work anyway. It's ironic, you're leaving me here in London to go to my hometown without me. I wish I could go with you."

He held her silvery gaze, lit by mischief and laughter. What was she thinking?

She licked her lower lip. "What would you do if I kissed you right now?"

Speechless. He had nothing. He ran over the past few minutes in his mind, trying to catch up on where her head was at. A small smile played across her gorgeous lips.

"But the rules, you said . . . I'd shut the hell up and let you kiss me."

He froze, intent on her every move.

Sinead stepped forward, one, two tiny footsteps, almost on the edge of her doorstep. She reached up and wrapped her freezing cold fingertips around the back of his neck, then tousled his hair at the nape. Shivering from the cold and her touch, he closed his eyes. He needed a moment. God, he wanted her. More than ever. The anticipation was killing him.

The gentle press of her lips on his mouth sent his eyelids flying open. He sneaked a look at her up close, lashes fluttering closed, strands of sugar-silk hair drifting around her shoulders.

Then her scent hit him. Her taste, like wine and sweet summer flowers. It took him straight back to their private little world in the hotel in Singapore, when they'd been so wrapped up in each other, nothing else had mattered. For a while. He wanted it again.

Reaching out, he let his hands skim over the curve of each of her hips, then pressed his fingertips into the warm flesh through the flimsy material of her dress. So much for the rules.

The groan which rose up into his throat was embarrassing. Except she captured it with her kiss. Her mouth. Deeper, pulling him into her heat. He answered her request, stroking into her mouth with his tongue, tasting her, remembering her.

Too soon, she pulled back, resting her forehead against his. His breathing was too fast, his skin stretched to breaking point. At least, she seemed to be affected by him the same way. They were in this thing together, one hundred per cent.

"Jaysus, you know how to kiss. I wanted us to slow down, but when you kiss me, it's perfect." Sinead stroked her fingers across his cheek, down to his sharp-edged jaw.

"You're perfect." He knew she wanted him too. That was enough. For tonight. "You'd better get some sleep before your flight tomorrow. I'll say goodnight, Irish."

"Goodnight, Gabriel." Her voice quavered. A touch of regret? He couldn't say.

He could feel her eyes on him, a tangible touch, as he walked down the narrow path to his car. Only a couple of days, then she'd be back.

He could wait, no worries.

Chapter Ten

He was heading out of the office at 6 p.m. the next day when it struck.

Throb, throb, throb.

The pain was near blinding, the head-spin so sudden, his knees collapsed under him.

Gabriel sank to the office floor and rolled over to lie flat on his back on the carpet. Horizontal was an improvement.

The voice he heard hovering over him a few minutes later wasn't one he recognised. But he was already out of it. Liquid shapes swam in his peripheral vision.

"Gabriel! Should I call an ambulance? Oh God, is it your heart?" A dark-haired woman. She sounded panicked. Who-ever she was. He couldn't focus on her face, his vision was too blurred.

He rasped out some words. "No, migraine. Get Ryan." His voice sounded choked to his own ears.

The next thing he knew, his head was lifted off the floor and a pillow was placed under his neck. Much better. Then there was something cool on his forehead, easing the pain behind his eyes.

"Gabe, are you all right? What else can we do?" It was Ryan, crouched beside him. His best friend's face blurred as if he was in a car looking through a rain-smeared windshield.

"Take me home? I mean, back to the hotel."

"Of course, mate. Let's get you down to the car."

So hot. Sweating buckets, and his mouth was dry. Tongue like sandpaper. A darkened room, smooth cotton sheets wrapped around him. The hotel. London.

How long had he been down for the count this time? He shifted and glanced down his body. He still wore his business shirt and trousers under the covers. For the life of him, he couldn't remember how he got into bed.

Somewhere down the road or somewhere closer, his phone buzzed with a brain-shaking echo. A woman answered it, thankfully. No need to move.

"Hello, Gabriel's phone . . . Sorry, he's sleeping at the moment. Can I take a message?" She yawned. "No? Okay then. Goodbye."

Someone walked over and touched his forehead, put something cold there. Better. Someone was looking after him for a change. He wished it was his mum. He missed her.

If Sinead was here, she'd look after him. He missed her too.

He remembered something. He had to call Sinead, as soon as he could function again. He needed to hear her voice.

Melbourne, Australia

Sinead finally kicked back on the bed in the swanky Southbank hotel. It was good to stop moving. She swivelled her ankles, one by one, then stretched her calf muscles. The long-haul flight to Melbourne with two stopovers was a killer. She couldn't even remember what time zone she was in.

Luckily, she'd pre-programmed the Melbourne and London times into her phone. Her hand shot out sideways and banged around on the bedside table, searching aimlessly for the phone. She really should open her eyes. She flicked the lamp on and checked the time.

Late morning in Melbourne, but it was close to two in the morning in London, a day behind. Somehow, going to Australia meant travelling to the future. So confusing to a travel-lagged mind. Not to mention spooky.

She'd tried calling Gabriel when she'd had lunch in Dubai but there was no answer. He might have been in a meeting. Now he'd be in his hotel room. It was probably too late to call, but she couldn't resist. She dialled his mobile number, biting her thumbnail.

She couldn't wait to talk to him and hear the low rumble of his voice which reminded her of decadent chocolate syrup. Delicious and rich, probably bad for her, but so indulgent and downright yummy.

The phone clicked in her ear. "Gabriel? Hi." She waited, but there was empty space on the other end.

"Hello, Gabriel's phone." A smoky, sensual and definitely feminine voice hit her ears.

What the hell?

She rallied her brain and voice to reply. "Er, can I speak to him please?" It must have been his PA, secretary, whatever. She hoped.

"Sorry, he's sleeping at the moment. Can I take a message?" The woman yawned. She sounded tired, half-asleep herself.

No! Don't be in his room. Don't be in his bed.

Sinead tried not to jump to conclusions, but what else could she think? It was late, London time. He had to be in his hotel room, in bed with another woman.

Gabriel couldn't wait for a few fecking days, he had to go ahead and bang some random slapper.

What if it wasn't so random?

It could've been the sleazy woman from the club. Kitty. She'd been all over him like a cat in heat. Gabriel had shrugged her off then, but maybe not forever. Probably only while Sinead was around.

She cleared her throat and held the phone in a death grip. "No message." She couldn't muster a response when Phone Woman said goodbye.

Sinead squeezed her eyes shut, blocking out the images overwhelming her. Of course they were there anyway, inside her head. Gabriel leaning into Kitty's kiss, wrapping his arms around her. The two of them naked, thrashing around in his bed, in the throes of a mind-blowing orgasm. They'd probably be perfect together, the pair of them. Rich and beautiful, and so far out of her league. They were probably laughing at her right now. Or maybe not. Too busy basking in afterglow, robbed of speech, too tired to move. She knew what it was like.

Gabriel was amazing in bed – he'd obviously had plenty of practice. He'd said he didn't want anyone else, but would he really push another woman away? Why reject someone who was there with him, when Sinead was on the other side of the world? Especially when she'd been denying him the slightest touch, like a fool. He'd been the one to stray, but she'd pushed him away, even when he'd started opening up to her. Sinead had denied what they both wanted. She may have missed her chance with him.

She couldn't think about it anymore. Exhausted to the centre of her being, body and soul, she fell onto the bed fully dressed. Her spine ached, her legs were puffy, and her skin was dry as the desert in Dubai. Other secret places heated and throbbed and practically chanted Gabriel's name.

Stupid body.

Then there was the way her chest ached and her eyes itched. It could have been allergies, sure. Except it wasn't spring in either hemisphere.

Stupid feelings.

She didn't have it in her to do anything or go anywhere in Melbourne. Not in his city.

Stupid Melbourne.

All she wanted to do was sleep for about a thousand years. Then her phone beeped. She glanced at the screen and froze.

It wasn't Gabriel. No, it was much worse.

I'm coming for you. WHORE.

She threw her phone across the bed like it had scorched her. The tears came then, great wracking, flooding rivers carving a cavern through her heart.

London, UK

Three days later, back in her poky flat, Sinead camped out on her saggy sofa in her sitting room watching old movies. Anything with Brad Pitt from the nineties was the sure-fire cure for her man woes. Only it wasn't working.

It was a cold morning. She'd meant to sleep longer, but the time zones had her muddled. The miserable rain belting against her windows suited her mood. Grey, cold, relentless wetness. Floods of tears, they wouldn't stop falling. Only fictional heroes were going to make her feel better. And her favourite owl-print pyjamas.

She hadn't heard from Gabriel since she'd been home. Not one phone call or text message. It was lonely, flying back to London to find nobody would have missed her if she hadn't come home at all. After that kiss on her doorstep, she'd expected so much more. A one-man welcoming party.

Yuki had been otherwise occupied going to a twenty-first birthday party for a family friend. Deanna and her other work friends were off at some nightclub last night. She couldn't face it, dancing, pretending to be happy.

Dropping into her black mood, she snuggled under her fluffy mohair throw rug and prepared to ogle Brad. The shrill ring of her front doorbell shocked her out of her stupor. Then the excitement gurgled up, beyond her control. She sat up straight as a street lamp.

It had to be Gabriel. She wasn't expecting anyone and he was the only one she was pining to see, like a lovesick puppy missing her owner. She shook her head. Horrible analogy. She missed him, nothing more. Of course she was still angry at him too. But that wasn't why she was trembling.

She glanced down and shrieked. Clearly, she couldn't answer the door in such a state. Like she'd been mouldering unwashed and unwanted under her blankie – which she had. Pausing the *Legends of the Fall*, she took stock of herself in the reflection on the TV screen.

Dashing into her bedroom, she brushed out her knotty hair and slipped on her jeans, tossing aside the owl PJs. The long grey T-shirt was passable. A quick spritz of Evian water across her face might tone down her red and puffy eyes. She hoped. Then she was down the stairs in her pink stripy bed socks, before you could say big-hunk-of-real-life-handsome-blonde-hero. Except when she looked through the spy hole in her front door, he failed to appear.

In his place was a small, red-haired and slightly bedraggled woman who bounced impatiently on the front step, dancing to some music known only to herself. Bridie. Her little sister was the only one of her family she was still close to, after her own falling out with Ma five years ago. But Sinead still hadn't expected to find Bridie outside her front door.

Bridie had a way about her which endeared her to everyone. Always optimistic, funny and bright. Sinead could do with a dose of her sister's contagious perkiness, so she opened the door wide.

Bridie's green eyes twinkled. "Sinead! How are you my lovely? I've missed you."

Sinead pulled her sister into a quick hug. "Oh, Bridie, me too."

Reaching to smooth Bridie's dripping wet pigtails behind her shoulders, Sinead pulled her into the hall. "What are you doing here?"

"I had a fight with Ma and I had to get away. I got in the car and drove. Sure enough I ended up at the ferry terminal, so I came across to see you. Eight hours' drive later, here I am."

So like Bridie to drive from Dublin to London without a plan. Sinead nodded and hustled her sister up the stairs. They stopped inside Sinead's doorway and Bridie peeled off her sopping coat, hanging it on a hook on the back of the flat's front door. Shutting the door behind them, she pushed Bridie towards the sofa.

"Sit down, you must be shagged. Driving all night. You'll be half crazed. Do you need a coffee?"

Bridie settled herself on the far end of the sofa, near the sitting room windows. "Aye, that would be gold. I'm so tired now, my eye's twitching."

Sinead glanced across at Bridie, who squinted one eye and glared so her eyelid twitched. She looked remarkably like a fierce red-headed pirate.

Giggling, Sinead made her way into her micro-sized kitchen and flipped the kettle on. "What was the fight with Ma about this time?"

Sinead busied herself with arranging her blue Moroccan coffee mugs and sugar bowl on the countertop, waiting for Bridie's answer, and for the kettle to boil. Bridie and Ma had been getting into it lately, but Sinead didn't know the details. She suspected things were worse than usual.

Bridie shrugged and ran her fingers through her matted hair. "You know she didn't like my man Liam at all. Ma banned him from the house and then she tried to 'ground' me. I'm twenty-three years old, for feck's sake. Then she invited some sad baldy widower from church to 'woo' me. I politely declined, then I took off."

Sinead shook her head and laughed. Having been on the receiving end of her Ma's matchmaking attempts, she knew how badly they could end. "I'm sorry, that's awful. You should have told me you were coming and I could have got you a stand-by ticket to fly over."

"I needed time to think. It's not working out with Liam, even without Ma sticking her beak in. Can I stay here for a bit?"

Sinead poured hot water over some instant coffee bags and inhaled the revitalising aroma. Not as good as real espresso, but it was all she had. She glanced up at Bridie, with her hair braided. She looked about fifteen.

"Sure, you can stay. You'll be on the sofa, you know I only have the one bedroom. When I fly out again in a couple of days you can take my bed. You really need to move out of home. Get your own place."

"I know, but it's taking a while to dig myself out from under, and I can't get a decent job in Dublin to save myself."

Sinead sighed and something knotted in her belly. Her sister's situation was bad. But Bridie had to sort herself out and nobody else could do it for her. Indulged and coddled by Ma as the baby of the family, Bridie had been allowed to hang around home after dropping out of design college. After spending all her money on clothes and going out clubbing, she'd racked up a huge debt on her credit cards. Then there was a student loan she still had to repay.

Coffees aromas wafted through the room as Sinead brought the steaming cups across to the sofa. Placing the drinks on the second-hand teak coffee table, she rubbed her hands up and down her arms, feeling the cold.

Bridie looked at Sinead closely, narrowing her sparkly eyes. "You don't look so good yourself. Is it the jet-lag?"

"No, you're not the only one with man trouble. I met someone. Gabriel. He's beautiful and there's something special about him. I like him. But I'm not sure he feels the same way." She chewed her thumbnail until she realised she was eating red varnish. "He might've cheated on me."

"Slow down there. I didn't even know you had a boyfriend." Bridie sipped her coffee, emerald eyes peering at Sinead over the rim of the mug.

"It's all new. I only met him a week ago, but it's been intense."

Bridie tilted her head to one side, tapping her fingertip on her coffee cup. "So, you don't know him very well. Why do you think he cheated?"

Sinead told Bridie about Gabriel, the gloriously handsome businessman, how they'd been thrown together in Singapore, their hot weekend there. The perfect evening Gabriel had planned for her in London. Words stuck thickly in her throat as she explained about calling Gabriel and the conversation with another woman in the middle of the night. When she told her sister how Gabriel hadn't contacted her, even since she'd been home, she had to stop and drain her coffee. It had her doubting he cared at all.

Bridie stared, homing in on the cracks in Sinead's story. "But you don't know what really happened. Could he be working long hours? Could it be a woman who works for him? An old friend?"

"I don't think he has any old friends in London, but he could've been working late. He did say he's setting up a new office and working around the clock." She'd considered those reasons, but hearing Bridie mention them made them sound more reasonable. "Do you think I've been an idiot?"

"Not an idiot, but you could have judged too soon. Why don't you call him, or better still, go see him?"

Sinead nodded, pushing up from the sofa and putting down her cup with a clunk. "You're right. I'll have a shower and head out. You should get some sleep while I'm gone. We can catch up later."

Sinead ruffled Bridie's still-damp hair and paced towards her bathroom. She wanted to believe Bridie. Perhaps she'd judged Gabriel unfairly. It was something she'd been known to do, given her horrible track record with men.

She ought to give him the benefit of the doubt, to try to make something of the attraction and the 'something more' between them. This kind of pull towards a man was entirely new to her. It had to be a good sign. She crossed her fingers by her sides.

Gabriel groaned as he walked into the gym, the echoes inside the tiled space of the hotel's swimming pool bouncing off his brain. It was Thursday morning, two days since the migraine hit. He had to get going and get into the office. And later on, he wanted to see Sinead.

Still not completely functioning, he'd forced himself to go downstairs and get some exercise. He'd missed it over the past few weeks, along with enough sleep and balanced meals. All the extra hours at work and the travelling had obviously been too much for him. Not something he wanted to admit to himself.

This migraine was the worst he'd had in a year, knocking him out for almost two full days. Luckily he'd had Ryan and Charlotte, a young project officer from the new London team, on hand to look after him.

They'd both stayed with Gabriel, camped out in the hotel suite's living area. He'd hardly even met Charlotte before. It was a nice gesture for her to stay, although unnecessary. Ryan had been there until the early hours.

His phone buzzed in his pocket. He palmed it and swiped the screen.

Speak of the devil.

He answered Ryan's call as he strolled into the locker room. His voice came out croaky as an old man's. "Morning."

"Geez, mate. You sound rough. Charlotte said you were doing okay."

"Charlotte said? Since when is she your go-to girl?"

"She is in the office. She's analysing the European market, looking for new opportunities. She's brilliant."

Gabriel dumped his gym bag on a low wooden bench. "You don't have to sell me on her virtues. Tell her thanks for staying with me."

"Tell her yourself. You'll see her in the office later."

"Okay. And I'll quiz her about you while I'm at it. I reckon she's into you."

"No, really? Huh. She's too young for me. Now she's working for me." Ryan breathed out, a huff of air echoing down the line.

Gabriel recognised the pique of interest in Ryan's voice. And he'd overheard Charlotte talking to Ryan as he was leaving for the office that morning. There was banter going on between them. It was clear Charlotte liked Ryan and was keen to hang out with him.

Ryan might have been making excuses, but Gabriel could see Charlotte was exactly his type. Slim, brunette, sharp as a tack, but with a kind of innocence. She could be what Ry needed in London, living away from his close-knit circle of family and friends. The circle Gabriel had always envied. Ryan hadn't had a serious girlfriend in years, but he needed someone, in a way Gabriel himself never had. Until now.

Sitting on the edge of the changing room bench, he offered his two cents. "If you're interested, talk to her. See how she feels."

Ryan laughed in his ear. "Since when are you giving dating advice? Oh, and Gabe? Do me a favour and book a doctor's appointment as soon as you get home to Melbourne. Get your head checked out before you blow a gasket."

Gabriel rubbed his forehead in small circles. "Yeah, sure."

He ended the call, not sure whether to be worried at the fact Ryan was worried. Did that even make sense? His head still ached, a dull buzz like an electric drill had taken up residence in the background.

Ry's dig about dating advice stuck in his mind. Until Sinead had fallen into his lap, Gabriel hadn't cared if there was a woman in his life. But in the last week, things had shifted in his mind – his priorities, what he should spend his time on. Resolving to change his lifestyle and slow down was one thing, but so far he'd never managed to stick to it. And making connections with people – that was a whole different kettle of fish.

Gabriel's phone vibrated again, dancing in a circle on the bench beside him. He glanced at the screen, his face stretching out in a smile so wide he probably looked like a goofball.

A text message from Sinead. She wanted to see him, straight away. Warmth spread though his body, thawing something cold inside him.

He'd been itching to call her since he woke, but he could barely form words. He didn't want to mess up when he spoke to Sinead. He needed to be properly awake, in top form. He'd intended to wait and call her after his swim but she'd beaten him to it.

Keying a quick reply, he forced himself not to babble about how much he'd missed her. Instead, he suggested she meet him in the café next to the pool, gave her directions to his hotel and asked her to text again when she arrived. He'd have time for a quick swim before she got there.

Stripping off his T-shirt and loose sweatpants, down to his brief trunks, he bundled his gear into a locker. It had been years since he'd concentrated on swimming, but he used to love it. He used to be great at it. Time to give it another go. Grabbing a towel and striding into the pool area, he stopped near the top of the pool and selected a lane.

Gabriel stepped up onto a starting block and crouched in position, like it was second-nature, ready to dive. When he bent and sprang into the air then dove into the water in one smooth movement, his tension receded.

The blast of cool water against his skin instantly cleared his mind of anything but the need to keep afloat. To keep moving. He pushed himself through the water with strong overarm strokes, breathing in and out in steady rhythm.

Letting the power of physical sensation take control, like with Sinead.

The Tube ride to Gabriel's Soho hotel had been quicker than expected and it was a short walk from the underground station. She was bubbling with excitement, or was it nerves? Sinead couldn't wait to see Gabriel again. Although she wasn't sure what she'd do if she found he'd cheated on her. A sigh escaped her lips as she checked her phone. She'd texted when she was down on the street but he hadn't responded yet.

She popped out of the hotel elevator and tried to get her bearings. The glitzy marble and mirrored hallway sent reflections bouncing every which way, playing havoc with her sense of direction. Never mind, she should be able to find the café near the gym in the public area of the hotel.

Still shivering from the biting wind outside, she wrapped her short coat around her and scanned her surroundings. Checking the signs in the hallway, she headed towards large entrance doors set into a wall of glass.

Entering the café, she looked for Gabriel but he was nowhere to be seen. The only people were a table of older women enjoying cups of tea.

Wandering to the opposite glass wall overlooking the swimming pool on the floor below, she spied a lone male swimmer, slicing through the water like a shark. He was long and lean with tanned skin and broad shoulders. There was something about the way the swimmer moved with such effortless grace, absolutely in the zone. It was too hard to see any more details from a distance, but she had an inkling it was Gabriel.

Heading out of the café and down a short flight of stairs nearby, she soon reached the entrance to the swimming pool and slowed her pace on the wet tiles. She took a seat on a concrete bench against the far wall between two Roman style columns. It was definitely Gabriel, she'd know that profile anywhere. And those shoulders. She watched him, captivated, as he swam lap after lap.

After a few minutes, he slowed and neared the end of the pool near where she sat. Gabriel reached out for the edge of the pool and gripped it, coming to a stop and breathing hard. He braced himself on the tiles and lifted himself from the water, muscles tensing and releasing. He hadn't noticed her yet.

Rising up, water falling in his wake like a trail of shimmering crystals, Gabriel pulled himself to stand on the edge of the pool. Sinead could only stare and hold her breath.

He was magnificent – a god from an ancient world, a golden man of myth exuding power and strength. From his muscular thighs she'd like to bite, to the narrow waist, hard, rippled muscles of his abdomen and his broad chest with a smattering of dark blonde hair, he was perfection. Perfection glittering with moisture.

He reached up and ran his hands through his wet hair, slicking it back from his face, droplets tumbling. Putting on a further show as he flexed his biceps.

She swallowed, hard, trying to stop her gaze drifting lower, to the tiny Lycra swimming trunks that left absolutely nothing to the imagination. She couldn't stop herself. Everything was outlined and defined. No shrinkage problem with the indoor pool being so warm.

Sweet Mary, mother of Jesus. What a man.

For the life of her, in her hot and bothered state, she couldn't remember why she'd invented the rules. All she wanted to do was climb him like a tree.

He glanced in her direction and did a double-take, his eyes widening and a lazy smile spreading over his face. Her own expression was probably stunned-looking, when he strode towards her.

"Hello, Irish. You found me."

She nodded, raising an eyebrow. "Hello, yourself. Budgie smugglers? Really?" She'd picked up some Aussie slang on her travels.

Gabriel laughed at the comment on his swimming trunks.

She bit her lip and squeezed her legs together, ignoring the pulse between her thighs. And she took off her coat.

She'd barely regained her breath when Gabriel shook the excess water from his body and walked a few paces to a folding chair with a towel hanging on it. He'd begun towelling himself dry when he twisted from the waist and met her eye. *Pat, pat, dab, dab.* The towel was getting a workout drying all that bare, wet skin. She followed its path with her eyes.

Abs and pecs and biceps, oh my.

The way his clear blue eyes sparkled and the cheeky look he shot her, made it clear he read her dirty mind. She didn't care.

She breathed a deep sigh of satisfaction as he sat next to her, close enough for her to notice tiny droplets of water still shimmering on the blonde hairs on his forearms. Also the toasty-coloured hair on his chest. She couldn't think of another thing to say. His nearness was stealing her breath.

He dipped his head and whispered low. "I missed you, while you were flying. Glad you're back."

Sinead's insides flipped over at his words, but then she remembered she was supposed to confront him. Somewhere along the line, since her chat with Bridie and seeing him again, she'd lost her certainty he'd cheated on her. It didn't feel like the truth. His missing her and wanting to be with her – that seemed true. She wanted it to be true. She believed in honesty and needed his side of the story.

"I tried to call you the other night, but a woman answered your phone." She left it there, wanting his explanation, unprompted by any jealousy or anger.

"Ugh, sorry. I've been down for the count for two days with the worst migraine. I wanted to call you, but it took a while to get moving again. Today's the first day I've been back on my feet."

She nodded. His migraines were severe. But he hadn't responded to her pointed enquiry. "And the woman was?"

"Oh, Charlotte. Someone from the London office, a project officer. She was with Ryan and they helped me back here to the hotel. Ryan's my best mate, head of the London office. I'll have to introduce you."

She breathed out the stale air in her lungs. "So she wasn't some woman you picked up? I assumed . . ." She shook her head and looked down at her hands in her lap. At the chipped nail varnish on her chewed thumbnail.

"Sinead, no. She was being helpful, making sure I was okay. I didn't even know who she was, I was so out of it. Anyway, I think she was trying to impress Ry."

Her breath rushed out all at once. She hadn't known she'd been holding it.

Gabriel touched her arm, just for a second. "Hey, I told you I didn't want anyone else. I meant it."

Her eyelids fluttered closed. "I'm sorry. I have a few issues trusting men. I've been let down in the past."

She sensed him nod beside her. Then he reached out and touched her cheek, brushed it with the back of his hand. She trembled when he ran his thumb across her cheekbone, then brushed her hair back behind her ear. He stroked his fingers through her hair, over and over.

She didn't care about the no-touching rule now. Her breaths came short and shallow. Panting, really.

He'd moved closer. His swimming pool blue eyes were right in front of her.

"Is it okay if I kiss you now?" he asked in a low, ragged tone.

"Yes." Her voice was barely there, little more than a squeak.

Her eyes fluttered closed when he bridged the distance between them, bringing his lips down upon hers, gentle as a drop of rain falling on her from the sky. His kiss was soft but deliberate. He left it to her to set the pace, to let him know what she wanted. If only she could decide what it was.

Trying not to overthink it, she let her body take the lead and deepened the kiss. Like every time they kissed, a wave of desire washed over her and she was swept up in its wake. She groaned into his mouth as he fisted her hair and slid his tongue against hers.

When her hand crept to Gabriel's bare knee, skirting the hem of his towel, the pleasantly rough texture of his body hair under her fingertips and the hitch of his breath awoke her to the reality of her surroundings.

She pulled away from him. They were sitting in a public area, right next to a swimming pool where a bunch of grey-haired ladies were splashing about, ready for a water aerobics class. The ladies from the café. She hadn't even noticed them come in. Not the ideal place for an intimate moment. She was snagged in Gabriel's gaze and his eyes were intent on her face, drawing her in.

"We could go up to my suite, but I do have to get to work soon."

"No. I know I keep bending the rules, but I'm not ready to break them yet, alright?" Lord, she could have kicked herself. She had to keep on making things difficult. But even with the heat between them, she had to be sure of her own feelings this time. Before she jumped in at the deep end.

Gabriel continued to stare into her eyes. "All right, for now. But I want to see you tonight and kiss you again. In private."

Sinead couldn't focus completely on his words, while he stroked his fingertips up and down her spine. Even through her shirt, it was like he strummed a guitar, plucking her strings and making beautiful music with her nerve endings.

The words simply poured out of her. "Oh Lord, yes."

Sinead frowned in confusion at Gabriel's deep chuckle.

"I like it when you call me Lord."

She snorted at the cheek of his comment and smacked him on the knee. "Yes, my Lord. But I draw the line at curtseying to you."

"I would never expect you to, my Irish Princess."

Chapter Eleven

"We can make it work. We're a team, and I've got your back." Ryan relaxed on the black leather sofa, crossing one ankle over his knee.

Kicking back in the bright red, high-backed swivel chair in Ryan's office, Gabriel welcomed the relief surging through him. Ryan was right. They could make it work. Gabriel didn't have to be the only one in charge, the only one calling the shots. He had Ryan, plus a whole team to call on.

After his swim and a coffee with Sinead following their extremely hot, tension-filled kiss that morning, he'd experienced a clarity he couldn't remember feeling for years.

He no longer wanted to be CEO, and surprisingly it didn't scare him to acknowledge it.

Even a few weeks ago, he couldn't have made the decision without a gaping hole opening up inside himself. He'd asked himself the question many times: if he didn't have his job, what else did he have?

Until recently, the answer would have been terrifying. Now, with Sinead on the scene, he was starting to imagine a different path. Of course it was still early days and their relationship was up in the air, but if he could visualise a future with her, he could work towards it. If he could get his personal shit together.

He'd been dreading this meeting since this morning, worried Ryan would feel let down. The London office was brand new and Ryan hadn't been the man in the big chair for long, and he'd never had the ultimate responsibility to the Board, or the staff and shareholders. That was about to change, but Ryan had proved he was up for the challenge. Anyway, Gabriel wouldn't disappear completely.

Ryan's thick eyebrows knitted together. "So what's the plan? Let's think about your role. What are the parts of the job you enjoy? What do you want to focus on?"

The questions cut to the heart of the matter. Gabriel was glad they understood each other.

"I've always wanted to spend more time on special projects, new technology, what's going to set us apart from the market in a few years' time. The day-to-day problems and managing the financial side of the company, it's more of a headache than a challenge. The last thing I need is more headaches."

Ryan nodded and stood. He paced the length of his office. He liked to walk and talk, saying it helped him think. Gabriel swivelled his chair and gazed out the window at the London skyline and the River Thames below. Threatening grey clouds dominated the sky, but a hint of blue and gold peaked through. The view was an incredible reminder of exactly how far he was from home, but also how much he'd achieved.

"I agree. I had no idea your migraines had become so bad. You should have told me," Ryan said with a sigh.

Gabriel's guilt rose up from his gut and crawled into his throat, a tangible thing, a rope threatening to choke him.

Ryan stopped pacing and stared down at him. "It's okay, I get it. It's hard to admit you need help sometimes. We'll work it out between us. You need to change your lifestyle and look after yourself. Go see your doctor, get those tests." His friend pinned him with a stare saying he wouldn't take no for an answer. "And

I think Director of Innovation and Special Projects sounds like a winner."

Gabriel nodded, ignoring the way his throat constricted at the mention of doctors and tests. "Great title. I can work on a job spec and a project proposal. Then I'll chat to the PR guy and work on the information for the Board."

"And what's the situation with your mum? What did her carers tell you earlier?"

Gabriel rubbed the heels of his hands over his eyes and breathed deeply before he could answer. He hadn't mentioned the call. But Ryan knew Gabriel checked in every day with his mother's carers. It didn't matter, didn't change the facts. He'd spoken to the care facility after his catch-up with Sinead. It had made the conversation easier, somehow, knowing he had something to look forward to.

Gabriel looked out the window again as he spoke. "She's been sick with another infection but it's not an emergency. The head nurse said the antibiotics kicked in and she's eating again. But she recommends permanent care. I think I'll stay here for the launch party and then head home."

Home. His mother's house was the only real home he'd ever known. Since she'd become ill and gradually faded away, losing her memories and eventually forgetting her own son, the little cottage had lost the feeling of belonging and safety. His apartment had never been anything more than an investment and a place to crash. It was still as cold and soulless as the display apartment it once was.

"I'm sorry mate, that's rough. I'm happy to help however I can, with work or whatever you need. I could come back with you for a few days."

"Thanks, I appreciate it. But I think I'll ask Sinead to come with me. I'd like her to meet Mum, at least once."

"Phew, this is a whirlwind romance. It's serious?"

"Like I said, she's different. I'm attracted to her, but it's more than that. Attracted isn't even the word for it – I want her so much it's causing me actual pain. My head's not right when she's gone." He laughed at his own comment. His head was a problem these days. "She makes me laugh. I'm happy when I'm with her and stop worrying so much. I don't know, it sounds crazy."

Ryan smirked. "Not crazy, but you could be crazy in love."

It couldn't be true, of course not. Ryan was obviously trying to freak him out.

"Who are you, my best mate or a bootylicious pop star? Crazy in love? No way."

Ryan's laugh was more of a hoot. "Who are you trying to convince, me or yourself? By the way, when am I going to meet this woman?"

He crossed his arms. Challenge accepted. "How about tonight? If you wrangle yourself a date, we can all go for a drink."

Ryan rubbed his hands together. "You're on."

The cool night air rushed into the trendy Soho bar behind Sinead, but she snuggled into Gabriel's side, his arm around her waist as he guided her across the room. She was insulated by his warmth, and all melty-glowy like an ice cream cake covered in candles.

After treading only a few paces across the dark wooden floorboards, she heard a deep voice call Gabriel's name. She and Gabriel moved in one fluid motion in the same direction. Gabriel waved, took her hand, then steered her over to his friend's corner.

Sinead took the opportunity to assess the man and the woman seated on a velvet sofa next to a low table as she crossed the room. Gabriel's friend Ryan and his mystery date.

Ryan was tall and well-built, with dark and brooding good looks. He wore a fancy suit and a flashing white smile. He reminded her of a polo player, little as she knew about the game. Even from across the room he'd oozed self-confidence and charm.

The combination of Gabriel and Ryan together out on the prowl, intelligent and charming men in their prime, dripping with handsomeness would be a danger to the sanity of women everywhere. She was glad Gabriel was with her now. Although her own sanity was sometimes in question when she was close to him.

As they approached the couple, Sinead took in the pretty woman seated next to Ryan. Gabriel hadn't said anything about her. She was fairly young, early twenties, slim with dark brown curly hair and enormous chocolate-coloured eyes. Her lipstick was dark red, making her look a little older, along with her conservative grey dress and heels.

Ryan's date was nervous, judging by the way she sat, cross-legged, slightly apart from Ryan, tapping her fingertips against the glass of red wine she held in a tight grasp. Perhaps it was their first date?

"Hello, hello." Ryan all but shouted his greeting when they arrived at the sofa opposite where he sat. He gestured for them to come closer.

Gabriel drew Sinead inwards, close to his side. "Hi Ry. I'd like you to meet Sinead."

Sinead offered her hand and Ryan shook it firmly, but dropped it when Gabriel cleared his throat.

Ryan grinned, his eyes sparkling. "So pleased to meet you Sinead. You're the wonderful woman who has my friend all turned upside down and grinning like an idiot."

She laughed, taking an instant liking to Ryan. "Lovely to meet you too, Ryan. And I don't think Gabriel's an idiot for smiling. I love to see it."

Gabriel smiled then, his while face lighting up. She even saw a hint of dimple. Her belly flipped over in response.

Ryan motioned to his date then placed a hand on her shoulder. "I'd like you both to meet Charlotte. Although come to think of it, Gabriel's already met her."

"I have?" Gabriel tilted his head and frowned. "Charlotte, of course. Thanks so much for helping me the other night. I was so under the weather I can barely remember anything." He glanced at Sinead, lowering his voice. "Charlotte works with Ryan. She helped me when I had a migraine this week."

Sinead shouldn't have been jealous or distrustful of the other woman, but both emotions danced inside her for a moment. So this was the woman on the phone the other night. Charlotte offered Sinead a shy smile, and Sinead's opinion started to change. She didn't behave like any kind of seductress.

Sinead and Gabriel both shook Charlotte's hand, and settled into the cosy sofa.

"And she's seen Gabriel naked." Ryan raised an eyebrow, as Charlotte leaned close and swatted Ryan across the knee.

Charlotte shook her head. "I have not! Really, I haven't." Charlotte's face flamed bright red as she caught Sinead's eye.

Sinead's mouth had popped open. She closed it with an effort and bit her lip. Charlotte looked half stunned, half mortified. Sinead didn't think Charlotte had done anything untoward. Now she knew why Gabriel had warned Sinead not to take everything Ryan said to heart. He joked and poked fun, but he was a good friend to Gabriel.

"Someone tucked Gabe into bed the other night, and I know it wasn't me." Ryan beamed, dark eyes shining with amusement.

Sinead's chest felt tight. She looked down at where Gabriel's hand touched hers, resting on the sofa. It was comforting.

Gabriel frowned, rubbing Sinead's hand. "Fully clothed, Ry, steady on."

Twisting a curl of hair round her finger, Charlotte looked up at Ryan. "Yes, be nice. We don't want to make Sinead feel uncomfortable."

Charlotte looked uncomfortable herself, the way her eyebrows pinched together. Sinead watched as Charlotte stood, smoothing down her dress. "I'll go and order some more drinks."

Poor Charlotte, she looked as if she wanted to escape.

After asking for Sinead and Gabriel's drink orders, Charlotte wandered off towards the long, Art Deco style copper-panelled bar.

"What's the story with you and Charlotte?" Gabriel questioned Ryan as soon as Charlotte was out of earshot.

Ryan shrugged and leaned back. "She's a sweet girl, very attractive but you know, I'm her manager. I hired her actually. She's . . . smart. Surprisingly smart." A dreamy look passed over Ryan's face.

Sinead leaned forward, wanting the full story. "Where did you meet her?"

Ryan's expression brightened. "At a London Business School presentation, I was a sort of mentor. She was working for a big bank and oversaw development of an app for their credit card marketing division. It looks incredible. It was part of her masters of business administration. I reckon she'll be a real asset in analysing the marketing opportunities for the European expansion. We're already drafting plans based on her research. She's kind of brilliant."

Sinead's ears pricked up at the mention of Charlotte's studies. She'd long wanted to study, but she hadn't managed it yet. And Ryan sounded besotted with Charlotte. She didn't know if he realised it himself.

Gabriel leaned forward too. "Interesting. You're dating then?"

Ryan shrugged. "Having a bit of fun, I guess. Trying to meet some new friends in London, getting out and about. But I'm not exactly looking for my soul mate." Ryan paused, sadness or some other emotion making his mouth droop, and his eyes turn glassy.

Sinead tipped her head to the side and studied Ryan's face. His strong jaw and the harsh line of his dark eyebrows were half in shadow. He turned and caught Sinead's eyes.

Then a cheeky smile slid across his face. "Don't worry, Sinead, I won't lead Gabriel astray. He informs me his man-whore days are behind him."

Sinead snorted. Ryan was funny, but there was sadness there too. She guessed he used humour to cover up for more difficult emotions. Something she understood.

Gabriel groaned and put his head in his hands.

She crossed her legs and looked from Ryan to Gabriel. "Boys, behave yourselves now. Gabriel may have a whorish past, but I suspect it was his best friend who led him down the garden path. You might be the devil in disguise." Sinead winked at Ryan, who let out a chuckle.

"You were right, Gabe, she's funny. Gorgeous too. You should hold onto her."

"I intend to."

Sinead snuck a glance at Gabriel, who was already watching her with a broad grin on his face, and eyes full of heat. This night was important to him. She had the impression Ryan was like a brother to Gabriel and his opinion held a lot of sway.

Sinead swung around to face Ryan before Gabriel made her internal thermometer go haywire. "So Ryan, tell me about your job here in London."

"I'm heading up the European arm of Global Village, setting up new business relationships, especially with London society and business high-rollers. I'll be looking at partnerships with the airlines and hotel chains. But I guess I've got a bigger job ahead of me than I realised, since Gabriel's stepping aside as CEO. He'll have some more time on his hands, so you must be happy."

She cocked her head at Gabriel. "You're stepping aside as CEO?"

Why he hadn't told her about such a significant decision? Didn't he feel enough for her to confide in her?

"Yeah. I've been thinking about it for a while but I only made it formal today. I need to make some lifestyle changes, slow down and spend more time in Melbourne. Especially since Mum isn't doing so well."

"I see. I'm sorry to hear about your mum." Sinead almost whispered her last comment, and Gabriel brushed her hair back behind her ear. She shivered, rubbing her hands down her thighs.

Charlotte returned and placed their drinks on the table, smiling at each of them. White wine for Sinead, a pint of lager for Gabriel, another red wine for Charlotte. Ryan's Scotch sat untouched on the table but he grinned at Charlotte and patted the seat beside him. Charlotte sat close to him, but seemed unsure what to do with herself.

Sinead sipped her wine, tuning out of the conversation for a while. She went over Gabriel's comments in her mind. He wouldn't be CEO anymore, but he needed to stay close to his mother in Melbourne. He had to be worried about her and it was difficult for him to talk about it. But where did that leave the two of them? A long distance relationship at best. At worst? She could be waiting for him for a long time.

Gabriel's fingers threaded through hers, his thumb stroking in circles on the back of her wrist. He held onto her firmly, rarely letting go, seeming to need the physical connection. Her mind wandered to his swim, and their scalding kiss by the side of the pool. The promise of more kisses to come.

When the conversation filtered into her mind again, Charlotte was explaining her work situation. Sinead was being incredibly rude by zoning out. She tried hard to focus.

"I was astonished when I was accepted into the MBA program. Then I had to work out how to pay for it. I was so excited when this job came up with Global Village. I always wanted to work in the travel industry. I'd love to extend my horizons and see more of the world. Of course, I want to do so many things in my career, sometimes it's hard to choose which path to follow." Charlotte paused and concentrated her attention on Ryan as she spoke.

"It's like the Butterfly Effect. One tiny event or decision can change the course of your whole life. Meeting someone who influences you, taking a new job." Charlotte's story came to a conclusion when she frowned, then took another gulp of her red wine.

Charlotte's words struck a chord with Sinead, although probably not the way the other woman had intended.

She shifted forward, talking to Charlotte. "I know what you mean. When I met Gabriel, it was completely out of the blue. Then we were thrown together again, like there was something more at work than mere chance." She offered Charlotte a smile, but the other woman bit her lip and stared into her wine.

"Anyway, I admire you for studying and working at the same time. I've been thinking of doing something else. I'm a flight attendant and I love travelling to different cities, the glamorous side I suppose, but it can be draining. I've always wanted to go to university, but I don't know if I'm smart enough. I'd like to study business or marketing." Sinead surprised herself by voicing the idea aloud.

She'd never dared tell anyone she wanted to go to university. In her family, there was no encouragement to choose anything besides a low-paying job and having a couple of kids by the age of twenty-one. There was no need for a woman to pursue a career or use her brain. Of course her family had no money anyway, so Sinead had wrapped up the dream of an education and placed it neatly on a shelf until she'd earned enough to make it a possibility.

Gabriel leaned towards her. His hand was hot and huge on her back, inching downwards. "You should do it, Sinead. I know you're smart enough, there's no doubt in my mind you'd make a formidable businesswoman. You already speak several languages and you're a natural negotiator. Great at organising people too."

Gabriel sounded so certain, she really wanted to believe him. "You really think so?"

"Absolutely."

Gabriel's lopsided smile popped out, the one she loved so much.

Not *loved*. Liked. She liked it.

It warmed something deep inside her and made her throat constrict at the same time. When he leaned in to her and placed a gentle kiss on her temple, her heart nearly exploded, right then and there. Nearly detonated like a grenade. Because she believed it. He actually saw something in her, beyond her looks or the heat always flaring between them.

If the signals from her heart were anything to go by, it might be time to push the boundaries of their arrangement. She'd never been one to follow all the rules, and some were begging to be bent, if not broken. She was feeling pretty bendy.

Strolling to his nearby hotel, the soft press of Sinead's hand in his, even the biting winter breeze couldn't steal the warmth inside him. Gabriel wasn't imagining the way she watched him at the bar, the heat in her eyes.

This thing between them was going great, even if the physical side was progressing slower than he'd like. It could be time to chat to her about her rules, see if she really wanted to stick to them.

There wasn't much talk as they walked but it was comfortable strolling beside Sinead. Their footsteps formed a beat as they sloshed through puddles on concrete against the background noise of cars whizzing past, splashing as they went. The sounds of the city went on around them as always, but he was keenly aware of his pulse, his heartbeat.

Sinead shivered, pulling her coat around her with one hand, giving him the perfect excuse to wrap his arm around her shoulders. He rubbed his hand up and down her arm and her back. Keeping her warm. Nothing more.

He was already overheating, picturing the clinging knit dress under her coat. Bright blue, showing off her curves. Along with his new favourite knee-high boots. She looked hot, even if the clothes didn't provide much protection from the elements. He'd been holding back all night, trying not to run his hands over the places emphasised by the dress. Trying not to tear it off.

That thought had him marching, urging her forward. Faster. "Not far to go. Let's pick up the pace so you don't freeze your sweet backside."

"Okay, but I can't run in these boots."

"I don't think they're meant for running. They're more for indoor games."

"You cheeky man. What makes you say so?"

"I've got a very good imagination and I've been thinking about it all night. You in those boots, minus the dress, your legs wrapped around me."

"Oh." He soaked up the breathy sound she made, like she was picturing it too and it left her gasping. Like she wanted it as bad as he did. Like the very idea of it got her motor running.

"Yes, *oh*. Here we are."

She'd agreed to come back to his hotel, but maybe she only wanted a drink. Now they were approaching the main doors, he wasn't sure if she'd come upstairs with him or not. It didn't seem right to assume. He pulled her towards him and grasped both of her hands.

"Come upstairs with me." He didn't mean it to sound like an order, so he took her hand gently and let his gaze drop to her mouth. "I want to kiss you again and I don't want an audience."

Sinead's grey eyes sparked with molten silver. Her lips parted, then stretched into a wide smile. "Yes, okay."

He could swear his heart stuttered with the impact of her words, matched with her expression. So beautiful, but so scary. How did she shake him up so bad? What could she do to him if they got serious?

Gabriel wasn't paying attention to his surroundings since he was too desperate to finally get her alone. They made it through the foyer to the lift, then the doors were closing and he was locked inside the confined space. Alone with Sinead. He hit the button for level thirty.

He stood awkwardly next to her for a second, his hands forming fists at his sides. Then he stopped thinking and pushed Sinead back against the mirrored wall. She gasped, then reached out and grasped his shoulder.

Raising their joined hands up on one side of her head, he leaned in and stole a quick kiss. He placed his other hand on her hip, gripping her there, loving the feel of her warm flesh yielding to his touch through her dress. He kissed her again, biting her full lower lip, something he'd been aching to do for days. She tasted like fresh cherries, sweet and sour. His body responded to it like an aphrodisiac.

He tasted her again, licking along her bottom lip until she opened her mouth to him, tilting her head to give him full access. She melted into him, her tongue finding his and her body pressing against him in all the right places. He deepened the kiss. With a shudder, she swayed into him. He thrust his tongue in her mouth in time with the movement of his hips. So delicious.

She ran her hands over the front of his shirt, then pushed him back. "Stop."

He stepped away, breaking the contact between them. Heart pounding out of control, hands shaking. Stunned she'd told him to stop, apparently out of the blue.

"This is your floor, isn't it?" Sinead looked up at him from beneath her eyelashes.

The lift had stopped and the doors were wide open. He hadn't even noticed.

Gabriel took her hand and kissed her knuckles, then met her eyes. "Sorry, I guess I got carried away."

She nodded, hiding her expression behind her loose hair as she ducked her head.

They walked a few doors down the hallway to his suite. Swiping his key card in the lock, he opened the door and let Sinead walk ahead of him. He supposed he seemed like a gentleman, but he really wanted to watch her walk, the sway of those hips. He wasn't sure if he'd get any closer to her tonight, so he'd make the most of the view. She only went a few paces before stopping to remove her coat. No complaints from him. There was the figure-hugging dress again.

She turned to him and touched his face, stroking along his jaw. Suddenly every nerve ending in his body was on high alert.

This time he couldn't stop his more primitive instincts taking over and he went to her, skimming both hands down her sides, following the indentation of her waist, the curve of her hips. Her shaky exhale of breath said he'd had an effect on her. A good one, he hoped. But he stopped there, grabbed her coat and ditched it along with his own in the closet. He didn't want to push her.

Sinead breathed out slowly, and he noted her flushed cheeks and bright eyes. He'd done that to her, got her all turned on. The most gorgeous woman he'd ever seen.

He watched as she scanned the large, luxury suite. Acres of beige carpet and eight foot ceilings adorned with dangly chandeliers, met polished black tables and supersized modern art canvases. There was a dining table to seat about ninety.

She glanced at him as her eyes popped open. "This room is only for you?"

"Yes. I know it's a bit much but they upgraded me. I like the extra space in case I need to hold meetings here."

He walked past her, ushering her into the living area. The long and sleek black leather couch looked cold and uninviting, but he'd been picturing laying Sinead down there since he checked in. He'd hoped he'd have the chance to bring her here. But now he wasn't sure what to do with himself, or her either. He didn't want to stuff things up.

He got rid of his jacket, chucking it over an armchair. He liked the way her eyes roved over him, and the way her lipstick was all smudged.

He gestured towards the sofa. "Sit. Would you like a drink? There's a fully stocked bar in the kitchen."

"Thanks, I could use a whiskey."

He was surprised she wanted the hard stuff, but he didn't comment and decided to join her. It might loosen them both up. He strolled across to the kitchen, making himself relax, locating a couple of crystal tumblers.

When he poured the drinks in the open-plan kitchenette, he looked over the black marble counter to see Sinead settle back on the couch, exactly as he'd hoped. But she fidgeted with her hands in her lap and smoothed her dress down, inching it lower to cover her knees. Why was she nervous? Had he already gone too far with the kiss in the lift?

Gabriel fiddled with the overly complicated stainless-steel refrigerator with a built-in icemaker, adding a few cubes to each glass. The ice cubes tinkled against the glasses in the quiet room as he walked over to her.

Offering her a glass, he sat next to her. Close, but not touching. Not yet. "Irish whiskey. Only the best for you, Irish."

Sinead took the glass in her hand and raised it towards him. "Cheers." She took a great slug of her drink.

He hesitated, took a small sip of the smooth whiskey, which burned in his throat and warmed him from the inside.

Then he spoke at exactly the same time as she did. "I want to us to be together."

"This isn't really working for me," Sinead blurted.

For a long moment, he stared at Sinead, unsure of what she'd said. Then the jumble of words rearranged themselves in his head. And what a punch in the gut they were.

"Shit. Sorry, I'm not swearing at you. Did I stuff up? Kissing you in the lift?" His heart beat like a drum and his stomach churned, waiting for her to explain.

"No, it's not that. I mean the rules, they're not really working for me. I want you to touch me, and I want to touch you." Her voice was low and husky, tinged with nervousness.

Gabriel's heart pounded, faster, blood rushing through his temples, but for an entirely different reason than before. Not fear of scaring her off, or fear of rejection, now it was pure anticipation.

But he'd heard her hesitate earlier in the lift and he wanted to make sure they were on the same page.

"I want you more than anything, more than any woman I've ever known. But I need to know you feel the same. I need to know what you want."

She flicked her hair back and her eyes captured his. "I . . . want to call the shots. To be the one in charge. At least for now."

Images from his earlier daydream flashed through his mind. Sinead in her dominatrix boots and very little else, standing over him, telling him exactly what to do. A rush of heat flowed from his head, straight to the small brain between his legs.

He was definitely on board with the plan, whichever brain was concerned.

"You mean, you want to take charge in bed?"

"Yes, in bed, here on the couch. When we're together. When we touch."

He nodded. Clenched his teeth. Dammit, she was turning him on. He'd thought it had been all over for a minute. Relief, a warmth he couldn't name, and out of control desire waged war inside him. "Fine."

"Fine?"

"Yes." His voice cracked as he swallowed past the lump in his throat. She must have heard it.

He didn't care. He wanted her more than his next breath.

Sinead's words rushed out on a sigh. "Oh, Gabriel."

Oh, my goodness.

Gabriel had agreed to let her take charge. For a man like him, used to commanding a whole company, projects worth millions of dollars, making all the hard decisions, it was unbelievable. And yet she believed he wanted it. She'd heard the way his voice had deepened and cracked, and she could hardly ignore the obvious physical reaction he'd had to her words. The hard evidence was there right beside her, and she didn't want to simply sit next to him. She wanted to take charge. Now.

Climbing onto Gabriel's lap, she swung one leg over so she was astride him, her slinky dress creeping up her thighs. Then she wrapped her arms around his neck. He shifted and groaned, and she sighed. It was so good, so incredibly right, to be close to him again. She leaned down until her lips hovered a hair's breadth away from his mouth.

She took control, telling him exactly what she wanted. "Kiss me again, hard."

He responded as she asked, biting her lower lip, then sliding his tongue inside her mouth. Tasting him, caramel-whiskey infused with his spicy scent, his strong body pressed against her, it was almost too much. There was no stopping the surge of desire building within her, not with him stoking the flames.

She moved back, breaking the kiss and raising her head to expose her throat. Gabriel took the hint, shifting strands of her hair to one side so he could kiss her there. He nipped the tender skin with his teeth, making her gasp.

She whispered into his ear. "Take off your shirt. I need to see you."

Sitting back slightly on his thighs, she watched him unbutton his shirt with shaking hands. There was something delicious about a man as physically powerful as Gabriel, so nervous and excited because of her. She couldn't take her eyes off him. The triangle of taut, tanned skin he revealed as he undid one button after another, nearly had her coming undone.

Giving in to her impulse, she bent close and licked a line from his Adam's apple, all the way down the centre of his chest. His muscles bunched and tensed under her touch as she travelled down further. She blew against the still wet path on his skin. A whole body shudder was her reward. Then he pulled the sleeves of his shirt down his arms and tore it completely off.

She took a minute to admire him. He was so beautiful, so fine, she had trouble believing he was hers.

My man. She tested the concept in her mind. It had the ring of truth.

Running her fingernails lightly down his arms, enjoying the play of his bicep muscles as he tensed under her touch, she spoke the words.

"You're my man." She looked him straight in the eyes. Her heart ached as the vulnerable boy peeked back at her once more. "My beautiful, strong man."

Sinead kissed him again, a momentary touch against his lips. She reached behind her to the glass coffee table, picked up her whiskey glass and took a long, leisurely sip. His eyebrows crept up a fraction. Hopefully he'd like the next little surprise she had in mind.

Reaching into her glass, she pinched an ice cube between her fingertips and placed the glass back on the table. Raising her hand to eye level, Sinead showed Gabriel the ice. He raised his eyebrows into the full-blown 'what the hell' and his lips twitched up at the corners.

Then she lowered the ice to his throat, savouring his shiver and sharp intake of breath.

She slicked the ice from his jaw, down his neck, into the indentation at the base of his throat. She followed it with a press of her lips. Kissing and licking the trickle of meltwater from his skin, humming, breathing him in.

The teasing ramped up as she trailed the ice down his chest, swirling it around one of his nipples, which instantly hardened. His whole body tensed under her touch, then he groaned when she bent and sucked each taut peak between her lips. Delicious, silky smooth flesh and the contrast of coarse hair teased her senses.

Gabriel's hands moved to her backside, pulling her closer to his body.

"Wait," she warned. "Keep your hands down on the sofa." She was enjoying this so much, she wasn't ready for him to take over.

He complied, resting his hands on the leather seat on either side of his muscular, denim-clad thighs.

Sinead wiggled in his lap. His hands tensed and gripped the leather with white knuckles. This slow seduction of her man was what she needed. She needed more than a quickie, more than one night.

Using the ice cube on the other side of Gabriel's chest, she kept up her kissing torture, teasing and tasting. Finally, she traced a path down the centre of his flat stomach, around the dip of his navel, following the happy trail of golden brown hair to the low waistband of his jeans.

Stopping her hand, she picked up the remnant of ice and popped into her mouth. Leaning in and kissing his mouth deeply, she swirled the ice around his tongue until it completely dissolved in their combined heat.

The sound he made, God, the sound. It resonated in his chest, a groan so deep it vibrated through him. Almost desperate.

No more waiting. Sinead reached for the hem of her knit dress and pulled it up, over her hips, up over her head. Tossing the dress to the floor behind her, she sat in front of him in her sexiest, knockout silver and black lingerie, thigh-high stockings and boots. Warmth rose in her belly. It wasn't only the whiskey, it was the effect of his gaze. Their eyes locked.

"You can touch me now."

She took his right hand in hers, then placed it on the lacy cup of her bra, over the swell of her left breast. She sighed. The palm of his hand rested directly over her heart.

Then Gabriel flipped her over at high-speed, so she was giggling and gasping for air. He was kneeling between her legs and grinning, holding onto her thighs.

"I'm going to make you scream, Irish."

Mmm-hmm. Excellent plan.

Chapter Twelve

By the time he arrived at work the next day, he'd swum fifty laps and conducted a conference call with a potential European partner. Gabriel should have been exhausted. His mind was elsewhere, but he was full of energy.

After staring blankly at his laptop for a few minutes where it was set up on the boardroom table, he gave in to his lack of concentration. He couldn't sit still so he stood and stretched, cracking his neck. His muscles ached but he was awake, *alive*, in a way he hadn't been for a long time. Years, even.

The lightness was the result of the load lifted from his shoulders at work, combined with Sinead's assault on his senses the night before. She wanted him, and the relief flooded his system along with the ever-present heat. The way she'd teased him so relentlessly with an ice cube, his body tightened again just thinking about it.

Pacing before the boardroom's floor-to-ceiling windows, he allowed himself to feel the full force of what she did to him. He'd never known anything like it. They hadn't even had sex last night, not quite.

Once she'd let him touch her, he'd reacquainted himself with her breathtaking curves, running his hands over her breasts, before tearing off her bra, licking and then sucking the delicate pink buds into his mouth. Lavishing attention on her, one breast and then the other.

He'd urged her to sit back on the sofa, then knelt down in front of her and spread her legs wide, pushing her lace knickers aside and holding fast to her hips, tasting her most intimate places, pleasuring her until she screamed his name. He'd nearly gone insane listening to the breathy sounds she made.

Finally she'd focused on him, and bloody hell it was worth the wait. She'd bossed him around, laid him back and stripped him bare, then took him inside her hot mouth. He'd come so hard and fast, like an out-of-control freight train hurtling down the tracks, not stopping for anyone or anything.

Sinead had completely blown his mind. She owned him. The weird thing was, he didn't mind. He bloody loved it. He never believed he'd belong to someone.

The fact he couldn't keep seeing her long term made him want to scream. He stopped pacing and clunked his forehead against a cold windowpane, spreading his hands on the glass barrier. Looking straight down, London was at his feet. But it felt empty.

Sinead had left his hotel suite all too soon last night, needing sleep before she got up at four-thirty in the morning, ready to fly. She must be in Paris by now. She was only there for the day, flying a European leg or two before her next long haul to Melbourne in a few days.

It'd be close to midnight before she got home to London. She'd be too tired to see him. He missed her so much already, his gut ached. His skin prickled in anticipation of seeing her. Touching her again.

He paced, back and forth. Trying to calm his racing pulse, ignoring a raging hard-on. The core London team would join him in the boardroom for the meeting soon.

Calm the hell down.

He fell into a leather chair and pictured Sinead in Paris, drinking coffee on the left bank of the Seine, or walking through the Tuileries Gardens. He'd take her sometime. He'd love to see her in Paris.

But he needed his head in the game now. He scrolled through the notes on his laptop. He'd called the meeting to outline his new role and the way he and Ryan would work together from opposite sides of the world. He'd lined up a similar meeting for his Melbourne team in a few days.

When he'd be back home. On the wrong side of the planet for continuing to see Sinead.

Ryan flung the door open and barged in, obviously all steamed up. "Man, it never rains but it bloody well pours. Looks like we're in for a hostile takeover bid."

"What? When did this happen? Who the hell's making the bid?" Gabriel stared at Ryan's tense expression. All arousal was shot to hell. Looking down at his high-shine Italian shoes and stuffing his fists into his pockets, he braced himself for crappy news.

"I've been pinged the stock market report. Someone's buying chunks of our stock. I'm not one hundred per cent sure, but I'll wager it's Travel South."

Gabriel's head shot up, on high alert. "Bruce Champion? The sly bastard."

The older man's haggard, weather-worn face popped into his head, along with Bruce's threat from a few years ago. To make Global Village pay. Bruce claimed Gabriel had ruined a deal Travel South brokered with the major Australian airlines. Of course, Gabriel hadn't ruined anything, only informed an airline contact of Bruce's underhand deals with the regional carriers.

Gabriel had promised open and fair business relationships, which he'd delivered, along with access to a cutting-edge digital marketing platform. Bruce ran a successful chain of traditional retail travel agencies in Australia and New Zealand but he hadn't kept up with technology. Still, in Bruce's mind, Gabriel had become his mortal enemy. And now it seemed he'd follow through on his threat.

"Okay, let's get everyone in here ASAP, including our financial market guys and PR. Let's work through all the scenarios and see what we can come up with," Gabriel said.

A tight, scary smile stole over Ryan's face. "Battle stations?" He loved a challenge.

"Armed and ready." Gabriel's own smile stretched his cheek muscles. His excitement was forced. This was the last thing he needed.

Going into full business mode, he wouldn't have time to talk to Sinead for a while. He regretted it already.

Paris, France

The tune playing through Sinead's earbuds was perfect. Something about hearts yearning and Paris burning. Burning with passion all night long.

She nodded her head along with the song's upbeat tempo. Soaking up the atmosphere, sitting at an outdoor table at one of her favourite cafés on the fashionable Boulevard St Germain, she watched the sophisticated crowd. Beautiful couples holding hands, basking in the afterglow of whatever had happened the night before. Just like she was. Students reading, old people walking their dogs.

Waiting for Yuki, she sipped a perfect café au lait. She sighed as the bittersweet flavour filled her mouth. Then she checked her phone for messages. Again. Her heart pounded as a new text message popped up before her eyes. Not from Gabriel. Her stomach dropped with disappointment.

It was from Bridie. Guilt clogged her throat for ignoring her sister so thoroughly since she had arrived.

Bridie: U gone? Where to?

Sinead: Yes, left for work at arse crack of dawn. In Paris.

Bridie: OMG! Lucky bitch. Can I have ur bed? I won't defile it with boys. Promise!

Sinead: Sure. See you tomorrow morning. xxx

She laughed at her sister's silliness and promised she'd spend more time with her soon.

Her skin itched to see Gabriel, to touch him, but trying to build a bridge with her family was important. She and Bridie both had to go home to Dublin soon and face their mother, and a united front would help. They'd support each other if things went to shite.

Her fingers hovered over her phone, wanting to reach out to Gabriel. She could let him know he was on her mind. He certainly was. Last night had been heart-stoppingly spectacular. She'd never been so hot-to-trot. But it wasn't just physical. They'd looked at each other. Really looked. She'd seen him and he'd seen her, no pretence.

In Singapore they'd had a glimmer of a connection, now it was stronger. More real. And Gabriel had let her take control. She'd needed it, wanted it. To touch him, to take her time. He'd been more than happy. His hands had shaken when he touched her. She'd never had the power with a man before, no matter how much she'd wanted it in the past.

Somehow, he made her want to be unflinchingly honest, in words and through touch.

She couldn't wait another second. Words rushed through her head. Should she play it flirty or sincere? Closing her eyes for a moment, she blinked them open and typed exactly what she'd been thinking.

Can't stop thinking about last night. When we touched, I think you nearly exploded my heart. S xxx

She hoped he'd reply immediately, but after a few minutes of staring at her phone, there was still no response.

Then Yuki arrived right in front of her, making her yelp in surprise, scattering her thoughts.

Sinead pulled the earbuds out of her ears, stopping the music mid-song. "Hi, Yuki."

Her friend swished her shiny black hair. "Hi, sweetie. I need one of those coffees. And crepes I think. Mmm, definitely crepes."

Yuki scraped a chair along the floor and fell into the spot opposite Sinead, dumping paper shopping bags on the ground. Yuki had hit the boutiques as soon as they landed, but Sinead didn't have the energy.

Yuki tipped her head to one side. "What's up with you? Did someone raid your secret chocolate stash?"

"No, I'm okay. Waiting for a call. Hoping for a call." Sinead wanted to avoid the full twenty questions routine.

"From Gabriel? Did you see him last night?"

Sinead had seen him all right. Every glorious inch of him. Her face overheated, as she imagined Gabriel laid back on the leather sofa, naked and ready, waiting for her touch. She bit her lip.

"Hello! Someone got lucky, and it sure as sugar wasn't me." Yuki rolled her eyes skyward and let out an exaggerated sigh. "I miss Daniel."

Sinead patted her arm in sympathy. Then the phone vibrated on the table. She picked it up with eager fingers, nearly dropping it into her coffee. The message set her face aflame again.

Need you, so much. Want to be inside you. Deep and hard till you scream. Will await your orders tomorrow. G.

Sinead fanned her face with her hand and grabbed the glass of iced water in front of her. The ice cubes clinked as she drank, and an image of what she'd done with Gabriel formed in her mind. Cool ice cubes melting against his hot chest. She gulped down the water but it wasn't doing anything to cool her now.

Good Lord. She might explode in a ball of flame before tomorrow.

"Oh, baby. Give it to me all night long Gabriel, you big spunky CEO." Yuki was laughing her arse off at Sinead's expense, wiping tears from her eyes.

"Shut up, please. I'm composing sexy words." Sinead told off her friend, then quickly typed another message before she lost her nerve.

I need you too. Don't touch yourself till we meet. Want you hard, ready. I have plans for you.

She waited a long moment. No reply. Had she gone too far with the sexting? But then Gabriel's message arrived.

Argghh! Temptress. No more. In a meeting. Can't get up for a while.

Sinead tried to control her laughter and failed. Gabriel must have been covertly texting in a business meeting, hiding an impressive erection under the table. She gulped on a dry throat when she imagined crashing the meeting and taking full advantage of his predicament. Pulling him out of the meeting and dragging him to his office, or simply crawling under the table. Such a pity she was on the wrong side of the English Channel. Sinead suddenly remembered Yuki was there, and glanced up, trying to control her crazy reactions.

Yuki's dark eyes flashed, and her gaze was slow and appraising. "I've hardly met the man, but I like him. I like the look he puts on your face. I'm glad to see you so happy."

Sinead beamed, pleased her friend approved. "Yes. We're getting along great. Like a house on fire." *Like I'm in love with him*, she wanted to add.

She couldn't be in love with him though. No, of course not. She gripped the edge of the table, hanging on for dear life. Mad woman stuff. Lock her up and throw away the key, she wasn't fit for normal dating society.

"Now, let's eat. I need some sugary goodness to go with all the tales of your sexcapades," Yuki said, then signalled a passing waiter.

"Oh no, I'm not telling you any secrets. Except that the sex-capades have so far surpassed my very high expectations."

She couldn't wait to see him, although it would probably be the longest day of her life in the meantime.

All day, lusty-woman thoughts would be playing through her head on swift rotation.

London, UK

Gabriel finally had his body under control and his head screwed on. After Sinead's teasing texts, it was no mean feat. He glanced at Ryan, standing at the front of the room, presenting to the assembled team.

"The projections show, even if Travel South succeeds in buy-ing up all available stock from independent shareholders, they'll still only hold a maximum of thirty per cent. As founders, Gabriel and I hold thirty-five per cent. The majority of the other shares are held by investment companies and long-term Global Village staff," Ryan explained.

The hostile takeover situation was serious. Every seat was taken around the long board table and an extra row of seats had been added along the back wall to fit in the entire London staff.

Gabriel's attention kept straying to the modern artwork on the opposite wall. It was a dauby interpretation of a beach scene, gold and blue streaks dotted with colour to denote sunbathers. He'd much rather be there, with Sinead. He shook his head. *Focus.*

A question drummed through his mind. "Is it likely Bruce could gain a controlling interest?" Gabriel asked. He wanted to believe Bruce's bid for control of the company could be shot down.

"Likely, no. But not impossible." The comment floated on the air, piercing the otherwise silent boardroom. Apparently coming from a young woman seated at the back of the room.

Gabriel leaned over and peered around a few heads to make out her face. Charlotte. Not afraid of making her opinions known, even in a meeting with more experienced staff. He was impressed. Her attitude reminded him of himself or Ryan a few years ago.

"Charlotte, tell us what you mean." Gabriel encouraged Charlotte, but he heard a sigh from Ryan. Gabriel ignored him. "Go on."

Charlotte nodded and stood in front of her chair, straightening her black skirt. "Bruce could easily have been meeting with investment companies for a while, whispering about his grand takeover plans. Not to mention, he may have approached some of our staff about selling. Perhaps he's made them promises, begun planning his team in a new, larger company. I'd suggest he's trying to leverage the European expansion we've planned, for his own company's benefit."

She frowned and looked uncomfortable, then flopped down in her chair. Her expression reminded Gabriel of when they'd all gone out for drinks and Ryan had teased her. Not afraid to state her opinion to the group, but worried about what Ryan would think?

Gesturing to Ryan with his pen, Gabriel then spoke to the room. "I hate to admit it, but Charlotte may be right. I've known Bruce for many years and he plays a long game. This takeover bid wouldn't be a spur of the moment decision."

They needed a plan. His PR representative should be the first port of call. Michael was a young man with slicked-back hair and even slicker marketing speak. He was green, but outstanding so far.

Gabriel spotted Michael across the room, tapping on a tablet screen. He was probably already working on it. "Michael, I want you to get on the phone, online, whatever you need to do, and find out who Bruce has been meeting with over the past few months. Keep it discreet and start disseminating some positive messages about our expansion." Gabriel faced Ryan and nodded once. "Ryan, I think you and I should talk to our Melbourne team members."

Then Ryan spoke to the group. "Okay, meeting's over. I don't want a word of this discussion leaving this room. Charlotte, you're with me."

Gabriel walked to the front of the room, meeting Ryan where he stood. They waited for the other staff to exit before speaking. Charlotte approached, her brown eyes huge in her pale oval face. She might have been intimidated by the pair of them standing there, both years older, more senior and taller than her, looking stern. Hell, his jaw was so tight, he probably looked ready to punch heads. He softened his expression, offering her a smile.

He noticed Ryan did the same, except Ryan's expression hinted at something Gabriel hadn't seen there for a long time. Attraction. Infatuation. *Ryan and Charlotte.* He'd have to talk to his friend about it later.

Ryan lowered his voice, watching as the last of the team left the room. "Charlotte, you could have discussed your theory with me in private before the meeting."

"I could have, but you didn't give me a chance. You seemed to have other things on your mind." Charlotte's voice was soft and a little shaky. If Gabriel wasn't mistaken, she was off-balance because of Ryan. Something he'd said or done had upset her.

"Sorry. Now's not the time for that discussion." Ryan adjusted his tie, one of his "tells" when he was stressed. What had happened between the two of them?

"Mind telling me what's going on between you two?" Gabriel asked. More to watch their reactions than anything.

"None of your business," Ryan mumbled.

Charlotte glared at Ryan, as if daring him to explain. "I'm sorry, Gabriel. Ryan's being rude."

Gabriel raised an eyebrow. "No need for you to apologise for Ryan. I'm used to him." It was interesting to hear Charlotte speak for Ryan. He was sure there was more going on, but now wasn't the time.

"All right, back to business. Let's talk about this takeover bid," Gabriel said, then gestured for Ryan and Charlotte to sit down. They sat on either side of him, avoiding each other's eyes.

"I take it you want to put a stop to whatever Bruce has planned," Ryan said.

"Right. I don't want to sell my shares. I'd like to maintain control of the company we founded."

Ryan sat forward in his seat. "I agree. So we'll need to gather some more market intelligence, and head him off at the pass."

Gabriel nodded, then tipped his chin in Charlotte's direction. "We should let you get back to work, Charlotte."

Ryan spoke for her this time. "She's with me. I want Charlotte's take on this situation. I value her insight."

Charlotte was silent, but her lips twitched up at the corners.

"Fine. Charlotte, maybe as a fresh face at the company, you can find out things we can't. Meet with some of the major shareholders here in London and report to Ryan. I don't want Bruce alerted to our research and I have no interest in playing his game. I certainly don't want to get into bed with the dishonest old bastard."

"Really? Who would you like to get into bed with?" Ryan joked and deflected from the issue at hand.

"She's a beautiful blonde, Irish accent, funny and sweet, goes by the name Sinead. No big secret there. But back to the point, Ry. I need you to man up and lead this fight against the takeover. For reasons you know all too well, I'm heading back home to

Melbourne in a few days. I need to know I can trust you to manage things. So get your arse in gear."

Ryan sat up straight. "Gabe, you're right. It's more than I expected to be managing. But it's fine, don't worry. Char and I are on the case."

Ryan's more serious side had come to the fore. About time. Gabriel would leave him to it. He wanted to get out of there. He needed some air. But he couldn't help overhearing Ryan and Charlotte on his way out.

"Why does he have to go back to Melbourne so soon?" Charlotte's voice was muffled, but clear as a bell to him.

"He wants to get back to his mum. She's very ill and the prognosis doesn't sound good."

Charlotte gasped. "Poor Gabriel."

"I wish I could go back with him. He needs a friend."

Gabriel clicked the door closed behind him and leaned against it. His legs were heavy, too heavy to move. Closing his eyes and breathing deeply, he concentrated on what to do next. The here and now, instead of the hard path in front of him.

His time with Sinead had helped him forget about his mum's condition for a while. Now he'd been forced to remember, he only wanted to see Sinead. But he had a whole crap-tonne of things to do first.

He palmed his phone and marched towards his temporary office, preparing for his daily check-in. First he'd call Martha, his loyal PA, who no doubt already had an update from his mother's carers. Then he'd call the respite care centre and find out the latest, first-hand. From yesterday's call, he knew his mum had recovered from the infection and was stable. Once he had the facts he'd know whether he needed to fly home in the next few days, or if he could spend more time in London with Sinead.

Adding to his unpleasant to-do list, he had an afternoon meeting scheduled with Kitty. He'd already put off his least favourite business contact twice. He didn't think he'd get away with doing it again, as much as he'd like to avoid having to see her. Kitty's events management firm was organising the cocktail party for the London office launch. It was an important event and Kitty's high-society contacts would be essential.

He gritted his teeth and went to take care of business.

Chapter Thirteen

By the time Sinead snagged a cab at Heathrow and settled into the back seat, it was closer to one o'clock in the morning than midnight. Still, she wanted to direct the cabbie straight to Gabriel's hotel.

Even if they were both too shagged to actually shag, he'd welcome her and let her curl up with him in his luxurious hotel bed. By morning, she'd be ready to give him a proper hello. They hadn't had a chance to break-in his bed. Yet.

Oh God, she *needed* him. Her body was almost crying out for his touch. She shook off the notion. She wasn't so desperate to see him.

Sure, who was she kidding? She was buzzing with excitement and pent-up lust. Her day in Paris, the City of Love, emphasised her lack of companionship. Yuki didn't count in her current mood.

Making the boring, sensible choice and pulling up in front of her flat instead of Gabriel's swanky hotel was utterly disappointing. She paid the cabbie and grabbed her wheelie bag, stepped onto the footpath and stopped.

A cool breeze teased her hair across her face, tendrils coming loose from her ponytail. Goosebumps prickled at the back of her neck as she glanced at her front door. The overhead light was out. She always left it on, the neighbours did too.

A weird sense of foreboding gripped her as she trudged up the concrete path to her front door, listening to the sound of her own breath. The cabbie slammed the passenger door and roared off down the road. Too late to stop him or ask him to wait, or ask him to walk her to the door.

The street light behind her cast a weak yellowish glow along the path, where glints of light sparkled. Something crunched underfoot. Glass.

Her head flicked upwards and her gaze caught on shards of glass glinting where the light globe should've been. It had been smashed. It could have been kids, causing trouble, winding up her tough-guy older neighbour, Mr Robinson.

She shook her head. Surely there was nothing to worry about? Coming home late on a deserted street was spooky. It was one of those absolutely quiet winter nights with very little wind, only clouds of her own frosty breath tainting the chill air.

The tiny hairs instantly stood up on her forearms and at the nape of her neck, as cold dread prickled her skin. A sign her body didn't agree with her brain's assessment of the situation. She gripped her keys, then made a fist, letting one long key poke between her fingers. A makeshift weapon when used like a knife, as she'd learned in self-defence classes.

She hovered on the doorstep. Her body screamed, *danger.* Then her mind jumped in with a silent scream, the one name guaranteed to have her quaking in her boots – *Padraig.*

Ridiculous. The idea of her first boyfriend showing up uninvited at her place in London, it was mad. But who else would've sent her those text messages? Who'd harassed her even when she was living in Australia? Why he would bother her was a mystery, five years since she'd left him behind in Dublin.

Two years ago, the messages had turned nasty, making her uneasy in her own home. So when the opportunity came up through the airline to transfer to London, she'd grabbed it. Even though it meant uprooting herself from her home in Melbourne and a circle of friends she didn't want to leave behind. She'd thought a city the size of London would provide anonymity. But maybe not.

Bridie knew where she lived, and her sister had only just arrived. Someone else might have known where she was headed. Oh, God, Bridie had better be safe. Hopefully tucked up in Sinead's bed, fast asleep.

She glanced over her shoulder as she unlocked the door with shaky hands. Walking into the entry hall and slamming the door behind her, she paused. Her right hand fisted and moved towards Mr Robinson's door of its own accord. Should she knock and wake him?

No, she was a strong, independent woman. Of course she was. She could handle herself.

Creeping up the stairs, leaving her bag behind, she sucked in a deep breath. *Be brave, not stupid*. She kept her phone in her hand, in case of emergency. At the top landing, she peered over the wooden railing to the floor below. There was no movement, nothing suspicious.

But the skin-crawling sensation wouldn't leave her alone. She faced the door to her own flat as if it was about to rear up and bite her. Opening it slowly, with an eerie creak, she stepped inside. She shivered and left it standing open.

Sinead crept into the middle of the sitting room with quiet, cautious steps, the worn brown carpet muffling any sound. Turning her head to examine her familiar surroundings, her stomach dipped with a seasick lurch.

"Shite."

Things were missing. Her television, a fairly new flat-screen, along with her DVR. A vacant space where they should have been on her sideboard. They were probably the only things she owned worth hocking for cash.

Cash!

She scurried across to her kitchen. The red canister by the stove marked 'Cookies' was usually stuffed with a bunch of foreign notes leftover from her travels. Getting to the kitchen counter, she tore off the tin lid and it clattered onto the counter. It was completely empty.

Sinead's body shook but her brain clicked into gear. She'd been burgled. A bog-standard, garden-variety robbery. *Or not.*

She stepped forward a few paces and glanced at her bedroom, the door standing wide open. The bed was empty and the girly pink and purple covers were smoothed out, apparently not slept in.

Mind whirring furiously, spinning with the need to make sense of what had happened, she looked for signs of life. Bridie wasn't around. Nothing was broken, no furniture overturned. The front door had been locked, not jimmied or kicked in.

Someone had got inside and gone through her personal things. Someone had taken what they wanted and then locked the front door behind them. It seemed 'someone' was her little sister. Her heart thumped hard in her chest and she slapped her hand over it.

Shaking, shivering from head to toe, Sinead sank to her knees onto the hard tiles of her kitchen floor. The cold bit at her skin through her tights.

Bastards. You can't choose your family.

Why did they have to be so awful? Bridie was the only one she'd trusted. Now that trust was completely broken.

With fingers that froze and stumbled, she lifted her phone from where it'd dropped on the floor. She called the only person she wanted.

Gabriel answered on the second ring. "Sinead? It's one o'clock in the morning—"

"Gabriel, please come. I've been robbed . . . I think it was my sister. I'm all alone and . . . please come." Her voice broke on a sob. The tide of emotion was so strong, burning her lungs and rushing through her like a hurricane, she had no chance of holding it back.

"My God, Sinead. It's going to be okay. Keep talking to me, I'm on my way. I promise I'll be there soon."

She clung to the phone like a lifeline, listening to his husky voice in the darkness.

"I'm almost at your place." He'd kept her talking, to calm himself as much as her.

He'd probably broken most of London's traffic laws, but he didn't care. Gabriel arrived at Sinead's flat quicker than he'd believed possible. Still not quick enough to calm his pounding heart or to erase the 'what if' scenarios playing out in his head.

What if he hadn't been around?

What if she had no one else to call?

What if some psycho had been inside, waiting for her?

He couldn't think about it, any of it. Talking on the phone hands-free as he drove, Sinead had sobbed and explained the series of events. He'd pieced together a story which made him clench his teeth and grip the steering wheel with hands like steel claws.

Sinead's little sister Bridie had stolen Sinead's stuff, along with her trust. Sinead was shaken, but not surprised. She sounded hollow. Resigned. She mentioned something about her family always being on the wrong side of the law, as if it was to be expected. As if Sinead had known something like this would happen, and she somehow deserved it.

Angry didn't begin to describe his state of mind as he parked the car and hit the concrete, already running. Still on the phone, he stormed up to Sinead's front door, pounding the pavement with an unforgiving stride.

He tried to keep the anger from his voice as he spoke into the phone and knocked. "I'm downstairs right now. Come and let me in, Irish."

She mumbled some response, then her rapid steps echoed in the hall. All he wanted was to wrap her in his arms, hold her close. He'd help her forget the family who'd let her down. Pushing one hand through his hair, he leaned against the doorframe. Breathed in, and out. Calmed the hell down. No need to freak her out any further.

The lock clicked and the door opened a crack, revealing one side of Sinead's face. Red, blotchy skin and a tear-swollen eye stared out at him, startled and wary. Still beautiful, but he didn't want to see her scared and defeated expression. Never again.

"It's all right now." He reached out and sighed with relief as she flung the door open and fell into his arms. Sinking into him, pressing her face into the crook of his neck.

"I'm so glad you're here." Her words were muffled against his skin.

He made reassuring noises, running his hands up and down her back, soothing the tension he found there. Without another word, he bent and picked her up, one hand braced under her knees. He walked them inside and banged the door closed behind them. In his arms, she snuggled into his chest as he took the stairs two at a time. All he wanted was to absorb some of her pain, take it on so she didn't have to deal with it.

When they entered her flat, he swivelled around. There was a blank spot where the TV should have been. But he kept walking, right into Sinead's bedroom, only stopping when he deposited her softly on her pillow. He made sure she was lying comfortably, then sat on the edge of the bed. He'd imagined seeing her in bed tonight, but not like this.

Gabriel stroked his hand across her tear-stained cheek, as she stared up at him. She was shivering. She looked too vulnerable. He wanted to stay and look after her, but he had to ask.

"Do you want me to stay here with you tonight?"

"Yes, please stay." She patted the space next to her in the bed with her right hand.

He nodded, kicked off his shoes, and lay down beside her. He pulled the covers up over them. Wrapping his arms around her waist, he soaked up her softness, her rose-petal scent.

She went still. Her grey eyes held storm clouds. "I can't believe she did it. Bridie was the only one who was on my side. My family... They're basically arseholes." She squirmed as she spoke, shaking her head.

"Do you want to talk about them? Your family?"

His hand had travelled under the quilt, and he stroked her stomach in small circles over her shirt. He wanted to be there for her, as he wished he'd had someone to support him over the last few years.

Sinead breathed out slowly before she spoke. "When I was growing up there were only two paths to choose. You could work hard for little pay, raise a family, and live a simple life. It could've been my life story, once upon a time. Or, you could learn a few tricks, get by using other means. My family, my big brothers, they learned quite a few tricks. Petty criminals, I guess you'd say. People who get sucked into the life, they don't want anyone else to get out. Some of the men don't like women who speak their mind either."

A tick in his jaw went off, but he clamped it down, clenching his teeth. "Is this why you left home?" He didn't want to push, but wanted to know what happened.

"Aye, along with an ex who wouldn't take 'no' for an answer. He wanted to get married and have a bunch of kids. I wanted to go to university and see the world. It wasn't a happy goodbye. My family sided with my ex-boyfriend, all except Bridie. She always supported me."

He frowned, propping himself up on his elbow to look at her. "What do you mean, your family sided with your ex? They wanted you to marry him?"

A grim expression marred her usual beauty, her mouth a straight line. Gabriel didn't claim to understand the dynamics of a big family, but he was pretty sure supporting your family members, having each other's backs, was part of the deal.

"They *expected* me to marry him. Anything less would shame the family. I lived with him, you see? My family, especially my Ma, they're old-fashioned. I was *living in sin*, so I had to be married. The fact he was treating me badly was of no concern to them. I expected more. So I left."

Gabriel's hand stilled on Sinead's waist and he shivered at the flat, resigned tone of her voice. There was more to the story and got the feeling he wasn't going to like it. He hated the story already. The ex-boyfriend—there were no words for men like that.

"What do you mean, he was treating you badly?" His words came out slow and cold. He dreaded the question, let alone her answer.

"At the beginning he was sweet, taking me out to dinner, buying me flowers and wooing me in front of my family. They all loved him, especially Ma. He's handsome, a smooth talker. He had us all believing he was a good man. Of course he's best friends with my big brother Eamon and a local legend in the neighbourhood, being a Gaelic footballer. I thought I'd found a good match, even if I wasn't ready to settle down forever." She paused, taking a deep breath. Her body trembled. He squeezed her tighter.

"After a few months it all changed. He talked to me like I was nothing. Someone to be ordered around, to do his bidding. He told me what to wear, who I could see and what time to get home. Once we moved in together it was worse. He expected his favourite dinners to be ready for him when he got home and if the house wasn't perfect, he'd get angry. He drank too much and he had a wild temper." She lay still and squeezed her eyes shut. She was running out of steam. He hoped so. He wasn't sure he wanted to hear any more.

"You don't have to tell me. If you don't want to talk, I understand."

"He wanted me to get pregnant but I wouldn't. I kept taking the pill. By this stage, I was trying to work out how to leave. He wanted sex all the time and I didn't. At all. I encouraged him to drink more so he'd pass out early of an evening."

Gabriel's anger simmered low like a pot on a slow boil. He stroked her arm but her face was hidden away in the sheets.

"One night he came home in a rage because he'd heard someone say I was going to college. I was waitressing, taking language classes too, learning French and German. I wanted to be a flight attendant and it was the first step. He yelled so much and threw a bottle against the wall, but I still didn't expect it when he hit me."

Leaning over, he searched her face. "No, Irish. Tell me he didn't hurt you, or I'll have to track the bastard down."

Anger seethed under his skin like poison, but he pushed it down. Another angry man was the last thing Sinead needed. So he pulled her close to his body and kissed her temple.

"He hurt me, in more ways than one. But he only hit me once. He punched me right in the face, so hard, he fell back into the wall and hit his head. So I ran. I wasn't so stupid to hang around for more. I went straight to Ma. I'll never forget the look on her face when she opened the door to me. It wasn't welcoming."

"You were not stupid. You trusted him. The man should have cherished you and known what a wonderful woman he had in you. Instead he hurt you. It's not how a real man treats a woman, any woman. Especially a woman he's supposed to love, who he wants to marry."

Emotions crashed through him, pounding, sweaty fear and red-hot rage. A possessive streak took over. Sinead would be his, to cherish and protect. She was as vital to him as the blood in his veins. The pain in his gut was real, slicing through him with the idea of a man forcing himself on her, hurting her in any way. He wouldn't stand for it.

No one would hurt the woman he loved.

I love her.

His stomach clenched and blood roared through his ears. He loved Sinead. A few weeks ago the concept of loving any woman would've been laughable, but not now. He definitely wasn't laughing, but he was content lying next to Sinead, holding her. Content. Another word he'd never associated with himself.

They'd both gone quiet. Sinead was completely still, but her body was taut, tension radiating from her every cell. He wanted to make it better. Make her happy, heal her old hurts. If she'd let him.

"What happened with your mother?" He only wanted her to relax, get her talking again. Instead, she flinched.

"She took one look at my black eye, and told me to go home to him. She said I'd made my bed and I'd have to lie in it. I was second-hand goods and no one else would want me. I left for London that night." Sinead's body shook in his arms as her tears flowed down her face.

Gabriel went still, hardly believing what she'd said. Her own mother, sending her away. It'd been years since he could rely on his mum, but only because of her illness. When he was a kid she'd been his rock. She'd loved him fiercely, had always wanted the best for him. He could never imagine her turning his back on him if he was in trouble.

Sinead had been hurt, in danger. She'd had nobody to help or protect her. He wanted to make it right.

Kissing her temple again, he whispered into her ear. "She should never have said something so cruel. She was wrong. I want you. I want you to be with me, Sinead. Now . . . always."

She rolled over to face him, wiping her eyes roughly with the back of her hand. "You don't have to say so."

"It's true. I've never said as much to another woman. But I want you and I need you, so damned much." He wasn't sure what to expect, suddenly nervous, holding onto the woman who had come to mean everything to him.

"Oh, Gabriel, I feel the same way. Kiss me? Please?"

The pleading in her voice and the way her lower lip trembled nearly undid him. He leaned over her and touched the silky skin of her cheek, wiping away a tear with his thumb.

Then he kissed her, gently at first. Pressing his mouth to hers, he sighed as she parted her lips for him. Taking his time, he slid his tongue against hers, tasting her, roses and something else, sweet and intoxicating. Shifting his body so he pressed against her, he relished her fingertips gripping his shoulders, pulling him closer.

She was his, only his. So beautiful and brave. The only woman he wanted by his side. He'd show her exactly what she meant to him. Even if it couldn't be forever. Damn, he wished it could be forever.

The light filtering through the partially open curtains was soft, but it pierced her puffy eyes as she opened them. Gradually Sinead adjusted, both to the light and to Gabriel's presence. He was wrapped around her, and they were both naked in her bed. Warmth flooded her body as it came flooding back. The way he'd made love to her. So careful, so tender.

He loves me.

He hadn't said those exact words, not yet, but it was in every touch. The way he'd caressed her, stroked her skin. She trembled again, thinking about it. He'd whispered into her ear as he touched her. Words of comfort, then dirtier words. She loved those too. She loved all of him.

All of him seemed to be waking up now. He stirred beside her, his arm tightening possessively on her waist and his hardness against her hip. Relishing the way he squeezed her and pressed his lips to her shoulder, she snuggled against him.

She was so glad he'd been with her last night. When she thought of what Bridie had done, it made her so sad. She hardly knew what to do about it. She couldn't call the cops on her own sister, and she couldn't think straight anyway.

What would she have done if Gabriel had been back home in Melbourne?

Why think of it now? When she was feeling so warm. So safe. She had to go and think of him leaving, going on with his life on the other side of the world. His life without her.

Gabriel shifted, kissing the slope of her shoulder. "I love these freckles, right here."

He tucked his chin into the crook of her neck. It was such a sweet gesture, her heart fluttered and danced like a rose petal dropping to earth in a spring breeze. But then it came crashing down with a thud.

"What's wrong?" Gabriel asked, then stroked her waist, causing her to shiver.

"When do you have to go back to Melbourne?"

He breathed out, no doubt understanding her tension. "A couple of days. I've been checking in with my mum's carers. She's okay, but I don't want to be away too much longer."

The 'where is this relationship going' question hovered on the tip of her tongue. But she chickened out of asking the big question and settled for a smaller one. "Do you want me to visit you in Melbourne?"

"I'd love you to, I want to keep seeing you. Are you flying to Melbourne soon?"

The nervousness in his voice surprised her, but he could have been worried about the future too.

She nodded against his hair. "I'm flying in on Monday and I'll have forty-eight hours downtime in Melbourne. I'll be tired after the flight, but do you want to get together?"

"More than anything. I wish we could stay here together, like this." He squeezed her tighter, then moved his hand to cup her breast.

She gasped, closing her eyes against the sparks of pleasure flooding her body. Her mood instantly improved. All she could think about was the way he touched her.

Gabriel's fingertip circled her already taut nipple, sending white-hot shards of pure desire through her system. "You're so beautiful, Sinead. So sweet. I don't want to let you go. I want us to be together. I know it's early days, but is that what you want?"

"Yes." The word was a sigh against her lips, as she melted under his touch. "I want to be with you too. But it would be a long-distance relationship. Could we make it work?"

"We'll try. You'll visit me, I'll visit you. We can travel together. I want to make it work. Make it perfect."

She didn't think he was only talking about their travel schedules. His fingers were doing amazing travelling of their own, heading south, down the curve of her belly. When those clever fingers trailed lower still, she sucked in a sharp breath and all thoughts fled.

Only later, she realised he'd been trying to distract her. Whether it was to head-off any more relationship talk, or to stop her thinking about what her sister had done, she wasn't sure. No matter, it was her favourite form of distraction.

Chapter Fourteen

Later that day, Sinead stood in the Mermaid staff lounge at Heathrow, stuffing her gear in her locker, preparing to board a flight to Amsterdam. It was a short trip, an easy job for a Friday. No big deal. Her phone pinged in her hand.

The text message from Bridie startled her so badly, Sinead had to read it twice to glean any meaning from it.

Sinead, I'm sorry. Didn't want to take your stuff. Paddy made me do it. I was seeing him b4 I came to visit. Can't talk now, but soon. B.

Bridie had apologised, but it didn't give her any comfort. The rest of the message was too awful.

Paddy. Sinead's ex, Padraig. The name jumped out from among the letters on her phone's screen. Shaking, her legs dissolved. The world washed away behind her swimmy eyes. She sank into a hideous orange vinyl chair.

Bridie was seeing him? It was too revolting to contemplate. He could've even been with Bridie in London, ordering her around. Being a manipulative bastard, telling Bridie how to hurt Sinead.

He might've been inside Sinead's flat. Her mind jumped to the underwear missing from her drawer a couple of weeks ago. She'd assumed she had left a few items in a hotel by mistake, but what if he'd broken in before and stolen her personal things? Like that day, years ago in her first London flat. Her ground-floor bedroom window had been open, her underwear scattered across the bed. A note scrawled in angry red writing on a page torn from her diary: *I found you. You can't run from me.*

She'd been terrified. And she had run, or flown away. Far away, to the other side of the world. The transfer with the airline seemed like a good idea at the time. Not that it made a difference. Whenever she'd moved, he'd found her anyway.

Earlier, she'd said she was fine to work today. But Bridie's text, the implications, had sent her mind and body reeling. If Padraig wanted to hurt her, he'd find a way. If he knew about Gabriel, he'd target him too. Saliva pooled in her mouth, a sure sign she'd vomit.

Grabbing her phone again, she punched out a text to her supervisor, calling in sick. She apologised for the short notice, but hoped he'd understand. She'd been robbed. She wasn't feeling safe or ready to work. Wasn't it the truth?

Her supervisor responded and told her he'd find a replacement from the stand-by crew.

Clutching her metallic water bottle, she swallowed about a river's worth. She had to talk to Gabriel. He'd been sure the shock of being robbed was still too raw, had insisted she was in no fit state to work.

She'd suspected Gabriel was keen on staying in bed with her all morning. Brilliant idea, but she didn't want to set up an unrealistic expectation for herself. It wouldn't always be like this. Lazy nights of lovemaking, followed by even lazier mornings, kissing and touching, sharing breakfast in bed.

If only she could go back in time and tell Gabriel she loved him. Her heart pounded and she bit her lip. If she went to him, she could be putting him in danger. He'd never want her now, not when he understood how messed up her life was. She'd spent the last few years running, never admitting that was what she was doing. But she needed someone's help. She wanted it to be him.

With a mind full of her sister and her evil ex-boyfriend, she took a deep breath and planned her next move. She had to think of Bridie. The way Bridie had treated Sinead now took a backseat to the possible danger to her sister.

Sinead had never confided in her sister about the full extent of Padraig's controlling ways or what happened the night she left Dublin. Bridie must have heard something from their mother, but no doubt Ma had painted an unflattering picture of Sinead's actions, leaving Padraig as the golden boy.

She wasn't sure if it was wise to send Bridie a message, in case she was with Padraig. But she had to do something.

Pressing her phone to her ear, she called Bridie but wasn't surprised when it went straight to voicemail. Sinead didn't mess around with her message – she wanted to make sure Bridie heard her warning loud and clear.

The words came out in a gush. "Bridie, listen to me. I'm not angry with you, not anymore. But promise me something. Don't go anywhere alone with Padraig. Stay where there are other people. He's a drunk and a thug – he hit me once. I'm scared he'll do it to you. He's been stalking me. I should have told you the whole story before. I'm so sorry. Call me as soon as you can. Let me know you're all right." Her hands shook as she ended the call.

Gabriel would be at his hotel. It was Friday, but he'd finished most of his business or handed it over to Ryan. Gabriel had a day off and planned to work out in the hotel gym. Without stopping to call him, she headed straight for the Tube station and took the first train to his hotel.

Hopefully, in going to Gabriel she was making the right choice. And not the biggest mistake of her life.

He ran, man against machine. Boring as hell. Staring at the monitor on the treadmill, challenging himself to beat the record set by someone who'd been here before him at the hotel gym. Why he needed to win, he couldn't say. Habit maybe? Gabriel had always been motivated to win, even when he wasn't sure why he was running a particular race.

In business, he was often competing with himself rather than a competitor. There was often no need to push himself so hard. He slowed his pace a fraction. Now he'd organised to slow down the usually frenetic pace of his life, he worried he might be bored, or drive himself mad. But he had to try.

He'd been running for fifty minutes when he heard someone call his name. A woman's voice. He was in the zone and didn't look up immediately. Until she was right in his face, standing in front of the treadmill.

"Kitty." He lifted his head and acknowledged her but continued to jog.

What did she want now? He'd met with her and answered hundreds of questions already.

"Gabriel, so glad I caught you." She tilted her head and her lips stretched out tight, smiling without humour.

He didn't miss the inflection in her voice, as if she'd caught him doing something dirty. The way her eyes roved over his chest, partially exposed by the athletic singlet he wore, made him feel like a piece of meat. The rumour around town said Kitty was shopping for husband number three.

Oh, shit.

He might have made it to the top of her shopping list. Not somewhere he aspired to be. Both of her previous husbands were dead, for one thing. They'd been older businessmen and loaded. She was probably changing her specs, looking for a younger model. Pity for her, Gabriel didn't find her style of cold, manufactured beauty attractive.

Sinead's image flashed in his mind, the way she'd looked that morning, all bare creamy skin, soft and sleepy in bed. No comparison. Sinead was the one he wanted, the only woman he'd ever wanted to wake up next to.

He wiped sweat from his forehead with the back of his hand. "Can I help you with something? I'm not actually working today."

"I need your help with a few last-minute decisions about the cocktail party tomorrow night. I tried to talk to Ryan but his assistant said he was unavailable." She rolled her eyes, apparently finding it unbelievable Ryan, or anyone, would be unavailable to her.

He raised his eyebrows as he continued a slow jog. "Is this going to take long? I've got things to do today."

Not entirely true, but she didn't need to know. He had a few errands to run, including picking up a gift he'd bought for Sinead a few days ago. He didn't want to go back to Melbourne without her, but a gift might help to show her he was serious about continuing their relationship, even long-distance. He'd found something he thought she'd like. Something special.

Kitty crossed her arms over her chest, looking impatient. "Give me half an hour. Do you think you could stop running?"

"Okay, fine. But give me a few minutes to shower. I'll meet you in the café."

She titled her head, smiling with one side of her mouth. "Can't we go up to your suite? There's some budget figures I'd like to show you. You have a laptop upstairs with a secure company login, don't you?"

The request was reasonable enough, seeing as Gabriel often held meetings in his hotel suites whenever he was travelling. But the way her eyes had widened, overly innocent, made him wonder if she had ulterior motives, trying to get him alone. No matter, he was a big boy. There was no way anything was going to happen with her. The sooner he got the meeting over with, the sooner she could leave.

"Fine, come upstairs. We can walk and talk." He hopped off the treadmill and grabbed his gym towel. He slung it over his shoulders, wiping his face and chest.

Kitty watched the action, her gaze lingering on his biceps. He rubbed at his skin, feeling suddenly filthy. Not in a good way, like Sinead meant it. He ushered her out towards the elevators.

Kitty's smile was genuine this time, but it was all teeth, like a predatory animal.

Sinead knocked on the door to Gabriel's hotel suite, not sure whether he'd be in. He might be down in the gym or he could have gone out, seeing as he had a day off. After a few seconds, the lock clicked and the door swung inwards.

Sinead jumped. A woman stood in the doorway with a smug expression on her face. Kitty's red-slicked lips quirked upwards as she leaned against the doorframe, casually hoiking up her cleavage in her low-cut top. Then the woman made a show of running one of her long talon-like fingertips along her lower lip, wiping away lipstick like congealed blood.

Smudged lipstick.

It didn't take a genius to do some basic maths. A messed-up Kitty plus Gabriel's private suite equalled bad news.

Kitty tossed her black hair back. "Hello again. Sinead, isn't it? Look at you in your little hostess outfit. So cute."

The blatant condescension in Kitty's voice was enough to make Sinead want to either slap the woman's face, or burst into tears and run away. But she wouldn't give the cow the satisfaction. Sinead ignored her, refusing to speak to Kitty.

"Gabriel?" Sinead called his name, loudly, peering over Kitty's shoulder into the suite.

She couldn't see him anywhere. *Please don't be in the bedroom or the shower.*

Sinead didn't want to believe Gabriel would betray her, not after the night they'd shared, but she'd been disappointed before. Her judgement had sometimes been way off when it came to men she cared about. Men she loved.

"Sinead?"

Hearing his voice was a relief, but when he stepped into view in the living area, she had to take a deep breath. He was wearing a fluffy white bathrobe and apparently nothing underneath. His golden hair was wet, slicked back from his face and his feet were bare. Why were his feet so sexy? He was freshly showered and delicious. If they were alone, she would've jumped on him. But it looked as if Kitty had beaten her to it.

Her heart dropped like a lucky penny in the gutter. Yet another man had taken her in, treated her like a possession – one he was apparently ready to dispose of as easily as a dirty pair of socks at the end of the day.

Sinead rubbed her own arms, suddenly cold. "How could you? After last night? You said you wanted me. You wanted us to be together, always."

The short-lived satisfaction of seeing Kitty eyes widen in shock, didn't make up for the look on Gabriel's face. Pure outrage.

Gabriel marched across the room towards the door, thunder in his expression, furiously shaking his head. He was going to deny it. Sinead may have been gullible, but she wasn't a glutton for punishment. No, if he wanted Kitty, he could have her.

She was out of there so fast, she was already inside the lift before he made it out into the corridor. The tears came quickly, rolling down her face, not stopping when she heard Gabriel yelling for her to wait, or when he shouted at Kitty to get out of his way.

The lift doors closed and Sinead couldn't help feeling they closed a chapter of her life.

"Do you have any idea what you've done? What the hell do you want, Kitty?"

Gabriel couldn't contain his rage, not this time. He slammed his fist against the wall next to the door. His hand smarted, so he shook it. Breathing hard, he leaned his forehead against the cool plaster.

Kitty had probably ruined his chances with Sinead once and for all, and for what? So Kitty could try to bag and tag him? He'd made it clear he wasn't interested every time she'd come onto him.

Kitty had managed to wrangle an invitation up to his room, then he'd set her up with his laptop on the dining table. He'd excused himself to shower after his workout and expected her to access the budget files and get to work, or grab a coffee while she waited.

But she busted into the bathroom when he stepped out of the shower, laying a sloppy kiss on him. He'd pushed her away and told her to get out, but not before she'd copped an eye-full of him naked. And then Sinead had arrived.

God, he was as angry at himself as he was with Kitty. He knew what she was like and he was stupid enough to have taken her at her word.

Her voice came too close to his ear. "I thought you'd be sick of the air hostess by now and you'd be ready to move on to a real woman."

Gabriel clenched his fists by his sides and moved slowly to face her. Kitty stood with hands on hips, defiant and challenging him to take her on.

He'd take her on, but not the way she intended. If she put him to the test, she'd lose. He raked his hands through his hair and looked her dead in the eye.

"So help me, Kitty, if you don't get out of here . . . I'm going to ruin you. I've told Ryan he shouldn't work with you because you're unprofessional and underhanded, but I could go much further. Your business is built on a good reputation. I have a lot of contacts who'd be interested to know you've been sexually harassing me."

He paused and stared Kitty down, letting his words sink in. The male and female roles were reversed from the usual situation, but it was still harassment. Her eyes widened and she gasped. Finally, he was getting through to her.

"I've told you more than once, I'm not interested in you. But you kept coming onto me. In fact, you knew I was seeing Sinead. She's my girlfriend. Get it into your head. You and me? It was business. Now we're done. After tomorrow night I never want anything to do with you." He only wished he didn't have to attend the cocktail party at all.

Kitty narrowed her eyes. It was probably supposed to be threatening, but he wasn't buying it.

He pointed at the door. "Get out."

To his utter relief, Kitty spun on her towering heels and scurried out, slamming the door behind her. He didn't give her another moment of his attention. He had to focus on getting Sinead back, to explain.

I love Sinead.

The words had been in the back of his mind lately, and again when he told off Kitty. In the heat of the moment, the truth. He had to convince Sinead of his feelings, but he knew it would be tough.

The men in her life had treated Sinead like dirt and she probably expected the same from him. He'd disappointed her, badly.

Now it was time to make sure she'd never doubt him again. Because if the incident with Kitty had proven anything, it was this – Sinead's feelings, her love, were the most important things in the world to him. He wouldn't give her up without a fight.

Sinead stomped down the street, blindly sloshing through puddles. She hadn't wanted to go home, if you could call the place home anymore. Her flat was no longer a safe haven. In less than twenty-four hours, she'd discovered her home had been invaded, her sister had stolen from her, and it was likely her stalker ex had been in her flat and touched her personal possessions. He could be coming after her. It sickened her. All of it.

She'd most likely have to move again. It had been the pattern of her life for the last five years, running from Padraig, finding a new life and getting settled, only to have him come breathing down her neck again. She'd thought it was all over. This thing with Gabriel, the rush of emotions, it had made her forget for a while. But that couldn't last.

Now Gabriel had gone and cheated on her with Kitty, a creature she'd known was trouble from the first second Sinead had laid eyes on her. Her insides were raw, like she'd swallowed acid, and the tears wouldn't stop falling.

Her legs carried her a few streets over to one of her favourite London cafés, not far from Gabriel's hotel. She glanced up at the sign. Nude Espresso in Soho Square.

She'd settled into a black leather banquette seat and with a café latte, before she realised this was the place she'd mentioned to Gabriel on the flight to London. Before they'd been diverted to Singapore, when they first spoke. *Nude Espresso*. Teasing and flirting, both aware of the frisson of attraction. They'd butted heads but still clicked right from the beginning. Within a day, he'd crept into the empty space in her bed, and her heart.

Sinead wouldn't ever feel it again. No one would take his place. Pain ripped through her stomach and caused another sob to escape her throat.

"Can I get you anything else?" A young woman barista with a sleek bob of black hair stood by Sinead's table and gazed at her, forehead creased with concern.

"Oh, a new heart. Mine seems to be broken." Sinead wiped her wet cheeks and tried for a happy face. It hurt.

"You poor thing, I know how it goes. How about some chocolate mud cake?"

"Now you're talking. Bring cake. Stat."

The woman nodded. "On the house. Have a trashy magazine too."

Sinead blinked and accepted the copy of *Hello* magazine the woman thrust at her. She sat flipping through it, grateful for a distraction. In the background, the barista greeted a customer. Only she wasn't expecting him to sit right beside her. She squeezed her eyes shut for a second.

She wasn't sure whether he was real or a figment of her emotional state of mind. Still, when she rubbed her eyes, there he was in all his glory, wearing faded blue jeans and a battered old leather jacket. A sombre, pinched expression on his face. So handsome it nearly made her cry again. Why did he have to be here?

"Any interesting news in there?" Gabriel asked, frowning at her magazine.

She squinted, tears blurring her vision. "Prince Harry in Brazil, the usual goings-on. How did you find me here?"

"I didn't find you exactly. I wasn't sure where to start looking, but I walked this way out of habit. Ever since a stunning flight attendant recommended it, this is my favourite café in London."

"Don't flirt with me, not this time. You hurt me. What you did with her – I don't think I can forgive you."

She gazed down at the table and her coffee, avoiding his clear, crystal eyes. Forgiving him was the least of her worries. She could barely forgive herself for trusting him.

"I didn't do anything with her, please believe me. I told her to never come near me again. You've seen what she's like." Gabriel paused, resting his forearms on the table. His jacket had disappeared and he rolled up his shirt sleeves. "She showed up in the gym and convinced me she needed to meet about work. I was an idiot for listening, but I let her use my laptop in my suite and asked her to wait while I showered. I'd been running for nearly an hour and I needed one." He shrugged his shoulders, looking embarrassed.

She wasn't sure she wanted to know what came next. She stirred her coffee furiously with a teaspoon.

Gabriel's hand landed on top of hers, stilling her stirring. A little whirlpool still swirled in the milky liquid. "Kitty walked right into the bathroom and tried to kiss me. I pushed her away and told her to get out. Of course, that's when you arrived. I never did anything to intentionally hurt you, I swear."

Sinead didn't know what to make of his explanation. She wanted to believe him and she knew what Kitty was like, true enough. Sinead wouldn't trust Kitty as far as she could throw her. But could she trust Gabriel? She wanted to, more than anything.

"Was that really what happened? If you had sex with Kitty and I find out you lied to me, it's over between us. You won't ever see me again. Do you hear me?"

"I swear, she barged in and tried it on. But I turned her down flat. Sinead, I want to be with you, not her. Not anyone else. I told her to leave and stay away, or I'd tell all my contacts she's been sexually harassing me."

Sinead was still stuck on the first part of his statement. He wanted her and no one else. She so wanted it to be true. This had to be more than a one-sided longing on her part.

"One slice of medicinal chocolate cake." A waitress deposited the cake in front of Sinead. "Uh, sorry to interrupt. Is this man bothering you?" It was a different waitress than before, but Sinead realised she'd been watching her and Gabriel from behind the counter.

"No, he's not bothering me. He's apologising. So far he's doing a pretty decent job of it," Sinead said.

"Good. I mean, I'll leave you to it." Backing away, the waitress gave them some privacy.

"Pretty decent? Thanks, I'll take it." Gabriel reached over and took her hand, threading their fingers together. She let him, craving the contact between them, which always seemed so right.

Sinead shot a sideways glance at him. "Did you really call her out for sexual harassment?"

"I did. If she bothers me, *us*, again I'll make sure everyone hears about it. She'd be ruined."

He'd called them an 'us'. An 'us' had a future. Surely he meant what he said. "I wouldn't want to get on your bad side, Mr Bigtime Businessman."

"I don't have a bad side when it comes to you. You're most welcome to get on all of my sides."

Sinead laughed, great heaving breaths coming out in sputters, not quite normal. But she was getting there. She kissed him then, the gentlest brush of her lips against his cheek. He sucked in a breath. She'd surprised him.

"I'm so glad I found you," he said.

She wasn't sure if he meant finding her in the café or on the flight when they first met. It didn't matter. Squishy lovey-dovey emotions warmed her from the inside.

Gabriel glanced up at the blackboard on the wall. "What else is there to eat on the 'Nudelicious' menu? I'll need my energy if I'm taking you back to my hotel."

She snorted at his arrogance but didn't correct him. Sinead needed to completely obliterate Kitty from both of their minds and she had a few wicked ideas on how to do it.

Savouring her chocolate cake, she licked her spoon, allowing all her ideas to show plainly on her face. She savoured the way he swallowed and cleared his throat.

Chapter Fifteen

The hotel's fancy function room was packed, a sea of glamorous people parting to allow them entry. Gabriel grasped her hand and she followed slightly behind him, swaying in her high heels as he cut through the crowd like a yacht sailing through clear water.

Sinead took in the scene. Would she fit in with the elegant crowd? They were a mix of Gabriel's business colleagues and potential clients from London's socialite set. People milled around, chatting and laughing. The lights were low, except for a spotlighted stage at the far end of the room. Black chiffon curtains lined the entire wall behind it and silver accents shimmered around the Global Village logo on a lectern.

The cocktail party was already in full swing. In fact, it had nearly swung. A bunch of young women exploded with raucous laughter around them and others were busting out funky dance moves on a dance floor on the terrace.

She was out of step with the late night, hedonistic vibe. Sinead and Gabriel were fashionably late. Striding in after ten o'clock on the arm of the only-very-recently-former CEO had stirred everyone's interest. Gabriel was a handsome and eligible bachelor, making him, and them, the centre of attention. This was the first official company event Gabriel had taken her to. Women and men alike were sizing her up, assessing whether she was right for him. Had she passed the test?

She glanced at Gabriel, resplendent in a tux without a tie and slightly ruffled hair. He hadn't been worried about arriving on time. He'd been more intent on 'relaxing' with her in his hotel suite and she hadn't exactly fought the idea. Making up after their misunderstanding over Kitty had been an absolute pleasure, for both of them. She'd been wrong to assume what had gone on between Gabriel and Kitty. So wrong to think the worst of him.

He'd shown her how much he wanted her. Gabriel's focus and concentration was impressive, in the boardroom and the bedroom. After nearly a whole day barricaded in his suite at Gabriel's mercy, and sometimes, with him at her command, Sinead was the good kind of exhausted. Bone weary, jelly-legged and sporting a silly grin which anyone with half a brain could interpret from across the room. She was nervous, but also stupidly happy.

Gabriel leaned in and whispered close to her ear. "Have I told you how beautiful you look in this dress?" He ran his hand up and down her bare arm and his gaze tracked the curves of her body, making her skin tingle as if he'd tickled her with a feather.

"I think you may have mentioned it upstairs when you helped zip me up. Thank you for the dress, by the way. I love it."

Sinead hadn't wanted to go back to her flat, even to find a dress. When Gabriel had invited her to accompany him to the cocktail party, she'd had a minor what-to-wear freak-out. The little black dress was waiting in a glamorous black and silver box on the bed when they returned from lunch. Apparently the concierge service extended to shopping for stunning designer dresses, at least for super-rich businessman types.

Actually, Gabriel had asked about her favourite designers. She'd assumed they'd have to visit loads of shops until they found the right dress. But they were saved from having to traipse all over London. The Karen Millen design in the box was gorgeous, with a plunging neckline bordered by sparkling silver and jet black beads and a slim pencil skirt. Sophisticated but not overdone. Perfect.

Then he'd presented her with a double string of black pearls with a dainty silver clasp shaped like an angel. She'd almost cried. She may have sniffled a bit. He'd selected the necklace for her personally a few days ago, choosing something unique. The handwritten message on the enclosed card still sent shimmers of pleasure through her:

These reminded me of you. Special and sensual, with a rainbow of hidden colour to discover when you look closely. A treasure to keep forever. Your Gabriel.

His words had her melting, wanting to tell him how her heart belonged to him. She held back, needing more stable footing before she put herself out there any further. And she still hadn't told him about Bridie's situation or the possible threat from Padraig. It hung over her like a dark thundercloud, but she hadn't wanted to ruin things with Gabriel. Bridie hadn't called her back, but Sinead pushed it to the back of her mind.

Padraig had tainted so much in her life, she didn't want him to stain this new relationship with Gabriel too. Gabriel had been so attentive, she'd been wrapped up in their bubble again, safe from the dangers out there in the world.

So instead of blubbering or laying her feelings on the line with Gabriel, she'd tried on the pearl necklace and the selection of filmy lace and silk lingerie that arrived with the dress.

Now, touching the pearls at her throat, skimming her fingertips over their smoothness, heat rose in her belly. She remembered how pleased Gabriel had been with his personal fashion show.

The noise of the party swirled around them, but she looked up at Gabriel and everything else faded away.

"What's the naughty look for? I like it," he whispered in her ear.

"Mmm. I was remembering when you gave me the necklace." She sighed when he pressed his lips against her throat for a moment.

He hummed against her skin, then stepped back. "Hold that thought for a while. We need to say a few hellos now we're here. Let's grab a drink and find Ryan."

She nodded, craning her neck to see where Ryan might be.

Gabriel snapped up two glasses of champagne from a roving waiter. He passed her one and she took a sip. Gabriel spotted Ryan, leaning against one of the French doors leading out to the terrace. He had a circle of people around him, hanging on his every word.

She and Gabriel crossed the room hand-in-hand. They approached the group and Sinead noticed Charlotte standing nearby, frowning into her drink. Charlotte was quiet, perhaps feeling a bit out of place. Much as Sinead had felt when she first arrived. When Gabriel let go of Sinead's hand to slap Ryan on the back, Sinead sidled up to Charlotte. She wanted to help make Charlotte feel welcome.

"Hello, Charlotte. Excuse me if I'm talking out of turn, but are you all right?"

"Hi. I'm a bit tired I suppose, working late with Ryan. We've been analysing this hostile takeover issue." Charlotte's grin seemed forced, and the expression didn't reach her eyes. She downed her remaining drink in a final gulp.

Taking a sip of her drink, Sinead wondered about Charlotte's comments. Sinead hadn't heard anything about a hostile takeover, but it didn't sound like good news. She and Gabriel hadn't had much time for business talk. But she sensed there was more going on with Charlotte.

Sinead's gaze followed Charlotte's, looking over to where Ryan held court. The group of men and women gathered around him laughed at some joke he'd shared. They were too loud, too eager for his approval. Gabriel stood beside Ryan, then poked him in the ribs with a low laugh. A pained expression crossed Charlotte's face when she caught Ryan's eye, but she covered it quickly.

Sinead noted the furrowed eyebrows and apparent confusion on Ryan's face. She guessed he hadn't noticed Charlotte was feeling out of sorts.

"I have to get going. Excuse me," Charlotte spoke in an aside as she brushed past Sinead.

"Hope to see you again soon," said Sinead.

No one from the group seemed to notice Charlotte leave. But Ryan stared after her, his eyebrows cinched together. She didn't know what to make of the silent exchange. Before she could think about it further, Gabriel moved back to Sinead's side.

"Sinead, I'd like to introduce you to our London team," Gabriel began, then reeled off a list of names. They all merged together.

The team members were friendly and a little drunk, telling tall tales about this win or that project, of little interest to an outsider. She didn't absorb the details, but she noticed Ryan searching the room.

"If you're looking for Charlotte, she said she had to leave. I don't think she was feeling well."

"Ah, right. I might call her in a while." Ryan grinned, a cheeky glint in his eye. "Well, Sinead. It's great to see you again so soon. I hope you're looking after Gabe here."

Ryan elbowed Gabriel in the ribs so he let out a huff of air – a literal ribbing. Sinead didn't understand why men had to bash each other to be friendly, but the comfortable camaraderie between the pair was good to see.

"I'm doing my best. Gabriel's been taking wonderful care of me these past few days. And I don't want him to go home to Melbourne."

"Irish, you're selling yourself short. I've never been better cared for than with you. And we'll see each other soon. I promise." Gabriel wrapped his arm around her waist and pulled her close.

Ryan rolled his eyes and groaned, but it was good-natured teasing. "You two are sickeningly loved-up. Don't mind me, I'm jealous as shit. I wish I had a stunning woman like Sinead to keep me warm at night." He paused, checking out the crowd near the exit. "Speaking of stunning women, I should try to find Charlotte. Back soon."

Sinead and Gabriel glanced at the retreating Ryan, then met each other's eyes.

"Loved up, hey? Is it so obvious?" Gabriel asked, eyes on her.

Heat slunk up her throat and across her cheeks. Her heart wobbled. Had Gabriel meant to use the word "love", or was it the sexy image that grabbed him? Because there was a whole lot of sexy going on in his blue-eyed devil's stare. Ignoring the L-word for now, she moved closer to his side.

"Gabriel, you're getting me all hot and bothered. In public." She pressed her body into his, then wrapped her arm around his waist, drawing him closer.

Gabriel chuckled then placed his hand over hers. "I'd like to explore the 'in public' thing with you. Sometime."

She shivered although she was far from cold, as a host of delectable mental images presented themselves. "Aye, that sounds grand."

He moved his hand down lower on her hip.

Trying to distract herself before her hormones took flight and she jumped on him, she changed the subject. "Charlotte mentioned a hostile takeover, but I got the sense she was hostile towards Ryan. She seemed down, or she could've been sick."

Gabriel nodded, smoothing his hand over her hip. "Yeah, Ryan seemed a bit off when I called him today. I figured it was the discussions with the Board. I'll give him advice when he asks, but Ry needs to take the lead as CEO now. I'll ask him about Charlotte though. She seems like a nice woman. Smart too. It'd be a shame if Ry messed things up and pushed her away."

They were wrapped up in their own little bubble, deep in conversation, when someone on a microphone announced Gabriel Anderson was "in the house". Sinead looked up at him, to see a puzzled expression cross his face.

"I wasn't expecting speeches. Where did Ryan get to?"

They both scanned the crowd but before Sinead could answer, Gabriel was being escorted to the stage at the other end of the function room by a young man with slicked-back hair. Michael from PR.

As soon as Gabriel's back was turned, Sinead's senses went on red alert, prickles at the back of her neck warning of someone lurking behind her. Lurking, or loitering with intent to annoy the hell out of her.

Slowly twisting her head to the left, Sinead found Kitty, glaring at her. She'd obviously been waiting to talk to Sinead without Gabriel nearby. Sinead had known the woman would be here, since she'd organised the event. Gabriel had already warned her. That didn't mean Sinead had to waste time talking to Kitty.

Sinead didn't want to give the woman the time of day, so she faced the stage where Gabriel stood front and centre before a microphone.

"Welcome everyone to the launch of the Global Village Europe office. We've heard London calling for quite some time, so it's exciting to be here and see this new branch of the company becoming a reality."

Sinead's attention floated away and Gabriel's speech faded to background noise, when Kitty moved close enough to strangle.

She whispered into Sinead's ear. "He's magnificent, isn't he? So commanding and . . . what's the word? Dominant. He could have anyone he wants. You know he probably *has* bagged half of the women here. London's best and brightest. It would take an exceptional woman to hold onto him. Don't you agree?"

Sinead refused to be intimidated by this woman who'd flung herself at Gabriel but been rejected. Sour grapes were the flavour of the evening as far as Kitty was concerned.

Calm as you like, Sinead tipped her head to the side and simply stared at Kitty. Sinead didn't belong to London's elite set, but she was tougher than she appeared and she'd win a staring contest hands down.

Sinead held the other woman's gaze, willing Kitty to wither and die. If not die, at least get the hell out of her way for good.

Kitty's mouth pinched into an ugly pout. "Nothing to say, Sinead? I must say, I'm disappointed. Won't you at least defend your boyfriend's honour? His reputation precedes him, and he has a *big* reputation. Extremely big. Which I was happy to confirm in the flesh when I saw him naked. If you hadn't arrived I would've had him. He was ready for me, if you take my meaning."

Sinead's mouth popped open in shock before she could control herself. Her blood thumped through her body and her fingernails clenched into the palms of her hands. The thought of Kitty looking at Gabriel that way, it was too much to bear. Itching for a fight, she barely stopped herself from slapping Kitty back to whatever rock she crawled out from under. Instead, she held her head high and gave the woman some parting words to ponder.

"Kitty, if Gabriel wanted a woman who was begging for it, he could find one on a street corner. It may surprise you to know he prefers a stronger woman. Someone who loves him and wants to take care of him. Get out of my sight. I won't waste another word on you."

Sinead turned to face the stage, crossing her arms. Kitty's rough exhalation of breath, still too close to the back of her neck, made her skin crawl. "Bruce Champion is going to crush him." Kitty spat the words.

A moment later, the woman was thankfully gone. Sinead didn't know what Kitty was on about. Whoever that Bruce person was, he sounded like bad news.

Then it happened. They locked gazes across a crowded room, a moment she'd read about in all the best romance novels. But this wasn't romantic. It wasn't Gabriel flooded by a spotlight who captured her attention, it was a shadowy figure, barely visible where he leaned against a large column to the right of the stage.

Something about the way he stood made her mind click and whirr. The set of his beefy shoulders and the contained rage and strength, helped her recognise him despite the poor lighting.

Padraig.

He was there, across the room. She swallowed, her feet glued to the spot.

Okay, okay, okay.

She could run, but where? Taking a gulp of air, she squeezed her hands into fists by her sides so her nails dug into her palms.

Why was he at the party? Did he really follow her, or was there some legitimate reason for him to be there? He was an almost-famous footballer in Ireland. Perhaps he'd been invited? No, she didn't believe it was coincidence – he had to be there to cause trouble for her and Gabriel. She was stupid for ignoring the danger. Why hadn't she told Gabriel about Padraig already? Gabriel would have made sure she was safe from harm.

"How are you doing over here?" The deep, resonant male voice was far too close to her side and she jumped, suddenly scared and confused. Her hands trembled.

When she sucked in a breath and glanced to her right, she found it was Ryan who'd spoken. He stood only a few inches away. "Oh, Ryan, you startled me. I saw someone I used to know. At least, I think it's my ex standing over there." She waved towards the side of the stage.

Both Padraig and Gabriel watched her from their respective positions across the room. Padraig's gaze was a malevolent force, a magnet sucking her strength from her body, leaving her jittery. His dark eyes glittered in the low light.

On the stage, Gabriel inclined his head and shot her a familiar, lopsided smile she realised was for her alone. He calmed her, made her a tad steadier.

"Someone you used to know, like the song. The ex, is he a friend? Do you want to go and talk to him, get re-acquaint-ed?" Ryan waggled his eyebrows. It would've been funny, if she hadn't been on the verge of fainting dead away.

She crossed her arms, bracing herself. "No, he's no friend. I wouldn't ride him into war. I'm not going near him. Ryan, he's bad news. Could you get Gabriel for me?" Her voice shook and Ryan obviously understood she was serious. Serious and nervous.

He patted her arm. "Don't worry, I'll have him back in no time."

Ryan strode towards the stage, a man on a mission. She was alone, although she was in the middle of a crowd. She tracked Ryan's progress through the guests, up the steps on the left side of the stage and across to Gabriel.

Michael the PR rep was speaking, announcing a marketing and social media campaign, but the details buzzed in her ears like white noise.

Ryan tapped Gabriel on the shoulder and spoke in his ear, then Gabriel's eyes found hers. Gabriel's jaw clenched, his shoulders stiffened, thunderclouds seemed to hover over him. After a word to Ryan, Gabriel descended from the stage and moved in her direction. But she lost track of him when he dodged around a large group of people, blocking her sight line.

Her eyes flicked across to where she'd seen Padraig standing, but only a dark shadow remained. *Where was he?* Her heart stuttered in panic and she clenched her fists tight again, before she lifted her right hand to the necklace Gabriel had given her, stroking along the strand. The cool, smooth surface of the pearls was comforting to touch.

Craning her neck to find Gabriel over people's heads, she let out a low gasp when something touched her. Grabbed her. A large, hot and familiar hand grasped her waist from behind.

Padraig's scent assaulted her, the stale stench of cigarettes and alcohol in an earthy haze sent her hurtling back five years. To the night he'd hit her and left her with no option but to run.

Run.

It was her first instinct again, and she lurched forward to escape his grip. But he jerked her backwards, pulling her into his large body, wrapping his thick, tattooed forearm firmly across her middle. She opened her mouth to scream, but no sound came out, just a gush of air. And she couldn't move.

A cold wash of fear came over her like a bucket of ice water. He was always tall, but now he seemed even bigger and stronger than years ago. She was tiny and breakable in comparison. If she were alone her sense would've deserted her. But she remembered where they were – the party, the crowd, Gabriel on his way back.

Padraig couldn't possibly hurt her, not here and now. Her brain silently relayed these facts but her body shook. Then a blast of hot, rancid breath on the back of her neck made her freeze stock-still.

"Calm down, Sinead. I won't hurt you, I only want to talk." He trailed a fat forefinger along her arm. She winced and clenched her jaw shut. "I tried to forget about you after you ran off. Humiliated me. Stole my money. But I've been watching. Seen you acting like a cheap whore, flying around in your slutty uniform. I can soon make you behave. We're meant to be together. The last couple of months, your hot little sister nearly took your place, but the dumb bitch went to the police," Padraig said.

No. Don't tell me you hurt Bridie. She'd never heard back from Bridie, but surely she was safe. Her sister had friends here in London.

He circled his thumb around on her belly, making her stomach clench. Sour vomit rose in her throat. One positive thought rang through, chiming like a bell. Bridie had called the police. Her sister must be safe. *Please let her be safe.*

Padraig's fingers dug into her hip, as he pinched her, hard. "I'll leave you with pretty-boy businessman, but he can't keep you from me, darling. I'll be back for you soon."

"No, you bloody won't be back." Gabriel's voice came from in front of her, cold and crisp as the frost on her bedroom window on a winter morning.

Sinead raised her head and sought Gabriel's face. He stood a few paces in front of where Padraig held her pinned. Anger and defiance poured out of every inch of Gabriel's beautiful body, his arms crossed over his broad chest, jaw set hard as concrete. His eyes were fixed over her shoulder on the man who held her against her will.

Even with her wits scrambled, Sinead couldn't take her eyes off Gabriel. He was magnificent, like an avenging angel set on vanquishing his enemy.

Padraig's grasp loosened and she caught Gabriel's eyes for a second. The hardness in his expression melted, with a look full of support and love. It could have been love. A second later, Gabriel's eyes shot back above her head and locked onto Padraig again. That venomous look could've murdered Padraig. She wished.

Suddenly Ryan was by Gabriel's side, a woman standing right behind him. Sinead blanched, all the blood draining right out of her head. She closed her eyes to stop the wooziness. *Charlotte. Oh, God. Be gone.* Sinead didn't want Charlotte in danger too.

Padraig tightened his grip on Sinead's middle. His forearm was a tight band cutting off her circulation. Sinead could not deal with one more thing, one more drama. Her legs buckled and she wanted to cry or hit something, fear and anger battling to win out.

Ryan ordered Charlotte into action. "Charlotte, call the police and get hotel security over here. Now." Ryan's deep voice held an authority and calm Sinead hadn't known he possessed.

Charlotte nodded, her eyes wide, phone already in hand. She hurried towards a door at the back of the function room.

Sinead shuddered, as Padraig's hot breath teased the back of her neck. He held her too close. How would she ever get loose?

Gabriel and Ryan stepped forward a pace, slow and in control. They were both so tall and broad, one golden-haired man, one dark, opposites in so many ways. They were utterly terrifying as a team when they displayed that stance. Barely leashed violence threatened to break loose with the slightest push.

Gabriel stepped forward a pace. "Let go of Sinead, right now." His voice was low and menacing, a slow roll of thunder.

Padraig spat on the floor by her feet. "I don't answer to you, or your lapdog."

Her ex was overflowing with fury. The muscles in his forearm tightened on her waist once more, before he shifted slightly to one side, moving his hand across to her hip. He reached behind him with his free arm. What was he doing?

Oh, no. No, no, no.

He might have a gun. The man was fecking crazy, to be sure. Before he could grab her, she spun out of his grasp, stamping a stiletto heel hard into the top of Padraig's foot. His strangled cry of pain sent a short-lived rush of exhilaration through her system.

Padraig's mumbled, *"Bitch"* didn't worry her, because his hands unclenched. She was loose, but he grabbed for her again. She shook, stumbling sideways on wonky legs. A thudding noise filled her ears, maybe Padraig falling, but she didn't look back.

Gabriel reached her in a split second, pulled her close, and wrapped his strong arms around her back. A sob wrenched from her throat. Sinead leaned her head on Gabriel's chest, breathing in his comforting scent of spice and clean male sweat. He was so warm. So solid. Her pulse thumped in her ears.

Gabriel kissed the top of her head and pressed his cheek to her hair. "It's all right now. I've got you."

Peeking out from Gabriel's chest, she spotted Ryan crouched down over Padraig, who was flat on his stomach on the floor. She hadn't seen him, but Ryan must have overpowered Padraig when he'd stumbled. A whoosh of air left her lungs and she sagged with relief. Ryan had him pinned in place with both his arms.

A security guard in a black uniform ran up behind Ryan and dropped to the floor, frisking Padraig's prone body. Sinead gasped when the guard retrieved a handgun from its hiding place, tucked in the waistband at the back of Padraig's jeans. He passed it to a younger, brick-shaped guard with ginger hair, standing behind him.

The senior guard looked up at her, where she was safe in Gabriel's arms. His forehead creased, his kind brown eyes open wide. "Is everything all right now, Ma'am?"

"Yes. Thank you." Her voice shook. She couldn't form any more words. Her brain was too busy flicking through all the might-have-beens. She might have been stabbed or choked. *Shot.*

The guard rose to his knees, clicking handcuffs onto Padraig's wrists. "Mr Anderson, Mr McKinlay, we'll take it from here. The police are on their way."

Ryan rose in slow motion as the guard and his colleague took over, pinning Padraig down.

"Thanks Greg. I think this man is someone Sinead knew back in Dublin." Gabriel frowned down at her as he spoke. His eyes held a question, hurt hiding in the background.

Meeting his eyes, her face heated with shame. She should have told Gabriel everything. Should have trusted him. Now he'd think she was keeping secrets from him.

Wasn't it what I did? I lied to him, not telling him what he was getting into. Her stupid brain decided to chime in, heaping on extra spoonfuls of guilt.

Not only had she been a liar but a scaredy-cat. She'd been hiding her past. The violence and sadness she'd been running from for years. Gabriel might think she was still having some sort of relationship with Padraig, and would probably run a mile too. She wouldn't blame Gabriel if he never wanted to see her again.

She took a deep breath. "His name is Padraig. He . . . he was my boyfriend a long time ago. He's been sending me messages, harassing me, but he's never followed me like this. I think my sister filed a police report about him too." Sinead shivered as she spoke, her body chilled even in Gabriel's arms.

"You'll need to talk to the police later tonight or tomorrow, but don't worry for now. We'll take him into temporary custody." Greg tipped his chin upwards and spoke to Gabriel. "I'll contact you with an update soon, Mr Anderson."

"It's Gabriel, please. I don't want Sinead to be alone tonight, so she'll stay with me here in the hotel." He tipped his chin to her and she nodded. He kept his eyes fixed on her face as he addressed the senior guard. "You know how to reach me, or talk to Ryan. Could you post a guard outside my suite?"

"Of course."

The two guards hauled Padraig to his feet, then he raised his chin and glared at her. Beady eyes in a mean, twisted face. God, she hated him. How could she have ever loved him? Or fooled herself into thinking she did? How could she have let him dictate where she lived, what she did? How could she have been so stupid?

Gabriel smoothed his hand through her hair and squeezed her tight. Padraig couldn't hurt her, he was gone. No, not completely gone. What had happened tonight, Padraig's existence, it could threaten what she had with Gabriel. She breathed out slowly, jaggedly, her heart still stammering along a ragged beat.

"Irish, sweetheart, thank God you're safe." He ran his thumb over her cheekbone, then straightened up and extended his hand. "Let's go."

She nodded, hoping that Gabriel wouldn't push her away now. She linked her hand with his, wanting nothing more than to be out of there.

Gabriel tucked her into his side, keeping her close. The party raged on around them, sounds of laughter rushing into Sinead's ears again. People were oblivious to any kind of incident, or the fact she could have been shot.

Out of the corner of her eye, she watched Ryan, still tense, standing as if ready to pounce. Gabriel muttered his thanks and Ryan offered a tight-jawed nod in return. She couldn't string a sentence together now, but she'd be sure to thank him later. She owed the two men her undying gratitude, possibly her life.

If her time with Gabriel was over, the least she could do was thank them before she said goodbye.

Chapter Sixteen

Gabriel stood immobile by the bed, arms crossed over his chest, afraid to make a noise in case he woke her. Sinead was finally asleep after he'd urged her to take a warm shower. He'd been so tempted to join her. To take her into his arms again, smooth his hands over her silky skin, to kiss her and taste her. To never let her go.

He'd occupied his hands and mind by making her a mug of hot chocolate in the kitchenette. Then he made sure she drank it. She'd settled in his bed in one of his T-shirts, comfortable and sexy as hell. But she'd been shivering, probably in shock. Staring up at him with too-wide grey eyes, shiny with unshed tears.

Now she looked far too small and vulnerable, tucked into his king-size hotel bed, surrounded by an array of pillows with the black quilt pulled up to her chin. Her icy blonde hair fanned out around her beautiful face, her expression soft and untroubled in sleep. He wished he was as untroubled.

The drama, the fear, was over for the night. She was safe with him, right where he wanted her. But he couldn't seem to move. *He* was in shock. The arsehole, Padraig, could have hurt Sinead.

Gabriel could have lost her tonight. He clutched his gut, sick to his stomach.

In the short time since they'd met on a plane, Sinead had turned him upside down and left his whole life, his future, up in the air. It was unexpected and surprising. Completely the wrong timing. But he wasn't scared of what it might mean.

The truth hit him like a tonne of bricks. He wanted Sinead in his life and he loved her – he loved her vibrancy and optimism, her bravery, her caring and forgiving nature.

Sinead's sister Bridie deserved anger, even hatred. But Sinead had forgiven her, more concerned about her sister's safety and wellbeing than her own feelings of betrayal. Amazing.

There was a worry nagging at the back of his mind. He might not have done enough to win Sinead's trust. Maybe Sinead still wasn't confident in him, or that they could have a future together. Sinead hadn't felt she could tell him about Padraig, not the whole story. It hurt. She must have been terrified and he could have helped her. Still, he understood. Sinead had been running for her life, same as him.

Only in his case, the danger was inside his own body. His genes were a hidden landmine waiting to explode. He had to tell her about his mum's illness, how serious it was. Early-onset Alzheimer's was a dark spectre hanging over not only his mother but him too. It threatened his freedom, his autonomy, and his life. The bloody awful disease was often hereditary.

If his mother's example was anything to go by, he'd be reduced to a shell of a man by the time he was in his forties. By fifty, he'd be on his way out. His mum was only fifty-four and the doctors reckoned she didn't have long.

He sagged into the suede armchair by the bed, resting his head in his hands. He couldn't let Sinead see it, couldn't let her stand by his side and watch him decay. This was why he'd never got close enough to any woman to have a relationship.

While he hadn't been looking for it, love had found him. Struck him square in the heart like a Norse god wielding a bolt of lightning. He loved Sinead. Warmth permeated his body, spread through his chest and wrapped around his heart. It almost winded him.

He'd do whatever he needed to love her, to cherish her and keep her safe. If it meant leaving her, letting her go, he'd do it. Even if it killed him.

The buzz of his phone in his back pocket shook Gabriel back to consciousness. He grabbed it and rose from the chair, pacing into the suite's living area, quietly shutting the bedroom door behind him.

He glanced at the screen. Ryan calling. Answering, he kept his voice low. "Ry?"

"How's Sinead doing?"

Gabriel's lips stretched upwards as he ran his hand through his hair. Ryan was a good friend. The best. He'd put himself on the line tonight and Gabriel wouldn't forget it. "She's good now, finally sleeping. But she was pretty shaken up. It took a while to get her to calm down. I only got pieces of the story about Padraig, but it sounds like he'd been stalking her for years. I didn't know what to say. I can't even think about what could have happened to her." He ground his teeth together.

"Man, it makes me sick. The police will want to know the background. They asked if Sinead could come and give a statement first thing tomorrow. Sounds like they'll charge him with assault at least. Greg from hotel security said the bastard was spouting crap about Sinead and Bridie being whores and owing him money."

Gabriel breathed slow and deep, unclenching his jaw with effort. "I'll go with her to the police station. I don't want her under any more stress than necessary. If the arsehole's spreading lies like that she'll need me. Did you contact Bridie like I asked you to?"

"Yeah. She's okay, staying with an old friend in East London. Hiding out, really. She went to the police after she split with Padraig and he started following her. She sounded scared. She was going to call Sinead 'when the coast was clear', as she put it, then head home to their mother's house in Dublin. But she decided to hang around a while." Ry breathed out, loud in his ear.

"She was horrified when I told her what happened tonight. I don't think she had any idea the guy was so unhinged. I get the impression Bridie's a bit naive and Padraig duped her. I don't think she's a bad kid, just in a rough situation with debts. It's obvious she loves Sinead."

Gabriel breathed out slowly, stretching his neck from side to side. "Thanks Ry. I'll call Bridie and try to get some sense out of her. I wish I didn't have to fly home tomorrow night. I'd stay here, but I need to check on Mum. Sinead's flying to Melbourne in a couple of days, but it doesn't make it any easier to go."

"I'll look out for Sinead, don't worry. Get some sleep before you head to the cop shop."

He nodded. "I will, I'm dead on my feet. Thanks for everything tonight. Talk soon."

Gabriel ended the call and headed straight back to Sinead. He didn't want to leave her alone. He wanted to hold her close. Pacing around the bed, he stripped down to his boxer briefs, flung his clothes on the armchair and turned back the sheets.

He climbed into bed and scooted close to her, wrapping an arm around her waist. The gentle curve of her hip, her inviting warmth and softness had his body tightening and jumping to conclusions. But tonight wasn't about sex.

Breathing in her heady floral scent, their first day together in the Singapore airport hotel sprang to mind. Sinead had talked him into 'spooning'. Now it seemed like the perfect idea. He couldn't think of any place he'd rather be in the whole world.

· ❤ · ❤ · ❤ · ❤ · ❤ ·

Alone again. Sinead unlocked her flat the next day and stepped inside the eerily quiet and all-too-cramped space. It was depressing. Far from her ideal home. There was nothing holding her in London. Her closest friends like Yuki and Deanna were based in Melbourne. And Gabriel, of course.

London wasn't too far from her home city of Dublin, but the relationship with her family was so strained it didn't matter. Visiting and playing happy families wasn't high on her to-do list, especially after the incident with Padraig. Ma's sixtieth birthday party was in a week's time, but she couldn't go. She'd put off RSVP-ing and hoped it would go away.

Gabriel had headed home to Melbourne. She'd see him in two days, after her long-haul flight with a stopover in Dubai, but it seemed like an age. He had become a central figure in her life already. So mind-bogglingly attractive, she sometimes forgot to breathe in his presence. But he could be so much more. Someone she could depend on, someone to share everything with, even the difficult times. Although she may have scared him off. Her horrible family and the stain of her experiences with Padraig had ruined other relationships.

What if Gabriel had flown off to Melbourne, thinking how glad he was to be rid of her? How would she cope if he didn't want her to visit? She couldn't fool herself into thinking everything was settled with Gabriel. Everything was so new, even if sometimes it seemed she'd known him for years.

She walked into her living room and dumped everything on the sofa. Her carryall bag, the garment bag containing her evening dress, and herself. She sank into the puffy cushions with a *humpfh*, popping her feet on the coffee table. She sat staring directly at the empty place where her television should have been. The television Padraig had stolen. She squeezed her eyes shut.

Gabriel had been her rock earlier at the police station. The investigating officer was a kind man and didn't ask too many difficult questions. When the interview came to Padraig's treatment of her years ago, she'd stammered through. Gabriel sat through the whole ordeal, holding her hand. She hoped that meant Gabriel was standing by her. He was so stony-faced it was hard to tell what he was thinking.

The police helped her lodge an application for a restraining order against Padraig but she'd still have to appear in court. The idea was too much to deal with yet.

Her contemplation was rudely interrupted by the trilling doorbell. *Gabriel*. Stupid hope lit up her body, even though she knew he was winging his way to Australia. She dashed out of her flat and downstairs.

Hoping for a pleasant surprise, she failed to be sensible and look through the spyhole in the front door. She flung it wide open and gaped at the two unexpected visitors in her doorway. She rubbed her eyes. Bridie and their mother. *What the hell?*

She stared, without saying a word, crossing her arms over her belly. Probably quite rude, but she didn't care. At least they both had the good grace to look sheepish.

Sinead squinted at them. "Hello." It was a poor opening, but the best Sinead and her shell-shocked brain could manage under the circumstances.

Bridie flicked her hair back and huffed out a breath. "Hi, Sinead. Sorry to show up like this without calling, but we were worried about you. I spoke to Gabriel and he told me what happened with Paddy."

To her credit, Bridie did look worried. Her face was pinched so a sharp line appeared between her brows. Sinead had forgiven Bridie, but it would likely be a long time before she trusted her sister with her whole heart.

"What are you doing here?" Sinead directed this question at her mother, who was currently staring at her shoes. Clumpy, black, sensible old lady shoes.

"I've come to apologise. I know it's long overdue." Ma stared at Sinead, as if studying her face for a reaction.

Sinead returned the stare. Her mother looked smaller and older, diminished somehow. Her formerly golden hair was sprinkled with silvery strands and her pale, oval-shaped face was crinkled with fine lines.

It had been two years since Sinead had last seen her mother in person, since Da's funeral. She'd tried to talk to her mother then, but it was the wrong time. And Padraig had been there, chatting with her brothers. Still, Ma had never made an effort. Until now.

Sinead nodded once. "Come in then."

She wasn't sure if she'd lost her mind letting them in, but curiosity got the better of her. She itched to hear what her Ma had to say, while hating herself for being needy. Sinead gulped in fresh air, then turned her back on them. She trudged up the hallway stairs without checking whether they'd followed. She heard footsteps behind her, sure enough. Her shoulders tensed in anticipation of the conversation to come.

At the door to her flat, she paused and waited for them to catch up. She opened the door and stalked in without meeting their gazes. She had to compose herself. Plonking herself down in her raggedy velvet armchair, she let her guests take the sofa. She was all politeness and hospitality, truly. But she wasn't going to make this easy for them. Why should she?

"So, talk."

Bridie broke the ice, settling into one corner of the sofa and smoothing her wild red hair over her shoulders.

"I'm so sorry about your things." Bridie nodded once in the direction of the space where the television should have been. "It wasn't my idea. I didn't want to have anything to do with it. But Paddy came here to find me, or find you, I'm not sure. He threatened me. Lord, he was scary. He grabbed my arm so hard he left bruises. He was up in my face and his eyes were like an animal." Bridie rubbed her own arms, up and down. "I realise now why you left home like you did."

Sinead fought the sickness rising in her stomach. It was hideous, the truth of what he was capable of, what she'd allowed to happen to her sister. Bridie could have been hurt a lot worse. Heat prickled behind Sinead's eyes.

Sinead's gaze tracked over her sister, sitting huddled on the sofa, long hippy skirt bunched up over her combat boots. "I'm sorry too, Bridie. I should have told you the truth years ago. I was ashamed. I suppose I didn't want to talk about it. But I put you in harm's way. The TV and the other things, they don't matter."

Bridie's tears ran unchecked down her cheeks and she nodded, twisting the ends of her hair. Their mother had stayed silent. So when Ma exhaled a shaky sound, almost a gasp from a dying woman, Sinead flinched.

Ma sat forward and opened her mouth a couple of times before speaking. "I'm the one who should be sorry, Sinead. I sent you away when you needed me. I didn't want to believe what you said about Paddy although I saw the proof with my own eyes. He loved you. I didn't understand how he could hurt you."

Sinead's blood heated in her veins at Ma's ludicrous words. She must have been in total denial, to believe Padraig innocent. To believe he'd loved Sinead. What he'd done to her face, the way he treated her, it wasn't love. It had taken Sinead years to get over it.

She'd gone to Ma for help, the one person who was supposed to love her unconditionally. And she'd been pushed away. It compounded the break, fracturing something deep inside. Only when she met Gabriel had she finally decided to trust a man, to trust herself, and she'd begun to heal.

"I don't know what to say. He hurt me and abused me. You told me to put up with it. I needed my mother and I got nothing from you."

"I'm so sorry, it's given me pain for so long. Your Da was so ill at the time, I hardly knew what I was about. You'd had an argument with Paddy and it got out of hand. I thought you'd sort it out," Ma said.

Sinead got it then, finally. The scattered pieces came together in her mind, like when she and Bridie worked on thousand-piece jigsaw puzzles as kids. If she stood back she could envisage the complete picture. Her relationship with Padraig was a copy of the original blueprint, a reproduction, and her parents' marriage had been an ugly design. Her father had been a rotten, cruel drunk. Never really violent, but he shouted and swore, and took off for days at a time. In Padraig, she'd found herself a man cut from the same pattern.

Da had spent all the family's money on booze and gambling, then blamed Ma for never having enough food in the house. He'd talked down to his children, especially his daughters. Sinead had always been insecure around him. According to her father, she was a *waste of space*. Her Da's cruel words rang in her ears even now, like Padraig's taunts haunted her.

Ma had put up with it all. Of course she expected Sinead to follow her stellar example. Even if Sinead followed her into relationship hell.

Sinead shook her head, fingers trembling as she forced them to stay still in her lap. "Da wasn't ill. He was drunk. All the time, for years. You covered for him, always so worried about what people would think. Why didn't you worry about what your children would think? Your daughters? What do you think we learned from you?"

Her mother stared straight ahead and sobbed. "I know, I know."

Sinead sat forward, entranced, as Ma folded and re-folded her hands in her lap. Over and over again. Repeating the same pattern. Sinead took a deep breath. She'd inherited exactly the same nervous habit. It was time to eliminate old habits for good.

Ma sighed, looking at the floor. "It's taken me a long time to understand, to get my right self back again. Since your father died, I've been stronger. He made me doubt myself so I was afraid to make my own decisions. I wanted you all to be happy, but I didn't know how to help." Their mother glanced up and held Sinead's gaze.

"When Bridie told me what Paddy had done, to both of you, I understood. And Eamon called me, so angry, and told me Paddy is calling you both whores all around town. Now I understand what kind of man Paddy is. The evil kind. I told your brother in no uncertain terms to get himself a new best friend. Paddy is no longer welcome around our family."

Sinead stared. Only her brother's opinion would've changed their mother's mind about Padraig. Eamon must have been livid. About time too.

Ma sighed. "I know how hurt you must be. I'm asking for your forgiveness, Sinead."

The wide-open gaze her Ma laid on her was vulnerable, but too demanding. Sinead didn't know if she had it inside her to forgive. Not yet, at least.

"I'll think about it." It was the best she could offer.

Her mother ducked her head, hiding the expression on her face. "Thank you. Think about it, it's all I ask."

Bridie stood and hovered, then rushed towards Sinead with the force of a mini-hurricane. She was all flying red hair and lanky arms and legs, landing on the arm of Sinead's chair. She fell into an awkward half-hug around Sinead's shoulders.

"Can you forgive me?" Bridie muttered against Sinead's hair.

Words stuck on a lump in her throat. "I already have." Sinead raised her arms and hugged her sister close. Bridie was a bright spark in the shadows of Sinead's heart. She didn't want to live without her sister.

Then Ma was beside them, reaching for Sinead's face, gently wiping a tear from her cheek. A tender gesture, the first from her mother in a long time. Her breath hitched.

It was a start. She was on the road to a reunion with her family, even if it was likely to be a bumpy ride.

Chapter Seventeen

Melbourne, Australia

The sun was setting over Port Phillip Bay, casting a golden glow across the flat, calm water reaching all the way from the horizon to the pale sandy beach. Gabriel focused on the stunning view as he pulled himself onto the wooden steps of the sea baths where he'd been swimming laps. His muscles ached, but it felt good.

Dripping wet in his swimming trunks, he grabbed his towel and dried himself. He stood in front of the baths at Brighton, right across the road from his townhouse on Beach Road, millionaire's row by the bay.

It was one of the first places he visited when he came back to Melbourne, but not number one on the list. The first visit was reserved for his mum. But instead of returning to the familiar tumble-down wooden cottage he'd called home since childhood, this time he visited her in the aged care centre. A soul-sucking, white-walled prison for people who could no longer care for themselves and whose families could no longer look after them.

No, it wasn't a prison so much as a waiting room. They were all waiting to die. The people who weren't aware enough to wait on their own terms, like his mum, had others sitting by waiting on their behalf.

He towelled his hair dry roughly, probably leaving strands sticking out all over.

Seeing his mum so helpless was the real cause of his tension. *Don't think about it.* Not when he'd be going back tomorrow and the next day. Not when he wanted to call Sinead. He didn't want to sound all down in the dumps talking to her.

It was mid-morning in London, hopefully he'd catch her. Grabbing his phone from the gym bag by his feet, he called her, watching the shimmer of the sinking sun. He'd have to bring her here when she arrived. It was only another day, but it felt like an eternity.

His lips stretched out in a smile. "Hey Irish, how are you?"

"Better now I'm talking to you. I miss you already."

"Right back at you. Guess where I'm standing?"

"Is this a trick question? Like you want me to say, standing in your bedroom, wishing I was there too?"

"No, but I like where your mind's going. You'll be here in Melbourne with me soon. I definitely want you in my bed. You're booked in, like a date."

Sinead giggled through the phone. "Nice date. Very romantic." He was glad to hear her sounding happy. He'd been worried about her, after the drama back in London.

"I'm all sorts of romantic when it comes to you. Actually, I'm standing in my favourite spot in my home town, wishing you were here with me. Watching the sunset over the bay at Brighton Beach."

It was a stunning spot. The late summer sun shimmered across the water's surface, and still radiated enough heat to warrant a swim even at eight o'clock at night. He'd needed it. The tension in his neck and shoulders after the long flight from London had been bugging him. Hopefully his muscles would ease up with exercise and he'd stop another migraine in its tracks.

Sinead sighed, her voice airy as the breeze. "I know the spot, been there once or twice when I lived in Melbourne. You're right, it's beautiful."

He leaned on the jetty railing. "It's right across the road from my place. I want to take you to dinner at the swanky restaurant here, then I'll talk you into skinny-dipping . . ."

He could picture it. They'd eat a delicious meal at the restaurant on the beach. Seafood, something starting with the letter 'c', for Sinead. Crab omelette followed by citrus crème brûlée and champagne, perhaps. They'd watch the sunset over the water through the restaurant's full length windows with a panoramic view. Then after dinner, they'd walk on the boardwalk by the sea baths and he'd chase her into the water. He'd give her a head start, or kiss her senseless first. Yes. If she was here, he'd kiss her until her lips were swollen and her expression was fierce and fiery. He could've groaned with frustration.

Sinead giggled. "You dirty man. I'm not skinny-dipping right in front of the restaurant. Unless it's the middle of the night when everyone's gone home. I might let you talk me into anything then."

He ran his towel over his hair one more time, then wrapped it around his waist. Damn, if he wasn't half-hard already. "I like the way you think. When you get here, we can do as much night swimming as you want. What are you up to right now?" He wished he was there with her, to hold her close and make sure she was safe. And just to hear her laugh.

"Getting ready to meet Bridie for brunch. We made up, you know, after everything. She even brought Ma with her to visit me yesterday." From the slight tremor in her voice, he knew it was a sensitive topic.

He stood still, watching a yacht cross the bay near the horizon. "Are you all right? You don't have to talk about it, unless you want to."

She blew out a breath so it echoed in his ear. "It's okay. Ma asked for my forgiveness. She sounded genuine. She said she understands she was wrong to turn me away when I needed help. It still hurts, but I'll try to forgive her. Bridie too. She didn't know what Padraig was really like. She's too trusting. I was too, years ago. I know how easily he could have manipulated her, because he did it to me too."

His chest constricted when she talked about her family and her bastard ex. It was real physical pain, as if Sinead's hurt had been transferred to him, even half a world away. He didn't know how to make her feel better, he only knew he wanted to try. He wanted to be the kind of man who deserved her trust, her love. A better man.

"Oh, Irish. Do you want to reconcile with your family?"

"Aye, Bridie at least. But I'm so worried about her. She's got no real direction in her life and massive debts. I don't want her going home to live with Ma, with the rest of the family hanging around. She'll get dragged into working for my brothers. Next thing you know, she'll be stealing from stores for them, or breaking into houses." She sighed.

He wanted to reach out to her, make her feel better, and forget everything except how good it was when they were together. This long-distance thing was a killer, already. But he had the beginnings of an idea, something he could help out with even from so far away. He needed to call in a few favours.

"I'm sure it will work out for Bridie. She's young, there's still time for her to do something different. And you need to stop worrying about everyone else and focus on getting yourself on a plane tomorrow to come see me. But no chatting up the first-class passengers. I've heard some stories about flight attendants. Some of them are very naughty."

"Hmm, I'm sure. Don't you get any ideas about looking up your old girlfriends in Melbourne. I'm going to miss you so much, with you living in the upside-down hemisphere."

He needed to see her face, to touch her. "There were no other girlfriends, I told you already. A few women, acquaintances really. Nothing to worry about."

"A whole city full of random women to worry about, you mean. Promise me there won't be anyone else. Even if I don't get scheduled on Australian flights all the time and I can't see you for a while. Lord, listen to me. All needy and pathetic."

"I promise. No other women, only you. We'll be together soon. And don't worry about sounding needy," he paused, wanting to say so much. "I need you too."

Her voice came out breathy as the breeze playing over his bare chest. "I want to kiss you right now, but I can't. But I'll be thinking about it. Kissing you, touching you. All sorts of thoughts. Naked thoughts."

His groan was loud, even to his own ears. "Me too."

"I'd better get going. Bridie will think I've stood her up. See you soon."

"Bye, Sinead." *I love you*. He almost said it.

Sinead walked like a wind-up toy, operating on low batteries. She checked in to the familiar Southbank hotel in Melbourne's CBD with a friendly hello to the staff at the glossy marble reception desk.

When she made it upstairs to her room, she wanted nothing more than a quick shower and change of clothes before she worked out how to get to Gabriel's place. She should look up his address online or call a cab. Too much energy required.

She dumped her bag and flung herself on the bed, kicking off her high heels. More than twenty-four hours in transit had taken its toll, as usual. But this trip, she simmered with excitement. Usually she'd be down for a twelve-hour slumber, a *Do*

Not Disturb sign on the hotel doorknob. To sleep like the dead, or the terminally jet-lagged.

This time, she'd wanted to bypass the hotel completely and take a taxi direct from Tullamarine airport to Gabriel's apartment. But no, she might be presuming too much. He'd kind of invited her to stay with him at his apartment in Brighton, but not exactly. After their phone call twenty-four hours ago, when they'd practised dirty talk over the phone, she was bubbling over with excitement and plain old-fashioned lust.

She raised her weary self and made a cup of coffee, reading her online messages. Bridie wished her a good trip, and Yuki told her to behave. Not likely.

A riveted Yuki had sat through Sinead's saga of a story on the second leg flight from Dubai. She'd caught her friend up on her time with Gabriel. Then Sinead explained the horrible blow-by-blow of the whole weekend and the background on her stalker ex.

Yuki was steaming mad with Sinead for not telling her the whole story sooner, in fact, she got a smack on the arm for her trouble. But Yuki swooned when Sinead explained how Gabriel had looked after her that night and stayed with her at the police station the next morning.

Wandering to the windows, she looked out over the Melbourne skyline. Victorian buildings and silver skyscrapers and the Yarra River shimmering below in the sunshine. She wanted to be with Gabriel. Where would he take her? He seemed so excited to show her around his city. Even though she'd lived here before, she wanted to experience it with him. Not long now, and they'd be together.

She stripped off all her clothes in a nudie happy dance. Her skin was so hot, sparks practically flew off with her uniform.

One quick shower later, she was wrapped in an enormous white bath sheet and dialling Gabriel's number. No answer. Unacceptable.

But as soon as she ended the call, her phone buzzed and vibrated in her hand, startling her out of her daydreams.

"Gabriel?"

"Hello, Irish. Good to hear your voice. Have you gone through security yet? I can come and meet you."

Happy heat rolled across her cheeks. "I've checked into my hotel and had a shower. I'm all wet. And naked."

She exaggerated a little, hoping to hear his groan in reaction to her words. She loved that sound and he didn't disappoint. The noise out of his throat was all deep and rumbly. It shot straight to its target in her lady parts.

"God, Sinead. You're trying to kill me over the phone. But why did you go to the hotel? I want you to stay with me."

Her lips stretched in a smile so wide her cheeks could've split open. "All right."

"All right? I'm at work at the moment so I'm already in the city. I'll skip out early and pick you up. Give me half an hour."

"You know the hotel? The Southbank one."

"Yep, already on my way. See you soon. Stay naked, I'll come to your room."

"Okay. Be quick."

She was definitely trying to kill him and he wasn't complaining. Gabriel lay in Sinead's hotel bed, naked and relaxed. Should he wake the sleeping beauty lying beside him? No, not yet.

She'd jumped him at the door when he'd arrived. What a sight for sore eyes, wearing nothing but a towel and a pair of sparkly silver high heels. The towel disappeared in half a second and he'd been totally on board with whatever she had in mind. So much for taking her back to his place. Hotels had their uses.

Her plan involved a lot of kissing all over his very grateful body, while she removed his clothes and performed some kind of torturously slow sexy-dance. She'd left the high heels on, even when the dance became more horizontal and X-rated. Lucky they'd got through the preliminary round of getting to know each other before her jet-lag hit. Then she'd pretty much passed out.

The waiting was killing him. Looking at her lying next to him, bare, creamy skin only half covered by a crisp white cotton sheet, his relaxed mood suddenly wore off. He wanted her again and it was getting urgent. He needed her. Not in this hotel. He was damned sick of hotels; he wanted her in *his* bed.

Then she made a groaning, sexy noise, and to top it off, she wiggled her hips. He was close enough to feel the movement against his side. It did interesting things to his body.

Her mouth popped open. "Oh, Gabriel."

He leaned closer, examining her face. Eyelids shut, eyes moving rapidly behind the shutters. She was still asleep. Dreaming of him. His heart suddenly felt too big for his chest, like it might explode at any second.

"Yes, like that."

Fascinated and more than a little turned on, he watched as her right hand, which had been wrapped around her own stomach, pushed the sheet down lower. Her fingertips blazed a trail down the gentle curve of her belly to the Promised Land. A land he'd like to explore further.

She made another little noise, like a sigh. He couldn't lie next to her and watch, could he? It seemed creepy, like he was spying on her. But he couldn't tear his eyes away.

As a compromise, he leaned in and pressed a kiss on her throat, then whispered in her ear. "I'm here, sweetheart."

Her eyelids fluttered. "Mmm. I love you."

He froze. Hot blood pounded through his veins and his body tightened. Did she really say she loved him? It was all he hoped for, but she'd said it in her sleep so it probably didn't mean anything. Her eyes flickered open, drowsy and clouded over by the lingering dream and some emotion he couldn't read.

"Hi," she whispered.

"Hi, yourself."

"I was dreaming about you."

"Were you?" Of course she was, but he couldn't bring himself to mention what she'd said in her sleep.

"Yes. I'm glad you're really here."

Stroking the slope of her shoulder, he tried to speak. He tried to summon some bravery but chickened out. "Come stay with me?"

"Absolutely."

"But first I think I need to make your dream come true." Dammit, he couldn't wait a minute longer.

Licking a path from her breasts down to her stomach, he circled her navel and tasted her sweet skin. He couldn't get enough.

When he ducked under the sheet and moved down to trail kisses between her thighs, Sinead's moans made him a very happy man. He'd make her a happy woman too. At least for now.

Sinead squinted her eyes to block out the blinding sun reflecting off sheets of glass. The front of the designer townhouses opposite the beach were like mirrors on a hot, clear day. Where were her sunglasses? She held her hand up to shield her eyes. She wasn't prepared for the last blast of an Australian summer after leaving London's cool, misty winter.

They arrived at Gabriel's apartment in the late afternoon and sweltering heat. The heatwaves were visible, shimmering above the asphalt road like a gateway to another dimension. As if she was in a science-fiction movie and she'd stepped through a portal transporting her directly into the heart of summertime on another planet. She blinked her eyes a few times. Lord, she was so tired she was delusional.

Gabriel opened his front door and ushered her inside, placing his hand possessively on her lower back. It gave her tingles. She loved feeling she belonged to him, even if it was only a tiny gesture. He let her go as he hauled her suitcase over the threshold.

Stepping into the apartment, her mouth dropped open as she scanned the open-plan living space. It was elegant and modern as she'd expected, but minimalist to the point of being bare. Definitely the word for it. Bare.

Gabriel's apartment was like a space-age movie set, all blank white walls with one enormous flat-screen television, hard-edged grey leather sofas, dark metal and glass coffee tables and a black glossy kitchen with shining stainless steel appliances. No artwork, no photographs or magazines, none of the usual clutter lying around someone's home. It was like a hotel room or a younger man's bachelor pad, but even more sterile. Where was the reflection of his personality in this place?

Sinead spun in a circle, taking it all in, then came to a stop and watched Gabriel. He still stood by the door with his hands stuffed into his jeans pockets. His expression was closed off, eyes cool and distant. Waiting for her reaction.

She glanced over his shoulder and caught a flash of blue – the view out the full-length windows on either side of the door. She could see straight across Beach Road to the bay, water stretching for miles in a flat aquamarine line until it met the cloudless summer sky.

"Do you like it?"

"I love the view, it's amazing. The apartment is lovely too, but a bit empty. Are you still decorating?"

He shook his head, looking around the room. "I bought the place for the view, but I haven't spent much time here. With all the travelling and Mum's illness, I spend a lot of time in hotels and at her house. It is a bit empty."

Sinead felt something tighten in her chest at his words. This place wasn't a real home, any more than her London flat. He deserved better. They both did.

He strode towards her, closing the distance between them, placing his large hands on her hips. Sinead melted into him, like an ice lolly on the hood of a car at the beach. The imprint of his warm hand grasping her through her light blue summer dress made her lower belly clench. His touch warmed all sorts of places inside her, matching the heat on her exposed, sun-warmed skin.

Her hands landed on his chest, hot and hard beneath his sunny yellow T-shirt with a surf brand logo. His heartbeat thudded under her touch. She'd been surprised he'd worn something so casual to work that day. But he'd said lots of Aussies dressed down in the office unless they were going to a formal meeting. He wore the look so well, like a cross between a professional surfer and a male model. So delicious-looking he made her mouth water. Summer weather was growing on her.

Gabriel's eyes were as deep as the sea in the distance. "I want to take you to meet her. Mum, I mean. But I have to warn you, she's not doing so well. She's gone downhill and she doesn't seem aware of what's going on around her." He took a deep breath and the words came out low. "It's Alzheimer's. She's not getting better."

Her breath stalled. *Alzheimer's.* She knew it was something serious, but Alzheimer's was such a cruel disease.

His eyes now had a liquid sheen warning of imminent tears. *Poor, sweet Gabriel.*

She lifted her right hand to cup his face, stroking along his jaw, rough with the beginnings of a five o'clock shadow. She raised up on tiptoes in her flip-flop sandals and pressed a gentle kiss to his full lower lip, offering comfort through her touch. It was only a quick kiss, but the way he squeezed her hips showed he appreciated it.

She pulled away and stroked her fingers down his arms. "So let's go see her. We can come back here later and you can finish showing me around."

"Okay."

Sinead threaded her fingers through his and they walked hand-in-hand back out through Gabriel's front door. She needed to support him this time, and she was thrilled he wanted her by his side.

The ride in Gabriel's convertible BMW down sunshiny Beach Road and some unidentified highway left Sinead's hair in a matted tangle down her back. Her skin was dry after her long flight and now it baked under the unforgiving Australian sun. She wasn't looking her best and her fingers shook in her lap. She shouldn't be nervous, but meeting Gabriel's mother was a big deal. And sort of scary.

She straightened her short dress as she hopped out of the car, and stood tall as she entered the aged care facility. It was like a small hospital, somewhere in Melbourne's southern suburbia, a concrete block of blandness.

She walked beside Gabriel down a dull, cool corridor smelling vaguely of bleach. A blast of chilly air-conditioning cooled her skin in an instant. Gabriel's apartment seemed sterile, but this place took sterile to another level. The place gave her the creeps. She shivered, and she didn't think it was only the air-con. What exactly was she walking into here?

Walking close beside Gabriel they entered a lounge area and she took in the scene – a group of ancient, white-haired people sitting in wheelchairs in a lounge area, facing the television or the windows, blank expressions on their faces. Family members sat nearby, drinking tea and making polite conversation, with no response from their loved ones.

An old lady laughed at nothing in particular and a middle-aged nurse wheeled her back down the corridor. Sinead looked across to Gabriel, but he didn't say a word. Was he okay?

He took her hand when they came to another beige corridor, his grip strong and reassuring. They came to the first door on the left. Sinead noticed the photocopied sign on the door, which read 'Susan Anderson'. Underneath was a tacked-on Polaroid photo of a good-looking middle-aged woman with unlined skin, short blonde hair, distant, pale blue eyes and a pleasant smile.

Sinead's blood ran cold as the implications hit her. Gabriel's mother was still relatively young, only in her fifties. From what he'd explained on the drive, Susan was likely to be stuck in an aged care home for the rest of her life. A life which wasn't expected to go on much longer. Her belly rolled over, sick for Gabriel and his mother. For a life cut short and a son's pain still to come.

Gabriel grabbed the door handle and pushed it open. Sinead took a couple of hesitant steps into the room behind him, her flip-flops thwacking on the floor tiles and Gabriel's deep inhalation of breath echoing in the otherwise silent room.

Tension bunched in Gabriel's shoulders as he spoke. "Hello, Mum. I'm back to see you again. I've brought someone to meet you."

There was no response from the woman who sat half propped up on an adjustable hospital bed. Sinead stepped to Gabriel's side and grasped his hand, then took in Susan's serene appearance. She didn't move. Her hair had been brushed into a smooth bob and she wore a casual T-shirt and track pants, as if she was about to go jogging at any moment. But that wouldn't happen. The thin plastic tube running into Susan's nose and the drip attached to her arm belied the idea. They were the only outward indications of her illness.

Sinead tried to meet Gabriel's mother's eyes. "Hello, Mrs Anderson. I'm Sinead Kennealy." Wondering what else to say, heart thundering in her ears, she tipped her face up to Gabriel's. "I'm Gabriel's girlfriend. Someday, something more. I hope."

Eyes widening ever so slightly, Gabriel went still as a statue. Sinead's cheeks heated at the bombshell she'd let slip. *Whoops.*

She trained her eyes back to the woman in the hospital bed. The pristine white sheets beneath Susan's legs were unruffled.

Gabriel tugged on her hand and led her to the two visitor chairs by the window. He pulled both chairs across to the side of Susan's bed and Sinead sat down. She crossed her legs and planted her hands in her lap, a lump rising in her throat. Sinead was out of her depth, not sure whether to talk to Gabriel, or stay silent until he took the lead. Was he regretting Sinead's being here?

Standing at his mother's bedside, Gabriel was calm and gentle. He bent to place a kiss on his mother's cheek and brushed his hand through her hair. Then he sat heavily beside Sinead.

Gabriel patted her hand. "Why don't you tell Mum a bit about yourself? I'm sure she'd like to hear from someone besides me and the nurses for a change."

She nodded, glancing at his face. He offered a taut smile. "Sure. I'm originally from Dublin, as you can probably tell from my accent. But why don't I tell you how I met Gabriel. It makes a funny story."

Sinead's mouth turned upwards as Gabriel placed his hand over hers, rubbing his thumb in tiny circles across the back of her hand.

She spoke for some time, telling Susan the story of her relationship with Gabriel so far. She explained how she lived in London, but visited Melbourne often. Sinead couldn't imagine going about her business in London without him. Susan breathed evenly, but had no other reaction to anything Sinead said.

A doctor in a white coat knocked on the door and entered, smiling as she laid eyes on both Gabriel and Sinead. A plump woman with kind eyes, Sinead guessed in her mid-forties. The name 'Dr Maria Fiorini' was printed on her name tag.

"Hello, Gabriel. Nice to see you again and with another visitor too. I came to give you an update on Susan's treatment plan. Is now a good time?"

"Yes, it's fine. Maria, this is my girlfriend, Sinead."

Hearing the girlfriend moniker from Gabriel's lips caused a little bubble of pleasure to burst in her chest and her face to light up. She probably had a silly grin on her face. The doctor raised her perfectly arched eyebrows. It didn't matter if Maria decided she was over-friendly.

"Hi, Maria." Sinead extended her hand to the doctor.

Maria sat on the end of Susan's bed and shook Sinead's hand. "Hello, Sinead, it's nice to meet you."

She retrieved a medical chart attached to a clipboard hanging on the foot of the bed and glanced over it briefly.

"Gabriel, as you know, Susan contracted a severe chest infection soon after she arrived here for respite care. We treated her with a high dose of antibiotics through an IV line. She's done well recovering and breathing on her own again, so the immediate issue is making a decision about her ongoing care. Alzheimer's disease progresses slowly in the initial stages, but now Susan's at a stage requiring a high level of care. I don't think she should return home, even with the nursing staff you organised. I'd recommend she remains here. But of course the decision sits with you as next of kin."

Gabriel shook his head and looked at the floor. When he lifted his head he looked first to Sinead, then Maria.

When he spoke, he sounded exhausted. "I understand. I've been expecting this, although I was hoping Mum could stay in her own home until the end. It's what she wanted."

Maria reached for his hand. "I know. But Susan hasn't regained her ability to speak since the infection hit. Even beforehand, she wasn't capable of making an informed decision. We're not sure how long she'll have left."

"Okay, let me think about it. I'll let you know tomorrow."

Sinead's heart stuttered. Poor Gabriel, it was the kind of decision no one wanted to make. She glanced at Gabriel now clenching his jaw, his eyes glittering. She wanted to hold him close, wrap him in her arms and let him cry or shout, whatever he needed. But not here. He wouldn't let out such emotion in front of his silent mother and the doctor.

"Of course, we can talk again tomorrow. I'll check on Susan now."

Maria made her way to Susan's side and completed her observations, checking the drip and making sure her patient was comfortable. Sinead supposed there was nothing more to be done for Susan now. She blinked a few times, not wanting to give in to tears, for Gabriel's sake. She didn't want him upset any further, he had enough worries.

Gabriel gripped Sinead's hand firmly, pressing his knee against the side of Sinead's thigh at the same time. His tension was palpable, radiating from his body like electricity.

She hoped he'd let her share the burden of his worries.

Lying on his back in the dark, unease crept over Gabriel like spiders crawling across his skin. With Sinead lying beside him in his own bed, he'd expected to find a sense of peace. But not after visiting his mum. The conversation with Dr Fiorini circled through his head in a never-ending loop.

Lurking at the back of his mind, like a monster under the bed, was the issue he'd pushed away for years. Now it reared its ugly head. It wouldn't get out of his face. He needed to talk to Sinead about the realities he was facing, what she could be facing if they made plans to stay together.

No. He needed to do more than talk. He needed to make a break.

The pain slicing through his gut at the idea of breaking it off with Sinead made it hard to breathe. He sat, raising his legs and resting his head in his hands. And he watched her. Memorised every curve, every detail.

Sinead was wearing his clothes, a loose white cotton shirt he usually threw on when he hit the beach or the gym. She'd never looked sexier, stretched out on his crisp white sheets, her long white-washed hair trailing over one shoulder.

In the dark she was all monochromes and curves in shades of white and grey, like an old Hollywood screen siren. But she was real, flesh and blood. So passionate.

The passion they'd shared still burned through his body. Sinead had taken him to a place where nothing else mattered but blinding pleasure, sharp and bright, like stars shining clear and true in the night sky outside his bedroom window.

He had no doubt she was his perfect match. But was it fair to let her tie herself to him, knowing the pain in store if she stuck with him long term? He already knew the answer.

He trailed his fingertips up Sinead's arm, then wrapped his arm around her, pulling her close into his body. He didn't want to let her go. He had some tough decisions to make, and soon. Meeting a woman like Sinead at all, but especially at this stage of his life, was something he'd never considered. It was terrible timing.

Giving up on sleep as a bad joke, he rose and got ready for a walk. It was almost dawn. He'd be alone and have some time to think across the road on the beach. Sometimes the fresh air helped give him clarity. He could only hope for a bucket load of clarity before breakfast, when he'd talk to Sinead again.

Where am I?

Sinead jolted awake, breaths short and shallow, disorientation making her head spin. The feeling often followed her on trips around the world. Where had she slept? Not a hotel . . . white walls, plain metal beside table. Gabriel's apartment. Her brain slowly caught up with her body, on high alert after her terrifying dream.

Padraig had been chasing her through a dark alley, her heart pounding a deafening beat in her ears, the whole scene awash with red, like a scene from a horror movie. A large, rough hand caught her and tugged her down to the ground, and she woke.

"Gabriel?" Her voice was shaky. She rolled over and patted the space beside her. He wasn't in bed.

She found her phone on the steel cube bedside table, checking the time in the half-light. Five o'clock in the morning. The sun was barely making its presence known, offering a scant sliver of lemon yellow light through the crack in Gabriel's bedroom blinds. She noticed a text message waiting.

Couldn't sleep. Gone for walk on beach. Back in time for breakfast. G.

Sinead had two choices – wait for him to come back as he expected, or go and find him. It wasn't much of a decision. She'd never been particularly good at hanging around and waiting for things to happen.

She was worried about Gabriel. There was something about the way he clung to her last night which left her uneasy. Talking to his mother's doctor had upset him. That might have been all. But the niggling feeling it was something more wouldn't leave her alone.

Hurriedly throwing on her summer dress and Gabriel's hooded sweatshirt, Sinead pocketed her phone and headed out of his apartment. Within a couple of minutes she was across Beach Road and walking along the damp sand by the water's edge, still unmarred by footprints. She grabbed her flip-flops in one hand and let the refreshing water wash over her feet.

It was a gorgeous morning, with the promise of heat to come later in the day. The water was flat and a slate blue-grey, with only a hint of a white foam when the miniature waves broke near the shore. She walked for a few minutes, enjoying the quiet and calm.

The famous Brighton bathing boxes came into view, framing the beach on the road side. The long row of multi-coloured, hand-painted wooden shacks were a tourist attraction and a magnet for amateur photographers. But at this time of day, she spotted only one figure sitting limp and folded over on the steps of one of the tiny houses, painted with a garish dolphin and starfish design.

Gabriel's head rested on his hands, and his shoulders shook in a rough rhythm. His pain squeezed like a tightly bound ribbon around Sinead's heart. She crossed the sand and approached, breathing deeply, preparing herself for the sight of his face.

He raised his head and his face was red and blotchy, damp with tears. She wanted to launch herself into his lap and hug him tight. But she moved quietly and sat close beside him on the wooden step. Taking one of his hands in hers, she wrapped the other behind his back. His body shuddered.

She rubbed her hand up and down his spine. "It's all right, you can tell me. What's wrong?"

He'd probably deny anything was wrong, though his heart was clearly breaking.

He shook his head. "It's everything. Mum, my job, you and me. All at once. I feel like I've been on a treadmill for the last fifteen years, running non-stop. Now someone's asked me to get off. I don't know what the hell I'm doing. Everything's changing. I love Mum but I can't give her the quiet end to her life at home like she wanted. I can't do my job like I should. Being CEO was getting to be too much and now the company might be torn apart in a takeover." He paused, glancing at her. "Then there's you. I can't give you what you deserve, Sinead."

Her hand stilled in position between his shoulder blades. "What do you mean? What I deserve, what I want, it's you."

He shook his head again, turning his troubled eyes towards her. "You don't know what you mean. You saw my mum yesterday. The disease, what it's done to her. It's an awful thing to watch someone you love degenerate. It runs in families, Sinead."

His voice dropped to a gravelly whisper and his eyes fixed on her.

"It's early-onset Alzheimer's. Mum was diagnosed at forty-two. In a few years, that could be me. Not being able to speak or eat. But first, I could slowly lose my mind. Forget who I am, forget how to work and look after myself. Forget who you are. I don't want anyone to look after me like a child. Especially you. You deserve a real life, without me."

Sinead's throat closed up. She couldn't swallow or get enough air. Gabriel could get sick like his mother? And soon. No wonder he was so worried. It was terrifying – nobody wanted to face such a terrible disease. But did he really think she'd abandon him? Go back to London like they'd never met, as if they meant nothing to each other? Apparently so. And here she was, thinking ahead to being together for better or worse, in sickness and health.

"I had no idea this was on your mind. Of course you're scared you might get sick like your mum, it's only natural. But you're getting ahead of yourself. You don't even know if you have this disease. You need to talk to a doctor, find out if that's what you're facing. But no matter what, I'm yours, Gabriel." She breathed deep, but said the words. She had to get them out. "I love you and I want to be by your side."

He scooted away from her, leaning his arms on his knees, trembling. "Don't say that. You *can't* love me, we only just met. I'm the wrong choice for you, Irish. I want you to go back to London and find someone else. A good man who can make you happy, give you children, have a full life. Forget about me."

She hopped off the step and stood on shifting sand, facing him. Her face heated, her annoyance rising up, unable to be contained. "Don't tell me what I feel. You're the only man I've known who's touched me body and soul. You protected me when Padraig came after me. You put yourself in danger to help me." She was waving her hand in the air, but forced herself to be still.

"You believe in me, make me think I can do more with my life. I *do* love you. I see the sweet man you really are, what you don't show the rest of the world. You see me, and I see you. I won't let you push me away because I know you're the only man I could ever be happy with."

He clenched his jaw so a muscle ticked near his ear. "You don't have a choice. I won't let you stick around until I ruin your life. I'm taking you back to your hotel and that'll be it. I'll say goodbye."

She blinked, not understanding this closed-off man in front of her. "Take me back to my hotel, say goodbye. But know this – I'll wait for you. I know you're having a horrible time at the moment with your mum. I'd stay and support you, if you'd let me. I'll be waiting when you're ready to come back to me."

He pinned her with those eyes, bluer-than-the-summer-sky. "Don't wait for me. There's no future for us. If I don't make a break now, I don't know if I'll be able to do it. When the time comes." His head dropped down, his expression hidden. "I need you to leave. Now. Before it kills me."

Sinead's stomach tipped and rolled like she was back on the plane in the storm, on the day they met. Only this time she might crash and burn. She stood, backed away, shaking her head.

She was trembling as she walked away from him. Back along the beach, back towards his apartment. Trudging through damp sand was hard work, it resisted and fought her every step. Her leg muscles burned with the effort.

She'd get her gear and be gone before he got back. There was no use talking to him anymore, not with the emotions threatening to choke her. Not with him stubbornly pushing her away.

She couldn't talk to him because he didn't even want her around. Her mind, her heart, rebelled at the idea. He was trying to protect her again. Or was he?

What had shaken her more than anything he'd said today, was what he hadn't said before. He had never once said he loved her.

Chapter Eighteen

Mermaid Airlines Flight 101, London to Paris

A familiar face leaned into the aisle as Sinead handed out multimedia headsets to the passengers. *Ryan*. Her airline-sanctioned smile slipped for a moment. What was Gabriel's best friend doing on her flight?

Ryan stretched out his long legs in the first class seat, seeming to occupy more space than his lanky frame required. He had a large presence, from his bright white teeth to his dark flashing eyes. Those eyes were trained on her, full of laughter under his shock of jet-black hair. He was an attractive man, but she had no interest in Ryan. Only one man would do in her present lovesick and depressed state.

Sadly, she wouldn't be seeing Gabriel anytime soon. Let alone jumping his bones like she wanted to. She hadn't heard a word from him since she'd fled Melbourne two weeks ago. She'd waited for him to show up at her hotel before she flew out, left him messages, but he hadn't returned her calls. After two days, she'd had to admit he wasn't changing his mind, and went home to London. Ever since, she'd eaten an extraordinary amount of chocolate, flown all her usual routes and done the best she could to summon a smile. An achy sigh rose up from somewhere near her heart.

Ryan raised a dark eyebrow. "My dear Sinead. Why the glum face?"

She crossed her arms and looked down her nose. "I'm sorry sir, do I know you?"

Her haughty question raised a laugh from Ryan, which hadn't been her intention. She'd hoped to head off the looming conversation with him while she was working.

"If you like, you can pretend you don't know me until we get to Paris. Then I was thinking we should have lunch together."

She lowered her voice to a conspiratorial whisper. "Is lunch really necessary? Wait, did Gabriel put you up to this?"

"Yes, it is necessary. I feel the need to share a lunch date in Paris with a beautiful flight attendant. And no, Gabriel doesn't even know I'm talking to you. At least, not exactly."

Gabriel must have known Ryan was going to see her though, which warmed something insider her. "What's that supposed to mean?"

Ryan scratched his jaw. "A few weeks ago, Gabe asked me to keep an eye on you. I feel I've been a bit behind the eight-ball with his request, so I want to make up for it. Have lunch with me. I have something to discuss with you."

Her interest was piqued, no denying it. What could Ryan have to say to make him grin like the Cheshire cat? She wouldn't rest until she found out what he was up to. She hoped it was some good news to do with Gabriel. Even if she knew she shouldn't get her hopes up.

She pursed her lips, then nodded. "Okay, I'll meet you for lunch. Text me when we get off the flight. Now leave me alone and let me do my job."

Ryan saluted her. "Yes, Ma'am."

She tottered back to the galley with her head held high, arm full of headsets entirely forgotten. She dumped them on a nearby trolley. Yuki was waiting there, bouncing up and down with excitement.

Yuki tugged Sinead's sleeve. "Who is that gorgeous man and where do you keep finding them? Is he your new boyfriend?" Her words ran together as they tumbled out of her mouth in an excited whisper.

Frowning, Sinead smoothed down her shirt. "No, of course he's not my boyfriend. My heart belongs to Gabriel. It's Ryan, Gabriel's best friend and business partner. He says he has something to discuss with me."

"Ooohh, it could be good news. Gabriel might surprise you in Paris."

Sinead's heart fluttered out of sync at the idea, but it was unlikely. The way they'd left things, Gabriel wouldn't be planning any grand romantic gestures. He was probably more down in the dumps than she was, with everything he had on his mind.

"I don't think so, but Ryan seemed pleased with himself. I need to find out what's on his mind."

Paris, France

Three hours later, Sinead arrived at the bistro Chez André near the end of the famous boulevard Champs Elysées. The place was a pleasant surprise, warm and welcoming, but not too horribly touristy. The dark wood tables and chairs paired with white linen table cloths dressed the place in elegance. The professional wait-staff, dressed in old-fashioned black and white uniforms, added to the authentic French atmosphere.

Ryan leaned back against a leather-bound booth style seat, smiling from ear to ear when he spotted her. "Welcome, Sinead. Sit down, relax. Would you like a café au lait or some champagne? Gabriel told me about your penchant for foods starting with the letter 'c'."

Sinead stared at Ryan as she sat opposite him, trying to catch up with his scattergun approach to conversation. "The coffee sounds good. Tell me what this is about, Ryan."

Ryan caught the eye of a passing waiter and gestured to his own coffee, ordering another.

He hit Sinead with a thousand-watt smile. "Gabriel is unhappy. Depressed, even. He won't do anything except work, sleep and visit his mum. He won't talk to me, except to tell me to bugger off and leave him alone. His PA, Martha, keeps calling me to complain about his never-seen-before level of grumpiness. I find all this fascinating." Ryan said this without a hint of concern. In fact, he was almost grinning.

Sinead was truly baffled, and her heart hurt for Gabriel. She bit her lip, biting back a few choice words too. "So he's depressed. It shouldn't make you happy, Ryan."

"You don't understand. You've gotten right under his skin. You're the only woman who's managed it. The only one he's ever given a chance. Since he sent you away he's been a shadow of his usual self. And guess what else Martha told me?"

She sighed, unfolding her fan-shaped napkin. "Please don't make me guess. Tell me already."

"All right. Have you spoken to your sister Bridie lately?"

The turns in the conversation were making her woozy, almost travel-sick. What did Bridie have to do with Gabriel's moodiness? "I haven't spoken to Bridie for a few days. What of it?"

"Did you know she's planning on applying for a work visa to Australia? Martha's been helping Gabe organise it. Apparently, he has a friend called Jay who runs an advertising agency in Melbourne. He's looking for trainees in graphic design. Loves travellers, young people with international experience."

This wasn't making any sense. "Bridie's applying for a trainee graphic design job? In Melbourne? But she isn't a qualified designer, and she didn't tell me anything about it."

Ryan grinned, tapping his fingers on the table. "Didn't Bridie study design at college before she dropped out? Doesn't she need a job and some help getting back on her feet? Martha says it's happening as we speak. Gabriel's arranging all of this to help Bridie. Now why do you think he would do such a selfless thing?"

Sinead sat back in her seat and gaped at Ryan. Her mouth was hanging open but she couldn't seem to control it. Gabriel knew how she worried about Bridie. He might have decided to help simply because he's a kind man, or he could be trying to make Sinead happy. The possibility took hold in her mind. Maybe he wanted to show Sinead he loved her.

She didn't know what to say. Her heart was palpitating too hard.

Ryan's eyes twinkled and softened. "He loves you, Sinead. I'd bet my life on it. He might not know how to tell you, but he's had no experience to draw on. His mum's illness and the business have been his world for so long, he's had no time for anyone else. When he told me he took you to meet her, well, it blew me away. He's never mentioned his mum's illness to a woman before, as far as I can tell. He hardly talks to me about it and we've been friends for nearly fifteen years."

A tiny, flickering candle of hope lit up inside her. Gabriel might still care. Maybe things weren't really over between them. She allowed the pleasure to play across her face, allowed the light to shine and the flames to lick and heat every part of her.

"Thanks Ryan. I appreciate you telling me all this. More than you could know." She patted the napkin down in her lap, not meeting Ryan's gaze.

"Gabe's a good man. Most people have no idea, but I do. He helped me through the hardest time in my life . . ." Ryan took a deep breath, raw pain twisting his expression. Sinead tipped her chin up to watch him. He continued, as if nothing had happened. "I know you see it too, who he really is. He deserves to be happy and I think you might be the one for him."

She blinked, hoping her verge-of-teariness wouldn't tip over into ugly snot crying. "Stop it now, before you make me cry. I love him, so much it scares the bejeezus out of me. I told him I'd wait for him." Sinead picked up a menu to hide her watery eyes and scanned the house specialties. "I'll have the Chateaubriand, frites and sauce béarnaise. Sounds fabulous."

Ryan grinned. "You're my kind of woman, Sinead. Steak and chips, no messing around. If Gabriel stuffs up I'll take you out in a heartbeat."

"You're all charm, Ryan. But despite yourself, you're a good friend." She tipped her head to one side and asked the other question that intrigued her. "What's happening between you and Charlotte, if you don't mind my asking?"

Ryan's face seemed to go blank, then he huffed out a breath. "A fat lot of nothing, but it's all my own fault. She wanted us to go together to the company cocktail party. As a couple."

"And . . ." Sinead prompted him to keep going. It was like pulling teeth, trying to get men to talk about relationships.

"And I kissed her. Really kissed her. In the office. It was completely inappropriate considering she works for me. Then I turned her down." He rubbed his hands over his face. "I stuffed things up. Now she doesn't even want to talk to me."

No wonder Charlotte had seemed upset the night of the cocktail party. Sinead hadn't had a chance to find out if Charlotte was okay, after all that happened with Padraig.

Ryan was watching her. She met his eyes, which sparkled, but were more serious than usual. "But you like her?"

"Of course I do. She's amazing. Beautiful and brilliant."

"So, what are you doing sitting here with me? Go back to London and make it right."

Ryan nodded, suddenly thoughtful. "Do you think Charlotte could really be interested in a bloke like me?

She smiled. "A big, strapping, handsome bloke like you, a CEO who cares about his friends and wants to see them happy? Yes, I think Charlotte could be persuaded."

Ryan grinned and finished his coffee. "Sorry about lunch, but I have to go." He rose from his seat and extended his hand. "Good luck, Sinead."

She shook his hand. "Good luck to you too."

Sinead relaxed into her seat, feeling infinitely better about lunch, men, Bridie, love, basically the whole world. All because of Gabriel.

Chapter Nineteen

Mermaid Airlines flight 360, London to Thailand, 30,000 feet above Thailand

T he plane dipped with mild turbulence and Sinead had to grip the armrests to stop herself from unclicking her seatbelt and dashing to a crew member for a weather update. She breathed out, long and slow. She was only a passenger today.

This flight was nothing like the other Asian stopover in Singapore. The typhoon. The storm that whipped up all the turbulence in her life. It was best not to think about it.

She gazed out the window. The best thing about flying to Thailand was the food. No, the weather. She looked forward to all of it. Once they descended below the light clouds it would be blue skies on the horizon and calm oceans as far as she could see.

It'd been two long weeks since she'd last spoken to Gabriel. A couple of days after her unexpected lunch in Paris with Ryan,

Gabriel had contacted her, leaving a voicemail message so sad it nearly broke her heart. His mum had another infection, she was being treated with yet more antibiotics. He needed to tell her how his mother was doing, he said. Nothing about his feelings, how he was holding up. But she'd read between the lines. He'd called her, needing to talk to someone. That was a good sign.

She'd called him back and endured a painful, stilted conversation. She told him she loved him and missed him. He said nothing, but she'd heard him sigh into the silence. God, how she'd wanted to wrap him in her arms.

It had been three days since he'd last texted, not that she was counting. Her phone was deathly silent and it was a bit strange, nothing more to it. She hadn't responded to his messages anyway. The ball was in his court. She was setting some boundaries and some firm ground rules. She was proud of herself, really. Even if her rules didn't always work out the way she planned.

If he wanted her, he would have to make the next move. He'd have to lay his feelings on the line. She couldn't be the only one to put her heart out there, ready to be stomped on, all red and squishy, bleeding under his feet. But she had an overactive imagination. There would be no stomping and no squishing.

After her short trip to Paris, she'd had a hectic schedule of flights from London to Sydney, thankfully avoiding Gabriel's hometown of Melbourne, then more European flights. Between each short trip she'd headed back to her lonely flat in London.

Oddly enough, the highlight of being in London had been hanging out with Bridie. Her little sister had been excited to share her news about her impending move to Melbourne to train as a graphic designer. When Sinead quizzed Bridie about exactly how this opportunity came about, Bridie clammed up. But she had asked if Sinead had talked to Gabriel lately, with a bright and hopeful tone of voice.

So maybe Sinead did have reason to hope. She crossed her fingers.

Time to focus on the here and now. The plane started its descent and she closed her eyes, smooshing her hair against the headrest. Soon she'd be relaxing on her first real holiday in a year.

Thailand, here I come.

She tried to summon some enthusiasm for yet another solo trip. Sure, it might be lonely. But maybe she'd meet some fellow travellers to chat to, or play bingo at the resort. She could go snorkelling and stare at the tropical fish. Or go fishing. They were all perfectly good activities for a single woman. It would be nice. Relaxing. There were stunning beaches and delicious food waiting for her. *C is for . . . coconut crab.*

If only she could have convinced Gabriel to be braver with his heart. He could have been here with her now, sitting beside her where he belonged. But she couldn't convince him to love her unless he believed it with his whole being, unless he knew it to be true. Gabriel needed to decide what sort of life he really wanted, and whether he had a place for her in his future. But he had to stay by his mother's side.

Sinead wanted him by her side for always but he had to choose for himself. He was being a blind idiot, so she'd wait him out. If only every second didn't drag on forever without him.

She should take up fishing. It might teach her patience.

Sinead emerged from the customs barrier into the solid Bangkok heat, fresh as a daisy. Hardly. The heat was only mildly softened by the air-conditioning and ceiling fans in the arrivals hall.

She dragged her suitcase behind her, unsticking her T-shirt from her back, and scanned the line of waiting tour guides and shuttle bus drivers. There should have been someone from her resort meeting her. Navigating around a bunch of rowdy Aussie girls painted orange in their fake tanner and their shorts and sandals, she came to a standstill.

Through the throng of travellers she spotted someone holding a placard with her name: *Ms Kennealy*. She gravitated towards it. Then she started in surprise, slapping her hand over her mouth, as the placard was flipped over to reveal a second slogan: *Irish princess*.

The man holding the card slowly lowered his arms and revealed his beautiful face.

She ran so fast her heart tripped over along with her legs and a zap of bright electric joy buzzed through her body. Sinead pushed past confused passengers, anyone standing in her way was liable to get a swift elbow to the ribs.

She had to get to him, her Gabriel.

Then she was right in front of him. She reached up to touch his face and he engulfed her in a breath-stealing embrace. Suddenly she was kissing him, revelling in the hot touch of his lips against hers, the taste of him like peppermint, coffee and home.

He kissed her right back like he meant it, giving her everything, saying so much without words.

Living in the moment, she melted into him and the whole world drifted away. And she knew. This was it, her real-life *Love Actually* moment.

Yay, yay, yay!

"How did you find me here?" she asked. When she pulled away, she hung onto his shirt so he wouldn't disappear.

"Truth? I called your mother. We had a long chat and she was very helpful when I told her I'm in love with you."

She narrowed her eyes. "The sneaky old woman. She never said a word. Wait, what did you say?" Sinead pulled further back to examine Gabriel's cheeky but smouldering hot expression.

"I'm in love with you. I love you, Irish, so damned much. I missed you like I was missing a limb when I told you to leave. I've been an idiot, about so many things." His head tipped down so their foreheads touched.

"I went to the doctor and finally had those tests. Scans and blood tests and memory tests. I'm fine, Sinead. They don't think I'll get sick like Mum. I need you to understand. And I needed to tell you I love you. I never believed I'd love anyone, or they'd love me back." Gabriel dipped his head and brushed his lips against hers.

She sighed in pure bliss. Even as her heart danced in one direction to hear he was healthy, she still wanted to smack him from the other direction for pushing her away, and for nearly breaking her heart.

"You're the only one for me. The most beautiful woman I've ever known, inside and out. You've shown me what I've been missing and I want it all with you. A real life, love, a partner, laughter and so much more. I want to belong to you. I'm yours, Sinead. You're everything to me and I'm not letting you get away ever again."

Her heart leapt, knowing it was true. He was hers. She held a finger to his lips, stopping the babble of words out of his mouth, although she loved to hear them.

She grinned like the lovesick fool she was. "Shh, Gabriel. I knew I loved you the second day we were together and you called me your naughty little trolley dolly." Touching his face, running her fingers over his stubble-dusted jaw, she hardly believed he was really there.

He'd come to find her, to tell her he loved her. She was getting woozy and she didn't think the heat was to blame.

Gabriel shifted and whispered against her throat. "You like it when I talk dirty, huh? So you're prepared, I've been working on some new material for tonight."

"Are you coming with me on holiday?" Hope welled up inside her again. They could be together properly, a real couple in love, building a future.

Gabriel pulled away and shot her a smile that made her mouth go dry. "Yeah, on holiday, and forever, if you'll have me."

Her heart went *pitter-patter-thump* and her thighs tingled in anticipation of the dirty-talking, amongst other things. "I'll have you all right. Every which way 'till Sunday and then some."

"That's my girl."

It was true. She was absolutely his. So she kissed the bejeezus out of him.

Chapter Twenty

Lonely Beach, Koh Chang, Thailand

The bliss was almost too much to take. Sinead lay on her stomach on a teak sun lounger facing the ocean, watching the waves lap at the perfect white sandy beach. She stretched out and arched her back like a cat, enjoying the slight release of tension in her muscles and the sunshine warming her skin. She could have purred with contentment.

Gabriel sat on the edge of the lounge beside her, massaging her back with coconut oil. The fragrance wafted through the air and added to the moment, a perfect holiday snapshot in real life. She was so relaxed, she was practically boneless.

Gabriel had picked up some moves from the Thai masseuse at the resort over the past two weeks and he seemed dedicated to looking after her, doing whatever would give her pleasure. She sighed as he untied the strings at the back of her skimpy white bikini and continued to roll and press her skin with his strong hands.

She sighed deeper. Almost a groan. "Mmm, lovely."

"Lovely like you."

Gabriel kissed the spot he loved, right below her ear. The same spot that drove her mad with desire when he teased her just so. He knew it too. Sinead shivered in spite of the sun beating down on them.

She properly groaned, squeezing her thighs together. "Don't do that to me here on the beach. We might get carried away." But she made no effort to stop him.

He kissed her ear lobe, making her squirm. "I don't think anyone around here would mind."

It was probably true, no one would care about semi-indecent frolicking on the beach. Lonely Beach was a hippy hangout for travellers from around the globe, where all levels of nakedness and combinations of dreadlocks, bikinis and tie-dyed clothing were perfectly acceptable.

It was such a slow, chilled-out way of life, compared to their normal hectic pace jetting around the world. Exactly what they both needed. Some time away from the everyday, to get to know each other and discover how wonderful they could be together.

"I was thinking about our talk last night," Gabriel paused. His hands stilled on her shoulders. "I don't want you to go back to London. I want you to come and live with me in Melbourne."

Sinead sat suddenly, wanting to see his face. At the last second, she grabbed hold of her bikini top and protected her modesty – what little she had left. His gaze flicked down to her barely covered breasts and that filthy look heated his eyes. Again. She didn't mind. In fact, her blood boiled and bubbled as she pictured what they'd get up to back inside their luxury hut further along the beach.

"Do you mean it? About living together in Melbourne?" It was what she wanted too, but she'd hesitated to suggest anything permanent yet.

He nodded, trailing his fingertips down her arms. "Yes, Melbourne, or somewhere not too far away. I need to stay close to Mum and the head office. I'd consider somewhere I could surf, like the Great Ocean Road. Bridie's going to be living in Melbourne. And I got you some admissions information for a business degree at my old university, with a major in travel and tourism. It'd be perfect for you. I love you more than anything, Sinead. I need you with me."

Good Lord, he was wonderful. He'd planned all that to make her happy. She studied his pinched forehead and the tight line of his jaw. He looked nervous about her response. The little ridge appeared between his eyebrows. He was adorable.

"We could . . . I do love it there. If I haven't already said it enough, thank you so much for everything you've done for my sister. The business degree sounds amazing too. You're so sweet, organising it for me." She paused for a beat. Now wasn't the time for half-measures. "Or, and this is just another option, mind you, we could get married here first and then find a house on the coast."

She almost laughed at the stunned expression on Gabriel's face. He'd completely blanked, as if his brain was still trying to catch up with what his ears had told him.

One corner of his gorgeous mouth tipped upwards. "Did you just propose to me? What is it with you always making the first move?" He pretended to be annoyed, but his eyes held bright summer sunshine which burst across his entire face.

She leaned closer, her gaze dropping to his full lower lip. "I guess I did propose. Someone has to tell you what to do in this love game, Gabriel, because honestly, you have no clue."

"Is that right? I haven't given you an answer yet, so don't tease me too much."

"Tease you? I've barely even started."

She'd tease him all right.

Sinead backed away, raising herself from the sun lounger, then turned towards the sea. With her back to him, she dropped her bikini top and ran across the sand, into the waves. When she was waist-deep in the water, she turned and waved at him. Her bare breasts bounced with the movement. She was being provocative, but didn't care about anyone else. Her eyes were only fixed on him.

She giggled as Gabriel got up and broke into a sprint, racing across the sand and splashing through the waves to meet her.

Then he stood in front of her, panting, his tanned and muscular chest bare, wearing only wet board shorts. A vision of manly perfection.

Sinead could've quite happily stood and stared at him for the rest of her life. But she'd rather hold him close and have Gabriel wrap his strong arms around her, for always.

"Yes," he said.

"Yes?" Sinead's voice held a question, not only about today, but about forever.

"I will. I do."

She squealed as he pulled her into him, and stole her ability to think with a mind-blowing, knee-shaking kiss. He lifted her and splashed water all around in shimmering, diamond-like droplets. Then he crushed her body against him, leaving no room for doubt. She would always be his and he would always be hers.

He would always love and protect her. He was her home. No matter where in the world they ended up, they would end up together.

Sinead had been lucky enough to find a little slice of heaven on earth in Gabriel's arms and in his heart. She wouldn't give him up, but would always hold tight to him. The man she loved. The man who would soon be her husband. She bit his lip.

He pulled back and whispered close to her ear. "I love you, Irish."

Kissing him with every inch of her soul, Sinead showed him the depth of her love.

My angel, Gabriel.

***

Read next...

Girl Under The Christmas Tree: A Steamy Holiday Romance Novella
Girl on a Plane series 0.5
A prequel or companion story to *Girl on a Plane*. This novella features Yuki, a girl looking for adventure before she became a flight attendant with Mermaid Airlines. When Yuki meets a handsome Irish CEO at the five-star hotel where she works, sparks fly. It's the week before Christmas, and Yuki knows it's forbidden for staff to fraternize with hotel guests. But Yuki might break the rules. . . for just one night!
Ebook & paperback

Hot In The City: A Romantic Comedy Story Collection
Girl on a Babymoon, Girl on a Plane series 1.5
This collection includes the special edition novella, *Girl on a Babymoon*! Catch up with Sinead and Gabriel, five years after they first met in *Girl on a Plane*. Now a married couple, Sinead and Gabriel are facing some big issues. An escape to a luxury tropical resort may be just what the doctor ordered. . .
Ebook & paperback

Heart Note: A Christmas Romcom Novella
A lighthearted holiday romance with a touch of mystery. Perfect for fans of *Love Actually*!
Heart Note features Lily, a curvy redhead shop assistant working on the perfume counter in a major department store in the lead-up to Christmas, and Christos, a smouldering security guard (possible Greek god?) who helps her to foil a perfume heist!
Ebook & paperback

Visit **cassandraolearyauthor.com/books** for details.

Pre-order now...

Girl on a Layover

A Steamy Romcom Novella, Girl on a Plane series #2
Yuki Yamimoto has a problem with billionaires. She knows it,
her Mermaid Airlines flight crew co-workers know it, and so
does her friend, Sinead.

Okay, maybe it's one billionaire in particular who Yuki's ob-
sessed with – Declan Moriarty, the charming, wavy-haired Irish
CEO she met years ago when she worked in a hotel in Melbourne. They accidentally shared a one-night-stand in his hotel
suite, then Yuki got fired into the bargain. It was totally worth
it, at the time. Until it wasn't. Declan was the one who got away,
the big fish she'd failed to reel in. The man who broke her heart.

When Sinead invites Yuki to her last-minute second-wed-
ding/renewal of vows/luxury getaway weekend, Yuki jumps at
the chance to go. After being publicly dumped and humiliated
by her ex-boyfriend in Singapore, Yuki needs to escape. It's only
when she boards the flight to Thailand that she realises Declan

may be invited too. After all, he's good friends with Gabriel, Sinead's gorgeous, entrepreneur husband.

Now it's panic-stations, as Yuki tries to work out how to be cool, calm, devastatingly sexy and totally mature. Piece of cake! But when she sees Declan again, he's as handsome as ever, and everything starts to go wrong . . .

Releases October 2023. Visit **cassandraolearyauthor.com** for details!

May 2023 Release

Dating Little Miss Perfect

A stand-alone contemporary romance novel perfect for fans of *The Hating Game* by Sally Thorne and *The Soulmate Equation* by Christina Lauren.

On an anonymous online dating app, LittleMissPerfect meets HotAussie007 and it's love at first click. In real life, a smart but spiky woman in STEM, research scientist Dr Eden, meets Finn, a laid-back Aussie marketing manager, at the big pharma company where they both work in California. When they are pitted against each other and forced to compete for special project funding, it's their jobs and futures on the line.

Eden just wants to win at life and in science. It's not happening! Finn makes things worse, with his annoying charm and muscular forearms invading her space. Whereas Finn is stupidly attracted to Eden but can't pursue her. He's stuck in the worst position of his professional life and can't see a clear way out. If he confides in Eden, or anyone, his whole life could blow up.

When they realise the truth about their online alter egos, dating is off the table. Can they ignore their inconvenient attraction, and work together to take down their unethical boss? Or will intense rivalry cause their IRL work lives and online love lives to collide and explode like a science experiment gone wrong?

Find out more at **cassandraolearyauthor.com**

Acknowledgements

I'd like to acknowledge the many people who have been involved in the various stages of writing this book. This second edition is something I'm especially excited about, as I always wanted to see this book in print. Now in 2023, it's finally happening! *Girl on a Plane* was originally published in ebook by HarperCollins UK in 2016, after I won the global We Heart New Talent writing contest. I appreciate the expertise of the editors who I worked with back then.

My fabulous writer friends have listened to me moaning about wanting to republish this book for many months, so thanks for putting up with me! A huge shout-out to my writing group, the Melbourne Romance Writers Guild. I joined the group after I'd finished the first draft of this novel back in 2015, but to those who helped me refine it, and then celebrated my success, thank you so much. Especially Michelle Somers.

Thanks to the equally amazing members of the Romance Writers of Australia, many of whom are also my friends (or just put up with my rampant fan-girling). Without your enthusiasm, expert writing and publishing knowledge, and the annual conference where I've soaked up information like a sponge, I'd still be wallowing in rubbish-first-draft land.

Last (but not least), thank you Melissa, whose experiences as a flight attendant inspired the idea for this story, although the story is not actually about you. No, really. Except for the part about always looking glamorous.

About Cassandra O'Leary

Cassandra O'Leary is an author, avid reader, corporate communications escapee and film and TV fangirl. In 2015, Cassandra won the global We Heart New Talent contest run by HarperCollins UK, and her debut romantic comedy novel, *Girl on a Plane*, was then published in 2016. She was also nominated for the AusRom Today Reader's Choice Award for Best New Author.

More recently, Cassandra has independently published several novellas and the story collection, *Hot In The City*, all while hanging out with her superhero husband and chasing her two mini ninjas around her home city of Melbourne, Australia. She loves/hates writing multiple things at once, and she has several more novels in the works.

Cassandra is a proud member of Romance Writers of Australia, Australian Society of Authors, and the Melbourne Romance Writers Guild.

Read more at **cassandraolearyauthor.com** and sign-up for newsletter updates!

www.ingramcontent.com/pod-product-compliance
Lightning Source LLC
Chambersburg PA
CBHW020330120726
47904CB00002B/363